Endangered Essence

Extra Elements Series, Volume 9

T. M. Kuefler

Published by T. M. Kuefler, 2022.

ENDANGERED ESSENCE

First edition. October 25, 2022.

Copyright © 2022 T. M. Kuefler.

ISBN: 979-8215807897

Written by T. M. Kuefler.

Table of Contents

To all of those roads that take us home.

ENDANGEREDessence

EXTRA ELEMENTS SERIES
T. M. KUEFLER

AND LET US BEGIN

HUMANITY NEEDED HELP.

The Drako's, a faction of extraterrestrials including deadly and advanced lizard like creatures, were slowly influencing Earth's politics for decades. For some reason only known to them, they finally decided to take complete control of humanity, or at least try to.

First, they released a disease. The spreading pandemic kept changing, mutating even as we struggled to eradicate it with vaccines. 80% of the human population died. That's when the Drako's came out of hiding and commenced their occupation of our planet.

The cities and more populated areas became deadly battle grounds. Many of those that weren't killed in the ensuing conflicts were enslaved. Experimented on, fed upon, tortured. Many were lost. Too many.

The survivors that managed to stay free reverted to guerilla warfare. They banded together and continued their fight from hidden bases. Fortunately, humanity found out that they weren't as alone in this fight as they thought.

Something called the Andromadan Alliance, enemies of the Drako's, extended their hand in aid to the surviving humans. Groups of the Nordic race descended to the human bases to join the humans in their struggle.

The Nordics are a light-colored race of extraterrestrial beings that were the first to appear. As it turns out, just like the Drako's, they and their counterparts had been watching Earth for a long, long time.

The Rocky Mountain Base, where we are located, is hidden deep inside one of the mountains along that extensive ridgeline. It is jointly run by both Lysander, a Nordic, and our human leader, Malachi. Lysander is the liaison between the Andromadan Alliance and the humans, while Malachi runs the human side of things. They seem to work together well.

WHAT ABOUT THE RANCH?

THE RANCH, OR THE PLACE that was once known as the Skinwalker Ranch, was liberated from Drako control by Coren and Blaze.

Coren is the oldest son within the Andromadan Guardian family. Blaze is his human Conversance. The other half of his soul. The two of them were kidnapped by the Drako's and brought to the Skinwalker Ranch where they were drugged and tortured. It was there that the duo found out about the human's that were working with the Drako's.

With the help of Blaze's long lost brother, Bane, they were able to free themselves and destroy that group of Drako's and the Ranch they inhabited. It was then that the Alliance was free to take control of the Ranch and start investigating the site and its ancient underground megalith.

Underground tunnels and caverns built to harness and distort the lay lines of the Earth. This power was fixed and returned to where it belongs by Coren and Blaze when they and Bane took over running the Ranch investigations.

Even though the area is no longer a magnet for extraterrestrials, the Alliance is still investigating the area and the secrets it hides.

HARVESTING THE FUTURE

MARKO, THE HEAD OF Operations and his now fiancé, River, along with pilot Merc Banyon, aka Wings, and weapons expert Dean Marshal, aka Scope, flew up in an Andromadan spaceship in order to attempt to hack into the Drako systems.

This was of course supported by not just the Base but the newest Andromadans to arrive at the Base, the Ancients. Four siblings that were part of the Ancient ruling family of Andromada, including the heir to the throne himself, Madron.

The group succeeded in their endeavors to harvest Drako information but ended up paying a steep price. They crashed and were trapped in the dangerous Peruvian jungle for weeks on end, running and hiding from the Drako's who tracked them.

Fortunately, the group was eventually recovered and returned safely to the Base. As for the harvested information, that is proving to be extremely helpful.

SHIFTING RACES

THE HORSE, BAILOR, turned out to be a little more interesting than the Base residents thought. As an equine divergent or more commonly known 'shifter', Bailor came out of hiding in order to claim his soulmates, Bane and Harper.

After a slight disagreement with Bane's family, the Andromadan Guardians, the newly formed triad moved to the Ranch and took over the day to day running of the investigation.

While everything resolved itself between Bane and his family, the troubled man was finally given the support he needed to heal from his time being controlled by the Drako Bosses. This helped

Bane accept his gift and his guides in way that would help lead him and the humans follow their destiny.

In the protection of his triad, Bailor introduced the Guardians and some Base members to another type of humanoid divergent, the canines. Specifically, wolves.

NO LONGER EARTH BOUND

MANY THINGS WERE REVEALED from the Harvest collected by Marko and River. One of those things was an encrypted file detailing an underground lab. A lab that was originally human run but was turned over to the Bosses at the beginning of the Drako occupation. This lab housed dozens of humans that boasted different sorts of psychic ability.

When Malachi and his team, plus a couple extra members, went in to retrieve the imprisoned humans they quickly found that the lab didn't just house humans. Locked away on the very lowest levels of the underground labs lived deadly creatures that were only ever described in myths and legends. These beings were all, unfortunately, freed on the night in question.

Amongst the chaos, one very unique woman was found.

This woman immediately connected with Catro, the youngest Andromadan Ancient. A male, that once complete, showed that he, like Royce, wasn't completely human, but was a reincarnated Angel.

EPILOGUE

LEAH

I was sitting on the end of my bed, staring down into my lap. My mind wouldn't stop. The hate, the self loathing, the pain. Oh God, the pain. I just wanted it all to stop. I needed it to stop.

Ember was finally gone.

I received the news this morning. Last night she tried to accuse Coren, one of the Andromadan Guardians, of rape and she was immediately transferred to an Egyptian base. Just as Malachi threatened.

I wondered when it would be my turn, when Malachi would show up with transfer papers for me. Not that it mattered. Nothing really mattered anymore. Not even the fact that after a year I was finally free of the woman's influence.

It didn't matter because in the end, Ember won. She changed me, damaged me so irrevocably that I no longer knew who I was. No, that was a lie. I was a bad, disgusting person who hurt others. I didn't deserve happiness.

I didn't even deserve life.

I didn't want life. Not anymore. Life was pain. Agony.

The boxcutter in my hand glinted in the light, mocking me for my fear. Someone worthless like me, no one would even notice. No one would even mourn, and I would be free. Two little cuts and the pain would be gone. And the world would be better for it. This world held enough problems without me and my caustic soul compounding those issues.

I set the tip of the razor sharp boxcutter to my wrist, right over my throbbing pulse. I didn't even wince when I pressed the tip into my skin and dragged it down my wrist towards my elbow. It didn't hurt even half as much as the pain in my heart. In fact, it felt like a release. Skin, flesh, veins, all of it spread open underneath the blade. Warm red blood spurted up, pulsing with the beat of my heart.

Switching the blade to my blood coated hand, I repeated the process on my other wrist. The blade clattered to the floor and I stared down at my upturned wrists, watching the mesmerizing rivers of blood flowing out. Down my arms and legs, over the bed and onto the floor.

So much blood.

I wondered where I would go after this, if I would get to see Uncle Declan again. Maybe. Maybe not. Maybe I was just too evil. I desperately wished it was different. I missed him so much. The last thing I wanted in this life was to see him again.

It didn't take long until my vision started to darken and my body became weak. For that I was thankful. No more pain. No more sadness.

No more.

Soon I would be free. Maybe I could be better in my next life. A better person. Smarter, stronger, more loving.

As for now, now I would fly.

My body slumped back onto the bed, the world spinning. Dark shadows slid across the walls and I vaguely heard a familiar voice scream in pain. My heart stuttered while it attempted to keep beating. I felt cold, numb. Everywhere except my wrists. Those were warm, hot from the blood that was still trickling out. The world slowly disappeared as I gave one last sigh of relief.

It was finally over.

MALACHI

IT WAS A LONG DAY.

After dealing with Ember's crap the day before, I was tired and ready for bed. I was about to stop by Zara's and pick up my daughter, Mali when I thought I heard someone call my name. Pausing in the middle of the empty hall I listened carefully. At first I assumed it was just my imagination then I heard it again. It was quiet yet loud all at the same time. The voice was familiar enough that I found myself following it. Unfortunately, as hard as I tried I couldn't place the voice.

Before I realized it, I was standing in front of Leah's door.

I frowned in confusion, wondering why the voice led me here then my mind flashed to the last time I saw Leah Rassmussen. The day that Chriton and I tore into her. She looked absolutely broken that day. But what was more surprising was how she drew away from my touch and refused to talk to me. Her reaction that day was completely out of the ordinary. In fact, most of her actions in the past year were out of the ordinary. Even after we lost Declan, Leah kept her shy but upbeat attitude.

While Leah and I were never truly close, we were friends in a way, connected by our mutual love of one person. Her guardian, Declan Rassmussen, took me under his wing when I first joined the forces and his team. He quickly became my mentor and best friend. Declan loved his little niece more than anything just as Leah obviously worshiped her uncle.

After Declan was killed, I took it upon myself to step up and keep an eye on her. From a distance. That wasn't one sided as Leah quickly took it upon herself to start sending me letters and care packages as she did with her uncle. I knew she was doing her best to keep an eye on me like I was her. Unfortunately, despite the breadth and depth of our association with each other, our relationship was still stilted due to my issues with boundaries.

As second in command I was quickly put in charge of Declan's team only to have the team completely change. Some of the members were reassigned, but the majority were honourably discharged. Before I knew it, I was basically leading a whole new team populated by a whole new crew of brothers. Brothers that still stood by my side to this day.

Sighing, I knocked on the suite door. Since I was already here I might as well check up on her. I grimaced at the thought of the incoming conversation. I really didn't want to talk to her. She changed so much in the past year that lately I really wanted nothing to do with her at all.

Shaking my head in disgust, I turned to walk away. This was useless, she wasn't answering anyways.

That voice came again, this time in an angry demanding hiss that sent the small hairs on my body standing straight up.

"Fine." I scowled and spun back around to knock again. When I once again didn't get an answer I started keying in the code that would bypass security. I didn't even know why I was doing this, listening to some stupid voice, but I was.

The door swung open and my heart stopped in horror.

Blood was everywhere.

The metallic smell inundated my nostrils while the horrifying sight of it staining the floor, the bed, and the legs hanging off the bed caused my mind to stop. Luckily, my body knew what to do.

Yelling, I frantically sprinted across the room and to the bed, just avoiding the boxcutter on the floor.

"Leah, baby, shit, what did you do? Oh God, what did you do?" I jumped on the bed and began shaking Leah's body. Her big grey eyes fluttered and blood spurted from her opened wrists. Terror flooded my being. I couldn't lose her. My words sobbed out as agonized tears flooded my eyes. "No, no, no. You have to stay with me, baby. Stay with me, Teach."

Feverishly messaging Medical, I sprinted to the bathroom and grabbed some towels. I tied them tightly around Leah's limp wrists in an attempt to stop the sluggish flow of blood while I prayed.

Her breathing was alarmingly slow, barely even there, her pulse thready and weakly stuttering.

"Please, Teach, please. Stay with me. Help is on its way." I begged the limp, dying woman while my shaking, blood coated hands smoothed over her ghostly pale face.

My heart didn't seem to be beating properly and I couldn't breathe. Everything around us was unfocused and time was moving sluggishly slow. The world was a violent swirling whirlwind with Leah's dying body right at the center. Leaning down I pressed my wet face to hers. "I am so fucking sorry, Leah. Stay. Please stay." I breathed against her lips, hoping that my breath would give her the strength to live.

A loud commotion at the door signalled the incoming Medical team. "Move." Dr. John James barked, running up on Leah's other side. I climbed off the bed and backed away while I watched John and his dedicated nurse, Daniel, work on the limp woman.

My mind was struggling with the fact that, after all this time of trying to keep her safe, I was losing her. That thought tore though me, destroying me. I spent two decades holding her at arms length and now for the life me I couldn't understand why.

"We are losing her." John stated through clenched teeth sending more shards of terror ripping though me. "She's lost too much blood."

"Here." I scrambled back onto the bed beside Leah, pushing my arm into the doctor's face.

"What the...?"

"Universal doner." I snapped out sharply, shaking my arm at him.

"Daniel." John turned to his nurse, but Daniel was already pulling out the equipment they needed.

In quick succession I was expertly hooked up to an IV that ran my blood straight into Leah's veins.

It was all happening so fast yet entirely too slow, all the while I prayed for my best friend's niece. A woman I kept firmly at the periphery of my life while not quite willing to let her go completely. A woman who I blamed when she began to change. Changes that, looking back now, I shouldn't have ignored.

These thoughts were only compounded when we finally got her to Medical and into one of the exam rooms. My arm was replaced by a bag of blood while John stitched up her wrists. When John told me that she was out of danger relief hit me so hard that I felt lightheaded.

Then, thankfully, she woke up.

And completely lost it.

Leah looked around with wild eyes. She started screaming and ripping at her bandages. Seeing her like that scared me to death at the same time it filled me with enough rage that I wanted to kill someone.

"What did you do?" She shrieked furiously, her bruised looking eyes filled heartbreaking pain. "Why? Why didn't you just let me die?"

I frantically launched myself from the chair and grabbed her arms in an attempt to stop her from hurting herself even more. She twisted and arched violently, screaming so loudly that I feared for her throat.

"Let me die!" She shrieked, her sickly pale face contorting horrendously. "I was finally fucking free! Let me be free!"

"Leah!" I yelled back, wrapping my arms around her and trying to contain the woman to no avail. John came bursting into the room, a prepared syringe in his hand that he immediately plunged into her arm.

Leah's struggles slowed and became lethargic, her head fell back across the arm I was using to brace her neck, tears rolled from her unfocused grey eyes and down her pale cheeks. The look on her face almost sent me to my knees.

"Uncle Declan, take me with you." She slurred one last time before her eyes closed.

"What the fuck was that?" John hissed, his eyes staring angrily down at the unconscious woman.

In complete shock, I could do nothing but shake my head. I wanted to maim, kill, destroy. It was my job to keep her safe and alive. A job I took on when Declan died. It was now clear that I completely fucked up, I failed her. I delicately laid the limp woman down on the bed, sliding a gentle hand down her soft yet disturbingly pale cheek.

"Check her wrists and keep a sharp eye on her. And call Dr. Daniels. I will be back." Filled with resolve, I left Medical and stalked straight to Operations.

"Marko. I need you to contact the Egyptian base. I want them to get every piece of information from that bitch we just transferred there." I hissed out my demand while I twisted a chair over to his desk and sat down beside him.

"I thought we had everything. They video taped it all." Marko gave me a confused frown.

"Not pertaining the Andromadans. This is about Leah." I told him, my jaw clenching with my anger.

Marko studied my face for a long moment before he nodded and got on it.

I moved over to one of the couches running the back length of the large, open room and waited for the information to start coming in. It didn't take long, and it was disturbing.

Returning to the chair beside Marko, he and I popped in some earbuds and watched the communiques as they came in. The residents of the Egyptian base were quick to interrogate Ember as per our request.

I was fairly shocked when the woman was only too happy to boast. She continually called Leah down while bragging about the power she held over the poor woman. Ember told them how she did it. Slowly, step by step, she manipulated Leah until the poor woman was completely in her control. Ember laughed as she explained how she kept Leah obedient with a mixture of mental and physical abuse. According to Ember a quick slap or pinch or even a slight stab to the leg went a long way. Mentally, she successfully convinced Leah that she was nothing, worthless. Leah was stupid and ugly and fat and disgusting. Ember shared that Leah ended up being persuaded that no one but Ember would ever care about someone like her.

That's when Ember came out with the kicker.

"If I ever see that bitch again, I am going to do so much more than that tiny little stab I gave her last time. I am going to fucking skin the ugly hag. Slowly. It's her fault that I am in this mess. Somehow she persuaded me not to kill that Blaze slut. Stupid bitch somehow fucking convinced me to ignore the slut and go after Coren instead. I made sure the bitch paid for opening her ugly assed mouth. But not enough. I will make her pay for fucking me over with her stupid assed advice. She will fucking regret the day she was born. If I just listened to my instincts then that slut would be dead and Coren would be where he belongs, under my heel."

"That is one severely disturbed woman." Marko breathed, sliding his fingers under his glasses to rub his eyes.

"Yup." I agreed through a set of clenched teeth, biting back my urge to fly to Egypt and kill the bitch myself. "Update the Egyptians with the new reports on Leah. Let's leave the decision of what to do with Ember up to them."

Marko nodded and his tattooed fingers began to flash over the keyboard.

"Report all of it then bury it, Marko. Complete confidentiality. Only accessible to you and me. Not even Lysander." Marko nodded sharply, his eyes in complete agreement with my order.

With a satisfied nod, I left Operations and returned to Medical. Leah was awake, staring listlessly at Dr. Daniels who was speaking softly to her.

"A moment please, doctor?" I asked, gesturing to Leah.

Dr. Daniels gave a sharp nod and left the room, giving us the privacy I requested. Sitting on the edge of the bed next to Leah, I reached out and smoothed my fingers down her tearstained cheek. She didn't move, didn't even blink, her eyes still staring at the spot Dr. Daniels recently evacuated.

"The Egyptians are currently learning how arrogant and boastful Ember is. She is turning out to be a fount of information." I whispered down to Leah.

I got a reaction with that. Leah's eyes squeezed shut and those tears started again, squeezing out from between her clenched eyelids.

"Why did you save me? You don't even like me. You never did." Leah asked, her voice so quiet I needed to strain just to hear it.

"I don't know." I didn't refute her claims, instead I leaned down to rest my forehead against the side of her head. "But know this Teach, I will never stop trying to save you."

"No more touching." She was back to whispering, her head jerking away from mine in a violent motion.

I drew back, stunned at her demand. Leah was a toucher, always was. Small, unintrusive things that only made people feel better. Until Ember's manipulations. Until Chriton's accusations. Now she believed that all touches were bad.

My heart pounded fiercely in denial. There was no way I was about to let that happen, not between us. My hand whipped out, gripping her stubborn little chin and directing her back to me. Placing my free hand beside her on the bed I bent down until my face was right in hers. "Mere hours ago, I found you covered in blood, your skin pale and ice cold. I am sorry, Teach, but after that I earned the right to touch you just so that I can make damned sure that you are still warm. Still fucking alive."

Her grey eyes filled with resignation and they fell to her bandages while she sighed quietly.

Healing from this was going to be a long, hard road for her. For the both of us. And the worst of it was that I didn't know if I would be of any help to her. But I was determined to do everything I could to try. My boundaries were officially blown to pieces where she was concerned and there was no way I was going to allow her to leave me. My heart couldn't handle it.

I decided that my first step was to approve a recent application for a volunteer at Care. A shy, introverted woman named Salem. A perfect foil to the shy yet kind Leah.

LEAH

"I AM SORRY. FOR EVERYTHING I did to you and your family." I began.

I was still weak from blood loss, my wrists freshly bandaged. My hands were clenched tightly on the long sleeves of the loose sweater I was wearing.

I was standing in front of Chriton with the rest of his family, the Guardians, standing protectively at his back. The Andromadan Guardians with their dark copper skin tone, black hair, and bright blue eyes. All of them tall and muscular with striking beauty. All of them carrying an innate deadly presence.

Biting the bullet, I came to their new suite so that I could apologize to Chriton. I apologized to Blaze and Coren the night I tried to take my life, but now I desperately needed to apologize to Chriton.

The whole family, even the dangerous looking newcomer with his eyepatch and white striped hair, was staring down at me with hard, unyielding eyes filled with hate and disgust. Chriton was looking to the side in his attempt to show me that I wasn't worth his attention.

I licked my dry lips and locked my shaking knees. I was determined to get through this. No matter what.

"I cannot tell you how much I regret doing the things I did. Helping Ember get to your brother. Touching you, a...assaulting you the way I did. Without your permission. Anything mean and rude I ever said about Blaze. All of it. I am truly sorry. I promise that from here on out, none of you will ever have to deal with me again." I finished before dropping my eyes to the floor and backing away from the door slowly.

I couldn't stop myself from jerking when I heard Chriton snarl, "Good riddance." Right before the door slammed shut.

I slowly walked away from the suite, praying that I would reach my own suite before the agony in my soul sent me collapsing to the floor.

Luckily my prayers were answered. I did reach my suite. I got just inside the door before my knees gave out. Exhausted, I laid on the floor, falling asleep as my tears flowed down my cheeks.

When the morning came I found myself tucked safely my bed surrounded by a familiar scent. Malachi. As much as I wanted to stay right where I was I forced myself to get up, out of the comfort that enclosed me, and go to work.

The weeks passed slowly after that. One day at a time. That's what Dr. Daniels told me during our weekly sessions. She clarified to me the reality of what Ember did, how she manipulated and twisted me. Dr. Daniels did everything she could to reassure me that I wasn't the person Ember convinced me I was. But Dr. Daniels was wrong. I was that person. I was the one who hurt those people, not Ember. I hurt

Chriton and his family. And for that, I was a disgusting worthless human.

For that I would pay.

In the meantime, I made damned sure to avoid any and all Andromadans.

Unfortunately, I couldn't really avoid Malachi DeMarques.

His adopted daughter, Mali, was in my class. A friendly kind caring girl that, like the father raising her, was far too adventurous. Not only that but Malachi was the human leader of the Base and thusly was able to track me down no matter where I was.

And believe me, he did.

CHAPTER 1

LEAH

My head was down, my eyes were trained on the tablet in my hand that was describing the new and improved class syllabus as I walked down the empty halls. I was happy that it now included the elements we agreed upon at the last teachers conference. The Nordic and Andromadan cultures were now being included.

Something painfully slammed into my shoulder causing me to gasp and clutch my arm. My tablet flew out of my nerveless hand and smashed on the hard rock floor. Usually, I kept a keen ear out when I was traversing the halls like this, so to have someone silently come up on me like this was such a surprise.

"I am sorry." I stated automatically, immediately stepping away from the person I inadvertently collided with. My eyes came up to see a familiar face with a set of bright blue eyes before darting away. Chriton. He was rubbing his well formed bicep while watching Diad bend over to pick up my smashed tablet.

Diad was one of the Ancients. As an Andromadan he had the tall, dark complexion of their race with bright green eyes that seemed to be specific to the Ancient family. He also boasted model good looks to go with the exotic features of his race. He was Salem's brother in law. Salem was my best friend.

I felt my heart stop and my face pale at the sight of Chriton, the man that I did everything I could to avoid. I only travelled the halls when the likelihood of him moving about was at its lowest. I spent most of my time when I wasn't working either at Care, the 24 hour daycare and Playcenter, or in my own suite. I always made sure to drop by certain areas like the library when I was sure that none of the family would be there.

"Leah." Diad smiled congenially at me, handing my broken tablet over to me. Diad and Chriton both bore similar joking, fun loving, caring attitudes with Diad, at least according to others, having more of a trigger temper.

"Thank you." I whispered, taking the tablet with a shaking hand. My other hand still clutched what I was sure was going to be a very bruised shoulder.

"How are you today?" Diad tilted his head at me and asked. This wasn't unusual as Diad was always very nice to me. In fact, most of the Ancients were.

"Good, thank you." I gave Diad a shaky but grateful smile. I was doing everything I could to ignore the man beside Diad while slowly backing away from the two men. "And, uh, how are you?"

"Good. When are you going to drop by the Cafeteria and check out my food?" Diad continued, his eyes narrowing on me. Diad was a chef and recently started helping out in the Cafeteria.

"Yes. I, uh, usually just eat in my suite. Then I have leftovers for lunches." I awkwardly explained, licking my dry lips. "I, uh, are you enjoying it?"

"I am." Diad said, his voice softening. "You should come by sometime. Check me out."

"Sometime." I nodded, feeling almost like one of those bobblehead dolls. While I had zero plans of going to the Cafeteria, I knew that I could at least be polite.

"Thursday?" Diad pressed, his green eyes watching me intently.

"I, uh, I have a parent meeting Thursday." I shared with him honestly. "I need to, uh, get going, get some papers graded." I stuttered and attempted to subtly slide around the two men.

A quick glance showed me that Chriton was still standing at Diad's side, his bright blue eyes centered down on the floor, his thumbs tucked into the belt of his black slacks. His white dress shirt stretched across his muscular chest in a way that masked yet displayed all of the dips and ridges that populated his torso.

"Some other time then." Diad nodded slowly, his body turning with mine.

Once I figured I was far enough beyond them, I gave Diad a relatively strained smile. "Yeah. Um, it was great to see you. Bye." I nodded and continued on my way down the hall as fast as I could walk, my eyes trained intently on the floor in front of me.

I could feel those bright Andromadan eyes, one blue pair, one green pair, burning into my back, following me down the hall. Needing to be away from them, no him, Chriton, and out of sight as soon as possible, I rounded the first corner I came to and sprinted away.

Reaching my suite, I messaged Operations to let them know about the incident and that I would need a new tablet. It didn't take long before I received a message back from Marko.

Leah, this is not a report worthy incident. No one was hurt. While this one is more important than the others due to the requirement of a new tablet, it still isn't enough for a full report. You don't need to keep doing this.

Yes, I do. As per Malachi. Ever since the incident with Ember and the Andromadans over a year ago, I made sure to report any and all incidents to Operations. Especially the ones that involved Chriton and the Guardians. Which weirdly enough was happening more and more often despite my attempts to avoid them.

"You shouldn't be here." I bluntly told the maddening man that showed up at my door half an hour later.

"Why not?" Malachi asked, his dark brown eyes assessing over me.

"Because I am fine." I told him with a roll of my eyes.

"I read the report, Teach." Malachi grunted, brushing by me and into my suite. I closed the door and turned to study him.

Malachi was a tall man of about 6'2. His indigenous heritage was written all over him. The beautiful dusky color of his skin that always made my fingers tingle to feel. His distinctive hawk like nose. His high cheekbones and sharp jaw. His dark brown, almond shaped eyes. The jagged length of dark brown hair that fell down to his cheekbones in the front and over the top with the back brushing the nape of his neck. He was extremely striking.

While I obviously noticed his good looks, I was a woman after all, I never allowed myself to see him as an attractive, available male. Mostly because from the moment I met him at the age of 8, he set his boundaries and maintained them throughout the whole of our lives. We may keep an eye on each other and keep in contact but beyond that we stayed out of each others personal lives.

Case in point, Mali, his adopted daughter. While I heard about him saving and adopting the child from the people around the Base, he, himself, never told me about her. He never asked me to watch her or to help with her. Not like he did with Zara or the others around Base.

Not that I didn't end up developing a close relationship with the kind yet daring girl when I ended up being her grade 1 teacher. Now though, with her recently moving into grade 2, I missed her. A lot.

"I was good. I didn't talk to him other than to apologize." I reassured the man, my knuckle coming up to my teeth.

"I know." Malachi mentioned, stopping behind the couch and leaning a hip against it. "Come here." He ordered with gesture of his hand.

"Jesus, Malachi. I just told you..."

"Leah." Malachi's voice hardened, his hand flipping over to point a demanding finger at the floor.

"You know, I am getting damned tired of your orders." I snarled at him, getting angry enough to throw something at the frustrating man's head.

"That's funny. With how fucking argumentative and stubborn you have been in the past year you should be getting used to them." Malachi clipped out, his dark eyes flashing. "Now get your ass over here so that I can check your shoulder. Or would you rather I dragged you down to Medical and have them deal with it."

"You are a pain in my ass, you know." I rolled my eyes and stomped over to him.

Using his long fingered hand, he gently pulled the shoulder of my shirt down far enough that he could see the bruised flesh underneath. "You are one to talk." He noted, running his calloused fingers gently over the area. I couldn't help but shiver when his breath brushed over my unprotected skin.

"You're breathing on me." I explained to him when his amused eyes darted up to mine, telling me he noticed my shiver. That was happening a lot, especially in the last couple of months, me reacting in some physical way to his presence. It was confusing, these new feelings.

I could only blame it on the fact that for the past year, Malachi was around a lot more than usual. And those boundaries of his, they seemed to be a lot more flexible. There was now touching and talking. He actually asked me how I was doing in a way that wasn't just small talk. It even appeared like he truly wanted to know, like he actually...cared.

"Diad dropped by Operations. He was concerned with how strange you were acting. He said, and I quote, 'she was very pale looking, almost terrified. All she seemed to want was to get away from us as fast as she could. She has never reacted that way before.' When he wouldn't leave it alone, I was forced to show him the reports." Malachi explained softly.

"Y...you told him?" I gasped as sharp pains pinned my chest. Diad knew what I did and now the rest of them would. Salem would know what a truly horrible, disgusting person I was. She would irrevocable stop talking to me. I would be all alone once again.

My agonized eyes dropped to the floor, my mind whirling, spinning darkly. Maybe it was for the best. She was too good for me anyways. I didn't really deserve a friend like her. Alone. That's really what I deserved.

"Leah!" Malachi's sharp voice and the hard hand he used to grip my jaw brought me back. My hand automatically came up to remove his, only for his fingers to tighten warningly. I hated when he did that. "I only shared the reports that pertained to Chriton's grievances. Nothing else. And I told him all of it was completely confidential. He assured me that he wouldn't say anything. To anyone."

I forced myself to take a deep shuddering breath in and nod slowly. It didn't matter if Diad told anyone, he himself would still look at me differently. I didn't know if I could stand that.

"Teach?" Malachi pressed.

"No, I, uh, I am fine." I told him. "It's ok."

"You are lying to me." Malachi clipped out, his face hardening, his fingers finally releasing me.

"No." I shook my head, gave him a shaky smile. "And yes. It hurts that he now knows. But its for the best. He, they, should know what kind of person they are letting into their lives. It's, uh, better this way."

"I hate that you see yourself this way now. That's not who you are. That was never who you were." Malachi sighed and studied me with his dark brown, almost black eyes. "That is not the bright and kind girl Declan introduced me too."

"Yeah, well, Uncle Declan is gone." I hissed bluntly, automatically darting away and circling around the couch to the other side of it. I needed to get away from the exasperating man. He knew just how to push all of my buttons.

"You don't think I don't know that." Malachi snapped angrily. Unlike his kindness and touches I could deal with his anger.

"Do you?" I asked softly, pushing him even further.

Malachi's eye narrowed on me at my subtle hint that he was still hanging on. "Teach." Malachi started only for me to cut him off.

"Look, I don't see myself any certain way. I only see the reality of who I am." I shrugged at him.

"Teach." Malachi repeated with a soft growl.

I gave him a smile, trying to reassure him that everything was going to be fine. "Really, Malachi." I vehemently reassured him. "It's fine. All of it is fine. You don't have to worry anymore. You can let go and move on."

"Yeah, you know damned well that is not going to happen. I think you should come stay with Mali and me. At least for a couple of days." Malachi brought up, his eyes taking on a strange gleam.

"No." I shook my head in denial. "That's not a good idea. Seriously. I am not about to do anything. I am just going to go to bed and try to forget about today."

"Hmm." Malachi hummed, running his dark eyes over me, assessing me in an intense way that he started to do in the past year. I wasn't quite sure if I liked the strange way it made me feel or if I hated it. Either way, I couldn't find it in me to stop him from doing it.

"Malachi." I practically begged.

Malachi nodded and slowly walked to the door, pausing for a moment to take one last look at me. "Call me, Teach. For anything."

"I will." We both knew that I lied.

Once the door to my suite closed behind the man, I felt relief drive over me and send me into a state of exhaustion. I was tired. Tired of being me.

Crawling into bed, I was immediately asleep in moments. Unfortunately, sleep wasn't the mindless outlet I thought it would be, but then it never was. Realistic nightmares were becoming my new best friend.

MALACHI

"JUST CLEAN IT UP." I ordered from the chair I was sitting on in my dining room.

"It needs new stitches, you dumbass." Leah snapped from where she was bent over my shoulder.

"Just clean it up and slap some of that tape on it." I turned my head to look at her narrowed grey eyes.

"What does it look like I am doing?" She demanded.

I barely bit back my grin at the attitude the woman was giving me. An attitude that developed the moment I saved her life. An attitude that I gloried in bringing out. If I kept her fighting then there was no chance of her giving up again, and there was no way I was going to allow her to give up, not again. Plus, that sexy little attitude got to me every time.

"Besides, if I go to Medical with ripped stitches I am pretty sure that Zara will actually tattoo her name on me." I winced at the thought.

"So instead, after you ignored doctors' orders to be careful, you took on a lizard all by yourself only to have the thing throw you across a room. You slammed into the side of a table, flipped over said table and 'somehow' ripped your stitches. But it's ok because in the end you killed it." Leah stated sarcastically while she rolled her eyes at me.

She finished cleaning the wound up before using her fingers to press the spread edges of the laceration together. I grunted at the pain that radiated through my already aching shoulder.

"Sorry." Leah whispered, her breath brushing over my ear.

"Don't be." I advised her. She really shouldn't be. Despite the pain I was still enjoying the feel of her hands on me. "Just get it done."

"I will if you hold still." She argued, making me chuckle. "God, why do I put up with your ass?"

"That sounds like a you question." I told her with a mischievous grin.

"Just give me...there, I got it. That should hold it." She finished with my shoulder. "If you don't screw around."

"Who the hell would I screw around with?" I joked, shivering at the cold feel of the antibacterial cream she was slathering over my shoulder.

"Why are you asking me? I don't know your tastes in women. I mean, beyond one night with Deliah, which to be frank, yuck." Leah stated, walking around me to go wash her hands in the sink.

She was wearing a pair of black slacks that cupped her thighs and ass beautifully. Those were paired with a long sleeved white button up shirt and a black vest. The shirt was unbuttoned just enough that I was able to get a glimpse of the delicious cleavage her fascinating vest pushed up. Leah was around 5'6 with long, golden blond hair that was braided back from her face and big grey eyes. Her face was heart shaped with rounded cheekbones and a wide mouth. She boasted a swimmer's musculature due to her chosen sport.

She was beautiful. Something I never noticed until the Drako occupation forced me to bring her in. Seeing the woman she became forced me to build and maintain even more boundaries. Not that I didn't always have boundaries when it came to her, when it came to everyone in fact. Well, everyone except my daughter. And Declan.

It was something I learned as a child from my parents. Always maintain boundaries.

Now, however, I no longer wanted boundaries. Especially not between Leah and I.

"Yeah, it was yuck." I shuddered at the memory of that night. It really wasn't a good night. At all. It took me no less than six showers after that night before I finally felt clean again.

Leah shot me an amused look from the sink. She crossed her arms and leaned a hip against the counter.

"Leah!" Mali cried, coming into the suite with Dr. Zara Hastings on her heals. Zara, a woman with hazel eyes and straight black hair, was pregnant with her third and fourth children after giving birth to her first and second children with her first pregnancy. Apparently the twin Nordics she was married to bred, well, twins.

"Uh huh." Zara studied me and my newly fixed wound with knowing eyes.

"I have enough tattoos." I told the doctor while I watched my beloved daughter bypass me and head straight to the smiling woman still standing at the counter.

"Hey, Mali-girl." Leah hugged Mali back in a way that radiated love. I smiled like I always did when I saw the way Leigh cared about my girl.

"You still should've come in." Zara scowled, walking towards me.

"It's fine, Teach fixed it." I stood from the chair while batting Zara's hands away. Walking into my room, I dug out a button up shirt and tried to shrug into as I returned to the main room.

"Here." Leah rolled her eyes and helped pull the shirt up over my sore shoulder when she saw the way I was wincing. "God, you are stubborn."

"Uh huh, I am the stubborn one in this relationship." Now it was my turn to roll my eyes.

"Well, since you have him well in hand, Leah, I am going to go save Krishnia from the twins." Zara grinned at our banter and gave us a quick wave before she left.

"Are you staying for supper, Leah?" Mali asked from the fridge she was digging in.

"Yes." I answered before Leah could.

CHAPTER 2

LEAH

I ducked my head to hide my smile at Malachi's answer. I couldn't lie, I was looking forward to spending time with Mali. While I helped the two make supper, I tried to ignore the way the three of us were working so close in the kitchen area.

"Shit." I gasped when I turned to dump the onion I finished cutting up into the pot of chili we were building and ended up walking into the side of Malachi's chest. My face ended up buried in his shirt covered underarm because he was stretching up to the cupboard above in order to dig through the spices.

His shirt was hanging open thusly his exceptionally muscled chest was mostly bare. Bulky pecs housed dusky nipples, abdominal muscles that dipped sharply, eight times to be precise, an interesting V that led down to what was kept between his legs. All of it enhanced with colourful designs.

To be honest, I wasn't sure about his opinion on having enough tattoos because I really liked the ones I could see. That was one thing that always fascinated me when it came to him, the pictures and designs that seemed to just appear on Malachi's flesh.

A Raven and Wolf sharing the upper part of one arm, a Tiger and a Python on the other. The forces tattoo on one of his forearms and a feather with Mali's name on the other. Those were the one's I knew about before I saw his shirtless torso for the first time today.

Now I knew he also had a number of others that were consistently covered by clothing. The tattooed leather necklace with its dreamcatcher pendant. A skull and crossbones on one shoulder blade. A dog tag carrying a familiar, beloved name on the back of the other shoulder. There was a number of lines of beautiful flowing writing down the right side of his rib cage. Straight down the center of his back, right over his spine, was a design of the solar system with the sun at the nape of his neck, followed by Mercury, Venus, and so on down the line of his back.

Malachi grunted and lowered his arm, his body adjusting slightly so that I could reach the pot. His eyes twinkled down at me when his fingers brushed down my back leaving behind an explosion of shivers.

"Sorry." I winced in apology. "I thought you were still over helping Mali with the tomatoes."

"Nope. She's got them." Malachi grinned and gave me a wink.

"Are these too big?" Mali asked drawing my attention over to the cutting board she was using. The girl was studying her cut up tomato with a frown.

I left Malachi to his spicing and walked over to her in order to examine the tomatoes myself. "Nope." I told her, sliding my fingers through her smooth blond hair. "Those are perfect. Go dump them in the pot."

"Can I do the celery, too?" Mali asked, jumping down from the chair she was kneeling on and carefully walking the cutting board over to her father who was waiting.

"Yup." I nodded, washing off the celery in question before handing it over.

"Grab the corn out of the freezer, please, Teach." Malachi gestured to the freezer while he continued to spice the boiling concoction on the stove.

"Sir, yes, sir." I mocked, giving him a sharp salute, before turning to dig in the freezer.

"Careful there, woman. I may start expecting that answer every time." Malachi chuckled, his eyes gleaming.

"Anything you say, Boss." I teased him by using his call sign, pulling the corn out and waving it at him.

"Holy shit. Are you actually teasing me?" Malachi gasped, pressing his hand to his heart and leaning way back. "Mali-girl, we now have experienced a new Leah element. Teasing."

Mali laughed and rolled her eyes at her father. "Leah teases me all the time. She always laughs and points out my smile after she does it and says 'There it is. There's that beautiful smile.'"

I smiled and shook my head at them while walking the corn over to the pot and dumping it in. "Here you go, Boss."

"Careful there, baby, I am finding that I really like it when you call me Boss." Malachi waggled his eyebrows down at me.

"Goofball." I rolled my eyes at him and turned to check on Mali.

After supper, I stood to start cleaning up. When Malachi tried to rise and help I placed a hand on his unwounded shoulder and pressed him back down. "Relax." I ordered him. "Mali and I got this, right Mali-girl?" I grinned over at Mali who returned my grin and jumped straight up to help.

"Yup." Mali agreed, carrying the dirty dishes over to the sink for me.

Malachi smiled warmly, pulling a tablet over and starting to work on it.

"Shhh." Mali whispered softly as I finished wringing the dish cloth out. She was tiptoeing away from her unconscious father who was bent over the table, his head resting on the arm that was curled in front of him.

"Come on, let's go do your homework on the couch." I urged the girl.

That was when I truly fell in love. With a couch. It was long and wide with the perfect amount of cushioning. Not to soft, not to hard. I wanted this couch.

After we finished her homework, Mali got ready for bed and showed me her growing reading skills by reading me her bedtime book.

"Leah?"

"Yes, Mali-girl." I was tucking her in one last time when she reached up to run her fingers through my loosened hair.

"I am glad that you stayed for supper because I miss you, a lot." She whispered, looking up at me with her beautiful brown eyes.

"Me too, Mali. I miss you too, Mali-girl." I told her, leaning over to touch my nose to hers. "Now, get some sleep, my darling girl."

"Ok, Leah." Mali wrinkled her nose and smiled at me.

After making sure her nightlight was on, I closed her door far enough to leave just an inch of a crack open before heading to the man that was still fast asleep. I walked over to Malachi, planning on waking him up but once I saw how exhausted he still looked, I decided against it.

Pulling a blanket off the couch, I carefully covered him up with it. My fingers smoothed his jagged hair from his face so that I could press a soft kiss to his temple. Then I turned the lights down and returned to my own suite for the night.

MALACHI

MY COMS, AN ALL ON in communication device that went around my wrist, dinging with an incoming message woke me up.

I didn't mean to fall asleep. And to be honest, I wasn't happy about the fact that I woke up with one hell of a stiff back and a wicked headache. I was also not impressed to see my suite quiet and empty. Then my fingers touched the blanket that Leah, the caring woman, obviously set over me so that I wouldn't get cold and I couldn't help but smile.

Looking down at my coms, I saw an incoming message from Grayson. A message that essentially tore straight into the whole of my being.

It contained a report involving Ranch security and the newest humanoid divergent group. The canines. At the end of the report there was an encrypted message left for me.

As per your request on any word relating to Leah, according to new Guardian intel, she is a Conversance. Chriton's. This is all according to Bane and has apparently been known since our initial introduction to the canine divergents.

This was a message I immediately sent to Marko with a request to flag any research the Guardians made pertaining to Leah or me. This way I would be notified with what they were looking at and when.

I knew if they thought Leah was theirs, Chriton's, they would attempt a deep dive on her past. And mine by association.

As for her being Chriton's Conversance, I knew what that meant. Soulmates. And to be honest, if I was a better man, I would step back and let him have her. But with the way my heart and very soul was screaming in denial I was pretty sure I wasn't going to be able to.

My hands possessively tightened on the blanket, pulling it closer around me.

CHAPTER 3

LEAH

Girl's night out.

I felt happy to be included but also extremely awkward. Mostly because the night was being hosted by Amber and Blaze in the Guardian suite. Amber was the Conversance of Callden, the father of the Guardian family.

If it wasn't for Salem begging me to come with them, I would be safe in my own suite watching urban adventurers tour abandoned buildings. Instead, I spent the night sitting beside River, keeping my mouth shut and my hands to myself. At least until Royce decided to use me as an example of the difference between freewill and destiny and how the two could go hand in hand. It was a heartbreaking example that hit way to close for comfort. Then she brought it all home with a disturbing reality.

If my Uncle didn't die like he did then Malachi would never have been made team leader. The team wouldn't have become what it was today and they wouldn't have founded the Base. Which meant that there was a large chance that the Andromadan Alliance wouldn't have decided to help Earth in the fight against the Drako's to the extent that it was and most of the women at the table wouldn't have found their soulmates.

It would be a very different world indeed. All because of one death. And for the life of me, I couldn't bring myself around to the thought of saving my Uncle at the detriment of everyone else around me.

My heart gave a pang at that thought, my mind travelling to when and if I would get to see my uncle again.

When Marko, Madron, and Catro arrived to walk us home I was relieved that the night was finally over. Girl's night, for someone like me, was a painful thing to live through.

Rising from the table with River, I joined the group just when Coren came striding into the suite. The Guardian dodged around everyone else only to catch my arms in his strong grip and spin me back around to the table. My mind immediately started screaming at his touch. No touching.

"Stay." He ordered me fiercely while glaring at the group in silent warning to not step in. "Chriton is on his way right now to walk you. He said and I quote 'She won't like it if I have to chase her down again.'"

Marko's angry eyes moved from Coren to mine before they softened. They seemed to silently reassure me that everything would be ok. I couldn't help but sigh when the group slowly walked out the door without me.

Sitting quietly, I kept my eyes lowered. Coren eyed me skeptically for a long moment before eventually relaxing. Harper and Amber rose from the table to clean up while Blaze walked over to Coren and buried into her husband's arms.

Seeing my chance, I took it. I wasn't stupid. There was no chance I was waiting around to be berated by Chriton, again. The sound of the chair I shot out of falling to the floor coincided with my shoulder slamming the suite door open.

"Fuck." I heard Coren snarl right before the suite door closed behind me.

I raced though the halls, frantic to reach the safety of my suite. Then I ran straight into a hard chest. A familiar chest. I knew that Malachi was a large, well built man. I saw it with my own eyes. I just didn't get the full picture until I slammed into all of that unmovable hardness.

"Teach, baby, what's wrong?" His long, blunt fingers caught me before I could bounce off him to the floor. I felt my heart skip a beat when I was held against the long, hard stretch of his body. I could feel his heat. I could smell him more so than ever before. Deep and soft, like a tickle in my nostrils.

"I, uh..." I stumbled, licking at my suddenly dry lips.

"Leah." Malachi's eyes stared down into mine, doing his typical assessment of me.

"I, uh, nothing. Nothing is wrong." I whispered, dropping my eyes from the intensity of his. I gave myself a shake and pushed my arms against his chest.

"You know I hate it when you lie to me." Malachi growled, his frustrating hand finding my jaw and bringing my eyes back to his.

"I, uh, girl's night. I tried to leave with Marko and the others, but Coren came back and demanded that I wait for Chriton. I couldn't. Once Coren was distracted, I ran out. I don't know why but lately, its almost as if, no matter what I do, they are always around. The Guardians. Chriton." I stammered out, trying to explain to him what happened.

Malachi's jaw tightened, his eyes taking on a frustrated, angry look. He knew something. I could see it.

"What do you know?" I demanded, clenching my fist and pounding it on his chest.

"Grayson told me something." Malachi began explaining. "You know what the Andromadan Conversance is."

"Bullshit." I cried. Feeling fury mixing with anxiety, I ripped myself out of his arms. "Bullshit. If I was his..."

"I know that." Malachi snarled back, his own anger written on his face. "I know, Leah."

If I was Chriton's Conversance like Malachi said I was, there was no way he would have been able to treat me the way he did last year. Not with the way the Guardians went after their soulmates with the single minded determination they did. Not with the way they cared for and protected their Conversances.

"No." I denied with a vehement shake of my head. "No, I can't be his. He showed me that."

"No, you aren't. Not yet." Malachi agreed with a sharp nod, his eyes flashing dangerously. "Fucking hell." He took a quick step forward. His hand delved into my hair, tightening around the back of my head. I was yanked up into his hard chest. I gasped when his mouth dropped down to cover mine.

CHRITON

YEAH, I WAS GOING TO kill him.

I was going to kill my friend.

I watched him touch and kiss my Conversance.

Leah.

Malachi held her in his arms, his hand buried deep in golden blond hair. Leah's fingers were clutching at his shoulders, her face tipped up to his. I could see the way they fed from each other. Deep, wet kisses filled with desire.

My heart jerked painfully in my chest.

I lost her.

After everything. I lost my Conversance. My soulmate. I knew that I didn't deserve her. Not with everything I did. I couldn't understand what happened, why I didn't recognize her as mine. But I didn't. And now she was in the arms of another man.

I didn't realize I even moved until I collapsed to my knees in the familiar warmth of my own suite.

"Chriton!" Amber gasped as she fell beside me, her hands shaking my numb shoulders. Everything was numb except my bleeding heart.

"I lost her." I rasped, causing both my brother and father to jerk their heads towards me. Shock was written all over them.

"What the hell do you mean, you lost her?" Dad demanded, striding over to crouch down beside me.

"Leah. And Malachi." I whispered, my mind replaying the scene over and over again. "I was too late. I lost her."

"No." Dad's hands fell to my shoulders, giving me a harsh shake. "No. That isn't the way it works. Not with Conversances. You didn't lose her. There has to be something we are missing. We will figure it out, Chriton, you can't give up on this and I won't let you."

"It hurts." I breathed, feeling the burn of tears sliding down my face.

"I know, son. I know." Dad cupped my face and reassured me. "But you can't give up."

"I need to go." I whispered, feeling that pain starting to override the numbness.

"Ok. Ok. We will go to the Ranch for a couple of days. Get away." Dad whispered, pulling me into a hug.

I didn't say anything. I couldn't. For the first time in the whole of my life the fact that I was slowly drifting away didn't scare me. In fact, I felt like I welcomed it. Anything to stop the pain taking over my body.

When we returned a couple of days later I was frankly surprised when Malachi tracked me down. I was sitting in my suite trying to force myself to get up off of the couch.

I glared at the door when it popped open and Malachi waltzed in.

"You know, I could kill you." I told him, my mind screaming for me to do just that. "But you are, were, my friend. And she chose you."

Malachi walked over and dropped into the nearest chair. "She didn't choose fuck all." Malachi grunted, his dark eyes assessing over my sprawled form.

"I saw you two. I heard her deny me right before the two of you kissed." I told him, my voice emotionless, that familiar numbness in full effect. At least it was better than the pain.

"True." Malachi painfully agreed with my assessment. "I did kiss her. For the past year I have been slowly, bit by bit, falling in love with her."

"Why now?" I demanded, pushing up from the couch, needing to get away from the man before I killed him. "Why not before?"

"That is a good question. One you should probably be asking yourself." Malachi irritatingly pointed out.

"I denied her. I didn't recognize her as my Conversance, and I fucking pushed her away. My own fucking soulmate." I yelled, gesturing angrily to the door.

"True." Malachi shrugged, relaxing back in the chair and cocking his arms up behind his head.

Pausing, I stared at the relaxed man. "Something happened beyond that. You know something." I stated, pointing at him.

"Hmmm." Malachi hummed, his eyes narrowing on me.

"Tell me." I demanded, stepping towards him. "Wait, why are you even helping me?"

"Because even though I am falling in love with her, you still affect her. She is hurt and confused and very lost. Right now, she feels as if she has no one she can truly count on. She doesn't even fully trust me. Which is probably in her best interest because I am about to betray her trust in a way that she is probably never going to forgive." Malachi sighed and leaned forward to grab the tablet off of the table.

"Why are you helping me?" I asked.

"I told you. I am falling in love with her. And if by any chance she can be happier with you in her life then I can do nothing but give her that." He said quietly, his hands working over the tablet.

"You would give her up?" My eyebrows rose in surprise.

"Fuck no." He chuckled derisively. "I would however give her the chance to make her own decision. For that to happen you need to know what actually happened last year."

I narrowed my eyes at him for a moment before I understood. He wanted to give Leah whatever would make her happiest. Even if it wasn't him. I couldn't help but respect the man even more than I did before.

"Show me." I grunted, jerking my head to the TV and retaking my seat on the couch.

"Yeah, yeah, hold onto your pants." He returned.

After another minute a number of videos started. The first one was of Ember being interviewed by the Egyptians. Fury rose sharply within me and my hands clenched tightly when I heard the conceited woman laugh and brag about everything she did to Leah and everything she planned to do to Blaze and Coren.

"I want to kill her." I stated baldly. Ember planned to kill my brother's Conversance only to have Leah somehow convince her not to. Leah essentially saved Blaze's life.

"Right?" Malachi hissed out from beside me.

The videos of Ember's interrogations changed to surveillance footage that was timestamped a year ago. The first was of the Library where Leah was apologizing to Coren and Blaze. I remembered Coren telling me about that. "I knew she did this." I pointed at the screen only to pause in confusion when I saw her helping herself to a boxcutter that was laying on the desk. Something neither Coren nor Blaze noticed.

The screen blinked and it showed Leah sitting on her bed. Her head was bent down to the boxcutter that she was opening and closing.

"NO!" I yelled and jumped up from the couch when she dug the sharp blade into the delicate skin of her wrists. Pain slashed through my whole body. My hands came up to grip my hair and my legs gave out.

My body was frozen cold as I watched her slowly collapse to the bed, her life blood flowing out around her. The video sped up until her door opened and Malachi stepped inside. "You saved her." I whispered, watching him work desperately to keep her alive before helping Dr. James do the same.

"Yes." Malachi confirmed quietly. He was bent forward in the chair, his elbows on his knees, his head hanging on his neck. "That was the night after Ember was removed from the Base. That was the night that I finally allowed myself see Leah."

"You have been there for her this whole time. What makes you believe that after all of that I deserve her at all. I left her to that. I wasn't there when she needed me most." I scowled over at him.

"You didn't know, so how could you have been there for her? You didn't even realize she was your Conversance at the time" Malachi's head tipped up to mine as he made an attempt to reassure me.

"Thanks for that." I laughed derisively.

"No problem, man." Malachi leaned over and grasped my shoulder.

"I think I know why. At the time she was so far under that bitch's thumb that she wasn't even Leah. All I felt when Leah touched me was disgust because she was essentially Ember." I frowned, reaching up and gripping Malachi's wrist.

"And she has done everything to avoid you ever since. You haven't been around her to see the difference." Malachi nodded in understanding.

"Yeah." I mimicked his nod, falling silent for a moment. "How does she taste?"

"Like sunshine." Malachi chuckled and shook his head at me in amusement.

"Have you?" I asked him softly, needing to know.

"No. Just the one kiss." Malachi thankfully denied.

"Will you tell me if, when?" I stammered awkwardly.

"Only if you do the same." Malachi narrowed his eyes at me.

I studied him for a moment before giving him a sharp nod. If he was willing to give me that respect then I could only do the same.

"So, what now?" I asked him.

"Now you take a trip to the Ranch, and I pray that she doesn't hate me for this." Malachi sighed, rubbing his face with his hands.

"I just got back from the Ranch." I frowned in confusion.

"Yes. But since Leah is going out for the weekend in order to make a documentary for the school I figured you might want to join her." Malachi explained, his dark brown eyes darkening even more.

"Yeah, I might." I nodded slowly, standing up and reaching a hand down to him. "Thank you, Malachi."

"Yeah." He scoffed at himself.

CHAPTER 4

LEAH

I was so excited to be heading out to spend the weekend at the Ranch. The school needed someone to make a documentary on the area and the investigation. I was quick to volunteer.

"Hey, Wings." I happily greeted the visually contradictory man with white blond hair and dark brown eyes. He was going to pilot me out to the Ranch.

Wings was one hell of a pilot and part of the First security team. Within the Base, there were three security teams. The First team was the one that took part in most of the outside raids and missions. It was also the team that was headed by Malachi and consisted of men from his spec ops team.

Wings was actually in a triad relationship, something that seemed to be more and more of a regular occurrence within the Base, with Madron and my best friend Salem. My first friend since Ember, well, my first true friend ever, really. Except maybe Malachi, maybe. To be honest I wasn't really sure what Malachi was to me. He was an enigma.

Since that kiss the other night, every time I saw him my mind replayed it over and over. His firm mouth moving possessively, parting my lips so his tongue could delve inside my mouth. His rasping tongue licking over mine, taking over and owning me in a way that felt safe yet erotic. Then there was the taste of him, addictive. And the way his strong hands held me to him. By the time he released me I was breathless and shaking.

All of it kept swirling through my confused mind until I consistently caught myself staring at his lips every time he was close.

This new change was weird. For me, Malachi was always just...there. But for the past year he has been...here. Very much here. And for some reason it didn't feel as wrong as I thought it would.

"Leah." Wings grinned at me. "Ready to go?"

I followed the pilot up the ramp and into the Drako spaceship we would be taking to the Ranch. How we got this particular ship was a completely different story, involving another triad. Whatever happened, it was ours now.

"I am." I smiled and handed him the bags I brought. Two of them. One was a camera bag, and the other was a backpack with a couple pairs of clothes and some toiletries. Since I was only going out for two days, I didn't need to take very much.

Wings stowed the bags into one of the storage compartments and guided me to the cockpit. It was a sparse area with only three seats. One was clearly the pilot's seat and set further back then the last two. Those ones were about three feet apart from one another and set in front of some panels at the front of the room.

Since this was my first time on a spaceship and I had no idea what to do, I set about examining the seats at the front.

"Leah." A familiar voice exclaimed happily. Looking over to the entrance I saw Royce and her husband, Catro. "Are you going to the Ranch as well?"

"Yup." I nodded with a nervous but excited smile. "Lysander agreed to let me go and document the dig sites for the school. I am going to get some pictures and video footage of the digs as well as record interviews with the people working out there."

"That sounds exciting." Royce, the beautiful, white-haired woman returned my smile, leaning over to give me a hug.

I was immediately filled with peace and soothing love. Royce always radiated that loving warmth, but it was so much stronger when she touched you. It was hard not to like and even love her.

The loud stomp of boots heralded another individual about to join us. I looked toward the door to see who it was when I felt my heart drop straight to the floor. My eyes were quick to follow.

Chriton.

Yeah, that Chriton. The youngest Andromadan Guardian. And the bane of my existence.

Tall, cut musculature. Beautiful dark complexion, bright blue eyes, medium length dark hair. Long defined jaw line, high cheekbones. Thick dark lashes that made him look like he was wearing mascara. Dimples in his cheeks and a very delightful little mole to the side of his left eye.

See, I was hooked on him the moment I first saw him. Love at first sight, maybe. Obsession at first sight, definitely. Unfortunately for me, he didn't feel the same way. Mostly because I was stupid and apparently easily manipulated.

Ember came into my life when I was at an extreme low and feeling really lonely. Glad to have someone who seemed to actually care about me, I was an easy target. She was a narcissist to the extreme. I quickly found myself falling in line with her wants because I was terrified of loosing my only friend and being all alone again. That fear was compounded by the abuse Ember enjoyed dishing out. After so much mental and physical abuse, I became exactly what she wanted, a mindlessly obedient bitch that hurt people who didn't deserve it. Blaze and Coren were some of those people.

Ember wanted Coren with a single mindedness that was terrifying and she did everything she could to trap him. And I helped her for some of it. In the end she was sent to different base. And I was inadvertently freed.

Ember was the one who forced me into acting when she caught on to the feelings I was harbouring for Chriton. She told me he would never notice me, I was far too plain, if I didn't step up and make him. In fact, she demanded I take action, so I did. I even kept doing it when he said no. Mostly because Ember kept pushing me, insisting that I try harder.

Then Chriton and Malachi both tore into me, stripped me of what little I had left. Chriton told me I was the last person he would ever want and both of them said that I was a horrible human being.

That was when I truly realized how far I fell. I even tried to walk away from Ember, but that didn't end well at all. It wasn't until she was removed from the Base that I was actually freed of her control and influence.

After the fall out, I turned myself inwards and gave up on having friends or even acquaintances, as much as I could with Malachi up in my grill all the time. I stayed far away from the Guardians and concentrated on my career and my kids while I attempted to make myself into a better person.

And it worked, for awhile. I even started to feel good enough and safe enough to make a friend, Salem.

Now it seemed like no matter what I did or where I was, Chriton or one of the Guardians appeared. And every time, I felt as if my heart was being clawed apart. I felt his words all over again, feeling them being pounded home over and over again. I was a horrible, disgusting person.

"Hey." Chriton gave Catro a head nod in greeting.

Catro lowered himself down into one of the two seats available and pulled Royce down into his lap. I felt myself blush when my eyes fell to the only seat left and the thought that I would have to share that seat with Chriton popped into my head. Sitting with him, on him. feeling his body against mine. My mind screamed no while my heart screamed yes.

Still to this very day, I yearned for him. But my head denied that yearning, telling me that I would just end up hurt all over again. My recovery last time was hard and dark. If it wasn't for Malachi I wouldn't have healed as much as I did let alone survived.

That was when another person entered the cockpit. A delicate looking female with long pale blonde hair and lavender eyes. She was very obviously Nordic. And absolutely gorgeous.

My heart jerked at the sight of her. There went my chance to have Chriton physically close to me. To be honest, it was probably for the best. Chriton could sit with her, and I could just lean against the wall. That would be best for my well being in the long run. I backed up to the railing that ran along the wall.

The woman smiled shyly at all of us.

"Fain." Chriton gestured the woman to the seat before, surprisingly, joining me at the railing.

Feeling his body heat against my side, I was at a loss of what to do. I needed to get as far away from him as possible, but I also relished the feel of that little bit of him brushing over me. I looked around to the others, hoping that one of them might be willing to save me.

Then the damned man bent over me and began to lock one of the harnesses that I hadn't noticed around me. I couldn't breathe, my heart was beating way too fast. He was too close. I could smell him. Smooth, like sex.

I was so glad for my clothing when the heat of his fingers swept over me with his actions.

"I, uh, thought..." I pointed at the chair Fain was sitting in, trying to say something, anything to get him away from me so that I could breathe.

"Taken." Chriton's grunt was his only answer.

Chriton finished locking me in and locked his own harness on. Then he pulled my side into his hard body. His long-fingered hand gripped my waist tightly. My mind screamed and cried.

No touching.

The heat of his body was branding itself into my side. I wanted to rip myself from him, but my body wouldn't move. All I could do was stand there, panicked and frozen.

I felt Chriton's hand tighten even more when the ship began moving. Once we were clear of the Bay, Wings put on the speed and we flashed across the sky.

We reached the Ranch in ten minutes. It was relatively fast considering the distance, but it was still ten minutes that were an agonizing hellscape filled with hopeless yearning.

Wings finally set the ship down on the landing pad. I felt my body unfreeze and my frantic fingers quickly unlatched the harness, needing to be away from the man and those toxic feelings that rose within me every time he was near. Ignoring everything else, I cautiously walked from the cockpit.

Once outside, Chriton, Catro, and Wings unloaded the boxes of supplies and bags from the ship before reloading it with items that were apparently being sent back. Bane, Chriton's brother-in-law, and Bane's husband, Bailor, arrived about halfway through to help them finish.

Bane is Blaze's brother. He, Bailor, and their wife, Harper, were the ones that brought home the Drako ship after they were kidnapped by the enemies.

Wings said goodbye to everyone before sauntering back into the ship. It lifted up and flashed off towards Base.

"Group hug." Chriton exclaimed, throwing himself into the hug with Royce and Bane.

Somehow I was yanked into the hug with everyone else. I was successfully trapped by Chriton's strong arm around my shoulders, trapping me in the awkward hug. I found myself trying to sink into myself and disappear.

I thanked God when Chriton's arm loosened, and I was able to duck myself out of the hug. Royce was also able to extricate herself from the hug leaving Chriton and Bane hugging each other.

Harper was talking to Fain, guiding the Nordic woman away from the landing pad and into the nearby village that was made out canvas tents and dirt paths. Only they were stopped when Chriton swung Harper up into his arms and spun her around.

Royce took my arm and gently backed us up until we were out of the way of Chriton's exuberant greeting of his family. Bailor was the next victim of Chriton's enthusiastic hugs.

It was interesting to see the physical affection he showed them. Back when he first arrived he was always quick to withdraw from any touch I tried to initiate with him. This was always followed with a look of disgust and a sharp word.

Fortunately, I only tried two times to physically touch him. And the only reason for that was because Ember forced me to.

Needless to say, lesson learned and now I made sure to never initiate contact with anyone, except Malachi. In fact, after Ember, I avoided all contact all together, unless it was one of my kids.

While the others were talking I slipped over to the baggage. Seeing my bags, I pulled my backpack on and hung my camera bag over my shoulder.

"Good. So, what's on the agenda first?" Bane turned slightly so he could include me in his question.

Excited to get started and actually see the Ranch, I smiled and patted the camera bag. "I want to get started right away, but I need to change into something a lot lighter."

"I agree, it's really freaking hot here. If you don't mind, Catro and I would like to tag along, see the sites with you." Royce agreed, shooting me a grin.

"Awesome. We will drop your stuff off in your tents, you can get changed, and we can get started." Bane grinned and gestured us forward.

I watched with amusement as Catro turned to grab the bags but paused. Bailor already had them. All of them. Ever single travel bag was slung over his neck, shoulders, arms, and hanging from his hands. I gave a surprised laugh at the bag covered man. Bane shook his head at his husband and gestured for us to follow him.

"Way to make the rest of us look bad." Chriton noted, slapping Bailor helpfully on the back.

After Bailor just barely caught himself from flying forward, he grinned arrogantly and started down the path.

We stopped at three different tents so we could drop our bags off and we could change before taking the bulk of the bags, Fain's, to the medical tent.

The canvas tent I was given was small but cool, the thick material reflecting the heat of the sun. There was a small dresser, a queen sized bed, and some end tables. There was also a light sitting on one of the end tables and a couple area rugs distributed throughout.

Setting my bags on the bed, I was quick to change into a set of short beige cargo shorts and a lace up sleeveless top. I pulled the camera from the bag but made sure to hang the bag with its extra batteries from my shoulder.

Leaving the tent, I made sure it was zipped up against the heat before checking over the camera to make sure it was working.

The next stop was Chriton's tent which was disturbingly right next to mine. I tried to ignore that knowledge as much as I tried to ignore the thick, vein covered arm muscles that Chriton displayed after he changed into a loose, sleeveless shirt.

Catro also changed into a cooler, sleeveless shirt while Royce, changed into a pair of jean shorts and a corseted sleeveless top.

Stopping at Medical, Bailor liberated himself of the rest of the bags then we all headed out on our tour.

Excited and fascinated, the camera in my hand came up and I did my best to get footage of everything. The tent village, the area around us, and the protective dome we were under.

Bane, Bailor, and Harper were a fount of information. Each of them where quick to answer my questions while we walked. Explaining what they were investigating there at the Ranch, why they were investigating it, and what they were finding. I was happily catching all of it with the camera.

I was loving the footage I was getting and was pretty sure that once I got it edited together it would be an awesome educational tool. Not just for the school but also for other bases.

With my mind on my work and my eye on the viewer, I felt a hand find my arm and I was pulled to the left. Looking around with a slight frown, I saw that Chriton was the one who pulled me to the side so that I could avoid a pothole that I didn't see. Thankful, I gave him a stiff smile before turning my concentration back to the camera.

Unfortunately, because everything was so fascinating and my attention was in so many places at once, this continued to happen. Chriton would place his hands on me for a moment while guiding me in order to help me avoid something. Each time I would feel the same heart stopping reactions that I felt in the ship race through my body while I thanked him in some way. I would also tell myself that I would pay more attention to where I was going.

But then it would happen again.

Bane, Bailor, and Harper took us around the various dig sites. Stopping in each area so that we all could investigate and I could interview some of the people working in those sites.

The archaeologists, anthropologists, and their teams were so helpful and willing to sit and chat with me. Most of them were delighted that I was doing this, showing me fragments of pottery or bones that they were finding before explaining what those fragments told them about the culture of people that once lived in the area.

I found myself so entranced with everything that it wasn't until we were walking down to the energy tunnel that I noticed Grayson Dodge, Malachi's best friend and the man in charge of the Ranch security, was now with us.

The energy tunnel was a circular tunnel that led to a large main cavern with a number of small caverns coming off said tunnel. It was the reason the Ranch became an investigation site in the first place. Coren, Blaze, and Bane were sent out to study the area because of the tunnel and the readings the Base found.

I was learning that the tunnel was built to divert and harness one of the Earth's lye lines so it could be utilized and changed into dark energy. The man who created it used the ancient civilization of that time to build the tunnel and caverns. He also used them for sacrifices in his efforts to divert and change the energy.

Coren and Blaze were the ones that reverted the dark energy back to light and returned the lye line back to its original position, making the tunnel and caverns powerless once again.

Once we were in the large main cavern of the system, I began to catalogue the area with the camera. There was hieroglyphics painted and carved on the walls throughout the cavern that they were still working to translate.

I was slowly turning with the camera when I paused on Royce and Catro. Catro caught a handful of Royce's hair and pulled her head back so that he could kiss her.

I felt a fission of jealousy mixed with want run through me. I wanted that. Not with Catro, but with someone who loved me. I wanted someone to hold me like that, kiss in that all encompassing way Catro was kissing Royce.

My mind flashed to Malachi and his kiss from the other day. The way it felt like he was trying to stamp his possession on me mixing with the desire that rose sharply within me. In that moment I wanted him like no other. Deep and dark.

My yearning was quickly replaced with the familiar pain of loneliness. The self disgust that followed was effectively shoved aside. Yes, I was lonely, but I was also finally starting to be content with who I was becoming and with my life. I was slowly returning to the warm, helpful person I was before Ember. I apologized to all of those I hurt during that time, even Chriton. Although that conversation had been fairly short and painful.

Royce moaned softly, rising up onto her toes in an attempt to get closer. Catro's hands found her ass and hiked her up.

"Woah. I am going to have to edit that out." I exclaimed causing them to turn their heads and stare at me.

Chriton chuckled and pointed to one of the hieroglyphs carved into the wall near the door, drawing my attention to it.

"So, what exactly happened here?" I turned the camera to Bane.

"Well..." Bane started but cut himself off with a frown.

Feeling fine vibrations travelling up my legs from the ground beneath us, I felt my heart drop in dread. Looking around the cavern at the others, I saw that each of them carried a worried look on their faces.

"Earthquake?" I whispered, lowering the camera slightly.

"No." Bailor shook his head. "This feels different."

"Maybe we should get out of here. Just in case." Chriton advised, looking around the area with a frown.

"Yeah." Catro agreed quietly, feeling the vibrations getting stronger. "Go."

Chriton grabbed my hand and dragged me with him as he raced out of the large cavern and into the tunnels. The ground shook violently, causing me to trip and stumble. Chriton yanked me closer, dropping an arm around my waist to pull me into his side.

I cried out, automatically covering our heads when the ground jerked hard and rocks began to fall around us. Chriton gasped, his body jolting in pain.

"Chriton." I cried, twisting to investigate his pain. A disconcerting grinding noise followed by ear piercing cracks immediately drew my attention.

I could barely see anything through the falling rocks and dust. I could just make out screams and yells through the loud sounds of the earth moving around us. Luckily I was just able to make out a darkened area about the size of a door in the tunnel wall. Praying it was one of the other smaller caverns, I shoved Chriton into it. The old wood cracked and broke under our weight and we fell into the room just in time.

A loud crashing roar signalled the tunnel caving in behind us, trapping us in the room and plunging us into darkness.

The world around us stopped heaving and the sound died down. The air in the room was thick, hard to breath, full of dust.

"Leah?" Chriton half coughed, half groaned from somewhere to the left of me.

"Yeah." I returned through my own coughing fit, slowly pushing myself up to a sitting position.

"Fuck." Chriton breathed in the heavy silence. "Are you ok?"

"Yeah." I returned again before adding. "You?"

"Yeah." He grunted and I heard the scuffing sound of his movement. "I am having a hard time seeing through all of the dust."

That's when I remembered the camera still in my hand. "Hold on." I whispered and checked the camera.

I was amazed to see it was fine and still working. Clicking on one of the buttons on the side it turned on the night vision causing the images on the screen to glow a soft green. Looking at the screen, I was barely able to make out the area through the swirling dust. I kept moving the camera around until I came across a small battery powered light sitting on a fold out desk. Raising to my feet, I used the camera to carefully maneuver over to the table so I could turn on the light.

Even though the light was small and thusly not very bright, Chriton still grunted and blinked at the sudden change.

Setting the camera on the table, I tried to wave away the dust and looked around the room. It took a bit for the dust to settle enough for me to see that the cavern was about the size of a bedroom. In fact, it looked like it actually was a bedroom at one time with what looked like the rotten remains of a bed, desk, table and chairs, shelving. All of this was strewn about the room.

"Well, that's fucking great." I sighed and ran my hand through my dirt coated hair in frustration. The door was completely blocked by large boulders. We were trapped.

I tried to push aside the extremely caustic thoughts of being buried alive. People knew where we were and I was pretty sure that they felt the quaking.

"Fuck." Chriton pushed himself from the ground and moved to the entrance so he could examine the cave-in.

Ear piercing yelling, screaming, and violent growling echoed from the side wall, causing me to gasp in fright and back away from the wall. I reached up to cover my ears when one of the high pitched screams filled with agony and death.

"What the fuck?" Chriton growled, staring at the wall before turning his eyes to mine.

The terrifying screaming continued, hurting my ears, reverberating dread through my system, scraping my nerves raw. I felt tears gathering in my eyes at the petrifying sounds that just never stopped.

Terrified, I kept backing up until my back met the far wall. I wanted it to stop, needed it to stop. Heat hit my side right before a long fingered hand caught the side of my head and pulled my face into a hard chest.

No touching.

I automatically jerked away, using my elbows to push the man away. Turning from him, my fingers tightened on my ears and my body dropped into a crouch, balling up as small I could to get away from the noise.

Concentrating on my breathing and keeping my fear fuelled anxiety under control, I felt him behind me, following me down. His body covered the back of mine, providing the heartbreaking safety of a warm male embrace.

I lost track of time while I trembled within Chriton's protective arms with my ears covered. I was so thankful when the screams finally stopped. Heart still pounding, I lowered my shaking hands and crawled away from Chriton's safety. I needed distance.

"I am ok." I whispered, standing and wrapping my arms around my middle. "Your arm." I gasped, my eyes catching on the large bruise forming along the side of his shoulder and arm.

Grabbing his wrist, I turned his body so that I could examine the swollen area. It looked really bad, but I was pretty sure nothing was broken. I gently ran my shaking fingers around the bruise not liking that he was hurt. I didn't know why I did it, but I leaned over and pressed a soft kiss to the area.

When I realized what I did I immediately dropped my hands from him, horrified, and quickly backed away, lowering my head to hide my face. "Sorry." I cringed to myself, remembering that he told me to keep my hands off of him.

No touching.

Horrible people didn't deserve to touch.

Chewing on my knuckle, I chanced a peek over at him, waiting for him to drop the hammer and start yelling at me again.

Chriton was watching me intently with those bright blue eyes of his, eyes that seemed so much brighter in the shadows of the room. His chest rose with a deep breath and his eyes thankfully moved from me to the walls enclosing us. I drew my own deep breath, he wasn't going to yell at me. At least that was something.

"Leah, I need to assess the situation and check on the others." Chriton informed me in a strange voice while setting his hand in the cavern wall. "I might be gone for a bit."

Studying Chriton, I didn't really understand what he was talking about. How was he going to check on everyone from here? I did know that Andromadans carried gifts, mental and physical, that made it so they could do some pretty unique things. I did not know what Chriton's specific gift was.

The only thing I felt like I could do was agree. "Ok." I whispered with a slow nod. Chriton turned his head to study me for a moment.

I jolted and felt my heart stop when Chriton turned back to the wall and stepped into.

"What?" I gasped in bewilderment and stumbled to the wall.

Running my hands over the smooth, solid rock that Chriton just disappeared into, I felt my anxiety kick in.

I was alone.

Chriton left me.

My heart told at me that he would be back, he wouldn't just abandon me trapped under rock and stone. He wasn't that man. But my mind denied that vehemently, screaming at me that I was now completely alone and buried alive. I had no food, no water, limited oxygen.

Closing my eyes, I forced myself to breath and think. There was absolutely no way I could dig myself out of the surrounding rock, so that wasn't an option. I really was trapped. Before my mind could begin screaming again, I forced myself to look at the reality.

Death wasn't so bad. It was just change. That's all, just a change.

Afterall, just over a year ago death seemed so easy. At least this wouldn't be self inflicted. And who knows, maybe my next life wouldn't be so painful. Maybe I could actually come back as a good person.

As always, there was Uncle Declan.

Really needing to take my mind off of things, I carried the camera to the back wall. Sitting down against the wall, I wrapped my arms around my raised knees. Holding the camera up so I could see the viewscreen, I began watching the footage I took during the day. My mind was editing the film as I watched.

The clock on the camera told me that about half an hour passed when Chriton reappeared back in the room. I felt my heart squeeze with relief, my eyes blinking rapidly to hold back my tears.

"Leah?" He asked in a low voice, his eyes moving around the room.

"Here." I called softly, lowering the camera slightly.

"Hey." He greeted with a smile, coming over to drop to his knees in front of me. His hands came up to cover one of my arms and one of my knees causing me to stiffen up. "Sorry for taking so long. I had to travel back and forth a bit."

"It's ok." I reassured him, giving his worried eyes a stiff smile. "What did you find out?"

"Everyone is alive." Chriton began, his blue eyes running over my stiff posture. "Bane, Bailor, and Harper are trapped another small cavern. Grayson, Catro, and Royce are still in the main cavern. The whole tunnel came down and everyone is completely trapped. Coren is here and working with everyone to try and get us out. The thing is, due to the earthquake the area became very unstable. If they try to dig out one area, another will cave in. They are working on a plan but its going to take time."

"Ok." I nodded slowly, turning my eyes down to the long fingers surrounding my limbs. "Do, uh, do you think you could ask them how much air I might have?"

His eyes jolted wide, taking on a stunned look. "What are you talking about?" He quietly hissed, scowling angrily.

"The air. It's heavy, unmoving. How much time do I have before I run out of oxygen?" I reiterated, wanting to know.

"Fuck." Chriton's eyes filled with anxiety, and he turned to examine the room. "I don't know."

"You should go." I told him causing his head to arrow back to mine, his face filling with confusion.

"Leah.." He began but I cut him off.

"No food, no water, no air." I pointed out firmly. "Three weeks with no food, three days with no water. With the size of the room, I am unsure how much air I have, and I would really like to know. There is also the fact that you can leave, get out, and you should."

Chriton's eyes narrowed and his mouth tensed with fury. "Do you seriously think I would abandon you?"

"I don't know. I don't know you. All I know is that if you can save yourself, you really should." I pointed out the fact that I really didn't know him. I knew about him, but I didn't know him.

"I am not leaving you." Chriton stated firmly, cocking his head to study me with an unnerving intensity.

"You are taking up my air." Needing him safe and gone, I dropped the bitch hammer. "We have less time with two of us using the oxygen than I would if it was just me."

That did it.

"Motherfucker." Chriton grunted in frustration before he glowered and prowled back into the wall.

I swallowed through the tightness in my throat and dropped my head to my knees. Sobs ripped from my chest, tore into my soul. I did what I needed to. Now at least he would be safe and free. Not hopelessly trapped, buried alive like I was. Wanting to preserve the light, I grabbed it from the table and stumbled back to the wall. Once I retook my seat, I shut off the light and allowed my sobs to echo into the black.

CHAPTER 5

MALACHI

I came striding out of the ship, not stopping even when I was handed a tablet holding all of the information I ordered. The night was dark with no moon and very little stars. Luckily, the tent village that was created for the people working on the Ranch was lit up.

I scanned the information on the tablet as I made my way straight to the dig site in question and down a dirt incline that led to the tunnel entrance. The whole area was lit by large construction lights.

"She is alive." I stated to Coren who was running the retrieval efforts.

Coren shot me surprised look when he saw me. This was the first time I stepped in on an incident like this. Unless my team or I were specifically requested then I trusted my people to handle it. That surprise turned to understanding when he fully comprehended the statement I made. "She is. For now." Coren confirmed with a sharp nod and a pair of narrowed eyes.

"And the others?" I demanded, handing the tablet off.

"So far everyone is alive and well but for a couple lacerations and bruises. Nothing life threatening." Coren detailed, his eyes returning to his own tablet.

"Where is your brother?" I barked out causing the man to turn and glare at me.

"What the fuck does he...?"

"Where is Chriton?" I turned furious eyes to the Guardian and demanded once again, my voice sharp and unyielding.

"Here, Malachi." Chriton sighed, walking out of the rock tunnel wall Coren and I were standing beside.

"The tunnels are completely blocked?" I questioned him, running an assessing eye over the dirt stained man. I didn't like the look of the bruising that was colouring his shoulder.

"Yeah." Chriton nodded, grunting when I reached over to grip the unbruised part of his arm to pull him closer to the light so I could check the damage.

"Leah?" I asked, carefully feeling around the bruised flesh.

"Angry, fighting. Giving me shit." Chriton told me in a frustrated voice.

"Good." I advised, ignoring Chriton's shocked look. "Anger is good. Anger will keep her going. Keep her angry, Chriton."

"Got it, Boss." Chriton chuckled hoarsely.

"You two have the weirdest relationship." Coren gave us a confused look.

"You have no idea." Chriton told his brother before turning back to me. "She wants to know how much air she has left."

"Of course, she does." I rolled my eyes at that. "Tell her that she will survive long enough to feel the pain of my hand on her ass if she asks another stupid question like that."

Coren shot me a sharp look while Chriton surprisingly threw his head back and laughed. "Will do, man."

LEAH

A WARM HAND RUNNING over my hair brought my conscious back to awareness. Opening my eyes, I lifted my heavy head up and looked at the man crouched over me. The light was turned on and Chriton was staring down at me with a worried look in his eyes.

"Hey." I rubbed my eyes and straightened up. "Did you find out how long I have?"

Chriton shook his head, his mouth tight.

"Not long, huh?" I gave a derisive chuckle and pushed my tangled hair back from my face.

"Long enough for Malachi to spank your ass for asking stupid questions." Chriton whispered, tilting his head to study me.

"He's here?" I asked quietly, feeling more tears burn in my eyes. I felt extreme relief at the thought of Malachi standing on the other side of the rock and dirt tunnel, just feet away. I knew that Malachi would do everything he could to get me out.

"Where else would he be?" Chriton asked.

I wasn't sure how much time had passed but I was getting thirsty. "What time is it?" I asked, frowning down at my coms to see that two hours passed since the cave in. "So, I take it it's just you that can go through."

Chriton nodded slowly. "My clothes as well. But that's because they usually have my living DNA on them. You cried."

Chriton reached out and ran his thumb down my cheek and I grimaced, feeling those tears welling back up. I swallowed and pulled my head away from his touch, not knowing how to answer that. My heart jumped when the hand Chriton had on my cheek followed, catching my chin and forcing my face right back to him. Just like Malachi.

"You run from me. Every chance you get." He rasped, his eyes glowing into mine. "For weeks now, months. Every time I get even remotely close you try to disappear. And its my fault. I fucked up."

"What are you talking about?" I asked, confused, while I tried to remove my face from his hand once again. He simply tightened his fingers on my jaw, holding me still.

"I denied you, I pushed you away, I hurt you. And I did it on purpose. When you looked at me, touched me, I was disgusted.

I hated your smell, your face, you body, the sound of your voice. Everything. I hated everything about you. I hated you. I wanted you gone, as far away from me as I could get you. And I set about doing just that, no matter how much it hurt you. I didn't care because you made me sick, and I wanted you gone." I violently shoved myself away from his painful honesty, scrambling across the floor until I reached the far wall.

"Leave." I demanded shakily, pain ricocheting through my whole being. I need him gone. He hurt too fucking much. His words mixed together, ricocheting through my brain, past and present beating at me. My fingers twitched, wanting to scratch, claw, dig deep into my own flesh. Anything to make the pain go away.

He watched me, slowly rising to his full height. "You were caustic. A bitch. A bully. Mean, selfish Weak." He continued, driving his point home like a stake to my chest, moving towards me one slow step at a time. "You were pathetic. And you wouldn't leave me the fuck alone."

"Please." I begged, feeling my chin and lips quiver in my effort to mask the upwelling of pain. "Leave."

"I was so fucking relieved when you finally did leave me alone. I was so glad when I didn't see you around anymore." He continued, driving that pain deeper still. "Then I was given the truth. I couldn't believe it. I didn't want to. I despised that truth. But I investigated it anyway. I looked into all of it, all of you. I found out everything. All about the manipulation and control you went through at that woman's hands."

My body jerked when his hands slammed into the wall around my head. The tears finally breaking free to slide silently down my face.

"So, you know. It doesn't change anything, I still did what I did. And it doesn't change the current situation. All it does is rehash shit that is dead and buried. Leave it alone." I hissed snidely at him. "None of it mattered a year ago, none of it matters now."

"That's not all I know." He swallowed hoarsely, reaching out to run his knuckles down my cheek.

My eyes squeezed shut at the bittersweet feeling of his touch. When I reached up to knock his hand way he caught my arm and held my wrist up. My eyes popped open at the feel of his thumb running over my scar.

"Malachi. He told you." I gasped, feeling confused as to why Malachi would betray that way.

"He did. And he hated himself for it, for betraying you. But he knew that I needed to know the full extent of your pain." Chriton clipped out his explanation.

"Why? Why did you need to know? You hate me, you despise me, you are disgusted by me, remember." I spat, throwing his own words back at him, twisting my arm loose.

"That's where you are wrong." He shook his head slowly at me, his eyes filling with what looked like pain.

"It doesn't matter. Your thoughts, feelings, don't matter. Not anymore." I brought my knuckle up to my mouth and chewed on it while I spoke softly. "Neither do mine. They cannot get me out. I have no food, no water, and I will run out of oxygen. Hopefully the oxygen runs out before the dehydration gets too bad. But either way, this is now my tomb."

"Why are you giving up so quickly?" He demanded angrily, slamming his palm into the wall.

"I am not giving up. I am accepting the reality of the situation." I argued that quiet voice, tilting my head at him. "You need to do the same."

"Fuck that." Chriton snarled and disappeared back through the wall.

CHAPTER 6

CHRITON

I snarled as I walked through the tunnel wall until I hit the outside. "That woman is so fucking frustrating." I growled at my brother and Malachi who were both bent over a tablet. "I can understand you wanting to spank her now."

"Right?" Malachi laughed in commiseration.

"She keeps talking about me accepting her death. I have no plans of ever accepting her death. But she won't listen to me." I ranted, stomping back and forth in front of the two amused looking men.

"Yeah, you are going to have to nip that in the bud. Take her mind off of death. Keep it on life." Malachi advised, his eyes darkening in that way that told me he was upset.

"Yeah, ok." I nodded slowly. "Since I am up here, have you two made any headway?"

"I have no fucking clue. I wish it was as easy as lifting the whole fucking thing and moving it but there is too fucking much that could go wrong. We need to figure out a way to shore up one area while opening up the other area. Which is fucking hard when we are running blind and dealing with three different areas that are connected but not connected. It's a fucking nightmare." Coren grunted, running a frustrated hand through his hair.

"Can you go check on the others? See if they have anything in their caverns that can be used to help." Malachi asked, frowning down at the tablet.

"Yeah. I'll be back." I nodded and disappeared back through the walls. First stop was Bane, Bailor, and Harper.

"Motherfucker!" Bailor yelped in fear and jumped about a foot high when I walked out of the wall of the small cavern they were trapped in. "I thought we made a deal."

"Sorry, man, hard times." I held my arms up innocently.

"Hard times? We are trapped in a small assed room where they housed a whole fuck load of dead bodies. This place sucks." Bane groaned from where he was leaning against the wall, his narrowed eye darting around the bare room.

"I take it someone is not happy that you are stuck here." I noted.

"Well, considering the fact that they were all murdered in horrendous fashions just to power a megalith built by what was essentially an evil scientist before being trapped here for all eternity. No, they aren't fucking happy. None of them are. And they refuse to move on." Bane growled.

"Yeah, it hasn't exactly been a picnic." Harper noted from her spot behind Bailor where he shoved her when I originally stepped into the cavern.

"Sorry. Everyone is working on it." I winced at the group.

"How's Leah doing?" Harper asked softly, stepping around Bailor to rush nervously across the floor to Bane. Bane caught her against him and bowed his body protectively over hers.

"Counting her breath's and pissing me off." I growled. "Is there anything at all you can use to help hold up the ceiling?"

"Chriton, there is literally nothing in here except us, one flashlight, and a bunch of angry spirits. Unless they want to hold up the ceiling for us, we got nothing." Bane clipped out, his voice weary.

Harper whimpered when the flashlight blinked off sending us all into complete black. Luckily, I was Andromadan and boasted certain talents like being able to see in the dark. It was on a greyscale and certain details weren't as sharp as they would be in the light, but it was still visibility.

"Seriously." Bailor yelled threateningly. "If you fuckers scratch her again..."

"No, Bailor, wait." Bane hissed.

"What..?"

"Shut up. I am trying to hear." Bane hissed again.

Cocking my head, I tried to listen and hear what Bane was hearing but all I caught was a soft whispering sound.

"One at a fucking time, please." Bane ordered. "That's better, now I can understand you."

The silence around us was broken up by the sound of someone pacing the length of the room. Someone who I couldn't even see.

"Ok, can we have the light back, please?" Bane's voice echoed eerily in the darkened room.

I slapped my hand on my neck and shot a glare behind me when someone breathed on me.

"Because otherwise we can't see. And if we can't see we definitely can't leave." Bane just finished his statement when the flashlight flickered back on. "Thank you."

"So..." I sent a set of raised eyebrows Bane's way.

"They said they would love to help us get the hell out but the biggest issue they have is they don't have enough energy. And our little bitty flashlight isn't helping them at all." Bane explained with a wince. "They really don't like us being in here with them."

"Ok, ok." I mumbled, pacing back and forth while thinking about the problem. "Sorry." I murmured when I crossed paths with the other pacer in the room and was flooded with cold. "Can they leave this room at all?"

Bane was silent for a moment. "No." He shook his head slowly.

"All right. Give me a little bit, I have to make one more stop then I need to go confer with Coren and Malachi." I told the group as I walked toward the next wall and cavern.

Once I reached the main cavern I was surprised to see it empty. After investigating a little I found a giant hole in the floor that appeared to be empty. Leaning over the hole, I called out. When I got nothing back I made the assumption that they must have tried to make their way deeper to protect themselves or even find a way out. Either way, with everything else I was dealing with, I wasn't about to go after them.

Returning to the surface where I could see the horizon just starting to glow I made my reports to Coren and Malachi.

"Ok, so we leave the largest cavern until last, just like we originally planned. It should stay stable enough for us to get at least one of the other groups out. Unfortunately, this crack right here is our most worrisome." Coren scowled as he pointed to the tablet and the jagged crack that extended over both small caverns. "Every scenario we have run ends up with us loosing at least one cavern."

Malachi sighed and reached up to rub the back of his neck before wincing.

"Sore." I asked, reaching over to press my fingers into Malachi's admittedly tight neck.

"Fuck. I have never been this tense in my whole life." Malachi groaned softly, twisting his neck in my hand so that my fingers gained access to the spots that needed it. "Not even when the team and I took a trip to Australia and decided to camp out."

"I haven't heard this one." Coren's head whipped up from the tablet he was working on, his eyes taking on an avarice gleam.

"Yeah. When I woke up to find five giant fucking huntsman spiders making a home out of my tent I was not a happy man. Then again neither was my team at the time when they ended up loosing all of their camping gear and one of the jeeps." Malachi explained with a soft smile of remembrance. "I can still remember Declan screaming for everyone to hit the deck when I whipped those grenades in there. When it was over all he could do was laugh. He asked how many grenades I used and I told him, one for each spider I saw."

"Declan?" Coren asked curiously.

"Don't be that guy, Coren. I know you decided to take a look at not just Leah's personnel file, but mine as well." Malachi shot Coren a knowing smile. "See, Marko cooked up this handy little program that tells him who is looking at what in the system. Certain files are set up so that certain people are notified when they are looked at and by who."

"Smart." Coren gave Malachi an impressed nod. "Be that as it may, this is the first time I have heard you speak of Declan."

"How often have any of you actually talked to me in a social way?" Malachi shot back accurately. "I mean other then Chriton here."

"Yeah, I see your point." Coren nodded in agreement. "I think I have something, but I don't know if either of you are going to like it."

"What is it?" I asked, stepping away from Malachi and his somewhat relaxed neck.

"Thanks, man." Malachi grunted at me gratefully.

"Do you remember when you first started using your gift? How you would always end up leaving your clothes behind?" Coren asked me.

"Yeah, it took me a bit to figure that one out." I agreed, remembering how dad started keeping robes in every room of the house for me because I came out of whatever I was walking through naked.

"It was because it wasn't your DNA. But when you were able to concentrate you learned to take the clothes with you." Coren continued.

"Leah isn't clothes coated in my DNA. Leah has a whole different set of DNA." I pointed out, crossing my arms.

"True, but what if you were able to cover her in your DNA? Just like your clothes." Coren added his opinion.

"Shit." I breathed, turning to look at Malachi. From the hard look on Malachi's face he knew exactly what Coren was saying, just like I did. If my DNA was on her, in her, I might just be able to bring Leah through the wall with me.

"If it gets her out..." Malachi gave a resigned sigh, his eyes darkening, his jaw clenching. "Do whatever you have to."

With a sharp nod, I stepped back into the tunnel wall.

CHAPTER 7

LEAH

B ored, I looked around the room, searching for something to do. I picked up the camera and started to record the items in the room. I spent an hour explaining everything I was finding before the battery started dying.

I replaced the battery and faced the camera towards one of the walls. Taking a small rock, I sat on the floor and began to carve into the wall. I talked to the camera the whole time while I used the rock to draw on the wall.

"What is that?" Chriton asked, sitting heavily on the floor beside me.

"Sponge Bob." I explained, pointing out the cartoon character. "See, he lives in a pineapple under the sea."

Chriton watched me with amusement while I sang the theme song.

"It's a kid's cartoon." I explained, grinning at him, remembering how much my kids love Sponge Bob.

"Here." He nabbed the rock from my fingers and drew four lines on the wall. Two horizontal, two crossing vertically, making a square.

Once he was done, he scraped an O in the top left corner.

Shrugging, I took the rock from him, careful to avoid actually touching him, and drew an X in the top right corner.

"I see that I am playing with an expert." I noted when the game came to a draw.

"Fuck yeah." Chriton stated proudly.

"How about this?" I drew out a number of vertical lines followed by a stick version of gallows.

"I don't know this one." Chriton frowned at what I drew.

"These represent the letters in words. You have to guess the words. In order to do that you guess a letter. If the letter is in one of the words then I write it in its spot. If it isn't then you get a body part added to the gallows. You have to guess the words before you have a fully formed hanging man." I explained the game.

"That is slightly disturbing." He very accurately noted.

"Especially when you realize that this is a kid's game." I laughed.

"Wow." Chriton gave me wide eyes before turning to study the lines. "E"

I wrote an E down at the end of the first word.

"A" Chriton added his next letter and gained a head on his gallows.

"R" I shook my head and added a neck.

"S" Chriton raised and eyebrow at me.

I wrote an S at the beginning of the first word.

"Did you seriously spell 'Sponge Bob'?" Chriton laughed.

"I figured we would start with an easy one." I grinned slyly at him.

"Gimme." He pulled the rock from my fingers in a way that had his fingers running over mine in a disconcerting way. "I have one."

Finding a clean spot, he began carving out his lines. There was a lot of letters that made up a fair number of small words. Once his gallows was built I began guessing.

"A" I received two A's.

"B" I received two B's.

Feeling confident, I shifted happily on my butt. "C"

I got a C.

"Are you just going through the whole alphabet?" Chriton asked with an amused look.

"No." I rolled my eyes at him. "D"

Chriton laughed but wrote down a D.

I now knew that one of the words was AND.

"N" Added three N's and proved me right.

Now I had AND and CAN. I was also pretty sure NOT followed CAN.

"O" I guessed and got an O

"T" Got me three T's.

Studying the words that were filled out so far I began laughing. "I like big butts and I can not lie."

"I thought that one would be hard." Chriton sighed dramatically, giving a pout with a full on lower lip jut.

"I see that you at least know some pop culture." I shook my head at his antics.

"What can I say? That song just speaks to me." Chriton grinned wickedly.

"Good to know." I couldn't help but smile.

I was enjoying our banter and the fact that I was actually learning about him as a person and not just as a concept. I always saw him. From the very first moment I laid eyes on him, I sucked up any information I could that pertained to him, and I knew he was far from perfect. But he was still an unrealistic entity that simply represented a painful time in my life that I was still recovering from.

Having him actually talk with me and even laugh was such a drastic change that I wasn't quite sure what to do with it other than enjoy the moment.

"Now that you know I like big butts, its your turn to share." Chriton handed me the rock and gestured to the wall.

"Ok." I said slowly, thoughtfully while I took the rock from him.

I took the time to think of what to share. Something light but personal. Something that would make him laugh.

I drew out my lines before adding my gallows.

"A" Chriton began with a sly grin.

Smiling, I shook my head and added the one A.

"Yes." Chriton rubbed his hands together gleefully. "B"

I laughed and gave him a head.

"Hmm." Chriton playfully narrowed his eyes at me. "C"

I laughed harder at the fact that he wasn't about to break the theme. I also added the one C.

"E" He jumped ahead, finally giving up.

The head got a neck, and I was feeling pretty proud of myself.

"O" He got his O.

"Yes." He exclaimed with an arm pump. "R"

"Nope." I denied and added a body.

"Son of a bitch." He swore and studied the wall for a moment. "S"

He got two S's and grinned proudly. "Yoga sucks!" He exclaimed, turning to me for confirmation. "Wait? You don't like Yoga?"

"When I first started it was ok." I shrugged. "But over time I started to hate it and it really began to suck. It's one of the reason's I quit."

"I thought you quit because of me." Chriton frowned at me.

"I quit your class because of you. There are other classes I could have taken." I pointed out accurately.

"I am sorry." Chriton said quietly.

"Why are you sorry? It wasn't your fault." I told him, turning back to look at the wall. "It started sucking long before you showed up."

"That may be true, but I clearly didn't help the situation." He acknowledged.

"Look. You had every right to say and do what you did, to stand up and protect yourself. Despite the why of it, I did assault you. I completely deserved what happened." I described softly, bring my knuckle up to my lips.

"You touched my arm, Leah. Yes, it was unwanted, but it was no different than something anyone else would to get someone's attention. There really was nothing assaulting about it except my illogical reaction to it." Chriton pointed out softly, reaching out and pulling my knuckle from my teeth before asking. "Was it your choice to do it?"

"Yes." I shook my hand free of his grasp and told him honest. "I was attracted to you. I was stupid and transparent to the point that Ember noticed. She was the one that, uh, advised me on how to get you to notice me. I followed her directions. I did it. Not her. Not you. No one but me."

"Would you have done any of it if she didn't force you?" Chriton pressed, pushing all kinds of triggers and sending my mind careening back into that dark. I definitely wouldn't have. After hours of therapy with Dr. Daniels I knew that now, but there was no way I was sharing that with him.

"It doesn't matter." I sighed, pushing myself to my feet so that I could get away from the suffocating feeling of his presence. My fingers were twitching again. "I did it. End of story."

I was walking away when Chriton caught my arm and swung me back. "Answer me, Leah." He ordered, showing a whole new piece of his character. This one was hard and demanding. Fierce.

"No. Ok. I wouldn't have done fuck all if she didn't force me to." I cried, yanking my arm from his grip. "I wouldn't have even been in Yoga in the first place if it wasn't for her."

"Fuck." Chriton rubbed his eyes wearily, his body still tense with anger.

"I don't know why we have to keep going over this." I hissed, my clawed hand coming up to my agonized chest, stepping backwards and away from him.

"Because I care." Chriton drop his hand and yelled.

"Bullshit." I disagreed with a vehement shake of my head. He didn't care. "You just think you do because of the current threat to my mortality."

"No. I cared long before this happened." He snapped, slicing his hand through the air.

"I am sorry for that. You really shouldn't have. Remember, I am a horrible person. I did bad things. Very bad." I whispered, stepping even further away from him, bringing my hand up and biting deep into my knuckle. I desperately needed that pain to help. Anything but what I was feeling right in that moment.

Chriton's hand caught my forearm and twisted my wrist so we both could see the scar running down the inside length.

"Talk to me." He snapped out harshly.

"You may have hated me but not as much as I hated myself. I allowed it to happen. I was weak and I allowed her to control me, change me into someone I hated. I am disgusting and pathetic. You were right about all of it." I screamed back, my lips shaking, my words stumbling.

"Leah, love." Chriton whispered, letting go of my hand and grasping my jaw once again.

"Don't." I stated, firming my lips and trying to push away from him.

I couldn't breathe, I needed him away from me. I needed to find my center. I was breaking, I could feel myself breaking. My hands becoming claws and raising to my head. Hurt. Pain. My fingers began to dig into my skull.

"Stop." He ordered, catching my arms and ripping my hands down, pushing me back into the wall.

Silent sobs welled up in my chest.

"Please." I begged, my body stiff against his, my arms cocked up between us in an attempt to hold him away, my face turned away.

"Leah, my precious girl, I need you to hear me." My sobs jerked in my chest, falling with heavy breaths from my trembling lips when his nose brushed over my cheek. "None of that was you. That manipulative, toxic relationship was not you. You aren't weak, you are so fucking strong. I am amazed that you lasted as long as you did."

"I didn't." I gasped out, shaking my head. "Disgusting. Horrible person."

"No, precious. Beautiful and strong. Everything I sensed and saw, everything that made me have that kneejerk dislike of you was her. She was all over you to the point that I couldn't see you." Chriton argued, his warm breath flowing over my face. "That night. It was late. Malachi found you. He dropped by for some reason. When you didn't answer he overrode the security. He found you, almost dead, bleeding all over your bed. He called Medical and did everything he could to keep you alive. They gave you blood, his blood, and stitched you up, kept you for observation. He investigated everything that happened and stayed with you."

My heart iced over at the description he was giving. My mind flashed to that day. I saw Chriton in the hall earlier that day and ended up dodging down a different corridor to avoid him. Ember was already thankfully gone. But I was alone, and I truly hated myself and all I became because of her. Chriton was right, she would slap me or pinch me or even kick me when I didn't do what she wanted. And that was only the least of it.

At that point all I could see was how I hurt Chriton and his family because of that woman. The pain was so bad that I wanted to die. The way I figured it was that no one would even miss me. Even if they did notice that I was gone they would be relieved. Before I really knew it, I was in my suite, on my bed with that knife in my hand.

A wicked sharp boxcutter.

I stared at my pale wrists while I cried. It would be easy. Two little slices, two little pains. They would be nothing compared to the bleeding of my soul. Then there truly would be nothing. It would be all over. The pain would finally be gone.

And it was easy. I didn't even panic when that blood spurted out and over my legs. Hot and sticky. Life. With sick fascination, I watched it flow out of me until my strength was gone, drained out of me just like the blood soaking the world around me, and I fell back onto the bed.

Relief calmly slid over me and my eyes slowly closed. I slept, finally at peace. I even ignored the far away voices yelling anxiously. They didn't matter anymore.

No more pain.

Then there was. So much pain. Agony in not just my heart and soul but now in my body as well. I opened my eyes to see Malachi sitting in a chair beside the bed.

When I realized I was alive, I started crying again. Angry, I was so angry. I screamed and fought, trying to claw open the stitches I could feel holding my skin together.

Malachi, looking wild eyed and furious, held my struggling body against his in an attempt to stop me from hurting myself. That was right about when John came in and jabbed a needle into my arm. Sweet sedation dragged me back into the peace of unconsciousness.

The next time I woke it was alone. But not for long as Dr. Daniels soon came in and began to talk to me. At the time I really didn't want to talk to anyone. Then Malachi returned and took over. He quickly became a pain in my ass. He was there for me constantly throughout the past year, with his orders and demands pissing me off. He pushed me into fighting with him and consequently fighting for myself. Now it was all for nothing.

My head was pulled forward by way of my jaw, bringing my focus back on Chriton. "Please, just let me die in peace." I begged.

"The day you apologized." He cut me off, giving me a slight shake. "In front of my family like that. I tried to ignore you, to not even acknowledge you. Despite seeing my reaction, you followed through. At the time I assumed that you were so pale because of the situation, but it was because you just got out of Medical. I didn't notice at the time, but I should've. Your eyes were dark and bruised, your body thin, too thin, so thin that your clothes hung off of you. You kept your fists clenched around the long sleeves of that loose sweater you were wearing, trying to hide the bandages on your wrists. After that, you just disappeared. I didn't see you again for nine months. Until I tracked you down. And considering that the Base isn't that big, that was quite the feat."

I clenched my jaw and tried to stop my crying. The man just wanted to torture me. While I prayed for it to end, I was done showing him my weakness.

"Why does it matter? What does any of this matter, now?" I demanded hoarsely. "It's over. All of it."

"No, it's not." Chriton snarled, his hand moving to grip the back of my head. "Mere days ago, I found out that I almost lost you, Leah, more than a year ago."

"What are you talking about? Lost?" I asked, completely confused. "Malachi told me about the Conversance. And you just mentioned that you didn't 'see' me because of Ember's influence. But that is absolute bullshit. I am sorry, Chriton, but your sister in law can literally disappear and Coren knew immediately."

"She still carried her own DNA. You didn't." Coren pointed out with a snarl before his eyes widened in realization. "That's why. You. Didn't."

"What the hell are you talking about?" I demanded, frowning up at the excited man in confusion.

"Fuck, yes!" He grinned, his eyes strangely intent, and shook his head right before he dropped it down.

I cried out when his mouth covered mine. His lips spread mine and his tongue was in my mouth. Chriton's tongue was in my mouth.

I could taste him. Different from Malachi but no less divine. I could feel his rough tongue moving, licking over mine.

"What are you doing?" I gasped, yanking my lips from his.

"If you need an explanation then I am clearly not doing a very good job." He said huskily, guiding my lips back to his.

My heart was beating so loud it was roaring in my ears. I whimpered into his mouth when his fingers delved into my hair, adjusting my head so he could kiss me deeper.

My cocked arms shifted until I was clutching at his sweaty, dirty shirt. I sucked on his tongue, plying it with mine causing him to moan softly. I felt that moan between my legs. My pussy pulsed and slickened until it felt like my underwear was soaked. Chriton's demanding kiss become more fierce, hotter, wilder until I felt as if my whole body was on fire.

"Chriton." I gasped when his arm circled my waist and I was lifted up against him.

My legs automatically closed around his hips and I moaned at the unbelievably giant pole that was pressing against my sex. Thick and long in a way I never knew a man could be. The friction from the grinding movement of Chriton's hips dug that pole into the seam of my shorts and along my clit.

"Precious." Chriton growled, dragging his mouth down my jaw until it found my neck. Once there he bit down hard and I almost combusted in his arms.

My pussy contracted violently and my hips jerked in his hold.

"My girl likes my teeth." Chriton rasped in my ear, nipping at the lobe with his sharp teeth.

"We need to stop." I gasped trying to get a hold of the situation, take back control. "Please."

"Yeah." Chriton breathed heavily, slowly lowering me back to the ground. "Yeah. You aren't ready for that."

"I just, um, Malachi." I whispered, backing nervously out of his arms.

"Yeah, I know. I saw." Chriton told me bluntly. "Do you have feelings for him?"

"Yes." I licked my lips and whispered.

"Do you, uh, have feelings for me?" Chriton asked with a worried frown.

"Yes." I nodded slowly.

"Ok." Chriton repeated my nod. Something about the situation and how he was acting just hit me as funny.

Once I started giggling, I couldn't seem to stop. Even pressing my hands to my mouth didn't stop the outflow of my laughter.

Chriton's head tilted towards me, his face taking on a softly amused look. "What's so funny?"

"Everything." I cried out through my laughter. "Everything. Three days ago, Malachi, a man that has been the most constant person in my life, kissed me. Like really kissed me. And I liked it. Like really liked it. And then...and then there is you. You kissed me. And I liked it. Like really liked it. And over all of that is the cave-in and the looming death factor."

"You won't die!" Chriton's voice snapped out, sharp like a whip.

"How the fuck am I going to get out, Chriton? You said it yourself, they can't dig us out because the other areas will collapse and kill everyone else." I argued back, laughing even harder and reaching up to grip the hair on the top of my head tightly. "No matter how much I care for you and how much I care for Malachi, I cannot change this. I never wanted that pain, any pain, for you or him. Not after everything I did. And now I am doing it all over again. Hurting you. I am nothing but pain for you."

"And what about you?" He stepped toward me, growling loudly.

"Aren't you listening at all? This isn't about me. I don't fucking matter!" I shrieked, feeling my body jerk with my rising sobs. "You should have just left like I wanted! Then I wouldn't be the one hurting you! Again!"

"Fuck." Chriton snarled and moved. My sobbing body was pulled into his arms. I clutched at his back while he surrounded me with his strength. "Leah, my precious love. So caring, so loving, so strong. I am not and will not leave you here to die, alone or otherwise. No matter what you say, nothing will change my mind about making you mine. You say you don't matter, but you do. You are *everything*."

"You need to leave, please." I sobbed, desperately needing him safe and happy with his family. He didn't need to be here to see me die. I would never want that. Not for him. "Tell them to get the others out, because we both know that three lives are better than one. And please, tell Malachi, tell him..."

"No." Chriton shook his head, stubbornly denying me once again. "Leah, precious, I need you to try something with me."

"I need you to go, be safe." I shook my own head. "Please."

"Listen to me, Leah." His fierce order caused me to hiccup and try to control my sobs. After long moments my crying finally stopped, and I was able to nod to him. "Ok, close your eyes and hold me as tightly as you can."

Doing as he asked, I pressed my trembling body into him and closed my eyes.

"Please work." I heard him chanting in my ear. His hands soothing up and down my body. I wasn't sure how much time passed, but I stayed as I was while he did what he needed to do, whatever that was it included a number of swear words.

Then warm tingles flowed over my body from the place it was connected to Chriton's. Those tingles were followed by a weightless, unsubstantial feeling. Any other time I would've felt disconcerted, but instead I felt...free and at peace.

"Yes1 Yes! Yes!" Chriton exclaimed and I was abruptly swept off my feet to be rocked against his chest. "Ok, precious. Hold on to me. We are going through the wall."

"What? Wait! I thought you couldn't take anything with you." My eyes popped open to look up at him in confusion.

Chriton set me down but maintained a hold on my arms. "You are very special. You, my Conversance, have the ability to mimic someone else's DNA if you are around them long enough. It's why I didn't see you, didn't feel you. With us connecting the way we did today, spending time together, kissing, you are now imitating my DNA." Chriton grinned excitedly.

"Oh my God." I outright laughed, my hands coming up to cover my mouth. There was a light at the end of the tunnel.

Chriton grinned before turning around to give me his back "Climb on." He crouched down while ordering me to climb onto his back. My arms circled his shoulders and my legs circled his waist. His hands gripped my knees. "All right. Let's do this. Malachi is going crazy up there. Close your eyes, precious, and hold on tight."

With one last smile, I did as he asked. This time the tingles and the weightless unsubstantiality came a lot quicker. I felt Chriton step forward and a sliding sensation moved over my nerves. Chriton kept moving and the sensation continued for long moments until fresh air hit my lungs and late morning air flowed over my body.

Opening my eyes, I saw the sun filled sky above us as well as about ten people staring at us with complete shock. Among others, I could see Coren.

And Malachi.

"Malachi." I gasped, feeling relieved tears popping into my eyes. I truly thought I wouldn't see him ever again.

Giving Chriton one last squeeze, I climbed down from his back and ran to the arms Malachi was holding open for me. Launching myself into the air, I hit him like a freight train and wrapped my limbs tightly around his torso. His strong arms caught me around my hips and shoulders. His hand gripped the back of my head, holding me to him while his torso bowed into mine. "Thank God." He murmured, his voice filled with shaking relief and gratitude. "Thank God. How?"

"Apparently I am a DNA mimic." I sobbed into his shoulder, my hands clutching at his neck and shoulder.

"Yeah." He rasped, his hands shifting around to grip the sides of my head and tilt my face to his. His dark eyes searched over mine for a long moment before his mouth dropped to mine. I couldn't stop myself from meeting him halfway, my heart filling in an almost painful way. It was feverish yet beautiful.

Hard lips spread with long sweeps of tongue. Sucking lips met with desperate demand. Desire flashed though me, deep and wild and completely focused on the man who had his dexterous hands on me. My hand sifted through his soft hair. My legs tightened around him, feeling the pressure of his abdomen shifting against me in a very delicious way.

Added to that was the feel of his long fingers curving around my thigh, his thumb circling down to press into the rise of my sex. A little lower and I would have that thumb right were my weeping pussy needed it. Just a little further.

Then he drew it all away. Malachi helped lower my legs to the ground but maintained his hold around my waist. Aroused and completely unfocused, I licked my lips and forced my mind back into working order. "So, uh, you shared."

"Shit, yeah. I am sorry, Teach. I felt like I didn't have a choice." Malachi winced, his hands sliding over my back. "Can I assume from that greeting that you don't hate me?"

"No, Malachi." I shook my head slowly up at him. "I don't hate you. I honestly don't know if I ever could hate you. But you should know that, uh, I kissed Chriton."

"Just...kissed?" Malachi asked, licking his lips and looking over my shoulder.

"Just kissed." Chriton's voice confirmed to him.

"Well, I guess that makes us even." Malachi nodded slowly.

"So, uh, what happens now?" I asked softly, twisting my head to look at Chriton.

"I have an idea." Malachi mentioned with a slight cringe. "But I really don't know how well it will work out. It could backfire in a major way."

"What is that?" Chriton asked carefully.

"They recently finished another four bedroom family suite on the lower level." Malachi brought up.

Coren started laughing loudly at that. "Are you seriously thinking of having all of you move in together?"

"It's a thought." Malachi shrugged, turning a set of questioning eyes from Chriton to me. "I mean, there is four rooms. One for each of us. And it would cut out any, uh, competition."

"He has a point." Chriton agreed slowly.

"So, do I get a say in the matter?" I asked, unsure of the thought of living with two very different males who I was separately developing feelings for.

"No." They both answered at the same time.

"Come on." I yelped when firm hands spun me around and threw me over Chriton's shoulder.

"My place first. I need a shower and I need to get Lucy." Chriton stated, walking up the dirt ramp.

"Where are you going?" Coren called after us.

"Back to the Base." Chriton called back to his brother.

"For crying out loud." Coren's voice echoed back to us just as the hairs on my body stood straight up followed by loud wooshes and cracks. Using my hands on Chriton's back I pushed up enough that I could see a glowing Coren moving astounding amounts of rock and dirt off of one area of the tunnels while another area collapsed. The dirt and rock were piled about twenty feet away and I heard Bane's voice call, "About damned time."

"Who is Lucy?" I shifted around and tried to look up at Chriton while I asked.

"My fox." Came Chriton's answer.

"You have a fox?" Malachi asked with a surprised smile.

"I do. I stole her from Amber. She's really sweet. Mali is going to love her." Chriton confirmed with a grin.

"Mali is going to love you for bringing in a fox. She's been asking for a pet since Guard found that damned cat." Malachi laughed.

"So, how do you want to do this?" Chriton asked as we reached the landing pad and I was finally set on my feet.

"I already have Lysander and the team working on my suite and Leah's suite." Malachi informed us to my irritation, pulling a water bottle out of one of his giant cargo pockets that he handed to me.

Both men watched in awe as I opened the full bottle and thirstily downed just over half of it in one go. Pausing, I took a number of breathless gulps of air in. "Hey, I haven't agreed to anything." I argued, pointing at the two maddening men.

Malachi's hand flashed out and those blunt fingers of his took a familiar grip on my jaw. "Leah, baby, I know you aren't arguing with your Boss."

"Shit. I knew that teasing you was going to come back to bite me on the ass." I moaned, slapping his hand away. "And that still doesn't mean I agreed to anything."

Malachi grinned and winked. "No, Teach, it isn't the teasing that is going to bite you in the ass."

"So, if he's Boss, what am I?" Chriton asked, crossing his arms and staring down at me with a set of raised eyebrows. I shook my head and began to drink the rest of the water in the bottle.

"Master." Malachi stated with a shrug.

I spit out a mouthful of water and cried out my denial, pointing a finger at them. "No!"

"Yes." Malachi laughed in amusement. "Boss and Master. It does have quite the ring to it."

"There is no way..." I argued.

"All in favor." Chriton called raising his hand. Malachi infuriatingly joined him.

"That is so not happening." I shook my head at them with eyes narrowed in warning.

"Majority passes. Names approved. From now on Leah will refer to Chriton as Master and me as Boss." Malachi stated as if it was an official decree.

"Nuh uh, no way. That is not the majority. Mali isn't here and she is part of this too." I yelled, stomping my feet angrily.

"Ah ha." Chriton laughed, pointing at me. "That sounds like a confirmation on the move to me."

"Damnit." I growled, glaring at the man. I closed the empty bottle and shoved it back into Malachi's chest.

"Yeah, I think I am going to like this." Malachi grinned and returned the bottle back to where he pulled it from before crossing his arms.

We all stepped back when the stollen Drako ship with Wings piloting came in for a landing. Once the ship doors opened I tossed the men one last glare and stomped inside.

I was right about to sit down into one of the only two seats when I was adjusted out of the way by a pair of hands on my hips. I rolled my eyes when those hands pulled me down to sit right on top of a hard set of thighs.

"What? No complaints?" Chriton breathed in my ear.

"Nope." I shook my head and shifted until I was resting comfortably against his hard chest. He was just as hard as Malachi. Closing my eyes, I hummed softly. "Wake me up when we get there."

Chriton chuckled and ran a set of fingers gently through my hair. I was so exhausted that I did indeed fall asleep for the ten minutes it took us to get back to Base. Chriton stirring in his seat caused me to jar awake and jump up from the seat.

"Woah there teach." Malachi caught my half asleep, stumbling body. "Calm."

"Sorry. Sorry." I whispered automatically, gripping his arm while I tried to get my foggy brain to work.

"Stop apologizing, Leah." Chriton cupped my face and turned my eyes up to his.

"Ok." I slurred out my agreement.

"She's fucking exhausted." Malachi noted from above and behind me.

"We all are." Chriton sighed tiredly. "Let's get this done as fast as possible."

CHAPTER 8

CHRITON

Leah was exhausted, weaving back and forth in a worrying way. Placing my hands on her rounded hips, I guided her through the halls. Her body relaxed back into mine as we stepped together, her head shifting against my dirty shirt. Really dirty. Both of us were coated in dust, dirt, and sweat from the cave-in.

My heart jolted happily at her easy acceptance of my hold. Every time she drew away from my touch, her eyes flashing with pain and self disgust, I felt it deep in my heart. And today I almost lost all hope of ever being able to feel her in my arms.

My beautiful Leah had long, thick golden blond heir with grey eyes. A rounded face, with a wide mouth, a straight nose, and uptilted eyes. She was medium height with curves for days. A thin waist jutted out to a roundly muscled ass and a set of beautifully powerful thighs. She also boasted a pair of perky, delicious breasts.

When she first came out of the tent in those shorts my dick hardened so fast that I felt like I was having a stroke. Her long smooth legs on display coupled with those shorts cupping her ass phenomenally and that tank top with its very convenient string running up the front. Her breasts strained the front of that top enough that they rose slightly over the top.

I wasn't sure what started it, my sexual attraction to Leah. After I learned that Leah was my Conversance I still had a hard time believing it. Until I tracked her down at the Farm one day just after her class arrived for a field trip. I remembered how I was turning around to leave, a sour taste filling my mouth at the thought of being in the same place as that woman. But then I heard her laugh. A soft warm sound that caught my ears and drew my head back around.

I found myself watching the woman laugh with the kids that were currently helping feed one of the newborn motherless calves. She was wearing a long flowing skirt and kneeling right in the dirt of the pen that the calf was kept in. The small boy that Amber was helping was giggling. Leah was smiling at the boy. Her face softened with warmth and happiness. My heart jerked at how different she looked right then. Beautiful.

After months of following her, watching her, I realized that the woman I originally met and the woman that I was seeing were two completely different women.

That woman was brash, arrogant, a bully in the worst way. This one was introverted, quiet, with soft yet sad smiles. She looked so small until she dealt with the children in her care and that warmth inside flowed out of her until she practically glowed with it. And then there was that delicious attitude. Something that I only saw when she was around Malachi. Something that I was extremely fascinated with.

I was slowly unravelling the mystery and now that it was all coming out, I was starting to understand it.

I sensed that this woman saw me the way I needed to be seen. I felt it in my heart. Not in the he's a Guardian and I want to 'test his power, wink, wink' type of way that every other woman saw me. No, Leah actually cared about me and my wellbeing.

For the past couple years, I felt as if I was slowly disappearing. Like my very essence was slowly drifting away from me. The more I used my gift, my ability, the less I felt like I was real.

Until the day that I joined bath time. Madron, his Conversances, and their roommates had a couple of jacuzzi tubs in their suite and we went over there one day for a jacuzzi evening. Leah, who was friends with Madron's wife, Salem, was there.

When it was time for the evening to end, I reached out to help Leah from the tub. She hid her cringe well when I caught her hand with mine. Yet, for that quick moment I felt my body center, my essence practically snapped back together. Relief crashed through me. Followed by joy, attraction, confusion, anger, obsession, and so much more.

She was quick to let my hand go, wrap a towel around that sexy little bikini she was wearing, and race from the bathroom. I found myself barely holding my arousal at bay and studying her intently, knowing that she was the reason for the inundation of emotions that were clashing inside of me.

That's when I knew irrevocably that she was mine, my Conversance.

Gently passing Leah to Malachi, I used my palm to open the door to the suite I shared with my family. They both followed me through the empty main room to my bedroom.

Both of them paused at the entrance, wide eyes darting around the disaster area that was my room. "Uh, what, uh, what?" Leah gaped in shock, now completely wide awake.

"I am sorry." I shrugged and pulled my dirty shirt off, tossing it towards the laundry. "I know it's a mess."

The shirt bounced off the top of the desk and the large number of items populating the top. It knocked over quite a few of those items sending them falling scattering and tumbling to the floor. Reaching into the jumbled cupboards, I dug out some clean clothes and threw them on the messy bed.

"Noooo." Malachi said slowly, still studying the room with bemusement. "I am afraid I may actual get lost in here and never find my way out."

I chuckled and clapped him on the back before grabbing up my clothes and heading to the bathroom.

"Chriton!" Leah's exasperated exclamation followed me to the bathroom.

LEAH

I COULDN'T BELIEVE the mess. I was amazed that he was able to sleep with the room like this.

"We have to do something about this before we can pack him up." I tipped my head back to look up into Malachi's dark eyes.

"Yeah." He nodded slowly in agreement, his eyes still darting around the disaster of a room.

"You, uh, pack the stuff in the cupboards and I will deal with the, uh, garbage and dirty...items." I planned.

"Yeah." Malachi nodded again. He turned to find a bin while I started on the mess.

First to get thrown into a pile outside the room were all of the clothes that were laying about the room. Dirty or otherwise, I didn't care. If they were not in the cupboards they went in the pile. Next was the dirty dishes and the garbage.

Luckily, there wasn't much of those and what there was consisted of empty packaging and water glasses. The packaging was put in the recycling and the glasses got washed and put away. Since I was already in the kitchen, I dug out a bucket. Filling it with hot soapy water, I threw a rag in it and carried it back to the bedroom.

The next was the clutter. All of it was washed before I handed it to Malachi who placed it in one of the bins he found. Knickknacks, books, office supplies, some weird looking electronic things, and various other items. Some of them made me blush when I realized what they were. Some of the things I had no idea what they were. But none of that mattered, because it all went in the bin.

Using the soapy water, I washed and wiped down everything I could as I uncovered or emptied it. The clothes from the cupboards were folded neatly and packed next.

"What are you doing?" The surprising sound of Callden's voice caused my heart to stop and my body to jolt about a foot in Malachi's direction.

"Packing. Can you find more bins for us?" Malachi answered, gripping my neck in a calming gesture and guiding me closer to the safety of his body. Callden was standing in the doorway with his arms crossing his chest. His eyes were watching us curiously.

"Did you find the fox?" Callden looked around the mostly empty room.

"Oh yeah, Lucy." I began to search the room to see if I could find the fox in question.

"Probably under the bed." Callden jerked his chin towards the bed.

Horror slid over me and I felt my face go white, I forgot to check under the bed. "I don't want to look." I gasped at the men. "Under the bed is always the worst."

Malachi grinned at me while Callden threw his head back in laughter. "I can't help you with that."

"Fuck." I whispered, eyeing the bed before making a decision.

Lowering to my knees, I bent over and lifted the sheet to look under the bed. Weirdly, it wasn't horrible. I pulled out more dirty clothes and some very intense looking books that definitely sparked my interest. Those were placed on the bed for Malachi to pack. I bit back my smile at Malachi's impressed whistle at the sight of those books. Then I saw a pair of glowing eyes.

"Hello, Lucy." I greeted, resting my relaxed hand on the floor and waiting.

She slowly inched forward until she could smell my fingers. After that she darted out from under the bed and raced around me with excited yips.

"Such a pretty girl." I laughed, petting her body and catching her when she jumped into my lap.

She yipped happily and licked at my chin once before sliding back under the bed. She returned seconds later with a slobbered and dirty stuffed toy that she dropped into my lap.

"Is this your baby?" I asked, picking up the toy and holding it out to her. "It's a very loved baby."

Lucy yipped, spun in a circle, and grabbed her stuffed toy from my hand.

"Your daddy is a mess. Do you want to help us finish packing up his mess?" I asked the adorable fox.

Lucy licked my cheek, grabbed one of the dirty shirts I pulled from under the bed with her teeth, and began dragging it to the pile in the main room. I grinned while both men laughed when she huffed and dropped the shirt in the pile.

"Such a helpful girl." I praised, petting her before rising to finish packing.

Lucy continued taking the clothes to the pile and we stripped the bed. Once the bed was remade with clean bedding, Lucy jumped on top of it, happily spinning.

"What the hell happened?" A damp but clean Chriton demanded from the doorway.

Lucy yipped and jumped into his arms. His eyes travelled over empty and spotless room in amazement while he automatically caught Lucy and gave her loving pets.

"We are done." I grinned, brushing my hands off.

"So, I see." Chriton breathed, absently petting Lucy. "Uh, did you find Lucy under the bed?"

Callden choked and walked away. Malachi grinned at Chriton and nodded. "Yes, she did."

"Shit." Chriton actually blushed.

"Don't worry, man. We all have our...thing." Malachi reassured Chriton with a knowing look.

"Sooo...?" Chriton's eyebrows rose with his question.

"No way, man. Not here and not now." Malachi denied with a firm shake of his head.

"We still need to do something with those." I pointed at the mountain of dirty clothes in the main room.

"Here." Malachi grunted and began to shove it all into another bin. "We can laundry it tomorrow."

"Sounds good." Chriton smiled in agreement. After setting Lucy down on the floor he hooked up a lead to her and we loaded the bins onto a trolly that was already waiting for us.

I began to push the packed trolley down the hall only to have Malachi reach around me and take over pushing. "Come on, mine next." Malachi said to Chriton who was walking Lucy beside us. Lucy was racing back and forth, smelling everything she could, her bushy tail waving back and forth.

We quickly reached Malachi's suite to see the door wide open with men packing bins onto another two trolleys.

"Dad." Mali called when she saw us walk into the suite. "We are moving."

She raced away from where she was helping Bear at the main room shelving unit and ran to her father. Malachi bowed down and hugged the girl who slammed into his abdomen. "Hey, Mali-girl, I missed you."

"I missed you too, dad." Mali mumbled from where her face was buried in her father's stomach.

"Shall we finish this up. We have all had a long couple of days and need to find a bed soon." Malachi told the girl.

"Leah." Mali exclaimed, running over to give me my own hug. "Uncle Scope and Uncle Marko are just about done packing your suite."

"That was very sweet of them. I will have to thank them." I told the girl, smoothing my fingers through her hair before noticing how dirty my hands were. With a cringe, I patted Mali to release me and my dirt caked body. "Your dad is right, let's get this done."

"Here, Mali-girl, why don't you watch Lucy for me while I help you dad and the others?" Chriton said, guiding the girl over to the couch and handing her Lucy's lead.

"I heard that you are going to live with us, Uncle Chriton. I am so excited. Is Lucy going to live with us too?" Mali smiled, petting the fox in a gentle fashion.

"She is." Chriton confirmed with a nod, stepping over to help Bear.

"Malachi." The man turned to me at the sound of his name and grinned when I pointed demandingly at his grey couch. There was no way I was going to let him leave behind that wide cushioned length of body hugging divinity.

"Of course, Teach." He gave me a dramatic bow before returning to the bin he was filling.

Chriton, Mali, and Lucy went with the next set of trolly filled bins that the men hauled down to the new suite. It took another two hours before Malachi and I finally finished the last of the packing which was good because I was starting to feel dizzy and shaky. Hungry and exhausted. Not a good mix.

I was closing the last bin when a wave of dizziness overcame me and I started swaying sideways in a way that I couldn't seem to get a handle on.

"Woah." Malachi emoted, his hard hands catching my waist.

"I am sorry." I shook my head in attempt to clear. "I think I am just hungry."

"Fuck, I bet." Malachi growled angrily, bending over to lift me up. He set me down on the counter and dug out a recently packed bag of mixed nuts, "Here, eat some of these." After opening the bag, he stepped between my legs and dug out a handful for me. I rested my very heavy head on his warm chest while I slowly plucked the nuts from his giant palm.

"There we go." Malachi said after I finished a couple handfuls. His hand under my jaw gently lifted my head up so he could examine my face. "You are already looking less pale."

"Ready?" Scope asked from the door as Bear and Woody carried out the last item in the suite, the couch.

"Yup." Malachi nodded and lifted my limp body up against his chest, bag of nuts and all. I kept munching on the nuts as Malachi followed the men through the empty evening halls. "Tired, baby." He soothed softly down at me, his chest rumbling comfortingly in my ear.

"Ummhmmm." I hummed softly, rubbing my face along the fabric of his shirt, my eyes drifting closed.

I kept eating, feeling the rhythm of his steady steps travelling down the hall, the stairs, then the hall again. A door opened and the atmosphere changed. The soft sounds of furniture and people moving around was soon followed by numerous farewells and the suite door clicking closed.

"Shit. She's exhausted." I heard Chriton voice.

"Yeah."

"Mali's room is unpacked and set up. She's already tucked into bed for the night." Chriton shared.

"Thanks, man." Malachi sighed graciously.

"I love her, too, you know." Chriton's voice said.

"I know that, Chriton. But that doesn't mean I can't thank you." Malachi chuckled.

"Are you going to put me down so that I can finally have a shower?" I murmured, patting Malachi's chest. I honestly didn't know how he could be holding me considering how much I stank.

"Sure thing, Teach." Malachi set me gently on my feet, making sure I was able to stand on my own before fully releasing me.

"Thank you." I patted his chest with the bag of nuts, letting them go into the hand he raised to grip mine.

With my eyes set on the open bathroom door and its call to cleansing, I stumbled towards it while pulling my disgusting shirt from my body and shoving my shorts down. The sooner I got naked, the sooner I could get into the shower. I was stripping out of my bra as I stepped into the large bathroom to see the relieving sight of my toiletries already set up waiting for me. Turning on the shower, I kicked my underwear off and stepped inside.

I moaned at the feel of the heated water running over my dirt stained flesh. With shaking hands, I washed myself from head to toe, twice, before I finally felt clean. Then, needing to feel completely clean, I shaved. My legs, my arms, my pubic hair, all of it. When I was done shaving, I washed once more before stepping out and wrapping a towel around myself.

It was then that I noticed that I left the bathroom door open. Oops.

I brushed my teeth and hair before shuffling out of the bathroom. Confused, I looked around the large open suite and wondered which room was mine.

"Come on, precious." Chriton gripped my shoulders from behind and guided me to one of the rooms with an open door.

Reaching the shadowed room, I was glad to see that the bed was already made. To exhausted to do anything else, I climbed up onto the soft bed and collapsed belly first. After a comfort finding shift, I was out.

CHAPTER 9

MALACHI

"Uh, Leah." I called, reaching a hand out to the exhausted woman that was literally stripping as she made a stumbling beeline straight to the bathroom. When she didn't seem to hear me, I dropped my slack hand and cocked my head at all of the delicious flesh she was revealing. I really wanted to bite the smooth flesh of the slight tummy I saw. And that ass. Her underwear was riding up enough that I was able to clearly see how mouth wateringly muscular her ass really was.

"Jesus." I breathed, wiping a hand over my mouth. She was reaching up to unclasp her bra. Then the maddening woman turned into the bathroom just as she pulled it from her chest, completely denying me the sight of those sexy globes.

"Fuck." Chriton breathed from beside me.

Giving myself a shake, I reached over and pushed Chriton. "Come on, let's go get her bed made so she can go straight to sleep when she is done."

Chriton licked his lips, his glowing blue eyes trained intently on the bathroom. "Yeah." He breathed before giving himself a shake. "Yeah. Let's do that."

We got the bed made in the room we decided was going to be Leah's, both of us taking pains to make it as comfortable as possible. Hearing the shower finally shut off we stepped out of the room and waited. Leah finally shuffled out of the bathroom and looked around with unfocused confused eyes. The beautiful, clean woman was still damp and only covered in a towel.

Chriton took the initiative and caught her shoulders, turning her around and guiding her to her room. The one right beside the bathroom. She walked into the room, gave a little sigh of delight and crawled up onto the bed. She collapsed, still in her towel, kind of, and was asleep in seconds.

Both Chriton and I moaned at the sight of the towel that was now barely covering the top of her ass and nothing else. I could see the sides of her breasts pressing out from where she was laying on her stomach. Not to mention the shadowed lips that peeked from underneath the towel and between her splayed legs.

Stepping forward, I carefully eased the comforter out from under her and covered her up with it.

"Goodnight, baby." I whispered, kissing her temple softly before making sure the nightlight was on and leaving the room so that Chriton could say his own goodnight.

Collapsing on the couch, I leaned my head back on the cushion and covered my eyes with my own shaky hand. I was completely drained having not slept either.

"So, what exactly is your plan here?" Chriton sighed wearily, collapsing on the other end of the couch and swinging his legs up into my lap. "We live together until she picks one of us?"

"Fuck no." I groaned, reaching down to adjust his heals off of my erection. "We both know that it's not exactly the usual triad. But it could be like the twins and Zara."

"Sharing." Chriton breathed softly, adjusting his hips on the couch. "Be a man, rub my feet."

"Exactly." I nodded shakily, absently doing as he asked, rubbing his feet. "Do you have a problem with that?"

"I felt absolutely sick when I saw you kiss her that first time. But since we talked, I don't have those feelings anymore. It's almost as if I have accepted you and her, because I am there too." Chriton murmured.

"Yeah, I felt the same when I first heard about your Conversance. Once I realized that I couldn't walk away from her but I just might be able to share, those feelings disappeared. It almost felt like it was meant to be." I mumbled, feeling my heavy eyelids blinking closed.

"That's it, meant to be." Chriton slurred.

And that was the last thing I heard.

Until there was a little girl giggling in my ear.

With a huge yawn, I gave my limbs a slight stretch around the warm body they were circling. The warm, hard body?

Tipping my head up, I looked down at the man that I was cuddled around. With a groan, my head fell back to the arm of the couch. Sometimes my penchant for cuddling was a royal pain in the ass.

"Good morning, dad." Mali giggled again. I opened my eyes to see Mali bent over the side of the couch and smiling down at me.

"Good morning, Mali-girl." I loosened an arm from around Chriton causing him to snort and stir against me. Reaching up, I pulled my daughter down so that I could kiss her forehead.

"Can we unpack so that I can eat? I am hungry. And I think Lucy needs to go to the bathroom." Mali continued, smiling down at me.

"Yeah. I got Lucy." Chriton grunted and rolled up until he was sitting on the edge of the couch. He rubbed his eyes before turning to squint down at me. "Did we cuddle all night?"

"Yeah, sorry. That's my thing. I am a cuddler." I apologized, my limbs quickly taking advantage of their freedom with a full, body shaking, stretch.

"I am not really complaining." He rumbled with a frown. "I honestly haven't slept that good in a long time."

I couldn't help but laugh at that. "Go walk Lucy. I will dig out some breakfast." I gave him a push to get him going.

Chriton nodded and attached Lucy's lead before taking her out. I stood up and after a quick detour to the bathroom I started digging into the bins for the supplies I needed.

"Here." Leah appeared beside me, dressed in a pair of loose cotton pants and a slouchy long sleeved shirt. She gently pushed me out of the way and began to hand me things. "I will dig, you start cooking."

"Sounds good." I agreed, grasping her jaw and bringing her face to mine so that I could steal a quick kiss.

"Mali-girl, can you put these in the fridge for me, please?" Leah asked, handing Mali some condiments she dug out.

With that Leah and Mali began to unpack the kitchen bins while I cooked up some bacon, eggs, toast and hashbrowns. Chriton returned and began to help by digging out place settings and setting the table. Lucy helpfully ran from person to person to see if any of us needed her help and Mali talked, telling a charmed Chriton and Leah all about school and her best friend, Atlas.

"I want to ask why you all decided to suddenly live together, but I am not going to. Because I don't really care. I am just happy that I now get to see Leah, and Uncle Chriton, and Lucy, everyday." Mali stated happily when we all sat down to eat our breakfast.

Leah smiled at my daughter, reaching out to run her hand through Mali's mess of a hair. "Me too, Mali-girl. Me too."

"Can we go swimming today?" Mali asked.

"No." I shook my head in denial. "Today we need to unpack and get Uncle Chriton's mountain of laundry cleaned."

"Then we have a family dinner to attend." Chriton winced and glanced over to Leah.

Following his gaze, I wasn't surprised to see her eyes drop to the table and her body tense right up. I watched as he reached over and covered her hand with his.

"Ok." Mali agreed, looking around the table with concerned eyes. She was obviously picking up on Leah's tension.

"It's going to be fine. They just want to show their appreciation for what Leah did for them." Chriton reassured the table. Leah's wide eyes snapped up to his, her face frozen with surprise. "I told them what Ember did, what she planned to do to Blaze, and how you saved Blaze's life. Believe me, Coren has already declared you his sister and dad wants to adopt you."

Leah's eyes darted around the table and her knuckle automatically came up to her lips. I sent her a warning glare which she ignored. She couldn't however ignore Chriton when he reached up and pulled that sorely abused knuckle out of her mouth.

After breakfast, everyone took turns using the bathroom and getting ready for the day. Mali came skipping out of her room and held up a hair tie to me. "Will you make my hair pretty, dad?" Mali asked.

"Sure." I nodded and she sat down at the table so that I could do her hair.

Chriton leaned over my shoulder with a frown as he watched me braid half her hair up into a flower, leaving the other half to hang down.

"How did you learn to do that?" He asked.

"Old YouTube videos and a lot of practice." I told him.

"Hmmm." He hummed, his eyes taking on a gleam.

"The videos might still be loaded on the system." I told him as I finished Mali's hair.

"Awesome." Chriton grinned excitedly. "I am so going to be the master of hair flowers."

Leah came out of the bathroom with her own hair tied up in a high ponytail. "Wow, Mali, that is beautiful."

"I know, right? Dad does a good job." Mali grinned and hopped off the chair.

"He really does." Leah cocked her head and smiled at me.

"I am a man of many talents." I grinned and gave her a wink.

"You should feel him cuddle." Chriton noted from the living room where he started to unpack bins.

"Really? And how exactly do you know this?" Leah covered her smiling mouth with her hand.

"They slept together. I woke up to find them both on the couch, cuddling." My daughter helpfully shared.

Leah's head fell back, and she let out a full blown laugh. The first one I'd heard in years. And it was beautiful. Chriton couldn't seem to stop himself, he stepped forward and took her mouth with his, clearly tasting that laugh. Deeply from the look of their moving lips and jaws.

After he let her go, his eyes came to mine and he smiled. "Sunshine."

We spent the morning and most of the afternoon unpacking and putting things away. Leah and Mali helped each other while Chriton and I helped each other.

"I am missing a book." Chriton noted, tucking the books that Leah found under his bed into his nightstand.

"Maybe." I shrugged, organizing his office supplies onto one of the shelves in the built in, wall length cupboards.

"I want it back when you are done with it. It's one of my favorites." He grunted, shooting me a knowing look.

"It looks interesting." I stated accurately. It did look very interesting.

"It is. There is this one scene that I think you will really like. It's very...heavy handed." Chriton winked over at me.

"I will keep an eye out for it." I chuckled.

When we moved on to my room, Chriton laughed when he came across my stash. He waggled his eyebrows at me and held up a long coiled length of whip in one hand and my black silk robe in the other. "I see that we seem to have some very similar tastes."

"Yes. I did notice that as well." I nodded in agreement. "Put them in the drawer." I jerked my chin to the bedside drawer.

"How do you feel about maids?" He asked, placing the items in the drawer.

"How short of a skirt are we talking?" I asked with a set of raised eyebrows.

"Underwear defining." Chriton grunted with a raised eyebrow.

"You do tend to be a dirty boy. I am thinking that a maid might be a good thing. We would have to find the appropriate uniform and convince Leah first." I noted, my mind flashing to an image of Leah dressed up as said maid in a very low top and a very short skirt.

"True." Chriton agreed with his own anticipatory smile. "But for some reason I think she will be fully on board."

"What makes you think that?" I questioned curiously.

Instead of answering Chriton simply shook the black robe out and gave me a knowing look.

"Yeah, I see your point." I chuckled, pointing to a hook on the back of the door.

"I want a blue one." Chriton stated, hanging the robe up. "I look very sexy in blue."

"I might be able to track one down for you." I grinned at him.

Once we were finished, we relaxed on the couch and turned on an adventure movie. Mali and Lucy cuddled up to Chriton while I pulled Leah back into my arms. She sighed and relaxed into me.

I was amazed at the change in her since she came out of the tunnels. How much she now accepted our touches, even reaching out with some of her own. The time spent with Chriton must have cleared up a lot and provided her the permission she needed.

CHAPTER 10

CHRITON

Supper that night was interesting. It started with complete awkwardness. I guided everyone to the Guardian suite keeping a firm hold on Leah's hand. I refused to give her even the slightest out.

Just about everyone was there. Amber and Callden, Blaze and Coren and their seven month old baby boy, Walker. Although Ryker, Amber's fifteen year old son, was running late and Bane, Bailor, and Harper were at their place out at the Ranch.

"Now I can finally do this." Coren growled as soon as he opened the door. He stepped right over and hugged a stunned Leah. "Thank you." I heard him whisper to her. "Without you I wouldn't have my Conversance or my son. Thank you."

"Uh, you're welcome." Leah rasped, awkwardly patting him on the shoulder.

While Coren was busy with Leah, I took Mali's hand in mine and guided her into the suite so that I could officially introduce her to everyone.

"All right." I stood with Mali's little shoulders in my palms. "This young lady here is Mali. Mali, I would like you to meet my dad, Callden, my sister-in-law, Blaze, and her son, Walker. My brother, Coren, is the one mauling Leah. And this lady here is my stepmother, Amber. Bane, my other brother and his partners, Bailor and Harper, are out at the Ranch but you will meet them later. As for Ryker, my stepbrother, he's around somewhere and you will meet him sometime tonight."

Mali blushed and smiled when everyone greeted her warmly.

"Can I get you some juice, Miss Mali?" Amber asked with smile.

Mali tipped her head back to her father and at his nod of confirmation she turned back to Amber. "Yes, please."

"Malachi?" Amber asked the man that was standing just inside the door, keeping a careful eye on Leah.

"I would love some juice, thank you, Amber." Malachi gave a grateful smile.

Coren finally let Leah go long enough for her to step into the suite. Unfortunately for Leah, she was immediately swept up by my father. He also received an awkward pat on the shoulder.

"Ok, let's give her a break." Amber luckily stepped in, guiding Callden away. Malachi, completely in tune with Leah, automatically paced over to the anxious looking woman. Her hand latched onto his in a tight, white knuckled grip.

"Thank you." Leah's lips twitched with the ghost of a smile.

"How old is he?" Mali asked, walking over to crouch beside the little boy that was standing at the edge of the couch, holding onto the cushions for dear life.

"Seven months." I told her, following her over.

"Ukka!" Walker screamed happily when he saw me, letting go of the couch and attempting to toddle towards me. Mali smiled and was quick to catch his waving hands, helping him keep steady so he could complete the three weaving steps towards me.

"He's adorable." Mali giggled and looked up at me.

"He is, until he doesn't get his way. Then he gets a lot less adorable." I winked down at the girl. Walker reached out from Mali to me and punched me in the chest with his little fist. "Ukka." He cried again with a happy grin.

"Remember, Walker, we don't hit." I caught his little fist and held it, looking sternly down into his bright blue eyes.

Walker's lip jutted out in a small pout right before he leaned forward and pushed his forehead into my chest. His way of apologizing. "It's ok, bud. It's all a learning process, right?" I cupped the back of his little head and looked down at him.

He tilted his head back and blinked his eyes up at me before resuming his usual half babble.

"He's smart." Mali noted with a smile.

"Everyone is in their own way." I told the girl, reaching out to cup the back of her head.

Mali smiled at my silent hint that she was smart as well and leaned into my shoulder.

"Supper is ready." Amber called to us.

I lifted Walker up to my chest with an arm under his booty and guided Mali to the table. Malachi led Leah to a spot at the table that was placed safely between Mali and I. Once seated, Mali immediately reached out to take my woman's hand. Leah smiled down at the girl, her eyes warm and filled with love. My heart gave a stutter at that look. I couldn't wait for the day that she turned that look to me.

I efficiently strapped Walker into his highchair and took my own seat.

Once we were all seated, the food was passed around and everyone began to socialize. My family kept it open and friendly for the newcomers. Soon Malachi and Mali relaxed while Leah unclenched, slightly.

Ryker was the last to join us. "Holy crap." He exclaimed in astonishment, literally sliding into his seat beside me after running into the suite. "So, get this. Jax and I were down on the lower level, practicing our sprinting and generally messing around. There was this weird stain on the wall and floor in the hall right by Gabe's suite. I pointed it out to Jax and do you know what he said? That Gabe told him that it was from a giant freaking spider. Gabe said it was massive. Bigger than a man. Apparently it tried to attack them one night and his dad killed it."

"I am pretty sure that either Jax was just pulling your leg." Amber informed her son. The rest of us were looking at Ryker with a mixture of pity and skepticism. There was no way a giant spider attacked anyone in the Base without our knowledge.

"No, he wasn't. I asked him why no one heard about it and Jax shrugged. He told me that he asked Gabe the same thing and that Gabe told him that he didn't know. I even asked what happened to the body. Jax said that according to Gabe, they took it to the Bay and incinerated it." Ryker stated earnestly, sounding as if he really believed this.

"Sorry Ryker, but I am going to have to claim bullshit." Dad grunted with a sympathetic cringe.

"If the Ancients or even the Base was attacked by a creature like that we would've been informed." Coren pointed out while pointing his fork at Ryker.

"Plus, there is no way Catro took on a spider that big all by himself. I get that he's different now but he totally would've died." I swallowed the food in my mouth before joining in.

"Uh, actually.." Malachi cut in with a shudder.

Everyone's eyes turned towards him in surprise.

"You cannot seriously believe this?" Coren looked at him in amazement.

"I saw it. Well, I saw the legs as they all were shoving them into the incinerator. The thing was huge if the legs were anything to go by. There are reports if you really want to see them." Malachi went white, his eyes taking on a haunted look as he described his memory. Mali leaned against her father in a comforting move while Leah reached around Mali's to grip the back of his tense neck.

"Seriously?" Dad exclaimed in disbelief, rising to grab his tablet. He returned to his chair while furiously tapping away at the tablet, trying to find what Malachi was talking about. Amber immediately bent over his shoulder so she too could read the information he was bringing up.

"Motherfucker." Dad snarled angrily when he obviously found what Malachi was talking about. "How the fuck were we not informed of this?" More time passed while he was obviously reading. "What the fuck?" He growled and tossed the tablet onto the table. "I am going to kill them."

I nabbed the tablet and began my own review. Video clearly showed the aftermath of the fight and the dismemberment and subsequent removal and destruction of the being that did in fact look like a giant spider. Scanning the reports, I was amazed to learn about the creatures plan to take out Malachi and how Catro, a reincarnated Watcher, defeated it. With a buzzing head I passed the tablet to Coren who shared it with Blaze.

Coren dropped to the tablet to the table with frustrated anger. "Why weren't we informed of this?"

"Shit, sorry. I didn't mean to put a damper on the mood." Malachi cringed out an apology.

"Actually, Malachi, you didn't put a damper on anything. Ryker was the first one who brought this to our attention. You just backed him up." I explained, driving an arm out and shoving my stepbrother straight off his chair.

Ryker yelped when he thumped to the floor. Leah frowned and was leaning passed my body to check on Ryker when my chair bucked harshly. The little shit tried to yank my chair out from under me.

"Hah." I exclaimed arrogantly, my hands flying down to grip the table and steady myself. "Going to have to try harder than..."

I cried out when the bottom front of my chair jerked violently forward sending me crashing back to the floor.

"What?" I heard Leah gasp when I was yanked, chair and all under the table.

Coren was quick to dive under the table with Ryker and I. That was when the fight truly began.

Coren, the asshole, got me in a sleeper hold, while I held Ryker down to the floor with my leg across the boy's chest. Ryker was far too well trained for a fifteen year old and too damned slick. He kicked out wildly, his heal connecting with Coren's shoulder causing Coren's hold to loosen on me. I immediately took advantage and rolled, kneeing Coren in the ribs.

Coren growled and launched himself towards me. Thinking fast, I flattened myself to the floor. Coren ended up landing mostly on top of me while crashing into Ryker. This sent all of us sliding into a chair violently. Luckily, the chair was empty and the sound of it clattering to the floor succeeded in breaking us up.

"I am confused as to why you are beating on each other instead of the one's that caused all of this." Amber noted from where she was standing safely in my father's arms.

"Best step-mom ever!" I exclaimed, jumping to my feet and swinging a giggling Amber around in my arms.

Once I set her on the floor, I started for the door. Coren and dad were right on my heals.

"Uh." Leah emoted worriedly. "Catro isn't here."

All three of us stopped in our tracks and turned to her with confused looks. She was standing beside Malachi with her arm around Mali.

"Catro and Royce are still out at the Ranch. Diad is watching the kids and, honestly, they have probably already travelled out there themselves to check on their parents after the cave-in." Leah explained to us, chewing on her knuckle. A knuckle that was quickly removed by Malachi which caused her to pause and shoot him a glare. "There is no point in doing it now when the only one technically available is Madron."

"Shit. She's right. I completely forgot." I grunted in irritation, running a frustrated hand through my hair.

"Let's finish supper. The food is still good even if our attempt at a calm family dinner is now a failure." Dad gestured, returning to his seat at the slightly jarred table.

"Too be honest, it is usually a failure." I pointed out with a set of raised eyebrows, making sure the rest found their seats before retaking my own.

"And whose fault is that?" Coren accused, his eyes narrowed on me.

"Ryker's." I exclaimed, throwing a thumb Ryker's way.

"Oh, yeah, blame the youngest." Ryker scoffed with a roll of his eyes.

"Well...yeah." I shrugged and bumped his shoulder with mine.

"Do they always act like this?" Mali asked her father.

"I want to so no, Mali-girl." Malachi chuckled down at her. "But I am slightly afraid it might be a lie."

"It would be." Blaze laughed, sliding her eyes over to her husband. Coren laughed, putting his arm around his wife and dropping a kiss to her upturned lips.

"I like these people." Mali giggled.

"That's good because we like you too." Callden leaned over the table and whispered at her.

I felt Leah's head turn to stare at something beyond me. When I realized that she was looking at Ryker I turned to him. He was looking back at Leah with smiling eyes. "Yo." He greeted with a chin thrust.

"Yo?" I exclaimed in a high-pitched voice. "That's your greeting?"

"It worked." Ryker grinned, pointing at Leah.

He was right, it did. Leah was now silently giggling into her fist.

"You're lucky, kid." I shot a glare to my little brother.

"I really am. I just gained another really hot sister." Ryker nodded in agreement.

"Not yours." I snarled at the boy, my arm circling Leah protectively. My mind knew he was joking but my soul screamed out its possessive instincts.

"Slow down on the cave man mentality. I am not going to steal your woman." Ryker rolled his eyes.

"Like you could." I grunted, relaxing my hold on Leah.

"I don't know about that. I did make her giggle with my awesome flirting abilities." Ryker bragged arrogantly.

"When he beats your ass, I am so making popcorn." Coren cut in, drawing my eyes over to see him watching us with amusement.

"Where's the faith?" Ryker exclaimed, rising his hands in the air in a frustrated gesture. "I have mad skills."

"I am sure you do. But I prefer my men a little older." Leah told the boy with a wincing smile.

Malachi laughed at that, reaching an arm around his daughter to grip Leah's neck. "Yeah, you do."

"Shush now." Leah whispered up to him. "There is a difference between sharing and caring and revealing and traumatizing."

"Yeah, Amber." Dad stated, turning knowing eyes to his wife.

Amber blushed and giggled. "Oops."

"I don't want to know." Ryker stated vehemently, pointing a finger at dad.

Leah fell quiet once again as she finished eating, watching everything intently. On the plus side she relaxed enough that I couldn't feel the waves of tension emanating from her anymore.

I couldn't stop myself from leaning over and pressing a soft kiss to her temple. I also couldn't stop from returning Malachi's warm smile when I caught his eyes.

Returning to our suite after a long supper and visit, Leah tucked Mali into bed before joining Malachi and I on the couch.

I felt my chest bloom with happiness when she smiled softly and curled into my chest. "Thank you." She whispered softly.

"No, precious, thank you." I returned, wrapping my arms around her and pulling her deeper into my chest. "Your forgiveness only compounds how beautiful your soul is."

Leah didn't say anything at that, instead she patted my chest and rose from the couch. "As much as I really want to laze around all night, I have school in the morning, and I really need to get to work on editing the Ranch documentary."

I smiled and watched Leah grabbed the camera that Coren returned to her before we left. Sitting down at the table she began to load the footage onto her tablet.

"Here." I stood, nabbing two of the controllers for one of the game consuls from the shelf and handing one to Malachi.

"You do realize that I am a soldier, right?" Malachi hinted as he took the controller.

"That doesn't mean you can manipulate a character on a screen." I challenged with a grin.

"Ok." Malachi shrugged and proceeded to demolish my ass for the rest of the evening.

CHAPTER 11

LEAH

"Up." A hard voice demanded and I was pulled from the blankets by way of a long fingered grip on my ankle.

"Fug off." I slurred, kicking out at the evil hand.

"Come on or we are going to be late." Chriton's hand dropped my ankle but fell to my hips to pull me up.

"Fer'ut?" I slurred again, getting angry enough to slap at those hands.

"Yoga class." Chriton stubbornly kept pulling me up from the bed.

"No. Yoga sucks." I grunted, now wide awake at the ass crack of dawn and being lifted straight off the bed by my hips. "Sleep, Chriton, sleep."

"Yoga won't suck anymore." He assured me, setting me on my feet and tossing a set of my workout clothes at me. Workout clothes that I thought I successfully buried deep in the cupboards of my old suite.

"Sleep." I threw the clothes back at him and leapt for the bed. "No." I whined when Chriton's arms caught around my waist before I could land. "Sle-ee-ep." I whined, trying to push his arms away while I kicked out at him.

"Dressed, Leah." Chriton ordered firmly, setting me back on my feet and handing me the clothes again before walking out and leaving me too it.

I grumbled various threats after him while I pulled my pajamas from my body and began to redress into the tight workout gear. Not liking the display of flesh from just wearing my athletic bra, I pulled on my robe and stomped out of my room. Most of my work out attire Ember picked out and was tight and body baring. And I hated it. For me, it was worse than wearing a bikini. Mind you, the only time I wore a bikini was when I was in water. As soon as I was out o the water, I was quick to cover up. The whole time I was wearing the skin baring workout clothing I felt incredibly uncomfortable.

Deciding that if Chriton wanted me to do this he could share, I stomped through his open doorway. Chriton had his shirt off and was in the midst of pulling a pair of shorts up over his lower half.

I swallowed hard at the delectable sight before me. Chriton's chest was sharply cut. Muscled shoulders and chest narrowed drastically to a rippling abdomen. Veins didn't pop out when he flexed, they didn't need to, they were already raised and snaking over his arms and torso. His legs were also muscled but not thick. His hips were perfectly slim, made for a woman's legs to wrap around.

His head turned to me at my entrance and he grinned proudly when he saw me running my eyes over him. Giving him a glare, I stomped over to his cupboard and began digging inside.

Yanking out a dropped arm tank top, I pulled it on over my bra and yoga shorts. The thing was huge on me so I caught the extra material on the side and tied it into a knot.

While I was doing that, Chriton finished dressing and strode out to the kitchen. Going to the bathroom, I dug out a hair tie from one of the drawers so that I could pull my hair back into a ponytail.

I was pretty sure I looked like crap but that was all I was willing to do. Walking into the kitchen, I crossed my arms and glared at the man that held two water bottles.

Chriton's eyes were running over me, bright blue and actually glowing. When his eyes finished their assessment of my body and reached mine, his mouth spread in a wicked smile. "Seriously thinking of changing my mind after that show, lady."

"Out." I ordered, pointing to the suite door.

Chriton held his bottle filled hands up and backed towards the door. "Come on, precious. Let's go get flexible."

"I really don't know if you will survive this relationship." I growled, following him.

Chriton chuckled and handed me my water bottle before taking my hand in his. I was still slightly amazed when he did that. A year ago, even a month ago, it seemed like an impossibility. Now it felt like a miracle. All of it. Him. Malachi. Mali. I was terrified that I would lose it but not as terrified as I felt at the thought of not taking the chance I was being offered.

When we reached the Guardian suite it was to find that Blaze was already up and dressed in her own workout wear. She was standing in the kitchen, filling up her water bottle.

"Awesome." She exclaimed excitedly when she saw me.

"See, you already have a yoga friend. You don't need me." I pointed out, turning to go back our suite for another hour of sleep.

"Nope." Chriton caught me around my waist and held me in front of him while we waited for Blaze to finish.

"But sleep. Please." I begged, tilting my head back to him.

"Leah, love, I promise, you will enjoy it. Just trust me." Chriton sighed, turning his own pleading eyes down to mine.

"Fine." I huffed. "But if you are wrong, you have to watch me read one of those interesting books I found under your bed. And when I am done, I am going to go straight to sleep."

"If I am right, you have to read it out loud to both Malachi and I." Chriton determined, guiding Blaze and I to the suite door.

"What books?" Blaze, ever the avid reader, asked curiously.

"Erotica." I told her bluntly as we walked down the halls.

"Oh." She blushed red and asked. "What type?"

"Role playing." Chriton described the bulk of the books.

"Are we talking like master and maid, catholic schoolgirl, Leia in the gold bikini, masseur promoting the happy ending, or is it more along the lines of dom and sub, puppy or pony play, furry's?" Both Chriton and I paused and looked over at Blaze in surprise as she listed off a number of different roleplaying scenarios.

"Blaze, my beautiful sister-in-law with a heavy emphasis on sister, I applaud your knowledge and interest, but this is one area that I will not be going into detail with you." Chriton told her with an unyielding look.

I couldn't help it, I joined Blaze's giggles. She linked her arm through mine and we continued down the hall with Chriton following behind us.

"I heard you packed his room for him. Why didn't you get rid of all of those godawful clothes?" Blaze asked curiously.

"What clothes?" I frowned, not really sure what she was talking about.

"You don't see it?" She whispered in amazement.

I stopped and turned to her in confusion. Luckily, we were now in the community area that the exercise classrooms were located around.

"See what?" I questioned, still not understanding.

"Look at him." Blaze gestured to Chriton with her hand. "You have to see it. Even a blind person could see it."

I turned to look at him like she demanded. He was standing behind us with his legs braced and his powerful arms crossing his chest. He was watching us with amused eyes, obviously listening to every word we were saying. He turned those amused eyes to Blaze, adding a raised eyebrow.

He was wearing another drop armed top that gave me an interesting peek at some side boob and the side of his sharp abdomen muscles. Seeing that masculine display of skin made my fingers itch to run along his bared sides. The look was finished with a set of long sweat shorts that fit perfectly, not too tight, not too loose. All together he really was a very attractive image.

"I am sorry, Blaze, unless it's the side boob, I still don't see it." I sighed, turning back to her.

"The shirt is neon yellow, the shorts are orange." She exclaimed almost frantically, gesturing even harder to Chriton.

My teeth found my knuckle and I looked back at Chriton. He turned his raised eyebrow to me while I once again studied him. He was indeed wearing a bright neon yellow top and orange shorts.

"Oh." I breathed when I took in the eye blinding colors. "I didn't even notice."

"How did you not notice?" Blaze asked in high pitched amazement.

"I don't know. I was busy admiring this area. Did you see these obliques?" I explained, reaching out to ride my fingers down the rivets running along his naked side.

Chriton threw his head back and laughed right before he caught me up in his arms and spun me around. My heart swelled happily with this loudly outrageous sign of affection. Something he only did with people he truly cared about. Something he was currently doing with me.

"I knew it." He exclaimed happily, setting me on my feet and pointing fiercely at Blaze. "I knew my precious saw *me*."

"Apparently." Blaze laughingly agreed, her eyes happily smiling for him.

"I, uh, what?" I looked between the two of them, now really confused.

"When Amber first moved in with us, she got rid of all of the bright clothes. She told him that they were very, very bad, for both his image and our eyesight. That's when we all, even Chriton, realized that he wore the clothes because it was a subconscious way to get people to see him. Something to do with his ability. Despite

Amber's attempts, the clothes eventually came back. When we asked him about it, he told us it helped him therefore he was just going to embrace it. Coren asked Chriton how he expected to attract his woman wearing crap like that. Chriton told Coren that his woman would only see him, not the clothes he wore. Because that's what he really needed, someone to see him despite everything else." Blaze lengthily explained.

"That makes sense." I nodded slowly before frowning at Blaze. "Has he always dressed like this for his workouts?"

"Yes." Blaze drew the affirming word out. "Right from the first day he arrived."

"Oh." I stated succinctly, really not knowing what to say to all that.

"Are you saying you have never noticed?" Blaze pressed with amazed eyes.

"He has smiling, happy eyes, and this fascinating mark right here only accents them. Then the dimples when he smiles. Such a good smile. Warm and affectionate." I pointed to the area's I was describing on Chriton's face. "It's hard to see the clothing when I have all of that to look at."

"Jesus. You two really do deserve each other." Blaze exclaimed in shock, shaking her head while turning to walk into the class.

"I didn't mean to make her mad." I turned wide eyes to Chriton, my knuckle lodging between my teeth.

"You didn't, Leah." Chriton soothed, reaching out to pull my knuckle from my mouth so he could lace his fingers through mine. "She's just having a moment, trying to change her thought process."

"I don't understand what is so confusing about it." I frowned, feeling his thumb circling the center of my palm.

"She doesn't understand how my clothes don't blind you. Especially considering you are actually wearing a piece of said clothes." Chriton explained, taking some of the fabric of the shirt I was wearing and rubbing it between his thumb and forefinger.

Looking down, I pressed my hand to my mouth in an attempt to cover my bark of laughter. The top was a bright lime green. Chriton chuckled and guided my down bent head to his chest, running his hand along my ponytail and down my back.

"It's not my fault you are so pretty you outshine your clothes." I laughed, patting his chest and turning towards the entry to the exercise room.

"Wait? Pretty?" Chriton called after me.

"Sorry. I meant to say gorgeously masculine." I turned, walking backwards, and told him mischievously while curling my arm up to make a bicep.

"Come here." He growled, curling a finger at me.

I shook my head with a smile. Reaching the door, I opened it and gave a flourishing gesture for him to proceed me.

"You know, in those books you found..." Chriton leaned down and breathed in my ear as he passed me.

"Oh, I know." I told him with a pointed look, silently telling him we would talk about it later.

Chriton shot me wink and pointed to an open yoga mat beside Blaze while he sauntered to the front of the class.

"All right, boys and girls." He clapped his hands to draw everyone's attention to him.

I moved over to the mat he gestured to and stood waiting for him to start.

Then the maddening man definitely took advantage of the teacher/student relationship. With each new stance, Chriton walked among the students making sure their stances were proper. This was usually done with a word and gesture or even taking the stance himself to show them.

Then he came to me.

Because I was in the back corner, no one noticed when he basically groped me while physical adjusting every one of my stances. Touching me, breathing on me, the soft humming sounds that fell from his throat, the smell of him filling my nostrils. He really was torturing me.

He would caress and grip my inner thigh when I was in the Warrior poses, along my side and arms when I was doing the Triangle's. The devious man even went so far as to straddle me and lean over to 'help' with my Supine Twist.

My whole body was burning, nerve ends tingling, limbs shaking, all from his touch. I was soaked and not just from sweat. The man had me so aroused that I was riding the edge of ultimate pleasure. I was pretty sure that one more touch would have sent me straight into ecstasy. Thankfully that's when the class finally ended.

"I changed my mind." I told him as we walked back to the suite, my voice slightly breathless. "Yoga doesn't suck. You suck."

Chriton grinned and wrapped an arm around my shoulder.

"I don't know why you are so happy." I slyly described. "As soon as we get back, I need to grab a quick shower and get to work. I am already cutting it close."

Chriton looked down at the coms device on his wrist to check the time. "Shit." He breathed in frustration when he saw how late it was.

When we reached the suite, I walked inside and was greeted by a little girl eating her breakfast and her shirtless father making lunches.

"Good morning, Leah, Uncle Chriton." Mali greeted with a happy smile.

"Good morning, Mali-girl." I returned her greeting, running my hand down her ponytail. "Good morning Malachi."

"Hmm." Malachi hummed, walking up to me and pulling my sweaty body into his arms. My hands landed on his bare, heated flesh, my fingers curling over his hard pecs. As usual, he took time to examine my eyes before leaning down and dropping a quick kiss to my mouth. "There's my Teach. I missed that light." He murmured against my lips.

I couldn't help but smile at that. "Thanks to someone dragging it out, kicking and screaming." I told him, leaning the slightest millimetre between us to nip at his lips. "Stubborn man. I don't know what I would do without you."

"Hmmm. If I have my way, you will never have to find out." He breathed back, nudging my nose with his.

"I need to get ready for work." I told him, drawing back. "If I don't hurry, Mali and I will be late."

"Go." Malachi ordered, pushing me to my room while landing a heavy hand to the meat of my ass.

I rubbed the smarting area while throwing a faux glare at him over my shoulder. I tried for a real glare but the feel of that pain resounding delightfully in my clit made it impossible.

Grabbing up my clothes, I darted into the bathroom to shower and get ready. Once the heavy mass of my hair was up and a light covering of make up was on, I dressed in a long, tight, high waisted black skirt and a dark blue button up blouse. Coming out, I walked to the kitchen to make my lunch only to have Malachi press a bag already put together into my hand. Then he tugged me back into his arms. "I really like this." He breathed, his groping hand running down my ass.

Chriton came out of the bedroom, Lucy on his heals. His step stuttered for moment when his eyes found me. I literally felt the heat of his glowing eyes glide over me.

"Bye, boys." I drew away from Malachi and knelt down to give Lucy some love before rising and calling for Mali to hurry up.

"Coming." Mali came racing out of her room with her backpack bouncing along her back.

Taking Mali's hand in mine, I waved goodbye and we walked to the school section.

CHAPTER 12

MALACHI

I was feeling itchy. On edge. It was so bad that during hand to hand practice that morning I almost broke Bear's arm.

After apologizing profusely, I sent him to Medical to get checked out. Then I went to my office to try and get some work done. Which was not easy with my unfocused mind.

When lunch time rolled around, I found myself moving. Leaving my office, I prowled straight to the school and Leah's classroom. The kids were just racing out to go eat their own lunches when I reached it.

"Malachi?" Leah gave me a confused look when I walked into her classroom, grabbed her hand and pulled her along with me. "Malachi." She called again, almost running to keep up with my fast pace.

When we reached my office, I slapped my palm onto the security reader to unlock the door and pushed her inside. Once I was sure it was closed and relocked I made my move.

"Malachi?" Leah questioned for the third time.

"Can't think." I grunted, ignoring her gasp in surprise when I pressed her into the wall. My hand automatically found the back of her head and pulled her mouth up to my descending one. Desire coursed through my system at the taste of her flowing over my tongue.

Leah whimpered and slid her arms up my chest and around my shoulders and neck, her fingers digging in delightfully. I growled into her mouth, my tongue licking deep, trying to taste as much of her that I could.

Needing closer, my free hand found her waist and pulled her hips into mine. The feel of her heat pressing against me sent the arousal that I was barely holding back roaring. Straight up. Thick and pulsing wildly.

My hand slid down her hip to her leg. When I tried to lift it in order to get even closer the fabric of her skirt got in my way.

With a furious snarl, I pushed back from Leah.

"Malachi." Leah cried out my name when I bent down, gripped the bottom of her skirt and ripped it right up the side, all the way up to her upper thigh.

"It was in my way." I told her, gripping her waist and lifting up against my body. My mouth found hers again just as my hand fell on her bare thigh, pulling it up and around my hip so that my dick could nestle were it wanted, right against her heated center.

"Yes." I breathed, sliding my lips down to her smooth neck while grinding my hard flesh into her.

"Oh fuck, oh God, Malachi." Leah shuddered in my grip, her hips jerking and driving against mine.

"Right there, baby." I whispered, nipping at her ear, the friction of our grinding rubbing the material of my underwear against the quickly moistening head of my dick.

"Yes, Malachi. Don't stop." Leah cried, her head falling into my neck, her lips sucking along the sensitive skin there. Fire. I was on fire. And only she could put it out.

"Teach, baby." I rasped. "I need closer."

"Yes. Closer." She trembled out her agreement.

My hand moved from her smooth thigh to the front closer of my pants. Leah pulled back enough that she could watch me. I could practically feel the heat of her eyes on me. My pants parted and I reached down to pull my painfully erect dick out of my underwear. It bobbed straight up between us, smooth, stretched flesh topped with an angry red dome.

"I, uh." Leah swallowed and shook her head slowly. Her wide eyes came to mine, her pink tongue torturing me by flicking out to moisten her kiss swollen lips. Desire and fear mixed in one.

"Not yet, baby. I know you aren't ready. But I do plan to leave you with something." I gripped her jaw with my hand, my eyes reassuring her.

"Fuck." Leah gasped when I pressed my tip into her underwear, circling it right over her swollen clit.

"God, you are absolutely soaked, Teach." I moaned at the feel of her wet underwear clinging to me.

"Yes." Leah cried, her hand falling to cover my prodding flesh, pressing it deeper into her slit.

"Shit, yes, Teach, just like that." I growled, my head rotating on my neck while I focused on pushing back the orgasm that almost consumed me. The feel of her touching the bare skin of my dick was the most divine feeling I ever experienced. I never, in the whole of my life, almost came just from a single touch like this before. My hips automatically began shifting, rotating, grinding my cock along the lips that were hugging around it.

Her hips met mine in a shuddering dance of pleasure. My head fell to her neck, my hand gripped into the wall behind her.

I groaned and my hips jerked when the next glide hit smooth, silky flesh. Burning hot and soaking wet. Leah kept directing my driving meat through her slit, making sure that it slithered along her clit. I could feel it, that swollen, pulsing, nub moving erotically up and down my cock. My balls began to tighten and rise in warning. I clenched my jaw tightly in an attempt to hold my rising orgasm at bay.

"Boss." Leah shivered and her eyes fluttered. Her beautifully flushed face filled with her pleasure and I knew she was right about to come.

"Let it happen, baby." I ordered, feeling my own orgasm right there at the sight of hers. My spine tingled and my muscles tensed.

Leah cried out and her hips began jerking erratically, her thigh shaking violently within my grip. I shifted my hips and rotated my head right into her clit in a hard, unrelenting way, driving her orgasm higher.

My balls clenched up and all control was gone. The pleasurable feel of my semen shooting out and into Leah's pulsing clit sent my head spinning. My own rapture rose to meet Leah's when my orgasm, our orgasms, just kept going and going. Leah twisted and shook in my arms while I kept washing her pussy with shot after shot of come.

I was still trembling when everything slowed down and I was finally able to think again. Leah was collapsed against me, her shivering body limp. Her mouth pressed softly into the skin of my neck.

I shifted my head and pressed a kiss to her forehead before gently releasing her.

"I, uh, we, uh, made a mess." Leah whispered, looking down at the white cream that filled the slit of her pussy and hid her little clit. My satisfied dick gave a slight twitch at the sight. Only one place would be better for my semen then right there and that was deep inside her.

"Yes, we did." I nodded, reaching over and adjusting her underwear until it once again covered her.

"Wait, shouldn't we, uh..?" Leah looked up at me with wide eyes.

"No." I shook my head at her, tucking my own sex back into my pants and doing them up. I reached out and pressed my fingers into her underwear, rubbing my cream deep into her pussy. Leah gasped in pleasure and arched into my touch. "You are going to wear me all day. Feel me against your most sensitive flesh. Smell me whenever your thighs spread even the slightest. Know that when you are ready, all of that cream I gave you today will be fucked straight up inside you. So hard and deep that it won't be until you are at work the next morning that it begins to drip out. Your pussy and the underwear that protects it was made to be covered with my come."

"What..?" Leah's breathing was fast and hard, clearly aroused all over again. Her little tongue darted along her lips, moistening them before she attempted to speak again. "What makes you think I won't just clean up once I get back to the school?"

"There's that attitude. Careful, Teach, or you will be returning back to school late and covered in a double load." I advised her with a wicked grin, reaching out to grip her jaw and bending down to speak against her mouth. "As for my orders, you will do as you are told for one reason and one reason only. Because I am your Boss. And despite your teasing...you like it." With that I dropped a quick, hard kiss to her lips before releasing her.

"You are such a dickhead." She growled at me.

"True, but then you now know exactly how much dickhead I am." I winked at my woman causing her to roll her eyes at me.

I chuckled and pulled her in so that I could hold her for a little bit longer before I was forced to return her to school.

Leah gave a happily contented smile and burrowed into my chest. "What do I do with you?" I whispered down at her.

"You are a smart man. I am sure you will come up with something. Well, something else." Leah laughed.

"Oh, I plan to." I grinned, looking forward to it.

LEAH

HE WAS RIGHT, I DID feel and smell him for the rest of the day. It was uncomfortably arousing. My pussy clenched and pulsed constantly under the erotically slick coating of Malachi's sperm. Just the thought of him on me this way made my thighs tremble. I was relieved at the end of the day when I was finally free.

I knew that Mali had dance class so I wasn't surprised to see Chriton meet us at the school doors so that he could walk her over. He was the dance teacher after all. After greeting Mali with a smile, he bent to kiss me only to pause. His eyes took on a bright glow and his nostrils flared as if he was smelling something. Those eyes dropped to my ripped skirt and the crotch it thankfully still covered. I couldn't stop myself from blushing a deep red. Chriton knew. He could smell Malachi on me.

"I take it you had a good lunch hour." Chriton grinned knowingly at me and continued with his original destination, my lips. "You feel like him. Which should affect my feelings, my desire, for you. But it doesn't. It only makes me want you even more."

With that, Chriton stepped back and reached for Mali's hand. I watched the two of them walk away with warm eyes.

When I returned to the quiet suite, I messaged Malachi to let him know that I was home while Mali and Chriton were at dance class. I changed out of my ripped skirt and top into something more comfortable. Settling at the table, I marked the homework I collected that day and checked my syllabus for tomorrow. Once I was finished with that, I opened up the Ranch footage and continued editing it.

I was so deep into it, I didn't notice the man that returned. Long fingers brushed my hair aside and a heated mouth nipped at my ear. "What do you want for supper?" Malachi's husky voice asked me.

"Hmm. Whatever you want." I murmured. His hand tugging on my hair tipped my head back. I smiled up at him with amusement when he tisked at me before taking his kiss. "Pushy man."

"Stubborn woman." He returned, releasing my hair and moving to the kitchen.

By the time supper was ready, Chriton and Mali returned from dance class.

After supper, I helped Mali with her homework before she went with her father to walk Lucy.

"I usually take her to the Garden and let her run loose." Chriton advised the two, giving the happy little fox a couple strokes before they left.

The door barely closed behind them when he was striding my way, his glowing eyes narrowed with determination. With a cry, I darted away from him. Laughter burst from my chest when he caught me within four steps. His hard arms circled my waist and lifted me up.

"Chriton." I gasped when he carried me to his room and threw me across the bed. Rolling over, my hands landed on his shoulders when his face buried into my neck. My giggles turned into pleasure filled whimpers when his lips and teeth caught the sensitive skin of my neck within their hold. His quick fingers delved up my shirt and covered my breast through my bra.

I shifted and arched against his hand, his mouth, seeking more. His smell, so different from Malachi's but no less arousing, filled my nostrils.

Somehow my shirt and bra were gone and my sensitive nipple was being sucked deep into the heated cavern of Chriton's mouth. "Yes, oh, shit, fuck, Chriton." I cried, my hands gripping his hair and pulling at his shirt. As good as he felt, I wanted to feel him bare against me.

With a grunt, Chriton straightened and yanked the offending shirt from his body. His blue eyes, glowing fiercely with his arousal, tracked over my naked torso.

"Beautiful, precious." He whispered, running his fingertips over my straining breasts and down my torso.

"Yes." I agreed, setting my palms on his chest and sliding them over his muscles.

"Fuck, precious." He rasped and shifted over my prone body. His legs spread mine, his hips settling between them. His lips found mine, his tongue rasping and twisting along mine. His fingers caught on the waistband of my lounge pants, pulling at the material there long enough for my hips to arch and twist up.

"Please, Chriton." I whimpered into his mouth, my body on fire, sensitive to every touch.

"Patience, precious." Chriton maddeningly voiced, his fingers still playing at my waistband.

Since he wasn't doing anything, I was going to. I jammed my hand between my stomach and his hip, my fingers circled and pulled at the burning muscle I found there.

"Fucking hell, Leah." Chriton's hip jerked, pushing his fabric covered spike even harder through my fisted hand.

His head dropped and his lips found my nipple right before his teeth did. That sharp, surprisingly arousing pain flashed through my body. Then his fingers delved into my pants and gripped my naked pussy in a deliciously tight hold.

"Yes. Finally." I gasped, twisting under his hold. My shaking hand released him only to dig into his pants to find delightfully bare flesh. Smooth yet snaking with the same veins that populated his torso. Long, thick. Longer than Malachi's admittedly disturbing length but not as thick. My tightened hand milked Chriton's flesh, revelling in the feel of its heat moving over my palm.

Chriton growled louder and nipped harder, his calloused fingers rubbing over my private flesh. The feel of his fingers manipulating over my clit in that way caused me to cry out with pleasure. Two of those fingers delved down and pressed into my entrance.

I gasped at the slightly painful feel of my muscles stretching around the surprising large intrusion of his fingers. A pain that quickly turned to pleasure when he began to thrust in and out of me.

"Oh, my God." I whimpered. "What are you doing to me?"

"Loving you." Chriton rasped, finally releasing my breast.

"It feels so good." I moaned, twisting against his driving fingers.

"Yes. It does." Chriton confirmed, his hips moving just as mine where, helping to drag his length along my jacking fist. My hand twisted and pulled in ways I only read about.

"Chriton." I cried. His fingers found a spot inside me that brought my body arching straight up and my orgasm crashing through me.

"Yes, Leah, my precious." Chriton groaned, his body shuddering against mine, the head of his cock throbbing in the palm of my hand before spurting molten heat right into its center. More and more until my palm was overflowing.

"Shit." Chriton breathed, his hips rhythmically pressing the moist head of his cock into my palm in the aftershock of his orgasm.

"Yeah." I winced slightly when he slowly pulled his fingers from my sore vagina.

I watched as he lifted those fingers to his mouth and licked them clean. Seeing him taste me that way made me wonder what he tasted like. I carefully pulled my cream coated hand out of his pants and brought it to my mouth.

After studying the glaze of white viscous fluid, I brought it up and licked some of it off. Salty yet delicious. Addictive.

"Fuck, Leah, you are killing me here." Chriton groaned, rolling off me and pulling me over into his side.

"The feeling's mutual." I told him, curiously eyeing the limp bulge in his pants. After a moment of thinking it over, I decided that I wasn't waiting. I reached down and pulled the waistband of his pants and underwear out so that I could see him.

"Are you peeking?" Chriton asked, tilting his head down to watch me.

"Yup. Curious minds." I confirmed, tilting my head so that I could see him better. Even satisfied he was magnificent. His sex was limp, laying up along the crest of his left hip. The head was a dusky pink, moist and squishy looking. The length was soft and relaxed, sheened with the leftovers of his semen. It was very interesting and I couldn't wait to see it hard again.

"Are you done?" Chriton asked, gripping my jaw and bringing my face up to his.

"Yup." I smiled and released his waistbands with a snap.

"And?" He asked with a raised eyebrow.

"It's very interesting looking." I told him honestly.

"That's it? Interesting? A book is interesting. A scientific study is interesting." Chriton exclaimed, sitting up and twisting to look down at me. "Not my dick."

"What? It is interesting." I shrugged, sitting up and reaching for my bra and top. After I got my bra clipped on, I shouldered myself into my shirt. "It was glorious when it was all stiff and pointy but now, it's interesting."

Chriton fell back to the bed with a laugh, his palms coming up to rub into his eyes. "That explanation was glorious. 'All stiff and pointy.'"

Chriton was still laughing when I heard the suite door open. Rising from the bed, I met Mali in the kitchen area where I was washing my hands. "Why is Uncle Chriton laughing so hard?" Mali asked, peeking around the doorway and into the bedroom.

"He's taking issue with my descriptive abilities." I shrugged casually.

"Why? I always thought you were great at describing things." Mali frowned in confusion.

"Not all things." Chriton walked out of the bedroom, his shirt once again covering his torso.

"Time to get ready for bed, Mali-girl." Malachi gestured his daughter to the bathroom before crossing his arms and smiling. "Do I want to know?"

"Something about stiff and pointy." Chriton told Malachi.

"Well, if anything it's apt." Malachi laughed, pulling me back into his arms.

"See. I am awesome at describing stuff." I exclaimed to Chriton.

"Apparently the opposite of that is 'interesting.'" Chriton grinned with amusement while he shared.

This made Malachi laugh even more.

CHAPTER 13

LEAH

Luckily the next day I was allowed to sleep in with no disturbances. I was also given time to actually eat my lunch. Unfortunately, when Chriton appeared after school, he directed Mali and I to the Guardian suite first as he needed to retrieve something he inadvertently left behind.

When we got there, Callden insisted that we stay for supper. Knowing that we weren't getting out of it, I shot off a quick message to Malachi to let him know what was happening.

Mali and I helped Callden cook while Chriton tore the suite apart looking for the thing he evidently lost.

"There you are." Chriton exclaimed, pulling a dark, metallic grey pad from the couch cushions.

"What is that Uncle Chriton?" Mali asked, running over to examine the item.

"It's an Andromadan long distance communication device." Chriton showed her the pad.

"How does it work?" Mali questioned curiously.

"It's like the coms devices only it's telepathically driven. All we have to do is set our hand on the pad like this," Chriton set the palm of his splayed hand on the top of the metallic pad, "And open up a link to the person or people that we want to contact. Unfortunately, only Andromadans can use it due to their telepathic abilities. The Nordics have something similar, although, because they aren't quiet as talented at telepathy as we are it works in a slightly different way." Chriton explained.

"That's so cool." Mali breathed, reaching out to touch the pad.

Malachi arrived at the suite right on the heals of Amber who was coming home from the Farm where she was the acting Veterinarian. Mali and Chriton just finished setting the table when Coren and Blaze walked in with Walker set on his father's arm. We were all just sitting down to supper when the suite door burst open.

"Gabe's back." Ryker exclaimed happily, racing into the suite and joining us at the table for supper.

Unfortunately, he sat down just as the Guardians stood up, their chairs shoving back from the table violently. Amber, an anxious look on her face, hurried to keep up with them, her hand catching Callden's in a white knuckled grip.

"Shit." I exclaimed, jumping to my feet and running after the group prowling down the halls towards the suites on the lower level. Malachi and his long legs easily caught up to me, taking my hand in his with a firm grip.

Callden stopped at the first suite, Madron's, and pounded on the door. Chriton and Coren took a braced legged, arm crossed stance behind their father.

"Callden." Salem greeted happily when she opened the door only for her face to turn confused when she saw everyone else in our group.

"I am sorry, Salem." I whispered out my apology, biting my knuckle.

Malachi immediately pulled my finger away and adjusted me into his side. "Do not take this on, Leah." Malachi growled down at me.

"But what if..?" I looked up at him and whispered.

"No, Teach." Malachi hissed, his hand coming up to grip my jaw in that intense way of his. "This is between them."

When someone said something inside the suite Salem opened the door wider and stepped to the side. Madron was in the kitchen, frowning at our group. "What's going on?" He asked slowly.

"Spider?" Callden asked, his voice low and deadly.

"Fuck!" Madron breathed, his bright green eyes widening with understanding.

Surprisingly, he darted into the bathroom that connected the two suites, Callden and Coren were hot on his heals. Salem, Amber, and I exchanged worried looks and ran after the men. Yells and loud crashing could already be heard from the suite by the time we reached the bathroom.

Entering the suite, I immediately saw Chriton jump out of the wall and land on Catro's back. Diad was yelling from under the dog pile of men on top of him. Madron was attempting to kick himself free only to have Callden yank him back in.

Catro gripped Chriton's arms and launched himself backwards so he could body slam Chriton into the floor. Catro groaned, rolling to his side in pain when Chriton did not hit the floor first. He didn't hit the floor at all. He sank through the floor. Which meant Catro body slammed himself backwards into the rock hard ground with breath stealing force.

"I fucking forgot." Catro moaned, almost cursing himself for his stupidity.

"Yeah, you fucking did." Chriton snarled, leaping out of the floor and trying to land an elbow into Catro's already straining torso.

Catro rolled to the side just in time causing Chriton's elbow to crack into the floor.

"You got fast." Chriton rasped in pain, gripping his elbow.

Seeing him in pain, I stepped forward to go to him, only for Amber to pull me back.

"Let them work it out." She advised, her eyes trained on the writhing pile of men that wasn't so much of a pile anymore.

Coren was holding Madron's head under his arm, rubbing his knuckles fiercely over the top of the struggling mans skull. Diad was sitting on Callden's chest, his knees firmly planted on the man's arms while he licked the sides of his face.

This was frankly surprising because Callden was extremely strong. Callden screeched out in disgust and jerked his face away from Diad's extremely wet tongue.

"Don't make me hurt you, boy." Callden warned loudly.

"Bring it on, old man." Diad mocked.

Callden snarled and snapped his head forward and to the side, slamming his forehead into the side of Diad's jaw. Diad yelped and flew to the side. Callden rolled, locking Diad underneath him and yanking his underwear up in a fabric ripping wedgy.

"Is it just me or are they seriously fighting like a group of teenage brothers?" Salem tilted her head and noted with astonishment.

"They always fight like that. At least the Guardian brothers do with each other." Amber explained, mimicking Salem's head tilt in her own study of the wrestling men.

"Yeah, so do the Ancients. I just never assumed that it would happen outside the family." Salem clarified.

"It's kind of understandable with how close the two families are." All of us spun around in surprise at the sound of Malachi's voice.

His arms were crossing his chest and he was leaning against the doorframe of the bathroom. Wings and Scope were standing beside him, watching the scene with amusement.

"Just so you all know, I am currently getting a flood of reports stating that it sounds like someone is being attacked. One even mentioned the sound of a dying cat." Malachi explained to us, gesturing to the coms on his wrist that was indeed dinging with incoming messages.

"Uh, I think that was Callden." Amber noted turning her eyes back to her husband.

Callden was back to yelling because Diad bit down on the outside of his thigh and was not letting go, despite the fact that Callden was batting Diad in the head with his own ripped underwear.

Somehow Madron gained the upper hand. He was now sitting on Coren's abdomen. Madron was pinching down on Coren's nipples and was twisting them for all he was worth while Coren writhed on the ground and tried to get him off.

Catro had Chriton wrapped tightly in his arms and was tapping his forehead demanding that he name 20 types of animals. Chriton struggled for a long moment before he sank through Catro's grip and into the floor.

"Stop cheating." Catro demanded turning in circle in his attempt to find Chriton.

"You're the one cheating, Angel boy." Chriton yelled from his crouch on the top of the table before flinging himself at the man sending them rolling across the floor.

One of the bedroom doors slammed open, crashing into the wall with a loud bang. "Enough!" Royce screamed furiously, her voice echoing in an ear splitting way that literally caused the sound of breaking glass to tinkle through the suite. She stomped out of the bedroom, her hair was a sleepy mess, her puffy eyes slitted with anger. "You all are screwing up naptime!"

She ran her threatening eyes over the group of frozen people before stomping back into the room and slamming the door behind her.

I turned my eyes to the males that were now untangling themselves and helping each other up.

"Why didn't you tell us about the spider?" Callden asked, turning his angry eyes to Madron.

"You couldn't have helped. It wasn't a normal spider." Catro stepped forward drawing all of our eyes to him.

"Obviously." Chriton rolled his eyes at Catro's understatement.

"No, I mean it wasn't really even a spider. That was just the flesh it took. It was a demon, one of the Fallen." Catro continued his explanation. "Your abilities would've been useless against it and you all would've died."

"Seriously?" Callden asked, raising his hand up. I gasped when it burst into flame. I heard he could do that, but I never saw it before.

"Seriously." Catro reached out and ran his hand over Callden's flaming arm, smothering the flames. "I won't lie, you are hot, but not the right type of hot."

Callden stared at Catro in shock for a moment before reaching out to rub his hand over his own cooled arm.

"Fuck." Callden breathed, looking back up at Catro with gleaming eyes. "Have you by any chance told your dad yet?"

Catro laughed and patted Callden on the back. "Royce broke it to him in a very effective way."

Madron joined his brother's laughter. "Shit, Callden, you should've seen his face. I have never seen such a range of emotions from him in my whole entire life."

"Why didn't you at least tell us, share with us what happened? We had to hear about it from everyone else or read about in reports." Coren asked, sounding slightly hurt, still rubbing at his obviously tender nipples.

"I was concentrating on other things." Catro jerked his chin towards the bedroom door where Royce was sleeping.

"I thought Madron did." Diad pointed at his brother.

"I kind of forgot. Sorry." Madron winced, rubbing the back of his neck. "Things were a little wild there for a bit. We were dealing with all of Catro's changes and the introduction of new family members. Giant spiders. Diad and Malachi's cuddle fest. Salem's pregnancy. The cave-in at the Ranch."

"You're pregnant!" I gasped happily, jumping up and down in excitement while turning to hug Salem. Salem giggled at my joy filled excitement, returning my hopping hug.

The woman that I considered a best friend was like me that way, she loved kids and always wanted her own. Now she was getting her wish. I was so happy for her that I wanted to cry.

"Wait." Chriton held up a finger, a frown on his face. He turned that finger to point at Diad and Malachi. "You two cuddled?"

"Fuck." Malachi groaned, covering his face with his hand. "Look. It just happened the one time. I was in a vulnerable place and didn't know what I was doing. It meant nothing."

"How can you say that?" Diad cried dramatically, giving him wide eyes and a phenomenally fake lip quiver.

Malachi shook his head at Diad with a slight smile. "Sorry man, but you really are just a friend."

"Ohhh. You've just been friend zoned." Coren nudged Diad with a wince. "Harsh."

"I don't know how I will ever recover from this." Diad sniffled loudly.

"Easily." Scope accurately guessed.

"True." Diad grinned wickedly. "So, Chriton, I hear you have your own news."

Chriton looked around the group and grinned. "Malachi and I cuddled."

"Fucking hell." Malachi dropped his head into his hand with frustration while everyone laughed around him.

"No, seriously, right now the three of us are still figuring everything out. Although, I will say this, after two whole days we are all melding together very well." Chriton explained to the group with a smile.

"It's not a triad?" Madron frowned in confusion.

"Not that we are aware of. But all of this seems to be, well, different from the usual Conversance." Chriton shared with him. "It could be due to Leah being a DNA mimic, or it could be something else. Either way, it is happening."

"Ok." Madron nodded slowly, his face still looking confused before he turned to look at Malachi then me. "It might be a little early but welcome to the family." Madron smiled at me, giving Malachi an amused nod.

"Thank you, Madron." I whispered, softly smiling in return. I felt Malachi step up behind me and pull me back into his chest. My arms came up to cover the ones he was holding me with.

"So?" I tilted my head back to look up at Malachi. His curious dark eyes came down to meet mine. "Do you just cuddle with everyone but me?"

Laughter sounded throughout the suite while Malachi blushed. I smiled and drew a finger over his cheekbone. I loved seeing the strong, experienced man blushing.

Back at the Guardian suite, we shared what happened with Blaze who stayed back with Walker and Mali. After supper we returned to our suite.

"What does 'Tuesday, BYOD' mean?" Chriton asked as we walked through the door.

"Bring Your Own Ducky. Tuesday is bath day." Malachi explained the words that Wings yelled out the door at us when we left their suite.

"Bath day, as in the jacuzzi?" Chriton murmured to himself for a moment before he walked right back out of the suite.

"Ok." I shrugged, walking over to the table to help Mali with her homework and work on my documentary editing. "Malachi, can you take a look at this? I feel like it needs something, like a cut or even a cut away. I just don't know for sure."

Malachi sat beside me and pulled my tablet towards him so that he could look over the part I needed help with. "A cut away." His fingers moved over the screen pausing and forwarding as needed. "Right here. Insert this footage there and make the explanation a voice over."

"Yes. That's it." I clapped happily.

"Leah, I don't understand this question." Mali pipped up, pointing at the question. Leaning over I looked it over before explaining it to her in a way I knew she would understand.

Chriton waltzed back into the suite carrying a large box that he set onto the table in front of us. "Fishing?" Mali frowned at the box, tilting it so she could see it better. It was indeed a fishing game. Something you would find at the fair. It boasted large plastic fish that opened and closed their mouths and fishing rods that were used to try and catch the fish.

"They are going to love this." I exclaimed, smiling excitedly up at Chriton. "They are so going to make it into challenge."

"That's the idea." Chriton smiled and crossed his arms.

"Smart man." Malachi laughed and stood to clap Chriton on the shoulder. "Time to get ready for bed, Mali."

Mali put her homework away and went to get ready for bed. Chriton was ready to join her for her bedtime book when she came out. I walked over and slid my arms around Malachi from behind, leaning into the strength of his back. He was standing at the kitchen counter making a tea.

Malachi hummed softly and dropped his hand down to grip my arm. "I don't know if you noticed, but somehow we all seem to be taking turns with things, like walking Lucy and tucking Mali in."

"I noticed that too. I can't say that I hate it." Malachi nodded in agreement. "Would you like a tea, Teach?"

"If you don't mind." I rubbed my face against his back before dropping a kiss to his spine. "This is surprisingly comfortable."

"Come on, Teach." Malachi chuckled, pulling me around so he could hand me my tea and guide me to the couch.

He sprawled on the couch with one leg stretched out across the cushions and one leg on the floor. He set his tea on the side table before pulling me down to settle between his splayed legs. After some adjustment, I was curled up in his arms with both of my legs bent up on the couch. My own arms were holding the ones he wrapped around me.

Malachi turned on a comedy show and we watched a group of comedians try to preform tasks. Warm and comfortable, I quickly felt my eyes drifting shut.

"No." I moaned softly when the comforting warmth I was wrapped in shifted away. Not wanting loose that warmth I clawed out and twisted my fingers into soft material that was covering hard shoulders.

"Shhh, baby." Malachi's voice sounded softly and I felt myself being lifted into his hard chest.

"Hmmm." I hummed happily and rubbed my face along his chest, fingering the material clenched in my hands.

I felt myself being set on a soft bed and whimpered when I felt him removing his arms. "It's ok, Teach. I am right here." He whispered, his fingers soothing over mine in an attempt to convince me to release him. I whimpered and opened my eyes to see his dark ones staring down into mine.

"It's ok, precious." Another voice, Chriton's sounded beside me. Turning my unfocused gaze to his, I saw his shadow moving before I felt his heat beside me.

I slowly released Malachi and rolled to Chriton. My hands found his bare chest and curled over his pecs. I felt his big hand cup my face at the same time the bed shifted and I felt Malachi's heat press into my back. Malachi's arm curled around my stomach as he shifted himself deeper into me.

"Hmmm. Now this is better." Malachi hummed softly.

"Much." Chriton noted, moving forward so his arm could join Malachi's around my waist and my head was able to press into the side of his chest.

My tired, sandy eyes closed, happy to be back in that comforting heat. "Love." I slurred just as I drifted away.

I woke up the next morning to feel as if something was off. I wasn't in my own bed and I wasn't alone. Two sets of heavy breathing echoed in the room. With a frown, I leaned up on my elbows and turned my head to see the two men in my life twisted together. Well mostly Malachi. His long limbs were wrapped around Chriton who was sprawled on Malachi's chest. The weird thing was that Chriton's limbs were spread out as much as Malachi's tentacling would allow.

"Come on!" I growled, reaching for my pillow and swinging it into their heads before rolling from the bed. I stomped out of the room to get Mali up and start making breakfast.

"Wha..? Shit." I heard Malachi groan after me. "Chriton, man, get up. You missed class."

I woke Mali up and she raced off to the bathroom while I walked into the kitchen.

"Seriously?" Chriton's voice groaned. "What the hell is it with your cuddling?"

"I told you, I can't control it." Malachi argued.

"Not that." Chriton returned with a grumpy growl. "The fact that its so damned comfortable that I never want to wake up."

"Must be nice." I called sulkily from the kitchen where I was cooking up some oatmeal with blueberries.

"Damnit." Malachi growled and I heard his feet slapping across the floor on his way towards me. "I am sorry, Teach." He apologized, hauling me back into his chest and burying his face into my neck so his lips could reach the sensitive skin there.

"You so owe me like three cuddles now." I tipped my head towards him and narrowed my eyes in warning.

"Believe me, baby, I fully plan to pay up." Malachi whispered huskily, his lips nipping at mine before sealing in a deep, breath sharing greeting.

"It's really not his fault, you know." Chriton noted, strutting across the floor towards his room. "I am just that sexy."

I laughed and drew back from Malachi to roll my eyes at Chriton. Malachi chuckled and shook his head. Releasing me with another kiss, Malachi left me for the bathroom. Chriton came out dressed in a pair of grey slacks and a black button down shirt.

He nabbed one of the bowls I was dishing up, taking his own wet kiss. "Cocky man." I reached up to smooth my fingers over his jaw.

"Yup. All stiff and pointy." He grinned and winked, nabbing another bowl when he saw Mali race out of her room, dressed and ready for the day.

After dishing up the last of the bowls, I got myself ready for the day with quick shower and a set of grey slacks and a long sleeved, thigh length black sweater.

Returning to the main room I was stopped by Malachi who was also newly showered and dressed in a pair of black cargo pants with a million pockets and a dark grey thermal. Malachi gave me a deep, wet kiss before heading off to a meeting. Chriton and Mali were standing at the counter making the lunches for the day.

I found myself thinking about how very different the men were. Different yet completely sexy in their own way.

Chriton was open and funny with more of a professional look. This wasn't surprising as he usually handled most of the Guardian paperwork and meetings. He also boasted a decently explosive temper. Although, it was extremely hard to get that temper to blow. Usually threats to his loved ones did it.

Malachi was quieter, more serious, not that he didn't know how to have fun because he did. His looks and bearing were completely with keeping of his chosen profession, a soldier. His temper was different and tended to be colder and more calculated. Malachi was the epitome of don't get mad, get even.

CHAPTER 14

LEAH

"What do you have on after school?" Chriton asked, handing me my lunch and cupping my cheek to turn my head up to his.

"Marking homework and working on the documentary." I shared, smiling warmly when he pressed his forehead to mine. "You?"

"Mali and I have dance tonight." He smiled at me. "You should come with us."

"Yes." Mali cried, skipping over to jump against my hip. "Please, Leah."

"Well, I am extremely curious and really do want to see the two of you dance." I smiled warmly, my minds eye bringing up an image of Chriton taking the time to teach a group of little ones how to dance.

"Then you really should come check us out." Chriton waggled his eyebrows at me.

"Ok." I agreed with a nod. My agreement sent Mali cheering through the room. Going up on my tiptoes, I brushed my lips over Chriton's ear. "Just so you know, I always check you out." I smiled and backed away towards the door.

"Yeah, you do." Chriton bragged cockily, giving me a saucy wink.

With that, Mali and I gave our goodbyes and walked to school.

CHRITON

THE EARLY AFTERNOON seemed to drag by while I finished up my work for the day. Finally, I was changed and heading to my dance class.

Entering the room that was booked for the class, I made sure everything was prepared and greeted the students that were starting to trickle in. Most of them were youngsters with a couple teenagers that carried previous experience with dance and wanted to continue with their chosen art.

The class was also mostly female with two males. Thusly when Leah arrived with Mali and I quickly swept my woman up so that I could greet her with a kiss there was a mixture of disappointed female groans and excited giggles. Leah smiled against my mouth and patted my chest for me to release her when she heard the sound of the feminine complaints.

Catro and his daughter, Atlas, arrived with Atlas quickly running over to join Mali and Catro approaching us. Leah greeted the Ancient with a warm smile that he immediately returned.

Catro took in my dance attire that was basically a clean set of workout gear with a set of raised eyebrows. "How are you not blind?" he asked Leah.

Leah rolled her eyes at him. "We just had this conversation with Blaze the other morning. He's owning it like a rockstar so leave him alone."

"Says the woman obviously blinded by love." Catro chuckled affectionately, shaking his head and walking over to sit on one of the benches that ran along the side of the room.

"I don't think I am blind." Leah complained, following Catro over to sit beside him on the bench. The two of them were soon joined by a number of parents that came to watch their kids.

I was guiding the kids through their stretches and warmups when I walked by at the perfect time. "Which one is yours?" I heard one of the mothers ask Leah.

"The little blond girl in the purple and the colorful one." Leah gave the woman an enthusiastic smile.

Catro, the normally quiet man, burst into laughter at Leah's description of me.

"Uh." The woman looked around the room, trying to find the second child Leah described but coming up empty. "Do you mean the instructor?" The woman asked, her eyes finally landing on me.

"Yup." Leah nodded, her eyes watching the class.

"Ok. Now that we have the boring stuff out of the way, let's practice the dance we started learning last week." I clapped my hands and the kids raced around to their starting positions.

I turned on the music and took my own position. Once the music started the kids began performing the choreographed amalgamation of Hip Hop and a popular Andromadan dance that I created. I watched them with a keen eye while I half did some of the moves with them and half advised.

Since each child was given their own separate choreography that was part of the whole, I would usually perform the child's assigned moves with them as I helped them. When the song ended, I went around and worked with some of them separately for a couple moments. Once I was satisfied, we tried the dance again.

This went on until it was time for cooldown stretches. I got high fives from the kids as their parents gathered them up and head out. Like usual, Mali helped me tidy up the class with Leah joining us.

"I didn't quite catch it. What did the woman say when you told her that I was the 'colorful' one?" I asked curiously, wiping down the bars.

"She called me a lucky...uh, lady." Leah darting a glance to Mali from where she was cleaning the mirrors, telling me that 'lady' was not exactly the word the woman used.

"And what did you say?" I asked curiously.

"I agreed. Then she told me that it was disappointing that such a good looking man dressed so horrendously. I told her that I liked it because I would never loose you in a crowd. She laughed and agreed that it would be a shame to lose sight of all the hotness that was you." Leah smiled, automatically giving me the rest of the story.

I returned her smile, happy with her answer. "I love the fact that you don't care about my clothes. Everyone seems to have some sort of comment on them."

"It's not that I don't care." Leah set the glass cleaner down and stepped up to me. She set her hands on my sides and tipped her head back to me. "It's just that I didn't notice the clothes because I was to busy seeing the man underneath them. Blaze said the other morning that you wear them because of your ability."

"I do. I don't wear bright colors for my everyday attire. But the workout wear, they are a comforting for me." I described, setting my hands on her shoulder and the side of her neck.

"I figured." Leah shrugged. "You disappear, walk through walls and stuff. The biology of being able to do that would mean that you have the ability to break your body down to its smallest cells so you can move it in those ways. Doing that repeatedly over time can have substantial physical and mental effects on someone. You probably started feeling as if you yourself were slowly disappearing. And from a physical standpoint, that very well could have been happening, loosing small pieces of yourself every time you used your ability. The bright clothes probably helped you make sure you weren't completely disappearing. People saw the clothes and thusly you."

"Just more proof that you see me. You ground me, keep me from disappearing. When I am with you, all those pieces that are drifting away snap back together. And I finally feel restored, complete." I explained to her gently.

"I hope that's not the only reason you picked me." Leah tilted her head, her eyes full of amusement.

"No, my precious." I leaned down, whispering in her ear and setting my hand on her lower back and tapping my fingers on her upper ass. "I told you, I like big butts. And yours is absolutely luscious. Even back then, I couldn't stop myself from noticing this beautiful piece of art."

Leah smiled and pressed a kiss to the corner of my mouth.

We finished cleaning and walked Mali back to the suite. Leah smiled happily down at the girl while they swung their joint hands and skipped down the halls together. Hearing someone coming down the steps behind us, I turned to see Malachi jogging towards us.

"Sorry, my meeting ran late." He breathed out heavily, telling me he ran all the way from the security meeting room.

"It's ok, dad." Mali's smile was reassuring as she gave her father's stomach a hug in greeting.

"What did you make for supper?" Malachi joked, grinning down at his daughter.

"Fried chicken." Mali's eyes were twinkling happily.

"Awesome. I am starving." Malachi exclaimed dramatically, palming open the door for us.

Leah laughed and walked straight into the kitchen to get started on fried chicken. Malachi joined her while Mali and I watched hair tutorial videos on the TV.

CHAPTER 15

MALACHI

After supper, Leah helped Mali with her homework while Chriton and I took Lucy for her nightly walk. When we returned I tucked Mali into bed while Leah worked on her documentary. After she was all finished, and successfully sent it off for the school to review, Leah collapsed on the couch between Chriton and I.

Feeling that familiar edginess rising inside me, I made my move. Leah gasped and grabbed my shoulders when she suddenly found herself straddling the hardness of my lap. Desperately hard. Her gasp died in my mouth. My lips spread hers so that I could eat at her mouth, my hand gripped the back of her head to hold her to me.

My hips drove up unto the spread of her legs, grinding my dick into her in search of the friction it was crying for. Leah rode my hips adding her own grinding twist and more delightful friction.

I growled and sat up when Leah whimpered and yanked on my shirt in a silent demand. I pulled that shirt off before resuming my feast at her mouth. I shivered when her small hands caressed over the flesh of my shoulders and upper chest and back.

Leah drew away from me so that her shirt could be removed by set of long fingers. I wasn't surprised to see that Chriton wasn't willing to just sit back and watch. Before she could return to me, Chriton's quick fingers divested her of her bra as well. She cried out and arched when Chriton's fingers pulled at the tightened buds of her nipples. I could see his mouth moving over the pale flesh of her throat.

Feeling my mouth watering, I cupped her breast around Chriton's fingers and drew it up to my hungry lips. I sucked that nipple deep into my mouth, flicking my tongue over the hard tip before adding a sharp nip. One of Leah's hands delved into my hair, fisting the strands painfully. Her other hand latched on to the one Chriton was stroking down her stomach.

Popping off her swollen, red nipple, I moved to the other one. Leah let out a whimper right before I let out a grunt when Chriton's knuckles scraped over the fabric covering my erection.

Once I was satisfied with the pleasurable torture I gave her nipple, I released that one as well. I dropped my eyes down to the knuckles that were shifting and dragging over me. They and the hand that they were attached to were buried in Leah's pants, obviously fingering her pussy. Added to that sight was the twisting and rolling of Leah's hips as they erotically ground over me.

I lifted my eyes up to Chriton. His glowing blue eyes were watching me, half masted with his desire. I jerked my chin to my bedroom. Chriton grinned and slid his hand free of Leah's pants. My eyes caught on his fingers, glistening with her arousal.

"No." Leah gasped when Chriton removed her stimuli and stepped back from her.

"Yes." I growled, wrapping my arms around her hips and rising with her in my arms.

"Malachi." Leah cried, her hands falling to my shoulders.

"We need more space." I told her, following Chriton into the bedroom.

I dropped Leah onto the bed and reached for my belt buckle. Leah's eyes dropped to my hand before darting to a now shirtless Chriton who was reaching down to undo her pants.

Leah, her eyes blown wide with her pleasure, lifted her hips helpfully when Chriton pulled her pants from her legs. Her underwear was red and silky looking, the crotch was deliciously darkened with her arousal. The wet material erotically clinging to the smooth lips of her pussy. My pants dropped to the ground and I gripped down on the root of my cock through my precum moist underwear.

Chriton leaned further over Leah and took her mouth with his. I could see their jaws moving as Chriton kissed her deeply. Leah cried out into his mouth when his fingers rubbed over that darkened spot on her underwear.

I growled softly when her legs spread nice and wide for his fingers. I watched, mesmerized, as he manipulated her soft flesh, rubbing over the swollen clit that I could clearly see poking out.

"Take them off." I snarled, wanting to see more.

"Yes, please." Leah begged, her hips rolling up with her demand.

"You really are bossy." Chriton shot me a grin and pulled her underwear off.

"Yes." I hummed, seeing that pink pussy spread for me. Wet, so wet. I could see her enlarged clit throbbing and her tight little entrance contracting. "Look at that pussy. She wants to be filled."

Chriton dropped his eyes to her vagina and grinned when he saw what I did. "Yes, she does."

"Is she wet enough?" I asked, climbing up the bed at Leah's other side. Bracing the palm of my straightened arm beside her head, I loomed over her. "Are you wet enough, baby?" I demanded, sliding my fingers through her wet heat.

"Yes. No." Leah whimpered up at me.

"Shall we see." I rasped, using two fingers to spread her pussy lips and pushing a third into her tight tunnel. Really tight. And burning hot. My dick jerked jealously, demanding to be inside her.

"She needs more." Chriton noted, his glowing eyes watching me work my finger in and out of her pussy.

"I think your Master is right, Teach. Your little pussy isn't wet enough." I looked down into Leah's beautifully flushed face.

Her eyes flared with desire at my use of Chriton's chosen nickname. "Wet enough for what?" Leah asked with a soft moan as I pulled my finger free of her vagina's strong clasp.

"For us to fuck." Chriton growled, shifting down to spread her thighs with his shoulders.

"Master." Leah whimpered when his tongue delved into her sex and his mouth slurped over her.

I gripped her thigh and pulled it up and out, opening her up more for him.

"Oh God." Leah gasped right before I covered her mouth with mine and muffled her cries.

I feasted on her mouth while the sound of Chriton eating her out filled the room. Leah moaned and jerked right after I felt Chriton adjust himself between her legs. Drawing away, I looked down Leah's twisting body to see his arm moving between her legs. His glowing eyes met mine and at my nod his arm began to work fast and hard, driving the finger he was fucking her with over the g-spot he obviously found.

Catching Leah's wrists, I pressed them to her chest and held them there with one hand. I used the other one to cover her mouth just in time to muffle her pleasure filled scream. Leah's eyes widened and her body attempted to arch up in a violently twisting motion. Her breathe sucked in and her face turned red. Those beautiful grey eyes rolled up and she began to convulse.

"Fuck yes! Come all over me, precious." Chriton snarled, his finger still working her gushing sex.

Leah's body clenched up and fluid squirted out to cover Chriton.

"Beautiful, Teach. Again." I demanded of the woman. She whimpered up at me right before she tensed and showered Chriton for the second time. "Good girl, so fucking sexy. I think you just may be wet enough to take him now."

Leah whimpered softly into my hand, her breathing hard.

"Up we go, baby." My hand left her mouth and I pulled her up using her wrists.

"Boss." Leah gasped, her voice shaky in the aftermath of the orgasms Chriton drove her to.

"Right here, Teach." I sat back against the headboard and after a quick adjustment of my underwear I pulled her into my lap with her back resting against my chest. My bare dick twitched happily when it nestled right between the succulent globes of her ass. Slick from her come and rapturously scorching, they clasped around me erotically.

One of my arms wrapped around her torso, my palm cupping her breast. My other hand delved between her legs that were spread around my own. My fingers rubbed and played over that delicate flesh, flicking and pinching her clit. My mouth fell to her neck and sucked the flesh I found there. Leah's hands found mine, clenching around my fingers, holding on to me in a way I prayed she never stopped. She gasped and moved against me, her head falling to the side to give me more room to work with, her ass erotically milking my dick.

While I was maneuvering us around, Chriton was removing the rest of his clothes. The man really was a veiny bastard. Those suckers snaked everywhere over him. Everywhere.

I was admittedly surprised at the length of his dick. It bobbed up a good nine inches. Now, I wasn't a slacker in that department, but I was at least half an inch shorter. I was, however, thicker. Not a lot, but enough to make a difference to a woman new to this. Thusly, I was glad I was letting him introduce her to the delights of penetration.

Chriton's blue eyes centered on us, glowing even brighter than before. He took his time watching us, his fisted hand moving slowly over his cock, stroking up and over the swollen head. I knew this worked over the sensitive glands there in a very pleasing way. In fact,

I quite often utilized that very same technique when I jacked myself off.

Seeing how ready he was, I spread my knees and thusly Leah's legs at the same time two of my fingers spread her lips.

"Keep her just like that." Chriton ordered, his voice hoarse with desire. With her wide open for him, Chriton crawled up the bed until he was kneeling between our legs.

Leah whimpered again and her fingers clenched around mine just as I felt his dick brush over the fingers I was spreading her with.

"Master." Leah cried out and her head twisted until her sharp teeth latched into my arm.

Looking down her body, I could see Chriton's dick notched at her entrance. His hips slowly drove him forward, through my fingers and into her open sex. His dick disappeared, inch by inch, until there was only an inch left. While he did that, I pressed and rolled a third finger over her clit.

"Look at how you take your Master, baby. So beautiful." I gripped Leah's jaw and twisted her face to mine. Her eyes were dark with a swirling mixture of pain and desire. "Are you ready, Teach? He's going to fuck you now."

"Yes, Boss. Please. I want Master to fuck me." Leah gasped out.

The sound of her words, delirious with pleasure, made my dick jolted hard and I almost came all over her. Chriton was in no better condition if the way his eyes flared and his jaw clenched. His hips drew back and snapped forward. Out of control.

Leah cried out and buried her face into my neck, her sharp little teeth once again finding flesh to latch down on.

My own hips began going, driving my dick along her ass crack. My eyes were centered down, watching Chriton's dick, slick with Leah's come and virginity, flashing in and out of her. All to soon he was thrusting his whole length into her, squeezing that last inch in and causing Leah to moan and claw at the two of us.

Every drive he made into her helped add to the dance my dick was doing along her ass. My arms tightened around her when I felt my own pleasure rising. The feel of her body moving against mine, the muscles of her ass cheeks clenching and unclenching around me was divine. My balls were drawing up and I could feel my sperm rising.

Clenching my teeth, my head fell back and I desperately held my orgasm off. I needed to feel her come apart in my arms at least twice before I would allow myself to go.

"Come." I snarled, my fingers pinching down around her clit.

"Yes, precious. Come on my cock." Chriton praised, his own jaw clenched.

Her ass contracted over my dick and I felt her pussy pulsing against my fingers with the orgasm that was rolling over her.

Leah's body shook and her breathing stopped with the intensity. Neither one of us stopped moving. Once Leah's breath whistled back in and her body relaxed, Chriton gripped her jaw and turned her face to his so that he could eat her lips. Leah gripped his shoulders and I felt him shifting. He kneed my legs closed and knelt with his ass on my thighs and her legs resting over his knees.

Closer.

His chest pressed into hers, successfully sandwiching her between us. In this position I could feel his balls pressing into mine.

While threesomes weren't a new thing for me and I knew that when two males were involved glancing touches were going to happen. It was just a fact of the situation. But this was no glancing touch. This was intimate. This was Chriton accepting me in a heartwarming way that was also equally perplexing.

Our pleasure seeking bodies moved in a whole new way. An immersive dance of entwined bodies. A full rhythmic massaging. It was slower than before but deeper, more profound. My eyes caught on Chriton's. He slowly drew away from Leah's lips, his own mouth moist and kiss swollen. He turned Leah's head, giving me her lips.

Not a stupid man, I fully took advantage. She tasted different and I could only assume that it was Chriton. I was tasting the mixture of the two of them. And I didn't care.

The friction between us finally succeeded in driving me crazy. The sound of pleasure falling from slack lips echoed in my ears. Fire travelled up my spine causing my mouth to tense on Leah's. Leah's lips pulled from mine as she cried out and Chriton snarled, his head falling back on his neck. My balls contracted and my dick throbbed out my orgasm. Shot after shot painted Leah's ass and back.

Chriton was tense, his hips twisting slowly. Leah was gasping and crying, her body violently bucking, arching back into my chest, her hands clawing and gripping. I felt a tingling woosh travel up my limbs to center right where my chest was connected to Leah's back. This was followed by a sharp jerking pain.

An agonized cry ripped from my throat and my torso arched in an effort to follow whatever was being excruciatingly torn from the inside of my chest. My heartbeats screamed to a stop and my lungs stalled.

I was having a heart attack.

I was dying.

That thought was compounded by what my fading vision saw next. Chriton's eyes were wide with worry and amazement, his face slack when two twisting whisps of light lifted from Leah's chest. These whisps rose up to join the one rising from his chest where they all seemed to swirl and mix together before separating and returning to their bodies.

My eyes darkened and everything faded away just as the pain diminished with a loud whomping thump.

CHRITON

"SHIT, FUCK, SHIT." I growled. Gently pulling Leah from the pale, unconscious man underneath her.

"What?" Leah gasped in horror when her eyes landed on Malachi. Her face paled with worry and her hands moved over his cheeks and face in an attempt to wake him up. She was sobbing, voice pleading, wide eyes overflowing with tears. "Malachi! Wake up, Boss, please, wake up. What happened?"

"I don't really know." I shook my head and began to check his alarmingly unresponsive body.

I remembered the look in his eyes and his agonized cry when the Conversance happened. I also remembered the souls that rose up out of Leah's. Souls. Two of them.

My fingers found his pulse. Deep yet fast. His breathing was the same. He was thankfully alive but beyond that I wasn't sure. I did know that he didn't look so good. Pale yet flushed, sweaty yet cold, breathing yet lifeless.

Madron, I need you. I called through our mental links only to receive nothing in return. I was guessing that he was either sleeping or busy. Either way, I needed his help. Now.

"Stay with him." I ordered Leah, jumping from the bed and yanking on my pants before slitting the bedroom door open and silently racing to the suite door. I didn't want to wake Mali. She didn't need to see her father that way.

Quietly leaving the suite, I proceeded to sprint down and across the hall to the suite that Madron shared with his triad, Wings and Salem, and their family, Scope, Marko, and River.

Stabbing my finger into the doorbell, I frantically rang it over and over again. I didn't care if I woke them all up. I needed help and I needed it now.

"What the fuck do you want?" Scope growled when the door was whipped open. Scope looked tired and furious.

"Madron." I gasped, racing over to the room that I knew was his.

"They are busy." Scope warned.

"Don't care." I growled, pounding on the door and calling, "Get dressed and get out here."

"I am going to kill him." I heard Wings snarl through the door.

"I would say go for it, but I love you too much." Madron grunted.

"I can take him." Wings growled back.

"He's a Guardian for a reason. Let me see what he wants." Madron clipped out right before the door opened.

"This better be good." Madron snapped out. Like me he was shirtless with a pair pants, undone, barely hanging onto his hips.

If you answered me the first damned time this wouldn't be an issue. Something is severely wrong with Malachi.

Take him to Medical. Madron slammed the door shut on my face.

Angry, I stepped through the door and into shadowed room containing two naked people scrambling for cover. My cocked forearm found Madron's neck while my advancing body propelled him into the wall behind him. *You know damned well I wouldn't be here if it was a simple as that. Stop fucking with me.*

Wings jumped from the bed and started towards us only for Madron to hold a palm up in a staying gesture. I was pretty sure that Madron was assuring Wings that he was fine because he was. My arm was only pressing lightly into his neck barely holding him to the wall behind him, the wall that it only looked like I slammed him into. It was all for shock value and used purely to force Madron to listen.

As Guardian to the Andromadan race I wouldn't hurt any of our people unless they themselves were a detriment. Or, you know, in play.

Shit. Madron's eyes examined my face before he patted my arm in a silent order to let him down. *What happened?*

The Conversance. I told the Ancient that was now following me back to my suite. Unable to truly explain exactly what happened, I sent him a visual of it all.

With a glance to thankfully see Mali's door still shut, we slipped silently through the suite to Malachi's door. We stepped into the room and quietly shut the door behind us.

"He won't wake up." Leah whispered, tears sliding from her wide worried eye. She moved Malachi so that his head and shoulders were laying in her lap. She cleaned him up and covered his lower half with a blanket. Her shaking fingers were sifting through his dark hair and over his upper chest and shoulders. She was dressed in one of Malachi's shirts.

"Let me see." Madron whispered, leaning over Malachi's prone body and setting his hand on the unconscious man's chest. Within a minute Malachi's head shifted in Leah's lap and he sighed. Madron removed his hand and sat down on the edge of the bed. "He's sleeping now, healing."

"What happened?" Leah sobbed, her knuckle finding her mouth.

"The Conversance. Between all three of you. Not just Chriton and you." Madron sighed with a slight wince.

"I don't understand." Leah blinked in confusion.

"You are a DNA mimic, right?" At Leah's nod Madron continued. "The Conversance happens when two or three soulmates join together and reach their culminations at the same time. From what Chriton showed me, all three of you came at the exact same time. Because you are a DNA mimic and was being held between the two of them at the time you were carrying both of their DNA. Malachi and you were tied so tightly together when the Conversance happened that your soul took his with it when it rose up to dance with Chriton's. Usually this doesn't hurt and really has no effect."

"From what I can tell, Chriton is your soulmate. But both you and he have lived past lives with Malachi. Probably a larger number of them if the connection you all have with one another is anything to go by. Both of you loved him in your own way. That connection was soul deep. But he wasn't a soulmate. In fact, from the read I got off of him, he didn't have a soulmate. Now, however, he has two." Madron paused in his explanation to run his eyes over both Leah and I. "The short of the long is that when your soul rose, because of the DNA tie at the time, it thought Malachi's soul was part of it. Your soul basically ripped Malachi's soul from his body to bring it along. Unfortunately, that is very painful and he really would've died if his soul wasn't returned as fast as it was."

"I did that?" Leah began to cry even harder. I crawled over the bed and curled myself around her from behind.

"No, Leah, you didn't do anything wrong. This is by no means your fault. Right now, I really need you to hear what I am saying." Madron reached out and took one of Leah's shaking hands with his. "There was no choice. You and he were basically one in that moment, just as you were also one with Chriton. Now, here is the kicker. When your soul, and Malachi's, danced with Chriton's, you all danced together and shared pieces with each other. You all became soulmates. You are all now each other's Conversance. And next time this happens, it won't hurt anyone."

"Why won't he wake up?" Leah stammered through trembling lips, her crying slowing slightly.

"He's recovering." Madron smiled gently at her.

"Is he still in pain?" Leah looked down at Malachi and rubbed her hand over his chest.

"No. He's completely whole and healthy. Well, minus the pieces he gave to you and Chriton but plus the pieces the both of you gave him. He's just exhausted. I am sure he will wake up in the morning feeling like a whole new man." Madron gave Leah an amused grin and a reassuring wink.

"Ok. Thank you, Madron." Leah nodded slowly, her wet eyes looking at him gratefully.

"It is not a problem, Leah." He soothed, cupping her face and pressing his forehead to hers. "Now you really are part of the family. There is no getting away from us. Ever."

Leah giggled before closing her eyes and sliding her forehead along his. I knew that after everything she had gone through she was fully memorizing this moment.

Madron slowly drew away and pressed a soft kiss to her forehead before rising from the bed.

"Chriton." He gave me a nod.

"Thank you, Madron. Please give my apologies to your Conversances." I returned Madron's nod.

"There is nothing to apologise for. You were right, I should've listened when you called the first time." Madron assured me before leaving.

After I heard the suite door shut with a soft click, I gently guided Leah's face to mine. "I am going to grab a quick shower and my pajama pants. I will be right back."

"Ok." Leah nodded slowly, her eyes still wet and swollen, worried looking.

"He will be fine and I will be quick." I assured her, dropping a quick kiss to her lips.

Leah sighed and nodded again. I knew that she really wouldn't be mentally ok again until Malachi woke up and showed her himself that he was fine.

After taking the fastest shower I could, I pulled on my pajama pants and returned to the room. Leah was bent over Malachi's prone body speaking softly to him.

"Your turn, love." I told her firmly. Leah shot me a look but didn't say anything when she saw the resolve in my eyes. "I have him." I assured her when she gently moved Malachi's head to the bed and slowly rose.

After she left, I maneuvered Malachi around the bed so that I could change the bedding. Then I dressed him in his own pajama pants and tucked him under the covers. Leah returned fairly quickly, still dressed in Malachi's shirt but now clean and damp.

"Bed, love." I lifted the covers so that she could crawl in beside Malachi.

She curled up against his chest, her leg cocked over his hip. I left her to get settled while I checked on Mali and made sure the suite was shut down for the night with only the battery run nightlights on.

Returning to the room, I crawled into the bed beside Leah and settled against her back. My movement shifted the bed enough for Malachi to let out a snorting breath. His body rolled into Leah and his arms and legs snaked around her, and me.

"I am pretty sure he will be fine." I noted into the back of Leah's neck.

"I finally got my cuddle." She tittered before relaxing between us.

I felt my own body relaxing right along with hers. All too soon I was falling deep into sleep.

CHAPTER 16

MALACHI

I woke up alone.

At first I thought that I really did die but then I heard Leah's voice followed by Mali's.

With a much needed stretch, I frowned at the weirdly heavy yet light feeling in my chest. That's also when I noticed how refreshed I felt. Sitting up, I pressed my fingers to the spot on my chest where I felt the ripping sensation the night before. Everything looked the same, in fact, other than the heavy/light feeling, it all felt good too.

My mind turned over every moment of what happened the night before and how it could have occurred. I kept returning to the same conclusion.

Then a thought jumped into my mind and I decided to give it a try. Gathering my strength, I closed my eyes and pushed one word out of my head and into the universe.

CHRITON!

Everything was quiet for couple of seconds before I actually got an answer back. My body jumped in surprise when Chriton's voice echoed in my head.

Fucking hell! Malachi, you asshole, you just scared the shit out of me. I am in the middle of teaching class and I literally jumped so high I sprayed my water bottle over no less than two women and one man. Bear really does not look happy with me.

When did Bear join yoga?

Yeah. That sounds like the question that should be asked right at this very moment.

Someone is sarcastic this morning. Could it because you prematurely sprayed all over Bear?

I blame you. I am assuming you talked to Leah. How are you feeling?

Surprisingly good. But no, I haven't talked to Leah yet. I am still in bed trying to figure out what happened. Considering the fact that I made you blow your water bottle load with just the power of my mind, I am guessing that I am on the right track.

What do you have?

Leah's a DNA mimic. I am guessing that's why I ended up going for the ride I did last night. Now I am part of the whole.

Nailed it. How are you feeling about all of that?

Nuh uh. Your turn.

Honestly. It feels meant to be, like it was supposed to be this way the whole time. I am just sorry about the pain you went through. You?

The same. I don't care about the pain. Although, I do feel like I could lift a fucking mountain.

Good. I am glad. Now go reassure our woman. She's been quite concerned over your unconscious ass.

On it. I closed the link with a smile and pushed up from the bed.

Stepping out of the room, I didn't get far before a flying body jumped into my arms. I caught Leah against me, one arm wrapping around her waist, the other coming up to grip the back of the head she buried in my neck.

"I am ok, baby. Better than ever, in fact." I soothed her.

"I was so scared that I would lose you." She whispered, drawing away and cupping my face with her hands. "I can't lose you, Boss. I can't."

"No, Teach, you won't. Now you are officially stuck with me. Body, heart, and soul." I told her, pecking at her lips gently.

"H-heart?" Leah stammered, her wide grey eyes searching over mine.

"Heart, Leah. I love you. I have loved you for a while now." I told her softly.

"I love you too, Malachi." Leah returned, her smile wobbly yet so filled with joy that I felt my already full heart filling even more. "I am pretty sure I fell in love with you the first time you grabbed my face in that maddening way you do."

"Thank God." I breathed, tilting my head to meet her lips. I proceeded to show exactly how much I loved her. Slow and deep.

When I drew away, I gently set her on the ground and followed her into the kitchen to help with the breakfast festivities.

"Good morning, dad." My beloved daughter greeted me with her own beautiful smile.

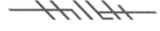

LEAH

HE LOVED ME. MALACHI loved me.

I rubbed a hand over my chest, feeling him inside me, right there beside Chriton. And it was the best feeling ever, carrying them with me like this.

I loved Malachi right back. Just as deeply and desperately as I loved Chriton.

Last night was a giant eye opener for me. The way they controlled me, the way they worked together to give me the utmost pleasure. I felt so loved in that moment it felt like my heart was splitting.

Then came the worry and appreciation. Malachi passed out, scaring the life out of me. And Chriton, just as worried for Malachi as I was, efficiently stepped in. The beautiful man made sure that Malachi was ok at the same time he reassured me. In that moment I realized exactly how much I loved both of them.

Mali and I were just finishing getting ready when Chriton returned from his yoga class. He walked into the suite, adorably sweaty. His eyes went straight Malachi and assessed over the man before Chriton smiled. His smile was filled with happiness and relief.

"Fucker." Chriton growled, prowling over the floor to pull Malachi into a giant, back pounding hug.

Malachi said something to Chriton that I didn't catch but caused Chriton to laugh and draw away.

"Uncle Chriton swore." Mali noted, watching the two men with confusion in her eyes. I did notice that three of us rarely swore when the young girl was around.

"He did indeed." I noted with a nod.

"Is everything all right?" Mali asked, clearly reading the room.

"Everything is fine, Mali-girl. You dad was just really tired last night, so it is a relief to see him so full of energy this morning. Nothing to worry about now that he got a good night sleep." I explained to the girl.

"Yeah, dad works too much. Sometimes he falls asleep on the couch. I used to get worried too, but now I know it's just because he needs sleep." Mali smiled and leaned against me.

"We will have to make sure he gets a good night sleep more often, right?" I put my arm around her shoulders and winked down at her.

"Yup." Mali agreed.

"Backpack, Mali-girl. We don't want to be late." I ordered sending the girl to her room to get her backpack.

Walking over to the men that were still talking, I wormed my way between them.

"Have a good day, Boss." I leaned up and kissed Malachi goodbye before turning to Chriton. I pulled the sweaty man's head down to my lips and whispered against his mouth right before I kissed him. "I love you, Chriton."

Chriton stood stunned for a moment before his arms wrapped tightly around me and lifted me against his chest. His lips went from slack to deep and almost frantic.

"Have a good day, Master." I whispered against his lips when he finally allowed me to draw back.

"I love you too, Leah. So fucking deep, precious." Chriton whispered hoarsely, his blue eyes glowing with his love.

Drawing out of his arms, I caught the sight of Malachi grinning proudly at Chriton as I directed Mali out of the suite.

"Do you love both dad and Uncle Chriton?" Mali asked, bringing up our relationship for the first time.

"I do. Does that bother you?" I paused at the steps we were approaching and sat down. I patted the space beside me for Mali to sit.

"No, not really." Mali sat down and frowned at me. "I knew that something was happening between you, dad, and Uncle Chriton. I mean, I have seen how Guard's parents act toward each other, and Aunty Zara with Uncles Rash and Krish. I know that love can happen between three people. So, I was kind of assuming that was what was happening."

"Um, yes. In a way. Right now, we all have feelings for each other and are currently trying to figure out exactly how we fit together. Yes, I do love both your dad and Chriton. And I do love you. Very deeply." I explained to the confused girl.

"Does that, uh, mean that we are going to be a family? Like, are you going to be my mom?" Mali dropped her eyes to the ground.

"I, uh, do you, uh, want me to be your mom?" I asked softly, silently praying the child that I loved so much said yes.

Instead of answering, Mali looked up at me with a set of wet, hopeful eyes.

"Oh, Mali-girl." I cried, pulling her into my arms and rocking her, feeling my own tears slide down my cheeks. "I would love nothing more than to be able to call you my daughter. But that isn't a decision I can make on my own."

"Do you think that Uncle Chriton might want to be a dad to me, just like dad?" Mali whispered into my shoulder.

"I don't know, Mali-girl, I can't answer that. But I can tell you that I have noticed how much he enjoys spending time with you. Speaking for myself, I enjoy spending time with those I love more than I enjoy anything else." I shared with the girl.

"Ok." Mali drew out of my arms and used her arm to wipe her tears away. "Thank you, Leah. For being honest with me."

"Anytime, my Mali-girl." I cupped her small face and gave her a smile filled with every ounce of love I carried for her.

"I love you too, Leah." Mali returned my smile. "And I really hope you become my mom. Just like I hope that Uncle Chriton wants to become my dad."

"Me too, Mali-girl. Me too." I held my hand out to her and helped her up. "Now, how about we both get to school. I don't know about you, but I am going to spend the day happy to have so much love in my life."

"Me too." Mali giggled up at me.

It was in the last hour of school that I got a message from Malachi. My Boss was heading out on an Op.

Taking a deep breath, I prepared myself for a long night. After school Mali and I decided to track down Chriton. We found him arguing with his father in the Garden. Chriton was facing us with his arms crossed while Callden was facing away from us.

"I swear, Chriton, that damned fox just knows. No matter where I go. Even if I haven't started actually working in it yet. When I leave for the day everything is fine then when I get here the next morning there it is." Callden gestured sharply down to the upraised dirt plot the two of them were standing beside. There in the middle of the plot was obviously Lucy's most recent manure deposit.

Mali started giggling when she too saw what Callden was gesturing to.

"I see someone thinks it's funny." Callden noted with a set of amused eyebrows, turning around at the sound of Mali's laugh. He grinned and swung Mali up against his chest. Mali smiled and hugged him tight around his shoulders. "How's my Mali-girl today?"

"Good. How are you, Uncle Callden?" Mali smiled at the man and cupped his face.

"I think a title change might be in order." Callden grunted, pressing his forehead onto hers. "Did you know that in Andromadan the word for father is mana and the word for grandfather is maj."

"I think that's a talk yet to be had, dad." Chriton warned, reaching a hand out to draw me into his arms. I smiled and slid my arms around his shoulders when he bent down to drop a tongue filled kiss to my lips.

"Did you tell him what happened last night?" I asked Chriton softly.

"I did. He's finding it vastly amusing and is completely excited to be a grandpa to an adorable little girl." Chriton shot a glance over my shoulder to Callden who was showing Mali some vegetation growing in the next plot over.

"She asked me some very interesting questions this morning." I shared with him.

"Really?" Chriton drew the word out, his voice filled with surprise. His eyes warmed with love when they fell on Mali.

"I don't really want to get into it without Malachi, but I do feel like I should warn you." I explained to Chriton.

"I agree." Chriton nodded, his gaze dropping to mine. "Although, I will say this, I already love her as if she was mine."

"Me too." I sighed, resting my head on his chest. "I hope he's ok. I never worried about him like this before. It was just who he was. I mean, it's still who he is, but now it's different because I love him."

"He's ok right now, they are still travelling." Chriton told me causing me to jerk back and scowl up at him.

"How do you know that?" I narrowed my eyes at him.

Chriton grinned and touched a finger to his temple. "Seriously? He got it first." I complained, crossing my arms and pouting. I couldn't believe Malachi already achieved the mental connection.

"You know an awful lot about the Conversance." Chriton noted with a set of raised eyebrows.

"Uh, Salem may or may not have shared with River and I." I brought my knuckle up to my mouth and gave him an innocent look.

Chriton's head fell back with his laughter at the same time he pulled me in for a rocking hug. "Well, at least I don't have to explain it to you. How does Malachi know? Because when he pushed his way into my head this morning I almost shit myself."

"He's close with all of them. Marko, Wings, Scope. Plus, he has become good friends with Madron, Diad, and Catro." I shrugged carelessly. "And he does run the Base with Lysander so I can only assume he tries to learn just about everything he can when it comes to the people who come here."

"True." Chriton smiled.

"Now that we have that covered, what should we make our Mali-girl for supper?" I patted Chriton's chest.

"Let's ask her." Chriton chuckled and guided me over to where his dad was teaching Mali to plant a row of carrots.

Mali decided on Chicken Fettuccine.

Later that night, after I tucked Mali into bed, Chriton shared that the Op was a success and the Team was on its way back. Apparently Scope, Woody, and Candle were injured and in need of Medical treatment. Malachi shared that he would be home as soon as he was sure that they were ok.

It was late when I woke up to the sound of a soft click. I carefully extracted myself from Chriton's arms before quietly stepping from his room.

A tall man completely covered in black except for his head stood in front of the closed door. He was sweaty and grimy, his hair a matted rat's nest. The black paint around his eyes was smeared down his face. His black uniform was ripped and damp. His goggles, balaclava, and gloves were dangling from his fingertips.

Malachi never looked sexier.

"Boss." I whispered running over to him. He bent and caught me against him, his arms holding me tight. "I love you, Malachi. So much that I refuse to let you go even though you smell absolutely godawful."

Malachi chuckled, setting me down. "Sorry, Teach, we were forced to crawl through some pretty extensive sewers."

"I know, Chriton told me." I wrinkled my nose and took his hand to pull him to the bathroom. "Come on, let's get you cleaned up and put to bed."

Malachi shut the bathroom door softly behind us while I started working on the damp uniform he was wearing. He set the things in his hand on the countertop and let me strip him down. The protective vest that covered his torso was the first to drop to the floor. That was followed by various filled holsters and sheaths and his heavy tactical belt, these were set on the countertop beside his goggles. His arms helpfully rose while I peeled off his skintight, black thermal. Before I began to work open the thick material of his cargo pants, I made sure to empty his pockets. Different types of stray bullets, a double bladed Karambit knife, a stiletto blade, a set of brass knuckles, and some other items I couldn't quite define. All of it was dumped into the sink.

Malachi stepped free of his pants when I finally got them undone and peeled them down his thighs. The last was his underwear, skintight and just as disgusting as his clothes. At that point I was feeling really bad for his poor genitals.

As soon as I got his underwear rolled down, I turned on the shower and stripped the giant t-shirt I stole from Chriton off. My underwear was kicked off as I pulled Malachi into the shower with me.

His eyes closed and he hummed softly while I gently washed his hair. I ended up biting back a smile when the paint covering his eyes began to run even more. With his hair clean, I moved to wash his face with a soapy face cloth. It took a bit of rubbing around his eyebrows and the corners of his eyes to get all of the paint off.

"There you are." I beamed after his face was finally clean.

Malachi watched me with his dark tired eyes as I slowly moved down his body, washing everything carefully. Kneeling down, I took his penis in hand and began to gently wash it down with the soapy cloth. "Poor thing." I crooned, finishing his dick and moving the cloth over his balls and between his legs.

Malachi's hand fell to the top of my head, his fingers delving into my wet hair. "There. I bet that's better, isn't it." I whispered, dropping a soft kiss to the sad looking limp flesh.

"Are you seriously talking to my dick?" Malachi asked, his voice hoarse. I ignored the way his cock thickened right before my eyes, stretching and lengthening until it curved up along his abdomen. I also ignored the reactionary arousal that was coursing through my system and the pulsing that was taking place deep inside my pussy. Instead, I concentrated on moving the cloth over his hips and between his ass cheeks causing him to grunt.

"He was dirty and he looked so sad." I looked up the long length of Malachi's body to meet his half lidded eyes. "Now he is clean. And look how happy he is." I nodded to his happily bobbing penis, my hands moving the cloth over his legs and feet.

Malachi shook his head and chuckled, "He's not happy. You woke him up and now he's hungry."

"Hmm." I hummed, finishing up his last little piggy before setting the cloth aside. "You may be right, he does kind of look like he's sitting up and begging." I noted before licking up his straining length from his root to his tip. My hands braced on his abdomen and hips and my breasts pressed into his thighs.

"Fuck yes, Teach, give him a treat." Malachi growled softly, his hand tightening in my hair. "He's had a long, hard night."

Looking up into Malachi's eyes again, I swirled my tongue around his swollen head before kneeling up and sucking it straight into my mouth. At that point I was so aroused that my thighs were shaking.

I moaned softly when his salty taste ran over my tastebuds at the same time his stretched glands glided over my tongue. The feel of him in my mouth was divine.

After using my tongue to investigate his tip and the edge of his crown, I sucked him hard and found out that my tongue really liked that pressure. My vagina clenched jealously, wanting to be filled and caressed by the burning heat in my mouth.

"Fuck, Teach." Malachi grunted, his hips moving, gently thrusting his tip along my curled tongue.

I gagged slightly when his tip nudged the back of my throat. "Sorry, baby." He whispered, drawing back.

Pulling off him, I eyed the length of his dick while I took a deep breath. "Leah...? Shit." Malachi snarled when I sucked him back in, deeper. I gagged again but kept trying until I succeeded in swallowing his tip into my throat.

I cried out when my mouth lost his dick and I was lifted from the floor. My hands gripped his shoulders and my legs circled Malachi's hips while he shut the water off and stepped from the shower. That divine penis of his slithered over my sex to rub right along my clit with every movement he made. It felt so good to feel him against me this way but I wanted, needed him a little lower, and a lot deeper.

I whimpered when he pressed me into the nearest wall and my eyes caught on something over his shoulder. Glowing blue eyes.

Malachi's knuckles glided over my pussy and I felt the rounded tip of his cock notch at my entrance. My eyes moved back to Malachi's black one's, seeing the dark desire written over his face.

"Boss!" I cried out when his hips curved inward and his dick started spreading me open. The painful stretch mixed with the pleasure of him gliding over my sensitive muscles. My fingers tightened on his shoulder and neck, holding him to me tightly. After what felt like forever I finally felt him seat himself fully. His root pressed into my entrance signalling that he was completely inside me. Almost painfully deep.

His head dropped and his lips nuzzled over mine. "I can't be slow and easy, baby. Are you ready for that?"

"Yes, Boss. Please. Fuck me." I pleaded, my lips nipping and sucking at his.

Malachi's jaw clenched and his hips drew back. He wasn't lying. It wasn't slow and easy. His hips slapped forward before jerking right back. Fast and hard. Rough and determined. His eyes took on a dark, dangerous look while his delightfully blood filled muscle slammed in and out of me. My cries of rapture were breathed into his mouth and while I held on to him with everything I had.

The nerves in my pussy roared to life and screamed in delight at the friction he was giving me. Within seconds I was riding the edge of ecstasy.

"Boss." I gasped into his mouth, my pussy clenching around him in a silent attempt to hold onto him. The friction of me squeezing around his jackhammering sex felt so good that when I did it for a second time it sent me spinning into orgasm. My body shuddered violently and my eyes rolled back in my head. My pussy began contracting around his dick, sucking desperately at the flesh that refused to stop moving through its grasping muscles.

Somehow he was getting even deeper, nudging painfully up against my cervix. It was then that I felt my orgasm take on a new level. With each harsh slap of his hips, my pussy spurted come out around him.

"That's my girl, give me that orgasm." Malachi snarled, his hands moving over me, gripping tightly around the globes of my ass and up around the back of my neck. His breath was falling from his clenched mouth in heavy beats, his cheekbones looked stretched and flushed.

Through it all he kept thrusting, seeking not just my pleasure but his. When I was finally able to think, somewhat, I decided to start that clenching thing again. Kegels. "Teach, you are squeezing my dick like you want to keep it." Malachi rasped.

"I do. Forever." I gasped, keeping up that delicious rhythm, loving the feel the burning hardness of his meat driving through my own tightened muscles. "Don't stop. Never stop."

"I won't, baby. Right here, forever." Malachi returned, his mouth finding mine, taking me over just as much as his dick was. I kissed him back, giving him all of it, everything I was feeling for him right in that moment.

My orgasm slammed through me, sending my mind soring. My pussy clamped down before it began to massage and spasm over the dick that Malachi planted deep inside me. Malachi's body tensed and he growled softly, always so silent while lost in the extremity of his pleasure. I felt that beloved dick swell and pulse with the substantial amounts of burning heat that was spouting from his tip only to be sucked deep into my womb.

Malachi's clenched mouth relaxed against mine and his lips moved softly in soft kisses.

"I love you, Teach." He whispered, his hand smoothing over my face.

"I love you too, Boss." I returned to him before looking over his shoulder and into those blue eyes. "I love you too, Master."

Malachi chuckled and shot a look over his shoulder. "And I thought she didn't notice you."

Malachi unhitched us and set me on my feet. My hand automatically dropped down to cover my leaking vagina. Chriton grinned knowingly and gave me a wink. "I love you too, precious."

"Wait. How long has he been here?" I asked, looking between the two men.

"Since the moment you stepped into the shower." Chriton shrugged nonchalantly.

"How come you didn't..?" I asked, gesturing between Me and Malachi who was turning the shower back on.

"Because you both needed it." Chriton stated, reaching out to help me into the shower. "I am sure Malachi would do the same for me."

"Fuck yes." Malachi grunted, his determined eyes meeting Chriton's.

This time it was Malachi who washed me down while Chriton helpfully waited with towels in hand. I was faintly surprised when he wrapped one of the towels over Malachi's shoulders before using the other to dry me off.

Looking around the room, I saw that everything was cleaned up. The sink and counter were empty, the dirty clothes and the vest were picked up off the floor. In their place was clean sleepwear for us. Malachi's pajama bottoms and another clean t-shirt of Chriton's.

I smiled up at my caring man, loving the way he took care of me. Us.

Once we were dressed, Chriton guided us to his room where I fell asleep tucked safely ensconced between the two of them with Malachi wrapped around us.

CHAPTER 17

CHRITON

L eah was gone.
     I woke up with Malachi tightly wrapped around me and no Leah. Extracting myself from Malachi's grasping grip, I headed straight to the kitchen to hunt down the woman I planned to drag to yoga with me. I sighed softly when I saw a note on the counter in front of the coffee pot.

Needed to swim. Coffee's set to go. Love you.

I knew that she preferred swimming to yoga, and I also knew that she hadn't gone swimming since we all moved in together. She was probably missing it. As much as I wanted to share my routine with her, I knew she was itching to get back to her own routine.

I was getting ready to head out for my lengthier Saturday yoga class when Mali shuffled out of her room. She saw me and grinned, her face lighting up in way I felt deep in my heart. Her happiness at seeing me was something I looked forward to everyday.

"Good morning, Mali-girl." I greeted, hugging the girl when she walked over and leaned into me.

"Where are you going?" Mali asked, tipping her head back.

"Yoga." I smiled warmly down at her, sliding my fingers gently through her sleep mussed hair.

"Can I come?" Mali asked, her eyes glowing with hope.

"Sure. Go get in your dance clothes." I jerked my chin at her room.

With a happy skip, Mali raced off to her room before skidding back out and into the bathroom. I couldn't help but chuckle at her excitement.

I filled up another water bottle for her and left my own message underneath Leah's.

Mali and I are at Yoga. Coffee's still set to go. Love you.

Mali came out of the bathroom and we headed out.

MALACHI

I WOKE UP TO SILENCE.

With a grunt, I sat up and glared around the disappointingly empty bedroom.

After stretching the kinks out of my sore, tired body I shuffled to the kitchen in search of someone, anyone. Moving to get some coffee going before relieving my bladder, my eyes immediately caught on the note in front of the coffee maker.

The first was obviously Leah and the second was Chriton.

While it was eerie to wake up in the morning to a quiet suite, it felt really good to know that they thought of me. After last night's Op, I knew neither one of them wanted to wake me, but they both still thought to leave me a note just in case I woke while they were gone.

Since it was officially our first weekend all together, I wanted to do something special with them. I just didn't know what.

Thinking for a bit, I realized that I wanted to do something that was just the four of us, something away from the Base.

Getting dressed, I left my own note and headed out to get my debriefing done so that I could put my plan into motion.

"Lysander." I greeted my Nordic counter part when I walked into Operations. Lysander, a tall man with long blond hair and stripped blue and white eyes, shared the Head of Base position with me. He was the main connection between human's and the Andromadan Alliance, or he was until the Andromadans started showing up.

We worked well together, keeping each other updated with daily meetings and messages. Lysander did tend to have issues with the fact that I refused to put his ass on the line when it came to security and retrieval. Just as I tried to do with the Andromadans. Unfortunately, the Andromadans were a stubborn lot and were inclined to do their own thing despite my orders.

"It's good to hear that everyone came back alive." Lysander noted, reviewing the report I wrote up while I was waiting in Medical for my guys to get treatment.

"Yeah. Unfortunately, the Cascades lost some people." I winced, sitting down at the conference table and using the tablet to bring up my report and a holographic image of the region.

The small base in the Cascades boasted around 50 residents. All of which lived under a reinforced metal dome that was well camouflaged to hide in the forest around them. The security set up was a mixture of old and new technologies. Every time we went there, I was always impressed with how the group utilized it.

When we arrived at the base last night after receiving their distress call it was to see the dome being circled by Drako ships. The first thing I noticed was the remote control machine guns popping up and down from the roof of the dome as they took shots at the blurring ships. Their gun men were good, but not as good as mine.

Once we were on the ground, we attempted to make it to the dome only to be blocked by the lizards that were already on the ground. In order to get Giggles, Bear, and Scope through the enemy and inside to those guns we were forced to make use of a back route that we knew about. A set of sewer tunnels. The leader of the Cascades was extremely shocked when we climbed out of that specific tunnel system smelling absolutely fantastic.

Once the ships were out of commission we only had the lizards on the ground to contend with. Those were efficiently overcome by my team and the residents of the dome who popped out of the extensive network of non sewer tunnels that were dug around the base.

In the ensuing scuffle, Scope ended up popping his shoulder out. Woody was clawed across his arm deep enough to need stitches. And Candle, well, he kind of blew himself up. For the umpteenth time. Although, I was forced to admit that it had been a while since the last time.

"Are they looking for some new residents? Some of the people from the Tacoma Op are asking for transfers. They are having a hard time with an underground base." Lysander noted, sending me the nine names that were requesting transfers. The transfers were signed off by Dr. Daniels, our resident Psychologist, Royce, and Marko.

"They have the space." I shrugged, checking over the reports on each of the individuals before signing off on them and forwarding the requests to the Cascades base.

"Good. So how is the...relationship going?" Lysander grinned and shut the hologram down before signing off on the reports.

"Interesting." I grinned.

"That's it? That's all I get?" Lysander asked, his eyebrows rising.

"If you want more, you're going to have to talk to Chriton." I told him with a chuckle.

"So, its like that, is it?" Lysander laughed with amusement, knowing that I wasn't about to share any Andromadan secrets with him even though he already knew about them. As the delivery of information within the Base went, Lysander and I made sure that we were the first to be informed about anything.

"Yup." I nodded. "I will, however, say this. There is a highly classified report that was made the other night that you might want to check out."

"Good to know, Malachi." Lysander gave me a smile and clapped me on the shoulder as he rose from his seat and left Operations.

"Nicely done." Marko grunted, flopping back into the seat that Lysander just evacuated.

"Thanks." I nodded at my friend.

"You know, I never said anything because I didn't think it was my place. I mean, we both know that I am not really one to talk when it comes to not recognizing the love of my life, but it's about damned time. For all of you. I have watched all three of you suffer, alone, for so many years. If anyone else in this Base deserves to be happy, you do. And I am really happy that you now have it. In so many ways." Marko shared with me in his quiet voice.

"Thank you, Marko." I nodded gratefully at my friend, a man I knew and worked with in one form or another for the past seven years. He was a man that I respected the hell out of. Marko was the one that actually found the Base. He came across the blueprints of an underground base that the government built before abandoning. He led us all here. As head of Operations, he was also hell on the computer. But then so was his heavily pregnant wife, River.

"Anytime, Malachi." Marko grinned before glancing at the emergency message that started ringing out on his coms and going completely pale. "Oh, fuck!" He jumped up from the table and sprinted from Operations.

"What?" I yelled, chasing after him.

"River is in labor." He gasped in between screaming for people to move out of his way. "She's not due for another month."

"Shit." I ran with him all the way to Medical while sending out various messages on my coms.

We slammed through the doors to see Scope clutching his shoulder and pacing in front of an open exam room door. Scope had a shock of dark red hair and light hazel eyes that clashed in an eerily good way with his naturally tanned looking skin. As for freckles, his face only boasted a couple interestingly placed ones while the rest of his body carried a thick coverage of them.

"Don't fucking worry about me. You help her." He snarled at the nurse that was trying to examine his limp arm.

"Get her to look at that arm, Scope." Marko ordered as we approached Scope.

"But River..." He growled, jerking his chin towards the room where Stand was working over a clearly pale and scared River.

"Luke is on his way." I reassured Scope a second before Medical's doors burst open and Dr. Luke Graden sprinted in with his nurse on his heals.

"Marko, give me a minute." Luke ordered as he passed us and into the room. Luke pulled on a pair of gloves and Stand stepped back so that Luke could reach River. Luke carefully felt over River's bare, distended stomach before he turned and gestured for Marko.

"Let them see the shoulder, Scope." Marko ordered before he ran into the room.

Luke was talking to them quietly, his hands still resting on River's stomach. Heated tears slowly started falling from River's eyes while Marko gripped her hand tightly. I didn't think his face could get paler, but it did.

Colleen, Luke's nurse came hurrying out of the room with Stand on her heals. Luke stepped out, his eyes angry yet determined.

"C-section?" I asked as he walked by me.

"Yup." He nodded sharply, striding down the back hall towards the surgery rooms.

Stand and both of the nurses were back in the exam room hooking a crying River up to IV's and getting her ready for the surgery. Scope was watching everything with the same fear that Marko was displaying.

"Hey." I turned and gripped his good arm. "She's strong. They both are. And so is that kid."

"I know." Scope swallowed, turning to look at me, his eyes haunted. I knew that the man was scared of loosing more people from his life. Scope was a foster child who was constantly shunted from home to home. He never truly found a family until Wings, Marko, and River.

"Come on." I forcefully guided him to the back so that we could watch the surgery. Luke was scrubbing up at the sink when he looked up and narrowed his eyes on us.

He flicked the water off his hands and into the sink before prowling over. Scope grunted softly when Luke felt around his shoulder. That grunt was followed by a pained hiss when Luke took his arm and gave it a quick twisting jerk. I cringed when I heard the shoulder pop back into place. "No lifting heavy items for six fucking weeks." Luke reiterated what he told Scope last night after the first time he popped Scope's shoulder back into place.

"She was in fucking labor. She couldn't even walk. What the hell should I have done?" Scope snarled at Luke.

Luke returned to the sink and began scrubbing up for the second time. "Oh, I don't know, maybe called for an emergency gurney. I mean, it's not like they are here for that exact reason."

"Sarcasm, thy name is Luke." Wings noted, joining us.

"Sarcasm is a friend when dealing with stubborn assed soldiers who refuse to take care of themselves. I have a man who literally popped his shoulder out of its socket twice in less then eight hours standing behind me. He is joined by another man who now speaks with an English accent because of a head injury he refused to get checked out before it was too late. And then there is the man who has popped open his stitches no less than fourteen times in the last two years." Luke finished his statement just in time to turn to his nurse who proceeded to glove and mask him.

"Give it up, doc." I crossed my arms and glared at the man. Luke and I had a love/hate relationship. I respected him just as much as he respected me. The man was a badass with an attitude and a great man to have at your back. He was also in a triad with Lysander and Nova. But, for some reason we frequently butted heads. He didn't understand the way me and my team worked while we didn't really enjoy being lectured by him constantly. What made us bond was the fact that we both cared and did our damnedest to save lives. Just in very different ways. Plus, I had to admit, the man and the way he had with words was damned amusing. "If I remember correctly, you didn't react the best either when Zara went into labor."

Luke ran a set of assessing eyes over me before giving me a sharp nod, acknowledging the hit. Stand and his nurse rolled River down the hall and into the surgery room. Luke's nurse and Stand started getting River ready while Stand's nurse helped Marko into a set of clean scrubs.

Once they were ready, Marko was let into the surgery room and it all began. The three of us men were watching for only a couple of minutes before Salem and Leah came running down the hall. Salem went straight to Scope. Being careful of the arm that Stand's nurse put a compression brace on, Salem pulled him into a grateful hug. Leah did the same with Wings, walking up and holding her arms open for the man to hug. Wings quickly took advantage of Leah's rare offer.

The women switched and Scope took advantage of his own hug from Leah. Salem wrapped her arms around Wings' middle to hold him tight while they watched the surgery.

After she was done hugging Scope, Leah came to me. Her eyes were worried so I made sure that she received a clear view of the surgery room by pulling her backwards into my arms. She relaxed into my chest, gripping my arm with one hand while reaching out to take Scope's uninjured hand with her other one. Within the next half an hour we were joined by others. The Andromadan Ancient's, Madron, Diad, Catro, and Catro's wife Royce.

We all watched as Luke and Stand worked behind the raised blue sheet while Marko sat on a stool beside River's head. Marko was smoothing his fingers over her face and through her hair as he spoke softly to her. River nodded slowly every once and a while.

Then I saw it. Luke's mask moved up in a grin right before he lifted a tiny, red, gunk covered, screaming baby up. It was clearly a boy. Marko's head shot straight up and he slowly stood, his eyes filled with amazed wonder. River started smiling and sobbing, tears of happy relief running down her face.

Stand reached for the baby, holding it while Luke cut the umbilical cord. Then the child was swept to the side counter with both parents watching with eagle eyes, waiting on bated breath. All the while, Luke continued working on River. We all heard Marko's gasping cry when Stand finally turned around with the baby wiped down and tightly wrapped in a blanket.

I felt Leah's shoulder's jerk and her head shifted until she was resting her cheek against my chest. I felt my shirt getting damp and my arms tightened, my body bowing over hers.

Stand careful set the boy in his shaking father's arms. Marko's shoulders jerked with a sob as he fell back to his stool and proceeded to hold the baby up so River could see him.

All to soon, Luke finished the surgery and River was cleaned up. Then Marko carefully set their boy in his mother's arms. Luke, Stand, and Colleen stepped from the room, giving the brand new family time.

"The baby is four weeks premature but other than being a tiny thing, he's fine. His lungs and heart are surprisingly strong." Stand told the group of us.

"There was no problem with the surgery. With a little tender care River will heal just fine." Luke grinned at us before turning to watch the family bond.

"So, when do you want to take the test, Teach?" I whispered to Leah as we walked back to our suite, bringing up our linked fingers to press a kiss to her knuckles. It was noon already as Leah refused to leave Medical until she got the chance to meet the new baby, Paladin, and check on both mother and father.

"What?" Leah frowned in confusion.

"Pregnancy test." I stated, my eyes carefully watching her reactions.

"I, uh, what?" Leah stumbled, her wide eyes coming to mine.

"Leah, you aren't on birth control." I reminded her softly.

Her eyes darted back and forth as she remembered how both Chriton and I came inside her. "I, uh, do you, uh, Boss?" She stammered, her hand dropping to her stomach, her brow furrowing.

I covered her hand with mine, "Baby, considering the fact that neither Chriton nor I made any effort to use a condom, I am pretty sure that both of us would love to have you pregnant with our child." I reassured her.

"We haven't even talked about...well, anything really. I mean, I know I love you both and would love another child, but beyond that. I don't know if you want to get married, if that is even a thing for, uh, this. I don't know if I am a mother and if Chriton is a father. I don't know." Leah gasped out, her voice anxious, her hands gesturing wildly.

"Hey, hey, hey, Teach. If you are worried then let's talk about it. Let's go back to the suite and talk. All of us." I caught Leah's arms and pulled her into my chest. "Ok?"

"Ok." Leah nodded shakily and drew back. When we returned to the suite it was to see Chriton and Mali playing a board game.

"How is the baby? Is he really cute?" Mali jumped up and ran over to us with a happy smile.

"He is fine, everyone is fine." I shared with Mali.

"And he's adorable." Leah exclaimed with a warm smile walking over to meet Chriton who was coming towards us.

Chriton bent to touch her lips with his before his head rose and his intelligent eyes met mine. He knew something was off.

"I think its time for a family talk." I noted, gesturing everyone to the couch.

Chriton's eyes told me that he was in complete agreement and he guided Leah to the couch.

"Does anyone mind if I start?" I asked, taking Mali's hand and leading her to the couch to sit beside Leah.

"Go ahead." Chriton stated, sitting in one of the chairs and stretching his legs out.

"Ok. I know we really haven't talked about things, we all just kind of agreed to play this all out. But now, with things going the way they are, I feel like it's the time to share where we all stand. I love you, Leah, and I am finding that I love Chriton. Not in quite the same way I love you but it's there." I paused as Leah giggled and Chriton rolled his eyes. "It is my greatest wish to have you both be part of my life, permanently, how ever that may come about. But, as you both know and seem to have accepted, I do not come alone. Mali also is part of this and is part of every decision I make."

Mali looked up at me with wide eyes. "If you want them permanently, then does that mean that Leah can finally be my mom and Uncle Chriton can be my dad, uh, mana?"

I crouched down in front of my daughter and brushed her hair back with a fingertip. "If that's what you want, Mali-girl."

Mali nodded sharply, turning questioning eyes to Chriton. His eyes stared into hers, starting to glow, and he bent forward and reached around me to take her hand. "Considering the fact that I already love you like a daughter, I would love nothing more than to be your mana."

Mali gave a giggling sob and swiped at the tears on her face before turning to smile up at Leah. "We are a family now. I have a mom, and a dad, and a mana."

"Yes, you do, my Mali-girl." Leah laughed softly, cupping Mali's face and dropping a lingering kiss to her forehead.

"Yup. A family." Chriton nodded softly, reaching out with his free hand to grip my shoulder. "All of us. Permanent." Our eyes met and I realized then that he was completely right. I was now tied to both of them in the most permanent way possible. Forever. My heart jerked in my chest before it began filling, full. I felt tears rise to my eyes.

Chriton's eyes glowed even brighter and a slow smile crossed his lips. I could see it, right there on his face, he considered me his just as much as he considered Leah his.

"What now?" Leah asked softly, still holding Mali's head against hers.

"Now, we go on vacation." I turned back to them and grinned.

"Vacation? What kind of vacation?" Mali straightened causing Leah's hand to drop.

"Camping. We are going to the Ranch and we are going to go camping. I set it up so that we will have some tents and a little camping area that is away from the village and the sites. It is close to a pond that the Ranch residents use sometime for swimming. We are going to take a week and spend it together, just us." I explained. "We are going to cook our food over a fire and go swimming. By the time we come home we will smell so bad no one will be able to stand us."

Leah smiled and shook her head in amusement at me. "Come on, Mali-girl, let's go get packed."

"Yes!" Mali exclaimed excitedly and jumped up from the couch. Leah followed the racing girl to her room where I heard them digging in the cupboards.

"You know, camping could be very, very interesting." Chriton rose, his eyes following the ladies. I rose with him, following his eyeline.

"Exactly. No one to disturb us." I grinned wickedly.

"Bring your whip, Boss." Chriton ordered softly, turning to his room to do his own packing.

"Planned on it, Master." I called softly after him.

Then I packed. Warm weather clothes for the day and cold weather clothes for the evening. Bathing suit bottoms for swimming. A couple books for reading and some toys for playing. Added to that was the usual sun protection items, and some boardgames and cards. Lastly were the toiletries. All of that was tucked into my giant duffle bag. My hard cased carry on was packed with my weapons and gear. Knives, guns, my brass knuckles. Goggles, vest, gloves, uniform.

Carrying it all out to the living room, I could see Mali's bags packed and set by the door. I could hear the girls talking in Leah's room. I set my stuff by the door and walked over to Chriton's room. He was packed but was sitting on the bed with his tablet in hand.

"I just want to get this done before we go." He murmured when he saw me leaning against his doorframe.

"Take your time." I nodded at him. "I am having the food and everything else delivered to the site for us."

"Hmmm." He hummed before falling silent for long moments. Then he grunted and set the tablet aside. "Let's do this."

"Let's do it." I grinned and held my hand out to him. He clasped it in his and pulled me in for a hug.

I closed my eyes and hugged him back.

"Come on, let's go." Mali called, hopping up and down by the door. Leah laughed, carrying a large bag out of her room. She rolled her eyes when I quickly relieved her of her load.

"You never know." I whispered to her, my eyes dropping to her stomach.

"You really don't." Chriton clearly caught my look and grinned almost maniacally at Leah.

Leah blushed bright red and dropped her eyes.

Chriton laughed and pulled her into his arms. "Come on, Leah, my precious, let's go camping. Maybe when we get back we will know."

With that we were off.

CHAPTER 18

LEAH

I smiled when my men were immediately accosted as they exited the ship. Well, Malachi was accosted, Chriton did some accosting. A tattooed and pierced Grayson Dodge, Malachi's best friend came jogging from the tent village and slammed into Malachi almost taking the unawares man to the ground.

Almost.

The bags Malachi was unloading did fall to the ground. Malachi laughed and twisted in Grayson's grip to give his best friend a giant bearhug.

When Bane and Bailor came ambling up the path behind Grayson, Chriton immediately dropped the bags he was holding and sprinted to the men. Bane, knowing his brother, braced when he saw Chriton coming and caught the flying man.

"Group hug!" Chriton claimed, reaching around Bane and pulling Bailor in. Bailor laughed and hugged the brothers' back.

Mali giggled and leaned against my side. I set my arm around her and we watched our guys greet their loved ones.

"Leah." Bane, finally extricating himself from Bailor and Chriton, came over and gently pulled me into his arms. "Welcome to the family."

"Thank you, Bane." I whispered, returning his hug. Out of all the people to welcome me, Madron's was the most touching but Bane's hit me the hardest and the deepest.

Releasing me, Bane looked down at the small girl at my side. "And this must be Mali. My new niece."

"Uh." Mali looked up at me with confused eyes.

"This is Bane. He's your father's brother in law. Another uncle." I introduced.

"He looks scary." Mali hissed softly, eyeing the dangerous looking man. I could understand where she was coming from. Bane did look fairly scary with his black eyepatch. Then there was the white hair on his head that carried two distinct black stripes. Lastly, there was the fact that the man was tall, muscled, and scarred.

"He does." I agreed. "And he can be. But only to bad people." I told Mali honestly. "I have heard that he is really sweet and protective over the ones he considers family."

Mali turned her gaze back to Bane and gave him a very clear assessment. "Ok." She nodded and held her hand out to Bane. "It's nice to meet you, Uncle Bane."

Bane chuckled and took her hand in both of his, holding it firmly but gently. "It's nice to meet you too. Tell me something, Mali, do you like horses?"

Mali nodded slowly, her eyes lighting up with delight.

"Then you are going to love my husband, Bailor." Bane motioned to the strange man with creepy eyes that were eerily reminiscent of a horse's eyes. This was not a surprise considering he was an equine divergent, he could shift into a horse.

Bailor smiled over at us and gave Bane a quick nod before he stepped back into the village.

"I don't understand." Mali frowned in confusion.

"Wait." Bane held up a finger before slowly pointing it to the path Bailor disappeared down. There, slowly clomping towards us, was a large male horse that boasted Bailor's coloring.

"Oh my God! Dad, it's a horse!" Mali exclaimed, covering her mouth with her hands.

Malachi laughed and joined us. Standing behind me, he slid an arm around my stomach and reached out to pat the stallion on his large shoulder. "It's good to see you, Bailor."

Bailor nickered in greeting at Malachi before bending his head to sniff and snort over Mali. Mali giggled and cringed away from the horses tickling. Bailor whickered and started to lip at Mali's hair.

"Thanks. Now we don't have to walk all of this over." Chriton grunted, throwing some of the bags over Bailor's back. Bailor turned and threateningly bared his teeth at Bailor. "This is what you get for showing off." Chriton shrugged his shoulders and pushed Bailor's head away from him.

Bailor swung his giant head over to Bane who simply shook his head and laughed. "You really should've known this was going to happen. It's Chriton. I am sure you remember how much he likes to use you as a pack animal."

"Uncle Grayson." Mali smiled warmly up at the man that stepped over to help Chriton load the horse down. Grayson grinned and bent over to lift the girl up against his chest in a giant hug. "I missed you."

"I missed you, too, Mali-girl." Grayson grunted, rocking the girl back and forth.

"We are going camping." Mali leaned back in his arms and cupped his attractive face. I wasn't sure if he was made more gorgeous because of his facial piercings and tattoos or despite them. Either way, they all somehow suited him, but then so did the green and black fauxhawk he used to sport that was now only black and slicked back.

"I heard." Grayson chuckled.

"Are you coming with us?" Mali asked hopefully.

"Not tonight. I have to work. But when I get my days off I will come out." Grayson told the girl.

"Ok. Did you hear? I have a new mom and a new mana." Mali bragged happily.

"Yes, I did hear." Grayson turned his gaze to meet mine and gave me a wink. I always liked Grayson, he was a brilliant goofball. He provided the perfect foil to Malachi's seriousness. "I can't say that I am surprised. It's about damned time."

"Leave it." Malachi warned his best friend.

"I have to hear this. I heard a little bit, but not much." Bane chuckled, taking over for Grayson to finish loading Bailor.

"He's always watched over her." Grayson laughed at Malachi's narrowed eyes. "Usually, it was just checking up on her, but there were two times that I know of when he got worse. At the beginning of the Drako occupation, and after everything went down last year. After we all arrived at the Base and he knew that she was safe he eventually backed off unlike this last time. This time he didn't back off, he just got worse and worse. I honestly thought they were going to kill each other at times."

"Are you happy now?" Malachi snidely asked his friend.

"Ecstatic." Grayson grinned gleefully.

"Shithead." Malachi rolled his eyes.

"I would never have killed you." I tilted my head back and looked up into Malachi's dark eyes.

"No?" Malachi's eyebrows rose sharply in disbelief.

"Nope." I shook my heard earnestly before dropping my head back down. "Just maimed."

Chriton laughed when he looked up and into Malachi's face. "Now we know."

Bailor shifted impatiently on his feet and whickered softly before turning and ambling away. Bane chuckled and we all followed the horse through the village. We made a quick stop at one of the tents to load even more supplies onto Bailor's back while he stood still and sighed wearily.

"Oh, stop whining. You know damned well you can use this to get something interesting." Chriton rolled his eyes at his brother in law.

"Oh, shit. Speaking of interesting." Bane snapped his fingers and jogged away.

Bailor snorted and continued walking. Mali rode on Grayson's back while Malachi bent down so that I could hop up on his. "Giddyap." I ordered, twisting around to slap Malachi's ass.

Bailor began throwing his head and whickering in what strangely sounded like laughter.

"You do realize that my hand is bigger than yours." Malachi grunted, holding his admittedly huge hand up.

"So it is." I whispered in his ear, reaching out and running a finger down the center of his palm. "I bet it is very strong...and firm."

Chriton, who was walking beside Bailor, stumbled. Catching himself, he cleared his throat and resumed his conversation with Bailor and Grayson.

"Careful, love." Malachi warned in a quiet voice, lowering his palm to grip the arm I placed around his chest.

"I wonder if it cracks like the whip you think you are hiding in your bedside drawer." I whispered with a nip at his ear. I smiled when Malachi stuttered just slightly in his walking. "Tell me, Boss, did you happen to bring that whip? Do you want to show me how well it cracks? Or does Master want to do that? Then I could tell you what is stronger. The hand...or the whip."

"Here." Bane stated when he caught up with us. He was slightly out of breath and handing me a small bag.

"Uh, thank you." I took the bag and started to open it.

"Yeah, that's not PG. At all." Bane warned.

"What is it?" I asked with wide eyes.

"Payback." Bane grinned, running forward to catch up with the others who were slowly pulling ahead of us. "From all of us."

Curious, I opened the bag just far enough that I could peek inside. "Oh my God." I gasped when I saw what was inside.

The first item was a set of silicone anal beads. The second item was called a Balldo that looked like a silicone cage with a tip like a bullet. It came with two round circles made of the same material. The last item was a long bulging vibrator with prostate massager that curved up along a man's taint.

"What is it?" Malachi asked, trying to peek in the bag.

I helpfully held open the bag for him to examine the items. Malachi's eyes widened and his cheeks tinged a bright red. Chriton, who Malachi was clearly sharing with, also turned a bright red. His head snapped sideways to glare at his brother.

Bane's coms arm was up and he was obviously recording everything. When he saw Chriton's reaction, he threw his head back and laughed maniacally. "This is so much better than I thought it would. Coren and Callden are going to love it."

"Shit. I knew it was going to bite me in this ass. I just didn't think it would be this bad." Chriton rubbed his neck, his face still beat red.

"This is going to be such an interesting week." I whispered happily.

"It is indeed." Malachi laughed huskily.

When we reached our camping spot, a nicely treed area that was indeed set beside a large swimming pond, we all began to unload. I noticed that there was already a large stack of wood waiting for us as well as a big, off the ground fire pit. Two large canvas tents and a gazebo were set in a semi circle around the fire pit facing the pond.

Inside the gazebo there was a picnic table in the center and a long wooden cupboard that ran along one edge. One side of the cupboard opened upwards to reveal an ice box filled with food items. The other side opened front ways to show dry goods. Both closed with a tight seal and were lockable.

The tents each boasted two queen sized beds, an end table with a battery powered lantern and a large rug covering the floor. There was also a set of shelves for clothing.

"Is there a reason for all of this?" Malachi asked, gesturing around to all of the amenities that were being provided.

"We decided to make it an official get away spot. So, all of this isn't just for you. And just so you know, there is an outhouse just through those bushes." Bane explained as a freshly unloaded Bailer clomped into one of the tents only to re-emerge minutes later, human and adjusting his clothing.

"What? No shower?" Malachi scoffed sarcastically.

"Nope. You are just going to have to rough it." Bailor grinned, clapping Malachi on the shoulder.

"Come on, Mali-girl, let's get unpacked and changed." I held my hand out for the girl.

We quickly put our stuff away on the shelves before changing into some cooler clothes. I dressed in a dark purple bikini and a pair of ripped jean shorts covered with a loose overshirt before wrapping a cloth wrist band around the wrist that didn't have my coms on it.

Mali dressed in her own one piece swimsuit and a long coverup. Before leaving the tent we both slathered on sunscreen and slipped on sandals.

All of the men were standing about twenty feet away on a rocky outcropping at the edge of the pond. Arms crossed, legs braced, beer in hand. Mali grinned mischievously right before she kicked off her sandals and took off. Considering how well trained every single one of those men were, I was amazed when none of them heard her coming. Malachi let out a yelp when his daughter slammed into his back sending them both careening into the pond.

The rest of the men stood stunned before they burst into laughter. I sauntered up to the group to see Mali and Malachi floating in the water splashing each other.

With a smile, I cuddled into Chriton's side, my hand resting on his chest. His arm automatically circled me. Grayson stepped up to us and set his hand on my shoulder. "He probably should've changed. Now he's going to chafe." Grayson noted, his head cocked to the side.

"Probably." I agreed with a nod.

"At least you were smart enough to change." Grayson noted just as his hand pushed hard on my shoulder.

Knowing how these things usually went once one person was pushed into water, I twisted my body down to the ground in front of Chriton. This did two things. With the removal of my body and a force to counteract the one he was dishing out, Grayson went flying forward, straight over the ledge and into the water. The second was Chriton. When Grayson made his move my hand tightened on Chriton's shirt and took him with me when I twisted to the ground, yanking and tripping him at the same time. He too flew over the ledge and into the water.

Standing up, I brushed my hands off before sliding a look to Bane and Bailor who both intelligently put their hands up in surrender.

"What just happened?" Chriton sputtered in confusion when his head cleared the water. His head jerked back, flipping his wet hair out off his face.

"I made an error in judgement." Grayson cringed.

"Yeah, you really did." Bane called the five feet down to them.

Malachi grinned and gestured for me to join them. I smiled and pulled my overshirt and shorts off, turning to hang them on a nearby tree. I kicked off my sandals and was turning back to the ledge when I heard Bane and Bailor start laughing again. Both men were pointing at the three men in the water.

Looking down at the water crew. Malachi was in the process of slapping Grayson in the back of the head while Chriton snarled intimidatingly at him.

"What happened?" I asked curiously. Feeling awkward and slightly self conscious, I wrapped my arms around my bare torso while I studied the water to figure out the best way to get in.

"All three of them glitched for about twenty seconds. Two of them obviously didn't like the fact that the third glitched as well." Bane explained, dropping his arm over my shoulder and looking down at me with a reassuring eye.

"Uh, ok." I frowned and took aim, feeling the need to get into the water as soon as possible. Chriton grinned when he saw my look and his arms came up to catch me.

I shot the man a fake glare when he didn't just catch me but took advantage of the situation by groping his hands over my ass and breasts. It was only when I splashed him that he stopped. Mali giggled and joined me when I pushed away far enough to get a good splash in.

That was right about when Grayson and Malachi came to Chriton's aid. Mali and I surrendered quickly when we found ourselves overrun and over splashed. All to soon, Grayson was climbing out so that the group could return to the Ranch.

"Watch out for chafing." Malachi called after his wet friend. Grayson flipped him off in return.

"Ok, I need to change." Chriton grunted, swimming over to the beach area beside the tents and sloshing from the water.

"Me too." Malachi stated, following him. Mali and I laughed when pounds of water flowed from their heavy looking, wet clothing.

Mali and I swam over to the beach and wading area while we waited for the guys to return.

I bit back my moan when I saw them walk out of the tent. They were both bare chested with knee length swimming shorts on. Malachi's were orange, white, and black. Chriton's were green, yellow, and white. I couldn't stop looking at all of that deliciously bare flesh. Twisting, bulging muscles. Darkened nipples, tight abdomens. Thickly muscled legs covered in dark hair.

Seeing the way I was ogling them, Chriton pointed at me, "Now you know how we felt." He walked over to the ledge and helpfully retrieving my clothes and our sandals. Mali grinned and threw her wet overdress up onto the beach, just missing her dad who was walking into the water.

Chriton set our stuff down on the beach before launching himself after Malachi. Malachi heard his splashing entrance and turned to him just in time. Malachi caught Chriton's upper body and twisted him over and into the water. Chriton clenched his teeth and maintained the grip he got on Malachi's arm, pulling Malachi with him.

Mali and I backed up from the frothing whirlwind of splashing water that the wrestling men kicked up.

Once they both stopped, Malachi started towards his daughter. Mali shrieked and laughed when her dad caught her around the waist and tossed her into the water.

CHAPTER 19

CHRITON

The sky was dark, the stars were out, and three of us were sitting around the fire. An exhausted Mali was tucked into bed and fast asleep.

After swimming, we cooked dinner and cleaned up. As the evening fell, and the temperature with it, we changed into warmer clothes.

Malachi was wearing a black canvas jacket that had more pockets than I cared to count with a pair of dark wash jeans. I was wearing a lined fleece jacket and a pair of canvas pants. Leah was swathed in Malachi's sweatshirt and a pair of my sweatpants.

"I have to pee." She stated, rising from the fire and walking behind the tents towards the bushes that housed the outhouse.

She was gone about five minutes when I heard a soft scuffing sound followed by a hiss. Straightening in my chair, I held up a hand and cut Malachi off from what he was saying.

Malachi froze and cocked his head, listening just as I was. This time I heard a low vibrating growl before something scrambled over the ground. It sounded as if something was moving through the trees and around the tents. Fast.

Shit. I heard Malachi voice in my head. I watched as he silent stood from his chair and took two steps towards the direction we last heard the sound.

There was a soft coughing sound and another hiss. More scuttling. This time it started near the lake and headed straight towards the trees and the outhouse Leah was in.

Leah!

We both started sprinting through the brush, desperate to reach the outhouse only to find it empty. Except for the clothes Leah was wearing. Malachi crouched down and gathered up the clothes, his eyes darting through the dark.

"Whose out there?" He called.

The growl came from over by the tents. We were halfway back when a loud cracking sound brought us up short.

I knew that sound. And I was pretty sure Malachi knew that sound as well. Especially if his gleeful grin was anything to go by. I returned his grin when he turned his gaze to me.

You go left along the pond, I will go right. Drive her towards the clearing behind the tents.

Then what?

Then we get to have a turn with the whip.

Moving with slow footsteps, I crouched down slightly and snuck quietly back to the tents. I may or may not have added a slight scuff every now and then while I moved around the tents and along the beach. Another hiss and a disturbingly close crack sent me lurching forward. I caught a flash of pale skin dressed in a jagged leather bikini darting around one of the tents and straight towards Malachi.

I pulled my jacket off and gave chase.

Once clear of the tents and deep in the clearing, Leah spun around with a growl and cracked the whip at me.

I jerked back when I felt the sting of air. The fabric of the t-shirt I was wearing split right down the center of my torso.

"What are you playing at woman?" I growled only to jerk back when she sent that whip cracking again. This time it was along my arm and shoulder to slice away more fabric. With a hiss she spun and ran.

Right into the waiting arms of Malachi.

Leah snarled and kicked out wildly when Malachi caught the whip and spun her around. He held her to his chest by way of the handle of the whip pressing into her collarbone and neck. Leah gripped the handle around his hands and struggled fiercely while emitting those fascinating little growls.

Her beautiful breasts were jiggling delightfully from where they were cupped and lifted by leather material that scarcely contained her. Her stomach was stretched out deliciously and her muscled thighs and calves were strained as she was drawn up onto her tiptoes. The little bottoms with their jagged edges barely covered the swell of her pussy let alone the globes of her ass.

At the erotic sight before me my dick was immediately hard and demanding its due.

"What have we here?" Malachi crooned, running his face along hers, forcing her to jerk her head to the side.

I prowled towards the two of them, pulling the remains of my shirt off.

"Men, bad." Leah growled animalistically, still struggling fiercely.

Gripping her chin, I pulled her face to mine and leaned down to her. "Very bad."

Leah snarled when Malachi knelt, forcing her to kneel with him.

"There's my love." I hummed, running my knuckles along her cheek. Malachi helpfully used the whip to force her face up to mine.

The sexy little thing before me bared her teeth at me and hissed.

"Such a wild little thing." I grinned wickedly. "Do you see that protrusion in my pants?"

Her eyes dropped to my pants and the protrusion in question. The swollen length of my dick was bulging out, tenting the fabric of my pants.

"Dirty man." she growled low in her throat. "Bad." Then she snapped her teeth at me.

Malachi gave the whip handle a hard jerk backwards. "That is not for biting."

"Bite bad man." She hissed back at him.

"No. Kiss." I coached hoarsely, sliding my finger through her hair.

"Kisssss." She drew the word out as if testing it, her gray eyes dropping down to the front of my pants. I felt my dick jerk harshly, spurting out precum in preparation of having her wide mouth stretching around it.

"Yes. Kiss. In your mouth." My hand fell from her hair to drag my thumb over her lips.

"Mouth. Food." She exclaimed hoarsely and leaned forward to suck and nibble on the protrusion.

"Fuck." I grunted in surprise while my hips jerked.

"Food." She licked the fabric covering me then she frowned, made an adorably disgusted face and pulled her face away. "No food."

"Tastes good." Malachi assured her, his eyes dark and filled with desire.

I used my free hand to open my pants and push them and my underwear down far enough that my demanding sex could pop out.

It was fat and pulsing, the head flushed bright red with my arousal. Leah's eyes dropped back to my crotch and I watched her pupils blow wide and her throat work in a swallow

"Baaad man." She gasped then grunted gutturally and began struggling once again. "Not food! Dirty! Blech! Bad, bad man!"

"Enough!" Malachi snapped out.

I gripped her jaw tightly, holding her in place and spreading her lips with the pressure.

She whimpered and raised pleading eyes up to me. She looked so deliciously edible. Her breasts were rising and falling with her heavy breathing. Her body held tightly to Malachi's while he pressed his head to the side of hers, his eyes filled with a wickedly gleeful gleam.

"Lick it." He demanded, using the whip to guide her head forward so that her lips brushed my dick.

She twisted herself violently only for him hold her tighter. "Lick." He snarled at her.

She darted her tongue out for the quickest taste. My sensitive flesh flared and tingled at the feel of her moist little tongue flitting over it.

"Again." I ordered harshly.

Leah whimpered and dragged the flat of her tongue along my flesh, running all the way up its length to the tip. Her whimpers turned into moans and her tongue kept licking. Her head tilted back and forth in her attempt to taste all of me.

"Such a hungry girl." I moaned softly. "Suck me, precious. Get all of it."

She hissed and growled but still dragged her mouth up my dick to rapturously suck the crown of my cock between her lips. Her mouth felt divine. Wet and hot and tight. Perfect. Her lips were stretched wide around me. She sucked on the spongy tip while rubbing the sensitive glands with her tongue.

"Oh fuck, precious." I groaned in pleasure, my hand tightening automatically on her hair. "You have one hell of a mouth."

"She really does." Malachi agreed hoarsely, tilting his head to kiss and suck at the line of her jaw and down her stretched neck.

Beginning slow, I started thrusting my dick along her tongue. When I pushed too far and caused her to gag I drew away. Leah snarled around my dick, bobbing forward to chase my cock.

"She wants it, don't you, Teach?" Malachi whispered into her ear. In answer, Leah's hand came up to claw her fingers over my abdomen.

Adjusting my hand in her hair, I thrust deep once again making her gag. By the fourth time, her throat opened up and my tip slid inside. She was looking up at me, her wet eyes filled with her hunger.

I kept working my dick in and out of her mouth, pushing further into her throat each time. Her talented tongue caressed over me while my meat made use of the friction of her esophagus. Rapture flared through me, and it felt like my semen was boiling for release.

"Yes, precious. Just like that." I breathed down at her, my chest rising and falling with my pleasure. "Fuck, you can suck cock, Leah. I really want to come in your mouth, but I want to come somewhere else more."

I pulled her head back and her swollen lips left me with trail of drool. I shivered when the cold night air brushed over my wet dick. Malachi rose from his knees, bringing her with him before releasing her into my grip. With one of my hands still in her hair, the other fell to the soft skin of her waist.

"Bad man." She whispered right before my lips dropped to hers.

I felt her hand slide up my abdomen, over my heavy pecs, up my neck and into my hair. I loved the feel of her hands on my skin. My tongue delved deep into her mouth, twining with hers. Leah whimpered into my mouth, and I felt her try to step closer to me. I moaned softly, feeling her soft, leather covered breasts press into my chest. I felt her fingers tightened in my hair right before she painfully yanked my head back.

"Dirty, bad, man." She spat, baring her teeth at me.

"I am about to show you how bad I really am, precious." I snarled and knocked her hand from my hair.

Leah gasped when Malachi spun her around and dropped her into the soft dirt. She fell to her back with a soft oomph, her legs splayed out.

"No!" She snarled, sitting up and swiping her clawed hand out at him when he knelt down at her feet.

"Son of a bitch." Malachi barked and jerked back.

"Ah ah." My hand flashed out to catch Leah's wrist right before she could reach him. Catching her other wrist, I muscled her back to the ground holding her wrists stretched up above her head.

She kicked out wildly at Malachi only to have him expertly push her thighs apart and crouch between them. Pressing a hand to her stomach, he held her twisting body down. Then he grinned down at her while his other hand came up, the blade held there flashed open. "No." She gasped when the leather underwear was expertly sliced up the sides and ripped away

"Bad man." Leah cried when Malachi gripped her thighs. His hands guided her legs up and around his shoulders. "I like to eat too." He pointed out as his mouth dropped down to eat her sex.

Leah's head fell back and she arched up into him with a pleasure filled cry. My dick pulsed at that delicious sound. Transferring both her wrists to one hand, I stretched over her body to slide the closed blade from Malachi's grip around Leah's thighs.

Malachi's dark eyes flashed open and glinted as I snicked open the blade and used it to slice open the front of the leather bra keeping me from Leah's luscious breasts. The material immediately spread and those quivering globes popped free. Pale and smooth, tipped with pink, hard nipples.

That was when Leah brought her foot up and violently kicked out at Malachi's shoulder sending him sliding back about a foot. At the same time the slippery woman twisted right out of my hands. I was so surprised in that moment, my mind was struggling to figure out what just happened and what to do about it.

Leah rolled to her feet and began to sprint away. She only got five feet because while my brain was trying to catch up Malachi's wasn't. The whip whistled out and locked around her arms and torso which caused her to jerk to a stop. The movement was so sharp that she almost fell onto her face before she was yanked backwards. Malachi was luckily already on the move, his arms circling her locked down torso and lifting her around.

That leather whip wrapped around her torso looked so deliciously erotic that I was forced to grip the root of my cock painfully tight in order to stop myself from coming right then and there. Her bared breasts were now plumped out and displayed from between the winding pieces of leather pressing around them.

She growled and hissed, kicking her legs wildly. "Bad man. Not food."

"Very well, Teach. If you don't want to feed us, I guess we will just have to contend ourselves with something else." The palm of his hand found her center, two of his fingers pushing into her pussy.

"No! Bad man. Not for bad man." She denied, shaking her head wildly and arching her body in an attempt to dislodge his fingers. Finding my feet, I prowled forward, gripped her jaw and guided her face up.

"Oh yes." I bent over her and soothed in her ear. "Perfect fit."

Malachi set her feet on the ground and spun her around before lowing her back to the cool dirt. This was all done so fast that she looked slightly dazed. Malachi set a foot on the whip still circling her arms and torso, holding her down. "Stay." Malachi ordered, stripping himself out of his jacket before pulling off his shirt and working his pants open. I grinned when Leah's eyes widened and dragged over the flesh he was revealing to her. My own hands pushed my pants and underwear from my hips and kicked them away.

Stepping over her, I knelt down until my hips straddled hers, allowing Malachi to remove his foot and finish undressing. Leah's eyes dropped to my cock. The angry, blood filled muscle was bobbing, pointing straight up her stomach to the eyes she was devouring me with.

"Beautiful." I whispered, my finger pinching down on one of the nipples peekabooing out from the twining leather and pulling it out.

Leah whimpered, her chest rising to follow my fingers.

"There's my love." I rasped darkly right before my mouth covered her other nipple. I sucked that delicious nub of flesh deep into my mouth, my tongue flicking over the tip while my teeth bit down painfully around it.

I felt Leah's body jerk and shudder against mine. Her legs shifted and trembled and she let out a gasping cry right before her breathing stopped for a long moment. Sitting up, I was amazed to see her face flushed with pleasure and her eyes rolled up in her head. Her breathing finally sucked back in. She blinked and her trembling body relaxed back into the dirt.

"Did you just come, Teach?" Malachi's voice asked hoarsely, his eyes staring down at her with surprise. My eyes caught on his dick when he knelt down beside us, his hand slowly fisting up and down that heavy post.

"No." She denied, shaking her head fiercely.

Malachi's hand flashed out and caught her jaw. "Since I have a strong feeling that you are lying to us, we are going to need proof."

I chuckled and shook my head before dropping back down to take her other nipple the same way I took the first. The orgasm she denied dragged her under for the second time. Leah whimpered, her body convulsing and gone. Straightening, I shift my hips back and lodged my cock at the entrance of her extremely wet pussy.

I grinned when Malachi bent over and covered her breathless lips with his palm. She arched and screamed when I plunged my dick into her. I could feel her tightness contracting with her orgasm, sucking at my thrusting dick rapturously. Needing deeper, I kneed her legs apart and dropped my hips down to hers, seating my dick root deep.

"Fuck." I breathed, my head hanging on my neck as I immediately withdrew and slammed back into her.

My hips slapped harshly against her as I fucked her. I relished in the rapturous feel of my dick shuffling in and out of her dripping hole. She always felt so perfect around me. One of my hands gripped her thigh in a tight grip, cocking it up and around my jackhammering hips.

"B-bad man." She gasped out when Malachi finally slid his palm from her swollen lips and down to her jaw.

"Good man." I shook my head, lowering my lips to hers. "Good man makes you feel good."

"Yes." Leah whimpered into my mouth. "Good man."

I felt the whip loosen from around her and her small hands immediately rose to clutch at my sweat slickened shoulders and neck. I dropped my torso down to her, my chest rubbing deliciously along hers. My eyes stared down, glowing blue, branding deep into her soul.

I grunted when I felt her leg give a shove and I was rolled to my back with her straddling me.

Her hands pressed into my pecs and her hips began to move while she rose and fell over me. Her eyes stayed locked to mine. The feel of her clenching and unclenching around me, providing my nerves even more friction was driving me crazy with pleasure. That coupled with her hips rocking my dick along her grasping muscles and I was practically gone. She looked like the goddess of divine rapture, rising and falling over me, forcing my pleasure higher and higher.

"I love you." She whispered down at me.

I felt her words deep in my soul. I could see my skin glowing as my whole being reached out and circled around her, my DNA dispersing around her, through her. I could see her edges turning fuzzy and mixing with mine.

"I see you." She whispered, running her hand up my torso and neck to cup my jaw and cheek. "My love. So beautiful."

She saw me, always. She was a part of me. Body and soul, deep inside me.

"Leah, my precious love." I cried out and everything snapped back into place. My hands glided up her sides and pulled her down tight to me. "I love you."

At my words, her head fell back and she flew. When I felt her coming around me, her strong muscles milking my cock, my own orgasm bowled over me, intense, deep. It blinded me to everything accept her.

By the time my mind snapped back into place, I could feel her body splayed over mine, trembling and limp. Unconscious. I could see our souls dancing before I felt mine return to my chest. Malachi was bent over the ground beside us, his hand soothing up and down her back, his concerned eyes running over her face. I could hear soft words falling from his lips in an attempt to wake her up.

Meeting his eyes with mine, I decided to try a different tact.

I have you love. I have you. Shit, Leah, precious, you need to wake up and talk. I am freaking out here, about to lose my mind. Malachi looks like he's about ready to kill someone. Come on, precious.

"Chriton? Malachi?" Leah whimpered, her head shifting on my chest before tipping up to look at me with a confused frown.

Oh, thank you God. I sighed at the same time Malachi voiced, "Leah, baby, are you ok?"

"I am fine." She reassured him softly.

I love you. I smiled and relaxed when I heard her voice in my head.

She's talking to me. I shared with Malachi, tapping my temple.

His eyebrows jerked up before his eyes narrowed on her. I watched as a slow smile spread across his lips and his eyes lightened with a mixture of happiness and relief.

"She's talking to me too." He whispered out loud, his hand reaching out to slide down her cheek.

I grinned and rolled her off of me to the ground.

"What?" Leah gasped when Malachi's hands caught her and kept rolling her until she was once again on her front.

"My turn." He crouched over her and breathed in her ear.

"You think so?" Leah teased with a smile, her hips swaying back to brush over his distended sex.

"It's only fair." Malachi brushed her hair back so he could press the side of his face into hers. His hips rocked forward, running his cock through the globes of her ass. "He got to be the first inside that little pussy of yours. It's my turn for a first."

Leah froze and jerked wide eyes back to him.

"Malachi." She gasped, her face flushing.

"Yes, Teach." Malachi growled softly, his palm falling sharply onto the side of her ass.

I felt my satisfied dick twitch at the sound of the cry that fell from her lips.

"Owe." Leah hissed, her ass jerking at the sharp pain.

Lube and wipes are in my jacket. Malachi voiced in my head as his hand fell again, this time on the opposite cheek.

I rose to find his jacket and the items he requested, my fully aroused dick relishing in the rhythmic sound of Malachi spanking our woman. Each blow was following by a teeth clenching cry from Leah.

Quickly returning, I sprawled in the dirt on my side, my head resting up on my elbow, and resumed my voyeurism. It didn't take long until Leah was begging Malachi to stop, tears falling from eyes filled with the sharp pleasure he was delivering.

Malachi gripped her beat red ass cheeks and massaged them in deep, hard rotations causing Leah to whimper and arch. He spread her ass cheeks wide and looked at the virgin asshole he revealed. Sitting up, I followed his gaze, uncapping the lube to coat the hand I was using to milk my aching cock.

Malachi reached a hand out to me, his eyes catching on my lube slicked sex and jacking hand before finding the tube I was setting in his hand.

"Ass up." He ordered, landing another ringing spank to Leah's abused ass.

Leah immediately obeyed, pushing her ass up but leaving her chest and head resting on the ground. Her fingers clenched into the dirt when he ordered her to spread her knees. I bit back a groan when he slicked his fingers with the lube and proceeded to fuck her ass with them.

She bit her lip and moaned, her face wincing as he worked to loosen her for his cock.

That wince soon disappeared and was replaced by pleasured whimpers. Malachi grinned when her hips began to move and grind against the fingers he was working in and out of her.

"Our girl likes a little ass fingering." I noted out loud, pulling my cock a little harder.

"Hmmm." Malachi hummed and removed his fingers.

"Ready for the big gun, precious?" I looked down into Leah's pleasure flushed face. "He's going to fuck you with his dick now. And that beast is very, very aroused."

Leah's eyes flared. Apprehension and anticipation. She was ready.

Malachi used copious amount of lube to coat his dick before fingering another fingerful into her ass. Bending over, I gripped the root of my dick tightly and covered her mouth with my hand. Which was a good call because Leah shrieked loudly into my palm and slammed her fist into the ground when Malachi spread her ass cheeks and pushed his dick into her ass. It took a little bit of pressure before he finally succeeded in popping the head inside.

His hands found her twisting hips and held her still while he steadily impaled her with his erection. He was about halfway through when the pain in Leah's eyes flipped to pleasure and her fisted hand returned to gripping the dirt. Her shriek turned to a gasping cry. Her wildly twisting hips slowed into a shuddering rock.

"There we go." Malachi groaned, soothing a hand over her lower back and ass while he seated himself root deep. "Fuck Teach, your ass is so fucking tight. I am not going to last long."

Releasing her mouth, I laid on my back beside her and watched Malachi snake a hand under her hip. Three of his fingers pushed inside her wet pussy and his hand gripped down. Every time he thrust, jarring her forward, this caused his fingers and palm to rub over her clit and g-spot. Leah gasped and her hips jerked against the onslaught of sensation the talented man was delivering.

Highly aroused, my legs cocked apart and my knees rose. My tightly fisted hand flashed up and down my sensitive dick, working my own pleasure higher. I could hear the suctioning sound of Leah's cream filled pussy around Malachi's fingers. An erotic sound that was mixing with the slap of Malachi's hips against Leah's upturned ass.

"Fuck." I breathed softly, rapturous fire shivering over my flesh at the erotic scene playing out in front of me. My eyes caught on a set of balls swinging back and forth violently with the harsh fucking Malachi was doing. My free hand dropped down to squeeze and massage my own balls.

"Boss." Leah cried right before her body tensed up and her eyes rolled in her head. I watched as her legs shook wildly, barely holding herself up while her hips jerked so violently that Malachi was completely dislodged.

Malachi snarled and reached for the wipes. He quickly cleaned his cock off before grabbing her twisting hips and slamming his dick into her pussy. His eyes gleamed and his jaw clenched with determination. His muscles tensed so tight veins started popping out all over. My hand quickened on my cock as I watched him fuck the hell out of her.

Leah gasped in a breath right before his driving cock sent her flying once again. My head fell back and my hips twisted against the pleasure of my own hold. I was so close. I felt my balls stiffen and draw up within the hold I maintained on them. I let them go and pressed my palm firmly into them, my fingers finding and pressing into a spot on my taint that was connected to my prostate.

I heard liquid spray over the ground followed by Malachi's hiss. My head turned just in time to see the stimulating sight of Leah's stretched pussy gushing around the dick jackhammering in and out of it.

I moaned and felt my orgasm edging. I barely held it back, waiting for the right time, keeping myself right on that edge.

Leah gasped a breath in, signalling the end of her orgasm. Letting go of my balls, I reached out and covered the hand Malachi was using to clench Leah's hips. His fingers shifted mindlessly until they were linked with mine and we were both holding Leah.

Her upper body was limp against the ground, her mouth lax with the pleasure inundating her body. Pleasure that, with a grimace, Malachi sent her flying right back into. Leah's unfocused eyes rolled and her body tensed before bucking wildly. I let go, my dick swelling and jerking in my hand, at the same time Malachi's eyes went foggy and unfocused, his chest bowed up and his hips jolted forward, shooting his come deep inside Leah.

At the same time, I felt my own burning semen splashing up over my abdomen and chest.

My glazed eyes watched Malachi as three souls swirled up and danced in the night air, mixing and swirling before returning back to their owners. Malachi's chest arched when his soul left him, his eyes wide with awe. When his soul returned his eyes closed slowly, the look on his face one of pure joy.

I could feel those pieces of his soul, her soul, now a part of mine. His was dominant, powerful, protective. Hers was delicate yet strong, light and filled with love.

I love you. I told him when his eyes blinked open. His gaze dropped to mine for a long moment, his eyes studying mine with a deep intensity.

I love you, too. He finally whispered back, his eyes softening and filling with that love.

Using the wipes, we cleaned up our limp, satisfied woman before wiping ourselves down. Damp from the wipes and leftover sweat, we all started shivering in the freezing night air. Now that we weren't busy with our minds focused on other things, we noticed how fucking cold it was out.

We quickly redressed Leah and pulled on our own clothes before I lifted Leah up into my arms and carried her to the tent. Malachi made sure the fire was out and everything was locked down for the night before joining us. He helped Leah into one of his t-shirts and a pair of shorts before tucking her into the bed beside Mali.

I turned the lamp off and changed into my own pajama pants at the same time as Malachi. Then we both climbed into the other bed. I hummed softly and hugged the arms that Malachi tentacled around me. It really was a fantastic sleep being cuddled by him.

CHAPTER 20

MALACHI

I woke up to the smell of cold, fresh air. I could hear the soft lapping of waves on the beach mixed with the crackle of burning fire.

My arms were full of a soft limbed woman. I was laying on my side with her held in my arms, front to front. Her head was laying limply on my bicep, the lax fingers on one of her hands were tucked around the side of my neck, just under my jaw. The fingers of her other hand were caught on the side of the waistband on my pajama pants. Her leg was cocked up around my upper thigh, resting just under her fingers.

My arms were wrapped around her, one at her head and neck, the other around her ribs and down her back, my hand resting on the upper curve of her ass. One of my legs was out straight while the other was cocked up between hers and somehow wrapped around her bottom leg.

"Hmmm." I hummed and buried my face into her neck, breathing her warm scent deep into my lungs. Leah shifted slightly, her head moving to nuzzle into my chest, her fingers moving from my waist band to slide up my side and curl around my bicep.

Newly settled, she emitted a soft contended sound.

My limbs tightened slight around her, my heart filling at the feel of her sleeping soundly in my arms. While waking up with Chriton was interesting and the sleeps were admittedly good, Leah was a different sort of delight, small and delicate, made to be tucked into the bow of my body.

Coffee's ready.

Biting back a groan at Chriton's words, I cracked my eyes open to see the sun lightened tent empty but for Leah and I. I stretched, my limbs stiffening and extending around the woman sleeping in them before I landed a sucking kiss to the soft skin of her neck.

Leah sighed and shifted slightly, her head slowly moving until her lazy eyes met mine.

"Coffee's ready." I told her, reaching up to smooth the hair from her face.

"I heard." She whispered, stretching her body up until she could press a kiss to my lips.

I smiled and took my time returning her kiss. Sliding lips and caressing tongues. I slowly drew back and unwrapped myself from around her. Leah gave me a playful pout before rolling from the bed. I watched her pull on the hoody she wore last night and run her fingers through her hair in a vague attempt to tame the silky mass.

"Come on." She grinned and reached a hand down to me. She grunted and ended up using both hands to pull my disobedient body from the bed. I chuckled and shouldered a t-shirt over my chest before stepping out into the cold morning air.

Mali was seated by the fire. Chriton was in the gazebo, standing at the counter and fixing coffees. Leah dropped a hand to the top of Mali's head as she passed the girl on her way to the gazebo and Chriton.

"Morning, Mali-girl." I greeted my daughter, cupping her chin and tipping her head back to mine. "How'd you sleep?"

"Morning, dad. Good. And you?" She greeted back with a smile.

Chriton dropped his hand to the arms Leah circled around his waist, her head resting against his back, a beautifully contented look on her face.

"Great." I nodded, feeling rejuvenated, renewed out here among nature.

I watched Chriton's head slant to the side and I knew they were communicating with each other.

Leah smiled and dropped a kiss to his shirt covered back before stepping back. Chriton turned and bent down for his own wet morning kiss before handing her one of the coffee cups. Leah ambled out of the tent and sat beside Mali to drink her coffee.

"Thanks, man." I entered the gazebo to retrieve my own coffee, my hand finding and gripping the back of Chriton's neck.

Chriton nodded with a smile. "Anytime."

"Pancakes?" I asked, my hand loosening on his neck and sliding down to his chest. My heart gave a jolt when Chriton's hand snapped out and covered mine in a tight grip, pressing it into his pec.

"Sounds good." He gave me a nod and released my hand.

With a couple pats to his chest, I turned to gather what I needed from the icebox and the cupboards. I started measuring out the ingredients into a bowl, mixing them together into a thick batter. Leah joined me in the Gazebo, digging out a pan and a spatula that she carried to the fire. She set the pan on the metal grill that Chriton lowered so that it could warm before coming back in and stealing the butter from me. After dropping a dollop into the pan, she returned to dig out the syrup and jam setting those and the plates and utensils out on the picnic table.

I carried the batter out to the fire and began to cook pancakes.

After we ate, everyone cleaned up before getting ready for the day. I pulled on a pair of long cargo shorts with a t-shirt that I cut the sleeves off of. Added to that was my old, worn baseball hat and a pair of sunglasses. Chriton was dressed similarly, only his shirt was a tank, his shorts were jean and his hat was actually a bandana.

I almost swallowed my tongue when Leah stepped out of the tent wearing a pair of similar shorts to the ones she wore yesterday, these ones made from a black cargo material. Added to that was another bikini, this one slick, tight, and black. That was covered by a loose knitted sleeveless vest that tied just under her breasts. Her hair was tied back in a braid and she was wearing a pair of sunglasses.

Mali was wearing a cute little sundress over her bathing suit with a floppy hat and her own sunglasses.

By the time we were all ready the morning sun was getting hot.

Mali and Leah sprawled on the beach on top of a blanket they hauled out while I dug out the fishing poles and proceeded to teach Chriton how to fish.

"Are we going to eat what we catch?" Chriton asked, attaching his chosen hook to the line before yanking his finger away and giving it a shake. Very familiar with the move, I immediately knew that he caught his finger on the pointed tip. This was proven doubly when he glared at the hook and stuffed that finger into his mouth.

"That depends on how big of a fish we catch." I smiled knowingly over to him.

"Just so you know, I want to hate this just for that alone." He clipped out informatively. "But I am kind of excited to catch a fish."

I chuckled at that and showed him how to adjust his reel so he could cast out and reel in.

"Watch." I advised him, demonstrating how to cast, my line smoothly flying out over the pond with a whistle.

Chriton nodded and tried to mimic my movements, only to catch my arm with his hook.

"Fuck." I yelped and grabbed at the line to stop any more ripping from Chriton's attempted cast.

"Shit." Chriton dropped the pole to the ground and reached out to grip around the hook that was lodged in the back of my arm. "Fuck, Sorry."

"It's not the first time." I assured him through clenched teeth. "Just pull it out."

"Shit, ok." Chriton nodded, his own jaw firming, His fingers caught around the top of the hook and carefully rolled it out of my flesh.

I bit back my groan of pain as the hook moved and jerked in the muscle it was imbedded in before finally sliding free. Chriton winced and pressed his palm to the bleeding wound. "I think you need a bandage."

I twisted around to see my blood dripping through Chriton's fingers and down my arm. "Huh."

Chriton rolled his eyes at my reaction and called to the ladies. "Mali-girl, will you grab the first aid kit for me, please?"

"What happened?" Leah sat up and eyed us with concern while gesturing Mali to the tent.

"Chriton needs more practice casting." I called to her with a grin, remembering when Declan and I took her out fishing the first time. She didn't hook me, but she did hook Declan in the back of his shoulder. Back then the hooks carried barbs so it was a lot more interesting when I was forced to take a set of pliers to the hook to get it out.

"He hooked you, didn't he?" Leah smiled, her eyes warm and unfocused, obviously remembering the same memory I was.

"Yeah." Chriton cringed, taking the kit from Mali and flipping it open.

"I know how you feel, Chriton." Leah shrugged, laying back down.

Chriton proceeded to clean my arm and tape a bandage over the wound before flipping the kit back closed. "Thank you, Mali." Chriton smiled down at her.

"No problem." Mali raced off to return the kit to were she found it.

"You hooked Malachi?" Chriton asked Leah, reaching down for his pole.

Leah shook her head slowly, "No, Declan."

"She got him good." I told him, stepping behind him and covering his fingers with mine to show him the appropriate actions. "Like this." I drew our arms back before swinging them forward, my thumb working the reel so that the line released and flew over the pond to land with a soft plop. I let his hand go and jerked my chin at the rod. "Now reel in, slow. The key is to make it look like a bug or small fish."

Stepping away from Chriton, I retrieved my own pole and cast out to my own spot. By the time Chriton made his fourth cast he had it down pat and I no longer inwardly cringed with worry.

"This is actually very calming." Chriton noted, moving over to the ridge we were standing on yesterday. He made another cast before sitting down at the edge with one leg hanging and the other cocked up with his pole arm resting on the knee.

"It is." I followed him up, making my own cast and sitting back against a nearby tree. I pulled my hat down low and just let the line ride.

"You and Declan were close." Chriton noted, his voice quiet and curious but unsure.

"We were." I confirmed, tipping my hat back so that I could look over at him. "I was 18 when I joined the service. A nervous young boy that wanted to help his country. After bootcamp hell, I was placed onto this team that was led by this big blond bastard who was 6 years older than me. He was one hell of a teacher and had quite the sense of humor. The worst puns and dad jokes you ever heard. I didn't understand until he took a video call one day. The tiny blond girl on the screen was giggling madly at his jokes. I found out that she was an orphaned niece that he and his mother were now raising."

"Whenever we got leave he insisted on dragging me home with him to stay with his family." I shared memories I hadn't thought of in a long time. "Looking back now, I learned how to be a dad from him, from watching him with Leah. Fuck he loved her. You could see it shining in his eyes every time he looked at her. And she loved him right back just as fiercely."

"Seven years we worked together, every fucking day. He taught me everything I know. How to be patient and understanding, how to give the men what they needed even if it was simply allowing them to joke and blow off steam in the middle of a serious Op. He taught me to trust and rely on the men around me. He showed me the meaning of love and sacrifice. He was my mentor, my best friend, my soul brother." My jaw clenched tightly at the next memory. "Then he gave his life for ours, the team, and I went home and told that tiny blond girl, then a fifteen year old teenager, that the uncle she loved more than anything else in the world wasn't coming home. Never again."

"I was given lead of the team. I didn't want it. To me, the team was Declan's not mine. Not that any of that mattered because after they saw what happened to Declan, most of the men applied to be discharged or requested a transfer. And I slowly ended up with a whole new team. The first was Grayson. Stubborn fucker walked straight over any boundaries I had and declared himself my best friend." I chuckled softly.

"And Leah?" Chriton delved.

"We weren't close." I stated bluntly. "Not like you would think with how close we each were with Declan. We both kept each other at arms length. Me, because that's what I did, I kept people at arms length. Everyone except Declan. Her, probably because she automatically sensed my boundaries and went with it. She does that. Strangely, none of that stopped me from keeping an eye on her, or her from sending weekly care packages. She started that shit after Declan died."

"Why?" Chriton questioned. "Why keep an eye on her if you weren't close?"

"I really don't know." I shrugged and sighed. "I would like to say it was in honor of Declan. And it might have even started out that way but after a few years it kind of became a need, even an obsession. I needed to know where she was and how she was doing. I needed to have my finger on that pulse. Maybe it was some sort of intrinsic instinct, a gut feeling of what was to come. I don't know, I just did it."

"But then so did she. When my team was turned spec ops, similar to what we do now, we ended up spending a lot of time on the home front working with our own government and I still received those packages. Someway, somehow. No matter where I was, I got that weekly care package." I grinned proudly at the thought of how stubborn she was.

"Hmm." Chriton hummed, a thoughtful gleam coming to his eye.

"What?" I asked him.

"Well, it just seems interesting to me. How, despite the boundaries you set when you met her as a child, you both hung on to each other just enough." He described, holding his finger and thumb about an inch apart. "Then, when I came along, one of the first things I ended up doing is helping you teach yoga before taking the class over. I knew you weren't a fan of teaching the class and was happy to hand it over. I also now know that Leah is not a fan of yoga at all and yet there she was taking the class that we both were teaching. It all just seems very interesting, that's all."

"Tell me something." I stated, reeling my line in and casting it again.

"Hmm?" Chriton raised his eyebrows in question.

"Are you attracted to me?" I asked bluntly.

"I have no fucking clue." Chriton chuckled. "I won't lie, you are a very good looking male, but right now you are just a very close friend."

"Yeah, I hear that." I grunted, relaxing back into the tree. "You will let me know if that changes, right?"

"Only if you do the same." Chriton pointed out the fact that he noticed the change in my assessing looks.

"I am pretty sure you will know when I decide." I laughed, knowing full well that he would definitely be able to tell if or when my feelings deepened for him that way. Although, I couldn't lie, with the way he was with Mali and Leah I was looking at him with new eyes. The way he accepted and even relished everything, mostly me being in his life and now part of his Conversance, was frankly astounding.

"Why aren't you mad?" I blurted out. I couldn't understand why I myself wasn't mad, I just knew that everything felt right and complete with him a part of it.

Chriton frowned as he thought about everything. "I was in the beginning. Believe me, I wanted to wipe you from existence. But then you stepped up and opened the door that I thought was permanently locked to me. You offered her to me and with her, Mali and you. At the time I could do nothing else but jump at it. I didn't know where it was all going, I just knew that I damned well wanted to be a part of it. As time went on things began to feel more and more right. When the Conversance happened it felt like something just snapped into place and it felt complete in a way that was so much more than what I hoped for. I already loved Mali. I was quickly falling for Leah. But you, you were a nice surprise and I found myself loving you just as much as them. Now I wouldn't change it for the whole of the universe. When you opened that door, you gave me everything. More than everything."

I didn't know what to say to that, so I just nodded and tipped my hat back down to cover eyes.

I yelped when I felt someone grab my ankle and yank me along the rock of the outcropping. "What the...?" I yelped and pushed my hat back just as my body spun out into the air and fell into the water.

"What the hell?" I came up sputtering and glaring at the man that was crouched at the edge of the ridge.

"That's what you get for not giving back." Chriton growled down at me.

"For fuck sakes." I grunted, swimming over to the beach and walking from the water. Leah and Mali were watching me with wide eyes as I stomped from the water and gave myself a shake right over top of them. Both girls squealed and ducked away from the water flying from me. I pulled my wet shirt from my body and dropped it on the ground with a wet smack.

"Shit." Chriton squeaked when I turned and sprinted up the outcropping. He tried to get away but tripped over his fishing rod. "Fuck!" He yelled as I caught him around the waist and we both went over the edge.

"I love you, too, you fucker." I laughed when his head popped up to the surface of the water.

"You are such a dickhead." He growled and launched himself at me.

I was ready for him and we ended up wrestling each other down before popping up and doing it again. A loud splash beside us brought us both to a stop so we could look around. Mali's head came up beside Chriton's with a big smile. She proceeded to splash him with long sweeps of her arm.

"Here." Leah gestured form the edge she was sitting on. I swam over and held my arms up, catching her when she slid off the rock. Her bikini clad body slid erotically down mine until she stopped with her hands on my shoulders. She tilted her head and smiled, right before she dunked me.

She also came with me due to the tight grip I maintained on her waist. I caught her neck and pulled her to me so that I could share my air with her, and my tongue. By the time I allowed us to rise we were both flushed and breathless.

Grayson was off that night and he decided to drop by for a fire cooked supper and some smores. After Mali was tucked into bed we all sat around the fire talking quietly.

"Have you had any incidents since the giant spider was destroyed?" Grayson's question sent shivers up my spine and my mind travelling back to that night.

I woke up to a security alert from Operations. They didn't know what was going on but the lower level lights and cameras were down and they were getting reports of weird noises. They also told me that Marko gave them orders to keep it quiet. Unfortunately, as high as Marko's clearance was, mine was higher.

Zara showed up to watch Mali for me just as I got the alert that the noises stopped and everything was back in working order. They did mention that the lower level residents were hauling something big and unhuman looking to the Bay.

I walked out of my suite and met Lysander on the way to the Bay only to step into my nightmare. Mind breaking. The familiar shape of thin pointy legs, longer than my mind could accept, were sticking out of the incinerator. At that point all I could do was tell myself over and over again that it was dead, the spider that was most likely bigger than me was dead. It was dead.

"No." I breathed and shook myself from the memory. "I haven't."

"That's awesome." Grayson grinned.

"You know, I don't think I have ever been present for any of the incidents when Malachi meets his phobia." Chriton noted, relaxed back in his chair with his legs straight out in front of him.

"My first time was interesting." Leah brought up with a soft smile.

"Fuck." I groaned, dropping my head back and pressing my palms to my eyes.

"One those big, black, wolf spiders. To be honest, I hated those things just as much as he did, they were huge and ballsy. It was the first weekend that Malachi came home with Uncle Declan. We were walking into the garage when one of those bastards dropped right down, almost landing on the top of Malachi's head. I remember shrieking and backing away. I also remember Malachi doing the same. Only when he backed away he pulled out his gun and took aim. Luckily, Uncle Declan relieved Malachi of the gun at the same time he slapped the spider to the ground. The spider ended up dead. And Malachi didn't accidently shoot an innocent bystander that may or may not have been passing by the garage at the wrong time." Leah shared, her gleaming eyes turning to meet mine. "It took him months before he would voluntarily go through that door after that. Even Uncle Declan checking the frame for him didn't help."

"I am sorry, but that entrance was horrible. It fucking attracted those things. Every time that door was opened, at least one of them dropped down." I explained, using my hand and splayed fingers as an example. "I swear it was like an amusement park for them."

"It was bad. I would shove the door open, wait a minute for them all to drop then I would run and jump through." Leah agreed with a nod.

"My first time was when we were deep in some African jungle, and we came across this huge web with the damned thing sitting right in the middle." Grayson explained, holding his hand up as an example. "I was still fairly new to the team and there was my team leader, frozen, staring at this web and spider like it was the anti-Christ. I swear, the spider twitched, and the Boss-man lost it. One of the older men spun around and literally sprinted away when Malachi turned to him. I found out later that it was because he was the one carrying the rocket launcher and he didn't want Malachi to steal it from him. Not that it mattered because Malachi opened fire on the thing anyways. By the time he was done, not only was the arachnid dead and the web in strings, but the surrounding trees behind it were gone. Malachi put so many bullets into them that he shot them in half. Luckily we were in an area where being silent wasn't a must."

"If silence was needed, I wouldn't have shot it." I shrugged, pointing out the many times when I successfully bit back my fear in order to save lives. It was definitely not easy and those haunting times still lived in my mind.

"Like the time you crashed the helicopter?" Grayson asked with a burst of laughter.

"I did not crash it." I growled, defending myself for the fiftieth time on this particular incident. "I would have had to have been flying it at the time to have crashed it. But I wasn't."

"Only because you jumped out of the damned thing before it hit the ground." Grayson laughed. "All because a damned spider was in it."

"It was a fucking bird eater. And if he couldn't handle the helicopter he shouldn't have taken it from me." I snarled over at my second in command.

"You have a problem." Grayson pointed at me with a set of raised eyebrows.

"Not anymore. Catro killed it." I argued back.

"Umm, he only killed the one controlling the spiders in that particular mountain. Not for the rest of the world." Chriton maddeningly pointed out.

"You are seriously looking for trouble." I warned him, my eyes automatically darting around to look over the area.

"I am just pointing out a fact." Chriton noted with a shrug.

"Yes." Grayson praised, lifting his hand to the man sitting beside him for a high five.

"As phobia's go, that one is extreme." Chriton kept pushing.

"Look, I have no idea why I am terrified of them, but I am. I kind of blank out and lose all control over my actions. The only times I have been able to even remotely control my fear is when I know death is stalking someone I care about." I explained with a shake of my head.

"You need to own it." Chriton looked over me with a set of assessing eyes. "It's a part of who you are. It makes you unique and individual. When I hear anything about spiders my mind automatically thinks of you. And I am still a virgin in that area."

"He's right, you know." Grayson agreed, jerking a thumb to Chriton. "I love you, man. A lot of people do. And your severe phobia is part of that. It's the same as everyone talking about Lysander's obsession with chocolate."

"I liked the fact that we both had the same phobia. It was one of the only things we had in common when I was young. And I wouldn't change that even now that we are both adults." Leah told me.

Reaching over, I caught her fingers in mine and brought her knuckles up to my mouth.

"What is Andromeda like, Chriton?" Leah changed the topic and asked Chriton.

"Well, precious, I hate to burst your bubble but it's very similar to Earth only with more land. It's more 50-50 when it comes to the land/water split. There are green forests and jungles. Mountains, rivers, lakes, deserts, ice caps. Our wildlife is similar but different. The Nordic home world is also like Earth and Andromada. This is probably why our races are so similar and we are breeding compatible even though humans are still such a young race." Chriton smiled as he explained, his eyes gleaming with happiness at Leah's question. "Although, the sky on Andromeda is more purple than the blue here and the sky on the Nordic home world is greener. But that is mostly due to the differences in suns and atmospheres."

"Do you think we might go there someday?" Leah questioned next, her eyes gleaming with anticipation.

"I would love for you all to see it, someday. But that is going to be something that is discussed in the future. Right now, Earth needs us and our life is here." Chriton told her honestly.

"Do you have a home there?" Leah asked, tilting sideways in her chair to relax against my shoulder.

"I do. Although, I am very rarely there. Like the Base, it's built into the side of one of the mountains. Unlike the Base, it has windows and decks and tons of fresh air. A beautiful mix of indoor and outdoor. Like most of our homes, it is made to fit in with nature instead of overpowering it. It is also built to outlast the years that I am not there." Chriton tilted his head back to look up into the sky, his voice going soft and quiet. "I honestly cannot wait to show it to you."

"Am I invited?" Grayson asked with a set of raised eyebrows.

"Come on, Grayson." Chriton groaned over at him causing Grayson to frown in disappointment. "I wouldn't be raving about it in front of Malachi's best friend if I didn't expect him to at least visit our home on Andromada."

Grayson looked down at his lap and smiled. "You know, I love it out here at the Ranch, under the open sky, out in the elements after years of being stuck in that mountain. But I won't lie, I miss my brothers in arms, I miss seeing Malachi and Mali on a daily basis."

"Mali and Malachi miss you too. Malachi has seemed very lost and alone since you moved to the Ranch." Leah told him, her hand soothing up and down my arm.

She was right. Since my best friend stepped up to run the Ranch security and left the Base I have felt lonely. Lysander and I maintained a good working relationship, but that really was it. Zara and her husbands helped out with Mali quite a bit, but we didn't hang out. The team and I would always consider each other brothers in arms, but we rarely spent time together outside of that. Other than Grayson, I really had no close friends.

Grayson looked over at me, his eyes filled with surprise. "You are always the one including me, not them. You are the open one, the friendly one, the one they all wanted around. Not me. I am closed off. I have boundaries. I keep people at bay. It's so ingrained in me that I often don't even realize that I am doing it. You are the type of person who doesn't see that shit." I explained to him. "You just accept and befriend."

"I guess. But you keep everything in order. You hold everyone together, keep us all going. I don't know how many times we've been trapped in fucked up situations where we all thought we were going to die. But you kept us all calm, you got us out. And you fucking care. Sometimes too damned much. You don't think I didn't see those fucking boundaries. I did. And I love that you have them because sometimes you care too damned much. No matter where we go, you collect people and no matter how much you try to withdraw from them you still take it all on. You blame yourself. Deliah, Guard, Slip, Ember, Leah, so many others. You blamed yourself." Grayson explained wearily.

"What?" I scowled at Grayson before darting my confused gaze to Chriton. He was rubbing his neck with a frown.

"Isn't this all just fucking beautiful?" A thick male voice asked from our darkened surroundings.

My trusty M18 Sig Sauer was palmed as I rose from my camping chair, kicking it out of my way. I felt Leah stand behind me, hugging into my back as I slowly turned, examining the area the voice came from.

Out of the corner of my eye I saw Chriton's unfocused eyes blink, his body slowly falling limp in the chair. Grayson was standing over Chriton with his own gun in hand.

I felt Leah shifting against me, her hands sure and quick as they moved over me before she turned and her back pressed into mine. I knew that she was taking aim with one of the other guns I kept on me.

"Is that any way to greet guests?" A suited man strolled from between the two tents with a grin. He was a short man with greying hair. Grayson froze and put his hands up when the muzzle of a shining black weapon pressed into the back of his head. A black haired woman with pale blue eyes shifted to the side of him. Her eyes were ice cold, emotionless. She was dressed in a suit just like the man.

Another two men stepped out from the sides of the tent, both suited and carrying their own weapons.

"Dante, I assume. How?" I demanded, wanting to know how they bypassed security.

"I believe you called the boy 'Slip.'" The grey haired man chuckled, stepping closer to the flickering light of the fire. "He was nice enough to slip a few DNA profiles into your medical database for me. You know, before he was murdered by your doctor." He gave me a nod when I showed my clear surprise at his knowledge. "Yes, I know about that. That damned doctor stole one of my best men. But in the end I got the best of him, because he never even realized that there was a number of extra profiles in his system."

"You obviously don't know everything." Grayson chuckled at the man, his eyebrows arched up with amusement. "The good doc has nothing to do with DNA profiles but keep thinking you got him over a barrel."

The grey haired man paused at that before his grin returned. "It doesn't matter. All that really matters now is the fact that I can in fact walk right through all of your fancy assed security and walk right back out with one of your leaders." The grey haired man walked over to the woman still holding her weapon on Greyson. He reached over and ran his fingers through Chriton's dark hair gently before yanking his head back. "And the coups de gras, I now have an Andromadan."

"No." I shook my head, my eyes meeting Chriton's. His gaze was unfocused, but I could see the denial in his glinting there. My mouth firmed and my eyes begged him. "You don't have an Andromadan." I stated to the gray haired man just as Chriton sank through the chair and into the Earth.

Leah's body relaxed slightly against my back and we both slowly raised our weapons up in surrender.

My gun dropped to the ground from lax fingers when one of the two men stepped forward and slammed the butt of his gun into my temple. Sharp pain slashed through my skull right as my mind went black.

CHAPTER 21

CHRITON

Everything was hazy and I was having trouble gathering my thoughts and focusing my ability. I struggled to get myself under control. I knew what I needed to do. I forced myself to focus on that and just that.

I needed to get to Mali, I needed to get her out of there. It felt like forever as I pushed myself through the dirt and rock around me until I was sure I was where I needed to be. I slowly stepped up and out of the Earth, luckily right beside Mali's bed. She was awake, curled into a ball on the bed and staring at the door to the tent with tears running from her eyes.

She jerked in surprise when she saw me before relaxing in relief. I held my finger up to my lips in a bid for silence before reaching for her. She darted a look at the tent door before silently crawling over to me. Once I held her safely in my arms, I slit open the back of the tent and ran silently into the trees.

Just in time.

I heard the men searching the tent for us before following us into the woods. I could feel Mali's body jerking against mine as she silently sobbed in fear. Finding a slight break in the trees, I slid down an embankment and into the pond. It was a straight drop off for which I was thankful for. Mali buried her head in my neck and tightened her arms around me. I silently shifted us along the pond edge until we reached an area that was clogged by overhanging bushes.

Dipping down into the water, I rose up inside the shell of the brush and waited. Mali snuffled softly as we listened to the men moving around us, following our trail before realizing that we went into the pond and were now lost to them. I heard them move back to the camp but stayed where we were. Mali stopped crying laying her head listlessly on my shoulder.

Hours passed slowly before my mind cleared enough that I was able to reach out to my father and brother.

It was a stuttering, stammering start before I was finally able to get what happened out. After talking to them, I desperately reached out to Leah and Malachi but got nothing back. Refusing to give up, I kept reaching for them, over and over again.

"Mana?" Mali whispered, her frozen body shaking against mine.

"I have you, Mali-girl." I told her through my own clattering teeth. "Help is coming."

"Dad and mom? Uncle Grayson?" Mali asked in a small, worried voice.

I closed my eyes tightly at the true realization that my Conversances were gone, taken by one of the Drako Bosses. My arms tightened around my terrified daughter, holding her close. "We will get them back, Mali-girl." I stated, my voice hardening with determination. "We will get them back." I wouldn't stop until I did.

At my words, Mali started sobbing again. "They took them, didn't they?"

"Yes, Mali." I confirmed through my own thick throat.

"Come on out, boy." Dad's voice called.

"Come on, Mali-girl, let's get out of here and make a plan to get our family back." Holding Mali, I ducked us back down into the cold water and came up clear of the brush. Dad was standing at the edge of another break in the trees beside the pond. When he saw us, he extended a hand down to help us out. Exhausted and frozen, I allowed him to pull us out but refused him when he offered to take Mali from me.

There was no way I was letting my daughter go.

Bane and Coren were ready with some towels which they quickly covered Mali and I with. We were guided to a heated truck and the medical team that was waiting inside. Dr. John James and his nurse checked Mali and I over as we were driven straight to the tent village. Mali and I showered and dressed in clean clothes before I tucked the exhausted girl into bed in one of the large tents. She held on to me tightly as I rocked her gently back and forth. When I felt her finally drift off to sleep, I rose to sit at the small table that was set to one side.

I bent over the table, exhausted, still unfocused and erratic. Setting my face in my hand, I used a thumb and forefinger to rub at my sand coated eyes.

"We found blood." Bane told me, sitting down beside me. "In three different places. I am guessing that they were knocked out before they were taken."

"I figured that was what happened when I didn't hear any noise from them." I sighed, my mind doing the same thing it did at least every fifteen minutes, reach for them. "Did you find the DNA profiles?"

"Zara is on it as we speak. She found two. The female and the older male." Dad said, carefully sitting on the edge of the bed so that he didn't disturb the little girl sleeping there.

"Dante." I stated the name I heard Malachi say.

"The Drako Boss?" Bane hissed, his head twisting to look at Bailor who was standing just inside the tent flap. Coren was standing beside him, both men stood with their arms crossed.

"Yes." I snarled out, my hand fisting tightly with the anger brewing deep in my soul.

"We need to get Marko on this." Dad stated, standing from the bed and striding from the tent.

"Lysander. The First team needs to be readied to go in. We need to talk to Chern." Coren grunted, rising his coms and typing away as he followed my father out the door.

It took around forty-five minutes for dad to return from the Base with a ship full of people he figured we would need. In the meantime, Bane and Bailor worked on getting another tent connected to mine for everyone to meet in. A couple small tables and one long one was brought in along with a large number of chairs. There was also a whiteboard and a peg board along with a number of electronics that they were getting set up.

Seeing all of this, I wanted to scream at them. All of them. Time was running out. And they were fucking around. Instead of watching them, I closed the flap between the two tents and paced. My mind planning. I could just walk right in there and take them out. I could. I could kill one man at a time, making my way through until I reached them.

My hands fisted and un-fisted as I paced furiously. All I needed was a direction and a set of blueprints.

I heard everyone arriving and bit my tongue. My head rotated on my neck. I needed to be patient, work with them.

For now.

Chriton, brother. Coren's voice called me into the room with the others.

I stepped into the room and moved my gaze over the group gathered. Marko's voice was coming over someone's coms from where he stayed behind in Operations. A holographic image of the world was spinning in the middle of the table.

Lysander was working with Chern, talking with the man quietly. Coren and dad were standing beside Bane in front of the white board writing information down as it was given to them. The First Team, now missing two members, were sitting at the long table checking over their weapons and reviewing the information that was coming in.

I turned slight when I heard Mali shifting in the bed, holding the tent flap open so that she could see me. "Mana." She whispered, her wide worried eyes coming over to me.

"Come here, Mali-girl." I whispered hoarsely, bending down to catch the girl who climbed from the bed and raced towards me. I lifted her up against my chest and turned back to see the group of people staring at us with varying stages of worry and apology.

Mali wrapped her arms around my shoulders and cuddled deep into my chest. My hand automatically came up to cup the back of her head protectively.

"How is she?" Rashnia asked, his eyes, one blue, one green, assessing over us.

"Worried. Scared." Bane darted a look over us, answering for me.

"Here." Rashnia stepped over to take her from me.

"No!" Mali screamed sharply, her arms tightening around me until I could barely breathe.

I soothed my hand up and down her back, narrowing my eyes in warning at the man. No one was taking my daughter from me.

"Sorry." Rashnia cringed and held his hands up while backing away from us.

Mali relaxed slightly and my eyes caught on the hologram zooming in further and further. North America, the eastern side of the USA, Georgia, Sea Island. There was a huge sprawling compound that surrounded a large mansion. My eyes took in every detail I could.

"Ok, this is the place that Dante reportedly calls home. These are the most recent satellite images we have been able to retrieve. Unfortunately, they are at least three years old." Marko started describing. "The place is walled up and protected worse than any prison I have ever seen. The only two ways in I have been able to find are here and here." The map lit up yellow in two areas along the outside of the compound, one to the north and one to the west.

Shifting my gaze over to the whiteboard, I read over the information there.

"From the information that we gathered from Chern and Bane it is extremely secure." Dad turned from the board and began sharing all of the information they gathered. "Bane unfortunately doesn't have much as he only visited the place once, but Chern was one of Dante's, uh, well, men and spent most of his time there. According to him there are around fifty people that work for Dante. They are all housed in separate groups around the compound." Marko helpfully lit up those in green on the map.

"Night shift consists of ten guards. Two watching the cameras in the main security room while the other eight make rounds around the house and compound." Dad pointed out those areas as they lit up blue. "There are around eight brainwashed zombies that are housed separately from the rest of the security." That area was orange. "There are two or more on shift at all times with at least one as personal security for Dante himself. With Chern's help Marko was able to track down those people in the harvested files."

Lysander rose from his seat, his hand gripping Chern's shoulder in a reassuring way. Pictures of those people began to show up in the hologram along with their names, ages, and defining features. My eyes latched on to one of the two women. A familiar woman with black hair and icy blue eyes. Nephthys. That was the name they gave her. Egyptian goddess of death, darkness, and the protector of souls. My mind latched onto the last part of her description. I prayed that part was apt even though I highly doubted it.

"She was there." I rasped out, staring into the emotionless blue eyes of the woman. "She had her weapon pressed to the back of Grayson's head."

"I want in on this." Chern stood as soon as I finished speaking, his eyes slightly wild looked. I turned to look at him, his eyes darting between the image of the woman and me.

Having received all of the information I needed, I quietly stepped back through the tent flap into the bedroom tent before I silently walked from that tent and made my way to the ship. Well, ships, as it turned out. Not only was there one of the Andromadan ships there but there was also the stollen Drako ship.

"Are we going to go get them now, mana?" Mali asked softly.

"Yes, Mali-girl, we are." I told her, my voice hard and unyielding. I stepped up into the Drako ship and turned to the cockpit just in time to hear two pairs of boots come racing up the path behind us.

"Get your ass seated." Wings grunted, sliding into the pilot's seat. "They haven't noticed you gone yet but they will soon."

I was sitting down into one of the two seats available with Mali in my lap when Scope came sliding in. "Go, go, go!" He exclaimed, jumping into the other seat.

I felt the energy belts surround us right as the ship lifted and flashed away. I bit back my yelp when the abrupt change in speed pressed me back into the chair.

"You get it?" Wings demanded.

"Fuck yes." Scope grinned and held up my weapon. A half blade sword made specifically for me. The energy in it mimicked my own energy and DNA enough that I was able to take it with me when I went through solids.

"Why?" I asked the two men why they were helping me.

"If it was Madron and Salem..." Wings left his sentence hanging, silently telling me that he would do anything to protect his Conversances.

It took us around ten minutes to reach the compound.

"Shit, something's wrong." Wings snapped, his eyes moving over the darkened, clearly abandoned building below us.

"Nobody's here." Scope breathed.

"Let's see what we can find." Wings growled in a frustrated voice and brought us in for a landing.

Scope stood guard over Mali while Wings and I stepped from the Drako ship. Moving slowly and silently, we searched through the empty compound finding nothing. No sign of life. In fact, it looked like no one had been there for over a year.

More and more I felt as if my soul was shredding. My mind kept calling for them, screaming. I knew they weren't dead, my soul told me that. But beyond that I didn't know.

Wings and I were stepping from the building and returning to the ship when my knees suddenly gave out. Pain slashed through my body. Agony. I felt my neck and back arch so far backwards that I was staring at the upside down building behind me. My body was seizing with the pain, I was blind and deaf for it. It was all I knew.

Malachi! My mind screamed out right before the connection cut off.

"Chriton! Shit, Chriton!" Dad's voice screamed in my ear.

I took a deep breath in, choking on the blood I inadvertently breathed in. I was collapsed on the ground with the lower half of my knees trapped under me. Dad's hands were red from where he was wiping the blood that flowed from my eyes, ears, mouth, and nose. My body hurt, like a giant bruise. I felt his hands shifting me over to a more comfortable position on my side.

"They are gone." I rasped helplessly, my fingers clawing along the cement I was laying. "If I can't find them, how do I free them?"

"We will find them." Dad gripped my shoulder, giving it a shake. "We will, Chriton."

Instead of answering him, I pushed him away and stumbled to my feet. Unsteadily, I walked to the Drako ship and my daughter. Mali fell into my arms, and we cried together.

CHAPTER 22

MALACHI

I woke up to unbearable agony.

Electricity scorched through my body, stealing my breath and scalding the very blood in my veins. I clenched my teeth around the piece of rubber in my mouth in a failed attempt to hold back my high pitched screams of pain as my body arched and seized with the excruciating burn. I vaguely heard Chriton screaming for me in my mind, but I shut down the connection not wanting him to feel this.

My body fell back to the chair I was strapped to when the electric current stopped. My heart was beating so hard that it literally hurt. My head was an explosion of pain.

"Oh good, you're awake." The grey haired man grinned from where he was standing beside a machine with nobs on it. "Now we can talk."

With red tinted eyes, I gazed around the room I was in. Bare cement walls with a couple lights attached to the ceiling. I was strapped to a metal chair that was set in front of a TV. The chair was obviously adjustable with a number of attachments.

The heavy metal door opening brought my eyes around to see two lizards step into the room followed by a Grey. I knew I was in trouble. And I knew what I had to do. The failsafe.

It was something Declan taught me. He said that no matter how hard we may try to protect the information we held inside our minds, sometimes that just wasn't possible. Thusly, he came up with what he called the failsafe, a way to effectively destroy any access to the knowledge that was housed within our memories.

"Fuck you." I grinned, slamming my head back into the spot needed sending me straight back into unconsciousness.

APOPHIS

I WOKE UP AND STRETCHED, my muscles burning from my extensive training yesterday.

I couldn't remember anything beyond the last weeks. Weeks that effectively taught me my place in this world. I was here to obey. I would do anything for my Master. And today was just another day for me to prove that.

Standing from my bed, I pulled on my suit, shaved my face, and trimmed my hair down into its usual buzz cut. Ready for the day, I stepped from the room and travelled to my Master's large office suite. Entering the room, I smoothly walked over to my Master's side where I stood until I was given my orders for the day.

I was quickly joined by Nephthys and Hel.

"I have a treat for you today." Master rose from his desk chair and gestured for us to follow him. "All of you." He chuckled and guided us down to the basement where he kept the humans.

The cages were mostly empty as he recently shipped the bulk of them out. All but two. A dark haired man with a broken jaw due to his inability to shut up and a woman that smelled disgusting and looked even worse. Her face and body were a mass of swollen, bruised, bleeding wounds. Her ripped clothes were smeared with blood. I knew how badly she was injured. In fact, I was the one that put the majority of those wounds on her.

Her eyes flashed with hope when she saw me. That hope died a quick death. She may hope that I wouldn't hurt her again like I did so many times before, but she knew deep inside that hope was useless.

I tilted my head and stared down at her emotionlessly, waiting for my Master's orders.

"Apophis. Pull the bitch out and chain her there." Master order, pointing to a set of rusty chains hanging from the ceiling.

I obediently unlocked the cage and reached inside, grabbing the woman's arm and hauling her out of the cage towards the chains.

"No. Stop. Please. Don't do this. You really don't want to do this. Please remember." The woman screamed and fought against me, begging me to listen to her, to stop.

I ignored her, quickly locking her wrists into the chains.

"When are you going to learn?" Master asked the furious looking woman. "He is completely mine. He does everything I tell him to. You are nothing to him anymore. And today, I am going to prove it to you. Irrevocably."

"Fuck you." The woman spat into Master's face only to have her head snap to the side with the immediate backhand I delivered to her.

"Apophis." Master wiped his face off with a handkerchief that he disposed of by dropping on the floor. "Fuck Nephthys. Hel, strip the bitch's back of her skin." Master handed Hel a whip before stepping back to observe.

Obeying my Master, I moved over to Nephthys, running my hands over the curves of her body. I felt my sex dutifully getting hard, ready. Nephthys was a beautiful woman and to be honest, I was hoping to be able to get my dick inside her. Master had given me orders to fuck others before, mostly women with the odd man thrown in, but Nephthys, she was one I was truly attracted to. Master was obviously showing his appreciation of my pure obedience by giving me this gift.

Nephthys moaned softly, grinding her ass back into my hard groin. I heard the whip whistle and the woman cry out in pain, but that didn't matter. All that mattered was the glorious woman in my arms.

My fingers slowly stripped her of her clothes, revealing smooth, clean flesh. My mouth sucked at her skin, my fingers caressing. My lips found hers, found her neck, her breasts, her tight stomach, all before finding the delicious wetness between her thighs. Her taste went straight to my head. She cried out with the pleasure I was giving her, her own hands delightfully caressing over my flesh.

Then I was just as naked as her, stepping between her thighs and thrusting home. The burn of her wet pussy spreading around my dick made me feel far too good. I groaned out my pleasure as my hips snapped back and forth. My dick fucked in and out of her tight tunnel, her grip deliciously strong around me, delightfully milking and pulling at my cock. It didn't take me long before she was screaming out her orgasm on my cock. I followed her right into that ecstasy, feeling my balls emptying themselves deep inside her.

"Do you want to know a secret, my little bitch?" Master crooned. Stepping away from Nephthys I looked over to my Master to see him holding the limp and bloody bitch's face up to us by her matted hair. "She's ovulating. I guarantee you that he knocked her up." The woman's red, crying face crumpled with agony and Master dropped her head.

"Apophis, again. Hel, put the bitch back in her cage." Master ordered with a gleeful smile.

I couldn't stop myself from relishing in the proud feeling that rose within me. Master chose me for this duty. I stepped back into the spread of Nephthys legs. My hands glided up her smooth thighs to settle gently on her stomach, my mind already picturing her swelling with my child. All for my Master. My throbbing dick found the entrance to where it really wanted to be and foraged inside, determined to do its duty and breed.

CHAPTER 23

LEAH

My soul cracked in two. My heart was ripped and torn, throbbing with more pain than I ever felt in the whole of my life.

I was forced to watch Malachi fuck the ice cold woman, his face filled with pleasure and pride at the very thought of making her pregnant. His beautifully tattooed body, a body I always assumed was purely mine, slapped almost desperately between the beautiful woman's thighs. His thick dick, glistening with her juices, flashed in and out of her. Each sound he made, and he made a lot, added one more rip to my already ragged soul. The sight of his semen dripping out of her sex, giving her what should have been mine was the final nail.

My back felt like it was successfully skinned. My body hurt almost as bad as my broken heart and soul as Hel released me from the chains I was hanging from and dragged me back to the cage. I turned away from the sight of the man I once loved giving that love to someone else for the second time in a row. I wished I was wrong, but I could see it deep in his eyes, he truly wanted her despite his orders. Not me.

To him, I was nothing. Not anymore.

Ever since I woke up all those weeks ago, trapped in this damned cage, my life was filled with drugs that seemed to block out half my brain. Not to mention the constant pain. The pain of the evil man ordering a clearly brainwashed Malachi to hurt me, torture me, over and over again. Any and all ways. No matter how much I begged and

263

pleaded, no matter how much I tried to get him to recognize me and come back to me, none of it worked.

Malachi was completely gone.

Now there was only Apophis.

Grayson who was locked in the cage two down from mine was in just as bad, if not worse shape than I was. While I received my torture, usually at the hands of Apophis and the cold blooded woman, Grayson received his own torture. He used to yell threats and things at Apophis, Nephthys, and Dante when they dragged me out, until about a week ago when Dante ordered Apophis to shut him up. And he did by breaking Grayson's jaw.

Since that day Grayson seemed to go downhill more and more. I knew he was sick, probably with an infection. But there was absolutely nothing I could do about it. He would probably die from his wounds soon and I couldn't stop it. That knowledge broke me even more.

I felt blessed numbness settle over me.

I had nothing left.

I didn't care anymore.

There was no point in fighting this.

Silence fell in the room and I was once again left in darkness. I let my mind drift away to the faces that I still loved, the ones I was sure I would never see again. My beloved Chriton, my beautiful Mali-girl.

I missed Chriton so much that it was unbearable at times. I felt so lost and empty without him. At first I called and called for him. But when I got nothing back I knew it was the drugs. The drugs were stopping my ability to connect with him.

I spent most of my time in the cage picturing his face. His beautiful blue eyes. My heart yearned to feel his arms around me, loving me, protecting me. I wished so badly to see him, smell him, touch him. One last time.

The hope that I desperately held onto was now dead.

I knocked on the bars of the cage to let Grayson know I was still alive but I got nothing back. At that point I was worried that he actually was dead.

Two days later the door opened again and Apophis was once again ordered to pull me from the cage. I didn't even react this time, my mind numb and broken with soul deep agony. I was silent while I was strapped down to a metal table by Apophis. My unfocused eyes didn't really even see the ice cold eyes of the woman sticking the electrodes to my temples. Instead, my mind conjured up glowing blues eyes holding my safe and protected. My tortured body convulsed violently under the current that was being forced through it while my mind was with Chriton.

I couldn't do this anymore. I couldn't fight anymore. I wanted to, for Chriton, but I couldn't. I just wasn't strong enough. I stopped praying for Malachi to remember me or for Chriton to find me and I started praying for death. I prayed that today was the day they finally killed me. Instead, I was out of luck. After they were finished with me, I was thrown back into the cage.

"I do believe we finally broke her. Good job, Apophis." The grey haired man praised an emotionless Apophis. I ignored both of them, simply allowing my eyes to drift closed once again so that I could picture Chriton's cherished face.

That night, the evil, cold eyed woman came in to give Grayson and I the only meal we got for the day and the daily injection of the drug we received. After she left, I felt different, almost as if my mind was parting, opening just the slightest. Like the waving of a curtain in the wind. I could only attribute that to Dante ordering for me to be given a weaker version of the drug now that I was broken.

Malachi. I cried, wishing that he would hear me for once. *I need you. Please.*

Who is this? Why are you in my head, calling me by that name?
A harsh demanding voice returned. It was slightly disconcerting how
similar yet different Apophis sounded compared to Malachi.

That no longer matters. I whispered back to him. *The woman in
the cage.*

What about the bitch?

Kill her.

I only listen to my Master's orders.

Then why are you talking to me?

Everything went quiet for so long that I was afraid I lost him

Apophis?

Why do you want me to kill her?

*Because she is a threat to you, to your Master, to Nephthys. You need
to kill her.*

My eyes squeezed shut with the hot tears that were running from
them when I lost the connection again.

In more pain than I could cope with, I shifted and tried to get
more comfortable as I slipped off into mind freeing sleep. I was just
drifting off when a soft scuffing sound drew my attention to the front
of the cage. Apophis was crouched before the locked door, staring at
me. With his head shaved like it now was and his dark eyes dead and
emotionless, his face looked sharper, harsher.

Kill her. My mind automatically ordered, my body sliding closer
to the bars. I pushed my arm through the bars, holding my wrist face
up towards him. *The guides are already there, you just have to follow
them.*

His gaze dropped down, his eyes finding my scar. His hand came
up to rub his temple.

Do it. Do it. Do it. I chanted into his mind causing his hand to
dart out and painfully grip my outstretched hand.

I held back my wince of pain when he almost broke my wrist
with the violence of that move. I was yanked forward into the bars

and I stared deep into his empty, dark eyes. *Kill, kill, kill the threat, Apophis.*

A blade appeared in Apophis' hand and I felt relief course through my body.

Finally.

He set the sharp blade to my bent back wrist right over the scar and pressed. I sucked in a breath at the pain but kept my eyes on him. His eyes were centered down at the wrist he was cutting into, his forehead furrowed. The tip of the blade dipped easily into my flesh causing blood to well up and drip down both of our hands. *Here I come, Declan.* I whispered softly to myself, feeling peace settle over me at the thought of seeing my beloved uncle again.

Apophis paused, his eyes following the trail of my blood, his hands shaking just the slightest.

What are you waiting for? Finish it. I ordered him, feeling my anger rise. *Kill the threat, Apophis.*

I hissed when the knife fell from Apophis' hand, the point of the blade popping from my flesh to clatter to the floor. I felt my wrist crack when I ripped myself free from his biting grip and pushed myself to the back of the cage. Apophis watched me with those dark eyes of his. His usually emotionless face frowning in confusion.

Leave. Leave now and leave the knife. If you aren't strong enough to protect your Master then someone else will.

Apophis' head tilted to the side and his hand reached for the knife.

"I hate you." I whispered out loud to him, clutching my arm to my chest. "Now I know that along with having no heart and soul, you have no spine, no balls. Useless fuck." When I was done speaking I pushed myself into the corner of the cage and turned my face away.

I ignored the clang of the cage door unlocking. My eyes closed as my body was violently yanked from the cage. I didn't even open my eyes when his hand found my neck and lifted me up, straight off my feet. I let my body fall limp, dangling from the fingers that were tightening, closing off my air flow. I could hear my heart beating in my ears. The blood trapped in my head throbbed, the strain of my desperate lungs was painful to a panicking degree.

But I didn't panic.

I let myself sink deeper and deeper into it. One pound, two pound. The pain of my air being cut off by the man I once loved was mixed with the peace of the darkness that was descending over me.

That darkness deepened until I felt like I was cradled in it. Then I heard a cherished voice yelling angrily in my head.

You will release her right now!

Chriton. I had forgotten how beautiful his voice was. Deep and smooth, usually with a happy undertone of amusement. He wasn't amused, though, not right now. Right now, he was mad. Furious and demanding in a way I never knew he could be.

Who are you?

I am your Master! I am her Master! You will fucking obey me! You will release the man, Grayson, from his cage. You will bring him and the woman, Leah, to me.

My...Master?

Yes, your Master, Apophis. Your true Master. Feel it, deep in your soul. You know that you are mine. Now, release her and do as I say!

Yes...Master.

Good Apophis.

The descending darkness was ripped away when I was dropped to the hard floor and air rushed painfully through my throat and into my lungs.

My eyes cracked open to see Apophis unlock Grayson's cage and pull the man's limp form from within.

Apophis dragged him over and dropped him down beside me. Grayson's head flopped towards mine, his eyes were feverish, dazed.

"Grayson." I rasped painfully and reached out to take his hand only to have it removed from my reach. Apophis lifted Grayson's limp body into his arms and began to carry him from the basement.

"Move, bitch." Apophis stated emotionlessly, landing a foot into my stomach. I grunted harshly and automatically curled myself into a protective ball. "Get up. I can't carry you both."

I ignored him, curling deeper into myself, waiting for him to leave me to my peace.

Do not hurt her again, Apophis. She is MY property. Carry Grayson up to the main floor and let the other's in. I will take care of Leah.

Yes, Master.

Once you let the others in you will kneel on the floor and stay perfectly still until I tell you otherwise.

Yes, Master.

I closed my mind, not wanting to hear anymore. Not from that emotionless man. I covered my ears and felt sobs rising deep in my chest. My body jerked and tightened in on itself even more with the pain that ricocheted through me. Everything hurt, my body, my mind, my soul.

I didn't know how long I laid there on the disgusting floor before something soft was set over my body and a set of strong arms surrounded me, lifting my curled body up against a hard chest. I ignored the debilitating pain that flashed over my skinned back and buried myself as deep as I could into that adored chest. The fingers of my good hand clutched at him while my starved lungs breathed his clean scent in. There were no words exchanged as Chriton carried me out of that horrific basement and upstairs to a cavernous, sunlit, entryway.

Chriton.

He came for me. He freed me.

My heart and soul reached out for him, needing to feel him. And I did. I felt him. His DNA spread and glided over me, into me, holding me, letting me feel his love. I wanted to cry with the relief coursing through me but I couldn't. I didn't have any tears left. Fortunately, I did have him. Finally.

I felt myself being set back down on the floor. This time I was sitting up vertically instead of horizontal. My hand refused to release him, forcing him to crouch down in front of me. Chriton's glowing blue eyes stared into mine, his gaze filled with relief mixed with something cold and deadly. Seeing him like this, his frozen face and glowing body carrying the promise of death, I could clearly see the Guardian in him. It was evident that he had zero problem killing to protect.

In that moment I felt almost numb to everything but him. Chriton. My eyes closed in gratitude at the feel of his cold hands cupped my face. My head pushed deeper into his touch when he slowly bent his forehead down to mine. My eyes opened in time to see his squeeze closed with the pain he was feeling. When his eyes opened back up, he turned his head. Following his gaze, I saw Apophis kneeling on the floor beside Dante, Hel, and Nephthys. Apophis' hand was firmly clasped with a very bruised Nephthys'.

My eyes fell to their hands before shifting to Nephthys stomach. "She's pregnant with his child." I dazedly informed Chriton, tearing my gaze from the couple to stare out the door that led to freedom.

Desperately needing to be away from the pain this place held for me and wanting to feel the sun on my skin, I forced my fingers to release Chriton. When I rose from the floor on a set of extremely weak legs, Chriton rose with me, making sure I was steady. I held my blanket around my shoulders and shuffled slowly out the door and into the heated sunlight.

CHRITON

I TURNED HORRIFIED eyes down to the couple kneeling at my feet.

Apophis.

He didn't remember any of us. He was clearly physically attached to the woman at his side, and she was apparently carrying his child. I felt Leah's pain beating at me before it was efficiently cut off and twisted into numb acceptance. My soul screamed when I felt that coming from her. Her acceptance of Malachi's loss.

"What do we do now?" Wings asked, his voice filled with a pained hush.

I turned to the grey haired man, Dante. Dante watched me with narrowed eyes filled with threat. "Dante" I crooned down at the man. "I am sure you are wondering how we found you. Well, you can thank my man for that, right Apophis." I reached down a soft hand and ran it gently along Apophis' face.

"Yes, Master." He agreed, his voice emotionless, his body motionless. Mostly. I didn't see it but I felt it, the barest pressure being turned into my fingers.

"See, he was mine first. Always mine. They both were. And you took them from me. You stole his mind, his memories, and you thought you could make him into someone completely pliable. And you did. For his real Master. Who is not you. He immediately recognized me the moment I spoke to him. He opened right up to me and let me in." I shared with Dante, turning to draw my fingers along Dante's face the same way I did Apophis'. "You, however, don't need to let me in. I will let myself in." I smiled down at him, the stretch of my lips carrying death to their curve.

Dante went pale and began to scream when my fingers slowly moved down his chest, dragging them deeper and deeper through his skin and muscles. I allowed my insubstantial fingers catch and pluck along every nerve I came across sending excruciating pain strumming through the man's body. By the time I was done playing along the nerves populating his torso Dante was beyond begging. His body was convulsing stiffly, his eyes unfocused with pain, his mouth slack and drooling. I backed off and waited just long enough for his eyes to clear slightly and focus on me. "Please." He rasped, begged.

Wanting to extend his pain but not wanting to leave Leah alone much longer, I titled my head down to his arched body. I twisted my hand in his chest, gripped his heart and gave it a slow turn. He shuddered and screamed one last time before his body fell limp with death.

"That was, uh, creative." Wings swallowed, his face pale.

"Thank you." I stated quietly, straightening to my full height and looking down at the rest. "Apophis, look at me." My voice snapped out. Apophis' head immediately came up. His familiar dark eyes centered completely on me. It was slightly disconcerting to be the object of his full attention in such a focused way.

He was dressed in one of those cursed suites, his dark hair was shaved close to his head and he boasted a number of newly healed scars, telling me that he didn't go without his own torture. He was somehow bigger and stronger yet smaller all at the same time. Less vital, emotionless. A true automaton. The outside form was Malachi, but inside was someone else. Apophis. "You will enter the ship on the right. When we get back to the Base you will follow the man on the gurney into Medical and allow the doctors to examine you. That is where you will stay until I say otherwise."

"Yes, Master." Apophis nodded and rose to his feet, his hand slowly releasing the woman's hand. I didn't watch him as he stepped out the door. Instead, I looked down at the woman kneeling on the floor. "Nephthys, Hel, you are both going to go with this man here into the second ship. You will listen and obey to whatever orders you are given or I will kill you myself." I motioned to Chern who stepped through the door. I watched as the emotionless woman's ice blue eyes landed on him before they immediately dropped to the floor. To be honest, I didn't want to let them live at all. I wanted both of them just as dead as Dante was. But I knew Lysander needed the information they carried just as Marko needed the data Wings helped him harvest.

"Come." Chern ordered, eyeing me cautiously while holding his arm out for the two to proceed him through the door.

As soon as the entrance was empty of people I finally allowed myself to feel. When I first heard Leah's scream in my head, my numb heart jerked to life. After weeks spent concentrating on caring for Mali and desperately searching for the missing group of three, it was a dizzying relief to finally feel that blip of a connection.

The connection was weak, drugged, going in and out but it was enough. My body was on the move while my mind delved deep and clung hard. Through Leah, I was able to reach Apophis. What I found there was horrifying to say the least.

I set aside the pain I felt and followed our connection straight into the swamps of Louisiana. Wings, Giggles, and I took the Drako ship and flew straight here. My father and brother were quick to follow with Luke and Chern in one of the other ships.

Unfortunately for them, I was quick and was already hunting through the compound, a true spectre of death. Feeling right on the edge of loosing all control, I coldly and efficiently killed anything and everything that breathed, all the way up until I reached Dante's room. That was where I came across Hel and Nephthys, both of whom were very well trained and did everything they could to try and kill me.

Dante watched with gleeful eyes as his zombies took me on. I may have felt a twisted sort of pleasure in toying with the two, taking the time to inflict a number of painful wounds. Dante's glee turned to shock and disappointment when I stopped playing and expertly brought them down with an admittedly heavy hand. Unfortunately, as much as I tried to hold myself back, Leah's memories of her torture at their hands made that impossible. Needless to say, they were extremely lucky to be alive.

While I was doing that, Apophis obeyed my orders and opened the front door. Luke darted in to examine Grayson while Giggles and Wings moved throughout the rest of the house, taking out anyone I missed before helping me drag the three from Dante's suite down to the entryway. Dad helped Luke with Grayson, gently moving the feverish man onto a gurney and rolling him out of the building. Chern and Coren helpfully killed anyone they found roaming outside.

When I was done clearing the house, I dropped down to the basement where Leah was curled on the floor in a tight ball. Her hair was matted, lank, her skin dirty and, yes, she smelled, very badly. She looked like she had lost quite a bit of weight. But it was the lacerations and bruises that coloured ever inch of her barely clothed body that affected me the most. Her back was a swollen mass of ripped flesh. Whip marks. I knew from the flashes of memory that I gleaned from Leah that Apophis himself was the one who put most of the marks on Leah's body.

"Chriton." Leah's rasping voice echoed softly through the large entryway.

"I am so sorry, my precious love." I swallowed, turning to look at the broken woman standing just beyond the doorway. She still held the blanket I wrapped her with tightly around herself, hiding the blood and dirt and rags that covered her.

Her eyes watched me strangely, almost as if she didn't quite know if I was real or not. I knew exactly how she felt. I was having an extremely hard time letting her out of my sight as well. All I wanted to do was hold her tight to me and never let go.

"Why? It isn't your fault. As much as I want to blame.." Leah paused to take a deep breath in, her eyes blinking upwards for a second before coming back down to mine. "Him. It isn't his fault either. He doesn't remember."

"I don't know how to fix this." I held my arms straight out in surrender as something snapped inside me. The frozen chill of my murderous mindset heated into white hot fury. "How the fuck do I fix this?" I yelled angrily, my voice hollow and broken. I needed to fix it.

"You don't." Leah whispered softly, her own eyes haunted and heartbroken. "We don't. We just...move on."

"Move on." I rasped with wince, feeling my rage banking slightly. She was right. Even if Malachi was lost to us, we still had each other and I was determined to keep us together. The tears I was barely holding at bay popped into my eyes. Needing to feel her against me, I strode forward and carefully pulled her into my arms, holding her gently. "It's been over a month since I held you in my arms last." I whispered hoarsely, feeling my limbs shaking with all of the emotions swirling through me, mostly relief. "I was so scared that I never would again."

"Promise me, Chriton, promise that you will never leave me. Never again. You are the only reason I am still alive. It was the thought of you that kept me going. Kept me fighting." Leah sobbed and begged, clutching at me while breaking apart in my arms. I knew that, after everything she went through, she was just as terrified of loosing me as I was of loosing her.

"I promise, precious, I fucking promise. Not even death will succeed in pulling me away from you because I will just haunt your ass." I reassured her, my hands smoothing through her matted, caked hair.

I gently guided Leah back to ship that contained Grayson, Luke, Coren, dad, and Apophis. Chern went with Wings and Giggles in the other ship with Nephthys and Hel.

Leah would have followed me to the cockpit but when she saw Apophis sitting in one of the chairs, she turned and shuffled to the room that Luke and Coren were working on Grayson.

My eyes squeezed shut at the knowledge that this was the second time Leah silently showed her rejection of Apophis' presence. Instead of following her like my soul screamed at me to, I forced myself to step into the cockpit and take a seat at the front of the ship. I could feel dad's concerned eyes on me but I ignored everything around me and concentrated on getting Leah back to the safety of the Base and getting everyone examined.

CHAPTER 24

APOPHIS

I didn't like that they split me up from Nephthys. While she was a proficient killer and I knew that she could take care of herself, she was also hurt and most likely carrying my child. But the Master, my Master, must be obeyed. His words were law. As ordered, I followed the gurney with the man, Grayson, into the Medical place and froze, waiting for my next instructions.

I only stood there for a couple of moments before Master stepped into the room. His sharp blue eyes flashed over the place, taking in every little detail. Except me. He ignored me. But that was ok. I was patient. I learned that lesson well.

Master was a tall, dark complexioned man. Strong. Attractive with his well tamed black hair and bright blue eyes. I found myself fighting to stop myself from staring into those eyes. Then there was his sharp jawline and smooth lips. The long length of his body was encased in a black uniform that accented the muscles that were underneath.

The first time my eyes latched onto Master, I knew that what he spoke was true. This man was my true Master. I quickly determined that I would do anything for him. All he needed to do was say the word.

The dirty woman, bitch, as my old Master called her, shuffled weakly at his side, her hand tucked tightly into the fascinating strength of his long fingers. She was still disgusting looking.

My gaze caught on the caked, dried blood that travelled from the inside of her delicate wrist to the tips of her fingers. My eyes dropped to the floor as that memory flashed before me. Dark blood welling from a delicate wrist. A word, "Declan", whispered in my head. Something about it all just seemed wrong to me. So very wrong.

Another white coated doctor stepped forward and carefully guided the woman into one of the rooms that ran along the back wall. A bathroom from the looks of it.

I could feel everyone looking at me, but I kept my head down and my eyes moving, taking in everything I could.

Master came over, took my arm and guided me into one of the other rooms along the sides. My flesh and nerve endings fired to life under his firm touch, sensitizing to the heat and pressure of his fingers circling my bicep. He pushed me down onto the bed inside the room. One of the white coated people followed us in, a tall man with brown hair and a scruffy face. He examined me while asking a number of questions. I was taken into another room where they did more tests with some very big machines. After that, I was returned back to the original room I was in where my Master was still waiting. When I resumed my seat on the bed he ordered, "Stay" pointing his finger down at the bed. Then he prowled out.

He seemed mad. I could feel anger and frustration rolling off of him in waves. I didn't understand why he was mad. I didn't want him mad. I wanted him happy. That was my purpose. To make my Master happy, however that came to be.

Long minutes passed of hushed whispering before the voices started to rise.

"You are saying that you can actually fix this." I heard my Master say as he appeared in the doorway of my room and stepped inside. "You can help him retrieve his memories?"

"I can." The white coated man, doctor, nodded slowly, following Master inside the room.

"How?" One of the men who looked like my Master asked, also entering the room to stare down at me.

"The memories aren't gone, just inaccessible. It's a simple matter of reconnecting those connections which can be done through the use of electrical currents applied to certain areas of the brain." The doctor explained.

"Do it." The Master lookalike ordered the doctor.

"Wait." Master held his hand up to forestall the doctor before dropping his finger to me. "It should be his decision. He has a new woman and there is a good chance there is a child on the way. Maybe he doesn't want to remember his old life."

"We need him. The Base needs him. Malachi. Not this putz." The Master lookalike stated firmly, gesturing to me angrily.

"You don't think I don't know that?" Master snarled angrily. It was me. Master was angry with me. He didn't like me. "You don't think I don't fucking need him? What about Leah? Can you look at her and tell me that she didn't need him this whole fucking time? And what about our daughter? We all fucking need him, but it still has to be his fucking choice!" Master turned to me, his blue eyes glowing and angry looking. "Apophis, do you want to remember your old life? Your life before the man you recently called Master?"

I was surprised that my opinion was actually being asked. My opinion, my wants and needs didn't matter, they never mattered. Just Master's. But knowing my Master required an answer, I forced myself to think about it. Did I really want to know? The way they were all talking it sounded like something bad. I didn't know if I wanted to remember anything bad. But then, Master mentioned a daughter. I had daughter and didn't even remember her. A family, maybe.

The thought that stuck and truly made me think about it was the thought that maybe Master would like me better if I remembered.

"I want to remember." I whispered softly, praying that was the right answer. I knew that the punishment would be harsh if I did wrong. I clearly remembered my training and all of the pain involved. My muscles twitched uncontrollably with those memories.

"No!" The bitch entered the room. She was now clean and most of her open wounds were bandaged but she was still bruised and weak looking. Delicate. "No, Chriton. No." She hissed out through dry, cracked lips. I waited for Master to shut her up. Or order me to. She had no right to speak to Master that way and I was sure she would quickly be shown her place.

"He deserves to remember." Master surprisingly argued back. I was confused that he didn't punish her for her slight.

"No!" The bitch yelled before her voice dropped to an emotional quiver. "No, he doesn't. He doesn't deserve that pain, Chriton. Leave him be. Oblivious to us, but maybe happy. He has a partner that he clearly wants, maybe even loves, and a child most likely on the way. If he...remembers..." The woman paused, her voice cracking through the tears falling from her eyes.

I examined her words and realized that, despite the pain I dealt her, the bitch was trying to protect me. This woman always confused the hell out of me, now more than ever. Although, I did have to acknowledge that she smelled a lot better now. Cleaner, softer. That scent was almost addictive. My head moved just the barest towards her, my nostrils trying to breathe every bit of that scent in.

"He will know what he did, what he was forced to do because he didn't know better, he didn't remember, and it will break him. Just, please, let him be happy." Her quivering voice finished.

"And what about you, Leah? Will you be happy?" Master asked softly. Happy. I didn't understand this word when it pertained to me. There was no happy, there was only purpose.

"I don't need anyone else but you. I just can't be here anymore." The bitch stated firmly, her eyes darting to mine for the quickest second before jerking back up to Master's. Eyes that were swollen and bruised, black, purple, yellow, the whites reddened with broken blood vessels. "Just you, then I can...heal."

"I love that you want to protect him. And believe me, I fully realize what could happen, but it still has to be his choice." Master reached out and gently guided the woman into his arms where he held her like she was the most precious thing in the world to him. My eyes latched onto the muscles moving and shifting under Master's arms, my mind wondering what those muscles felt like.

Looking up into his blue eyes, I studied Master as he studied me right back. "Nephthys, do you love her?"

"I don't know what love is." I stated honestly, my mind latching onto the beautiful woman who I considered mine. My other Master gifted her to me, allowed me to put a child in her. It was my job to take care of her and protect her as well as I could under Master's watchful eye. If I didn't do a good job, not only would I be punished but so would she. And I couldn't let that happen. "The bitch is right, Nephthys and the child she carries are mine. If my new Master wills it, I will create a family with her."

"Then you really need to think about this carefully before you make your decision." Master advised, his eyes hardening. He was mad at me again. He didn't like me calling the woman by the name my old Master gave her. "And her name is Leah. Use it."

I nodded in agreement, thinking of Nephthys and the child she might be carrying. I would do right by her. As was my duty, my purpose.

"Would you like to meet your daughter?" Master asked, his eyes still studying me in an eery way.

I thought about that for a moment. A child. My child. I felt nothing when it came to this knowledge. But Master asked me so he must want me to meet the child for some reason. There was only one answer to that question. "Yes." I nodded, agreeing to meet the child they claimed was mine.

Master nodded sharply and lifted the metal bracelet around his wrist, typing something into it with his long, quick fingers. He took the woman out of the room but returned ten minutes later with a little blond haired girl's hand tucked tightly in his.

"Dad?" The little girl whispered, her big brown eyes moving over me. Those eyes were filled with so many emotions. Love, relief, confusion, pain. Emotions I didn't feel. Emotions that I could tell that everyone else was expecting me to feel.

"Hello." I greeted with what I was hoping was a warm smile. The girl, my daughter was admittedly beautiful and vaguely reminded me of the woman, Leah.

"Her name is Mali." Master said from his stance behind her, his hands settled on the girl's slim shoulders.

"Hello, Mali. That's a beautiful name." I told her honestly, reaching my hand out to her. The girl took a deep shuddering breath in and fell into my body.

My arms automatically surrounded her, gently holding her strangely familiar body. "I missed you, dad." She whispered, her voice shaking.

"I do believe I missed you too." I whispered back, rocking her little body. And I did. I missed her. Maybe not in my mind but in my body and soul. Those parts knew her, remembered her.

"Are you going to live with me again?" She asked.

"Yes." I confirmed, cupping her small face gently in my hands. "Me and Nephthys and our new baby."

"Who's Nephthys?" Mali asked, her eyes widening with confusion and fear.

"My woman. The woman who is carrying my child." I informed her. "You are going to love her. She is so beautiful. Blindingly beautiful. Just like you."

"But? What about mom? And mana?" The little girl whispered, backing away from me as tears slowly rolled down her face. Mom, mana? Who were these people? If the Master brought the child to me, he obviously wanted me to retake my spot as her dad and raise her.

"I am sorry, who?" I asked, frowning in confusion.

"Mana?" Mali whispered again, her head jerking towards my Master.

"Come, Mali-girl." Master bent over to pick my daughter up. "Let's give this man some time."

CHAPTER 25

LEAH

I didn't think I could break anymore. But apparently I could. I was sitting in the exam room next door, listening to everything, helpless to do anything.

I listened to Apophis voice his claim on the admittedly beautiful woman, declaring that they would all be a family.

Mali, my daughter, was so confused.

"Mana? What is dad talking about? What about mom?" I heard Mali exclaim in a high pitched, frantic voice.

"Mali, my beautiful daughter. You know how I told you that your dad doesn't remember anything before his time with the Drako's, well that includes your mother and me." I heard Chriton explain to the girl.

"Well, make him remember." Mali demanded sharply.

"It's not that easy, my Mali-girl. Because his memories were stollen he doesn't remember Leah or Grayson. And he did things...he, uh, he hurt them. Very badly. Your mother was trapped in a tiny cage, drugged and starved, beaten and tortured. While he, uh, chose another woman and this woman most likely is carrying his child." I cringed when I heard Chriton's stumbling words. "He's made the decision to be with this other woman, to build a family with her. If we push him to get his memories back, it will hurt him very badly because he will remember Leah and Grayson and he will remember every, uh, bad thing he did. That could severely damage his mentality."

"So what? I go and live with him, a man that doesn't really remember me and this 'perfect' woman of his?" Mali growled angrily.

"That is entirely up to you, Mali-girl. Your mom needs to be away from...here. So, I am moving us out to the Ranch. We would both love it if you came with us. But it has to be your choice." Chriton's voice got even quieter as he shared his plan with the girl. That plan almost sent me spinning right back into tears. The depth of the love I felt for him in that moment was indescribable. The protection and caring he was showing me was beyond words.

"You mean him. She needs to be away from him. The man who promised to love and protect her but hurt her instead." Mali stated, her voice loud and furious. "My choice is not with that man. That, in there, isn't my dad."

"Mali." Chriton sighed softly.

"Where is mom?" Mali demanded. This was followed by a rush of small feet sprinting into the room before stopping. My head lifted from the floor I was staring at to meet my daughter's horrified brown eyes. "That monster in there did that to her, didn't he?"

"He didn't have a choice. He was brainwashed like Chern and Uncle Bane were. And even if he did have a choice, he doesn't remember anything, he didn't know who she was when he did it." Chriton tried to reassure Mali to no avail.

Mali gave a sobbed cry and ran over to me. She scrambled onto the bed and into my arms. I felt my own tears rising to join hers. "I missed you, mom."

"I missed you too, my Mali-girl. So much." I returned, rocking her back and forth. "I love you. I love you." I started chanting, finding myself unable to stop.

I heard Chriton return to the room with Apophis.

"Your daughter doesn't want to live with you."

"I heard." Apophis returned emotionlessly. "I apparently hurt her mother. I am assuming the woman in question is the...Leah."

"Do you regret it?" I heard Chriton enquire with quiet ferocity. "Any of it? Hurting Leah or Grayson?"

"I am sorry to disappoint you but no. I did as I was trained to do, as I was ordered to do by my Master at the time. It is my Master's will that is my reason for being. And because I was good and obedient I received the gift of Nephthys and my new child. I cannot regret that." Apophis stated impassively.

"And what of the others that you once loved? Your daughter? Will you not regret losing her?" Chriton pressed, his voice becoming an angry hiss.

"Of course. She is mine. What makes you think I will lose her? Just because she doesn't want to live with me doesn't mean she won't have to. She is my daughter after all." Apophis' voice was confused. Confusion was the only emotion I ever saw or heard from him.

Chriton was quiet for a long moment. "Ah, but see, she is also mine. And her mother's. We both have just as much of a say when it comes to her wellbeing and living space. And she will be coming with us." This was followed by a slight scuffle. "Ah, ah, no arguing with your Master."

"Very well, Master." Apophis said obediently.

"Good boy." Chriton clipped out his praise. "While I am gone, this nice, green eyed man has volunteered to stay with you. You know, make sure you stay out of trouble. You can consider him a stand in for me. Listen to him. Be a good boy. And when I come back, you might just receive a gift. Not a woman, mind you. You apparently already have one of those. But something else. I also want you to think long and hard about those memories and whether you want them back or not."

"I do believe I will say no." Apophis' voice rang out.

"Not so fast there, my boy. See, if you really want your daughter back, you will have to remember. She has already said that you, as

you are right now, are not her dad. So, maybe, keep that in mind."
Chriton informed the man right before a door slammed.

"Come on." Chriton appeared in the doorway. He held his hand
out to Mali and carefully helped me up from the bed. "Keep me
informed. On everything." His hand tightened around the one Mali
slipped into his while his eyes turned to Coren, Callden, and Diad,
who I was guessing was now in charge of Apophis.

It didn't take us long to pack what we would need from the suite
and walk to the Bay.

"River and Salem wanted to say goodbye, but they also wanted
to give you your time. So, they made you a video that they sent you."
Wings told me, his voice quiet and remorseful as he attached my new
coms around my wrist.

"Thank you, Wings." I reached out and grabbed his thick wrist
in my hand. "All of you, for everything."

Wings gave me a sharp nod before guiding me up into the ship.
Ten minutes later Bane, Bailor, and Harper were meeting us as we
stepped from the ship. Chriton followed Mali and I down, his
movements slow as if he too was in pain. He didn't say anything
when Bane pulled him into a hug, although, he only gave his brother
a quick back pound before drawing away.

"Leah needs food and rest." Chriton shared, his hand settling
lightly on my side.

"Yeah." Bane nodded slowly, his eyes, haunted and broken,
sliding over me then Mali. "We got you. We got all of you."

After eating, we all were guided to a large tent that turned out
to be three tents connected. Two smaller bedroom tents were
connected to a bigger main room tent. It was all fully furnished and
stocked.

That night I jerked awake thinking I was still in the cages. I
calmed quickly when Chriton's strong arms surrounded me. For the
first time in weeks, I felt safe and loved. Desperately needing to

return that love, I ran my hands over his bare chest, arching up to find his mouth.

Chriton groaned and tilted his head down to mine, our mouths fusing together.

"I don't want to hurt you." Chriton whispered when I glided my hand down his chest to the band to his pajama bottoms.

"I lost you. I fucking lost you, Chriton. For days, weeks, I don't even fucking know how long. I couldn't reach you. And I honestly thought I would never see you again. That thought...I couldn't...I need to feel you. I need to know you are real and finally here with me. I need to feel your love." I told him, my voice shaking and fierce.

Chriton's beautifully glowing eyes shined wetly and his mouth found mine once again. His lips became frantic on mine, demanding. He needed to feel me as much as I needed to feel him. Those lips drifted from my breathless mouth and down my neck.

I shivered and caressed my hands over his back with firm, life affirming strokes. I gasped when he rolled us from our sides to his back. My hands fell to his chest as my knees automatically straddled his hips. He sat up and gently pulled his t-shirt from my body before his hands found my sides. The fingers of my good hand delved into his hair while we feasted from one another again.

I couldn't stop kissing him, feeling the pleasure of his lips and tongue rasping over mine coupled with the burning heat of his breathe. Life. It was his life mixing with mine.

My body shuddered in rapture when his hand slid down my panty covered ass and his fingers pressed between the lips of my pussy to rub over my aroused clit.

"Chriton." I whimpered, my hips rotating against his deliciously talented fingers.

"Yes, love. Show me how good it feels." Chriton praised, his eyes staring deep into mine, glowing brighter and brighter.

I felt him lift and the material around his hips shifted down until my thighs were hugging bare flesh. The burn of the rounded head of his cock replaced his fingers and rubbed over my clit. After a couple dragging strokes his dick slid far enough down to catch on my entrance, only stopped by the thin fabric of my underwear.

Chriton snarled into my mouth and his hand yanked my panties aside until his dick was moving along my pussy bare. The friction of his skin thrusting along my clit was divine. I was gasping and whimpering into his mouth, my hips moving with his.

"That's it, love." Chriton rasped, his hands on my rocking hips helping to guide me.

"Chriton." I cried, feeling my orgasm building deep within me. "Fuck, I missed your beautiful dick. Almost as much as I missed you."

Chriton chuckled and gave my lips a sharp nip. "It missed you too, love. More than I can ever describe."

"Show me." I whimpered out just as my orgasm shot through me. My hips jerked and my legs trembled. It felt so good that I could barely breathe with the pleasure. My eyes wanted to close, but I forced them to remain open and on his. I needed that connection to him. I need to see him.

Chriton's lips tightened over mine. His hand moved to shift his cock down to my entrance and he thrust inside me. He gave a gasping grunt and his eyelids fluttered with pleasure. His deeply seated entrance drove my orgasm higher. I could feel him so deep inside me.

My starved pussy gripped and massaged him. I started moving, riding him with slow strokes. His arm wrapped around my hips and helped me move against him, his own hips arching up to meet mine. His other hand delved into the strands of my hair.

I held him close in every way I could, my hand in his hair, my arm around his shoulders, my lips against his. My lungs breathed in every breath he breathed out and my chest pressed tightly to his. My pussy clenched around him in a purposeful attempt to hold him inside.

Chriton groaned softly when he felt my inner muscles rhythmically clamping around him. The feel of that extra friction sent my pleasure, his pleasure even higher.

"I love you." He whispered against my lips, his hand clenched in my hair. "I never want to let you go. Never again."

"I love you, too." I whimpered back, feeling his heart pounding against mine. "So much that it hurts without you."

Slow and gentle, we pushed each other up and over that ledge.

I cried out into his mouth as my sex sucked at his throbbing sex. Chriton groaned while his cock twitched and pulsed with his ecstasy, over and over again. Everything within me relished in the burn of him filling me. That burn spread like wildfire until all I felt was him.

My love, my Chriton.

It was deep and filled with so much love.

Then I watched as the wisps of our souls rose up out of our chests to dance together before returning to our bodies. I felt him there. Deep inside me. With me.

Unlike Malachi. I didn't feel him there. Not anymore.

He was lost to me.

I needed to let go.

And I would, with the help of the man I loved.

CHAPTER 26

APOPHIS

Master was mad.

He left me.

He left me in the care of another, but he left me, nonetheless. I didn't know what I was supposed to do now. The green eyed man now in charge of me, Diad, brought me to this suite that was apparently mine. Empty and cold.

Diad moved his stuff into one of the other rooms. A room that smelled like Master. One of the rooms had been mine. A third room held toys and little girl items that I was sure was my daughters. The last room smelled like the woman. Leah. Addictive. The first morning there I woke up to find myself in her room, curled tightly around her pillow. Her scent deeply ingrained in my nostrils.

It was a couple days later when Nephthys was finally brought to my door by a uniformed man that I realized Master truly did want me to take care of her. So, I did that. I did everything I could to make her comfortable in the room that was mine. For some reason my mind rebelled at the thought of Nephthys being in my daughter's room and I already took over the other room. That left my old room to Nephthys.

Most of the time Nephthys was quiet and distraught. Her pale blue eyes were constantly moving, her body always tensed, as if she expected to be attacked at any moment. Her and Diad did not get along very much. She was extremely erratic and rude. She could be quite violent, especially when she had an episode and lost control of herself. She tended to get very angry, destroy things, and threaten

Diad and I with bodily harm during those episodes. He would immediately snap at her in clipped voice, effectively stopping her in her tracks.

Seeing how uncomfortable Nephthys was, I cooked her meals for her, ran her baths, made sure to do everything I could think of to make her comfortable. We didn't talk too much. Words weren't normally exchanged between the ones Master owned. I did, however, make sure she went to all of the appointments and meetings that she was supposed to go to.

As the weeks passed, I felt her easing up around me, trusting me, slightly. I assumed that this was due to the fact that I didn't make any effort to touch her and I gave her space. I could sense that she clearly didn't want me to touch her, thusly if I could avoid that, I would. Unfortunately for me, it was one sided. She had no problems touching me whenever she felt like it which I was finding that I really didn't like.

Chern turned out to be very helpful when it came to Nephthys, and as a by product, her touching. He was someone that she seemed to care about and trusted more than anyone else. He began to spend not just days but nights in the suite, sleeping on the couch. I didn't care. As long as Nephthys was comfortable. Although, I did note that he didn't seem to like it when I was around.

The only reason I kept doing my duty when it came to her was because I knew my Master wanted this. He wanted me to take care of the woman he gave me. He may have left me but I was bound determined to do what he wanted. It was, after all, my purpose. I found myself counting the days until he returned for me. I hoped that he would be proud of me.

Then things changed, new knowledge was introduced. Nephthys wasn't pregnant and she wanted to move out. At first I disagreed. That wasn't what my Master wanted. But then Diad sat me down on the couch for what he called a serious conversation. He sat in one of the chairs and told me that it wasn't my place to assume what Master wanted. He told me that Master wanted me to start thinking for myself.

Did I truly want Nephthys?

He pointed out that I did everything for her while she did nothing but ignore me for Chern. Unless she was having an episode. It was during those times that both her and Chern seemed happy that I was there to help. Diad mentioned how I refused to allow her or Chern entrance into any of the bedrooms beyond the one I gave her. He also mentioned that, despite everything going on with her and Chern and the nonexistent child, I didn't seem like I truly cared about any of it.

"I don't." I told him honestly.

"Tell me, Apophis, what do you care about?" The green eyed man asked me, his eyes studying with a disturbing intensity.

My answer was fast and immediate, ingrained in me but still felt deeply in ways I couldn't really comprehend. "Master."

"You have had two Masters, Apophis. Which Master are you talking about?" Diad pressed, reaching out to grip the wrist that was hanging off my knee.

"My current Master." I stated firmly.

"You care about him." Diad said, watching my confirming nod. "So, you did all of this because you thought, what? That it would make him proud?"

"Yes." I nodded again. "If I make him proud enough he will return for me and I will be able to fulfill my purpose of standing by his side."

"Apophis, do you know the difference between knowing something and assuming something." Diad's head tilted to the side as he asked.

"Yes." I confirmed.

"Well, you seem to assume that your, uh, Master, fuck I hate calling him that. You seem to think that he wants you to do certain things based on what you see of his actions. Nephthys. You assumed that you were supposed to care for her because your last Master gifted her and her, well, womb, to you. And you assumed that your new, uh, Master, wanted you to continue doing that." Diad rubbed a hand over his face.

"Yes. Is that not true?" I asked, confused.

"It is not." Diad stated bluntly and I felt horror blaze through me. I failed. I didn't do what my Master wanted. No wonder he left me. "Listen to me, Apophis." Diad's voice brought my swirling mind back to the moment at hand. I failed once, but I refused to fail again. "Your Master only wanted for you to be happy. That's all he ever wanted. He thought that Nephthys was what you wanted, he thought she was what would make you happy. So, he stepped back so you could be, well, happy."

"Everyone keeps saying this. Happy. I don't understand this. There is only purpose. And my purpose is to obey my Master. To do his will." I whispered, rubbing at a strange pain that was building in my chest.

"Do you mind if I show you happiness?" Diad asked, his voice eerily soft.

"I...guess." My eyes darted around, not really sure what my answer should be. I hoped I picked the right one.

Diad nodded slowly and reached for the tablet on the table. A couple taps and the TV turned on, the screen showing a grass covered ground for a moment before the camera videotaping the scene rose and steady.

Blue sky's, green trees and grass. A group of people were walking and talking. My eyes latched onto a man that looked eerily like me. But different. His hair was longer, his face filled with emotions that I didn't, couldn't feel. A beautiful blond woman with big grey eyes was riding his back. Her legs were cocked up around his hips, her arms loosely circling his neck.

They looked, happy, deeply in love. The side of her peaceful looking face was pressed along the side of his. His head was tilted slightly, returning that press, making it look warm, intimate. I felt awkward watching it, almost as it I was intruding on something special. The man's eyes were smiling, his hands were wrapped around the woman, one at her thigh, one around her arms. The grip was firm in its ownership but gentle in its loving care.

Even with my troubles understanding emotion, my soul recognized it for what it was. Deep, abiding love.

The woman was smiling as she opened a bag in her hand and peeked inside.

"Oh my God." She gasped out in a familiar voice. Her eyes popped up and her face went bright red.

"What is it?" The man who looked like me asked, trying to peek in the bag.

The woman helpfully held open the bag for him to examine the items. The man's eyes widened and his cheeks flushed.

The camera moved turning to another group. A small, blond haired girl, Mali, my daughter. She was riding the back of a man I recognized as Grayson. The last man of the group was ambling beside a large horse covered in baggage. He was very familiar. My Master. His cheeks also flushed red and his head snapped sideways, those bright blue eyes of his glared right into the camera.

Laughter echoed through the mic of the camera. Close. Obviously coming from the person videotaping the scene. "This is so much better than I thought it would. Coren and Callden are going to love it." The laughing voice claimed.

"Shit. I knew it was going to bite me in this ass. I just didn't think it would be this bad." Master rubbed his neck, his face still beat red.

The camera returned to my lookalike. Both the man and the woman were smiling and whispering together. They both carried shining eyes filled with anticipation.

"Master." I whispered, turning to look at Diad when the video ended.

"Yes." Diad nodded, rewinding the video to pause on an image of the man who looked like me and the woman.

"Who are they?" I asked curiously, feeling as if I knew the woman. Her laughter, her voice.

"The woman is Leah." Diad stated, his eyes darkening before dropping to the floor between his feet.

"The Master's woman?" I frowned in confusion, this woman looked nothing like that other woman. This woman was clean, healthy, shining so bright it practically blinded me. "Who is the man?"

Diad's eyes rolled up to meet mine. "The man? His name is Malachi. The three of them, they were just starting to find their way, together. They were so happy, so in love. Both of them, Malachi and, uh, your Master, they would do just about anything for her. And she would, uh..." Diad stopped his eyes dropping again for a long moment. He cleared his throat and continued through a hoarse voice. "She would and has done...everything. For them."

"What happened to him? The man, Malachi." I asked, feeling as if my Master's anger towards me was directly linked to this man that looked so much like me.

"He's gone." Diad whispered, his fingers coming up to press into his down turned eyes.

"My Master is mad because he is gone and I am here." I stated causing the man's wet eyes to jerk up to me.

"Yes." Diad nodded slowly.

"I don't want my Master to be mad at me. It...hurts." I frowned, rubbing my hand to that weird pain in my chest. "How do I bring this man back?"

Diad was quiet for a long time, his eyes back to studying me with that disconcerting intensity. "You remember." He whispered, reaching up to press his fingertip to my temple.

I thought about that, my hand coming up to rub the spot he touched on my temple. "I remember." I whispered, my mind turning that thought over in my head.

I remembered the day it was original brought up. My Master wanted it to be my choice. The woman, Leah, she didn't want me to remember and at the time I thought that she was doing it to protect me.

Looking up at the image, Malachi and Leah, I realized that I was right. She was trying to protect me. No, not me. Him, Malachi. It would somehow cause Malachi pain for him to return. And me, I would need to essentially die.

If bringing Malachi back helped my Master in any way, I could do nothing less but return the man they loved to them.

"Very well." I agreed, my voice soft, my eyes staring up into Malachi's eyes.

CHRITON

I GOT MY UPDATES ON Apophis. Consistent and usually painful to read.

As per Leah's request. I didn't share them with her.

Apophis did indeed move Nephthys in. Diad said that they seemed to come to a strange agreement that neither one of us really understood. Apophis did everything he could to give her the care he thought she needed but beyond that Diad described their relationship as tentative friends and soon to be co-parents. Diad also made it known that, unless Nephthys was having an episode, Apophis attempted to avoid touching her. The same could not be said for her as she tended to touch him, both of the men actually, more often than either of them liked. This was done in either a platonic way or, if she was in the midst of an episode, violently.

According to Lysander, Chern was showing some pretty deep protective instincts towards the woman and was spending a lot of time in Apophis' suite with them. Diad confirmed this as well as adding his two cents. From his view of things, the woman in question was clearly displaying some sort of emotional attachment towards Chern. Apophis, on the other hand, was trusted to the point of a savagely abused caregiver.

Apophis noticed this but didn't seem very concerned about it. He just stubbornly continued to do what he could to help make the woman 'comfortable' despite the destructive violence, ignorance, and disrespect she still continually dealt him. Although, I was forced to see that the violent episodes the woman experienced was part of her extreme confusion and the deprogramming she was being put through.

After about two weeks out at the Ranch, I finally got the news I was waiting for, Nephthys was not pregnant. In fact, when Apophis and Diad insisted on walking her down to Medical so she could take the test she attacked them and screamed that she wasn't even able to have children. Luke was quick to pull out the ultrasound and determine that she wasn't lying. Dante had forced her to have her tubes clipped. It was an easy enough procedure to reverse but quite effective in stopping pregnancies. This new knowledge seemed to calm the woman slightly.

It didn't take Nephthys long to try to convince Apophis that she needed her own space. Which she really did if Diad and Apophis were getting as much abuse from her as I assumed they were. She was moved out by the next week. Days later I received my next set of news.

I wish to remember. Apophis sent me the message directly through our connection.

I know things haven't turned out the way you wanted them to, but that doesn't mean they won't turn out for the better.

There is no better for me. I am not meant for that. I don't even understand it. But he was meant for it. He deserves it and you deserve him.

Who was?

Your Malachi.

To say I was surprised at this statement was an understatement. I didn't even realize he understood who Malachi was.

You do realize what it means for you if he is brought back.

I fully understand. My life for his.

Not quite.

Yes. My life for his. The things I did, they weren't him. I want you to know this. I want him to know this. It was me. The control, the obedience, the nonexistent emotions. I fully understand that there is something intrinsically wrong with me. But that is me, not him. He is not me. I am not him.

Very well. I will set it up with Luke and let you know when.

Will, uh, will you be there, Master?

Yes. As much as I wanted to leave him to it, especially with the way Leah was healing and starting to return to her warm, shining self, I couldn't. Not him. Not my Malachi. I messaged Luke, getting the procedure all set up before letting Apophis know.

Leah, love, we need to talk.

I am in the tent, folding clothes.

Returning to the tent, I did indeed find Leah folding clothes.

"I have news." I cringed, sitting down on the bed to the side of the clothes she was folding into piles.

Leah paused and turned to me. Her eyes shuttering, waiting for my news. Right from the start she informed me that she only wanted to hear news pertaining to Apophis if it involved his death or the return of Malachi's memories.

"The procedure is a go for tomorrow." I told her, reaching out to take her shaking hand in mine.

"I can't." Leah swallowed, her eyes begging me to leave her out of it.

"I know. But I need to be there." I told her, my voice calm.

She gave me quick smile and a sharp nod. "I know."

"I will stay in contact with you. As much as possible."

"I know." She gave me another of those sharp nods.

"What are you thinking, Leah? I can guess what might be going through your mind right at this moment, but I can't be sure." I asked softly, praying that she opened up.

"It's nothing, Chriton, really. This isn't about me. It's about him. I can't imagine how hard it will be for him when he remembers what...he is going to need you to help him through this. I am really glad he has you." Leah gave me a wobbling smile.

"Leah." I pressed, knowing that what she said was true but it was also only half of what was churning inside her. When she shook her head in denial, eyes trained on the laundry her hands were clenched around, I demanded. "Leah."

No, Chriton! She snapped into my head, her voice filled with agony. *This isn't about me. This isn't about the fact that I forced myself to bury him because that was the only way I could find my happiness. I need him, all of it, to stay dead and buried. Because the alternative is the fact that one of the men I loved with every ounce of my being couldn't remember me long enough to stop the monster using his body from torturing me in every way possible. He did everything he could to break me, Chriton. And he succeeded. Now, when I see him, all I feel is hate.*

"Leah, my precious love." I stood to cup her face gently in my hands, feeling helpless in the face of her pain.

"Why didn't he see me, Chriton?" Leah cried, jerking herself out of my hold. The laundry went flying everywhere and she pounded her fisted hand into her chest. "If I was so deep inside his soul like he claimed I was then why didn't he recognize me like he did Mali? Like he did you? Because I am not there. I am nothing to him, Chriton. I am nothing. And I need to stay nothing. Because being nothing hurts a lot fucking less than...being broken"

"Fuck." I attempted to breath back my tears while tugging the struggling woman into my arms. "Feel me, Leah, feel me." I ordered hoarsely. "You aren't nothing, you are everything. Everything."

Leah stopped struggling when she felt my DNA start mingling with hers. "Only to you, Chriton. Only to you." She whispered, allowing herself to fall limply into me. For some reason the feel of us mixing and connecting this way always seemed to calm her, reassure her that I was still here.

"I need you to understand something, precious. This is completely Apophis' choice. He told me that he doesn't see himself and Malachi as the same person. And he doesn't want me to see them as the same. He told me that he was ready to trade his life for Malachi's." I shared with her.

"Will...he see it that way?" Leah's mouth quivered and she drew away, her eyes filling with heartbreaking knowledge.

"I guess we will see." I whispered, reaching out to brush my fingers over her wet cheeks. I wanted to hold her tight and tell her that everything would be all right. I wanted to protect her beautiful caring soul from any more harm. I wanted to, but I knew that I couldn't.

"Yeah." Leah sighed, giving herself a slight shake before her shoulders firmed. I hated that she felt this need to mentally and physically prepare herself for even more pain, but I loved her strength. "I love you, Chriton."

"Yeah, precious. I love you, too." I returned, feeling pride blooming in my chest. She might not be ready to deal with Apophis and Malachi. She might not ever be ready for that. But she was fully ready to stand by my side while I did what I needed to do.

CHAPTER 26

MALACHI

My brain felt like it was seizing over and over again while the pathways within started reconnecting. Doorways opened. More and more memories flooded in. Older memories rising to mix with newer horrific ones. What was once emotionless and analytical was now searing through my brain. Horror and agony shattered through me. Leah. Tears squeezed out from underneath my eyelids. My heart stuttered to a stop before it resumed beating. My chest struggled to continue drawing in life giving air.

"Shit." I heard Master's, Chriton's voice snarl.

"It was just a skip. We expected it." Another voice, Luke's voice advised.

More knowledge fell into place.

Grayson begging me, fighting for Leah, until I broke his jaw. Leah, fighting and begging, pleading for me to return to her, to stop hurting her. My fists finding the give of her muscles and bones. My hands working the whip that I used to open her flesh with. And so much more. Electrocutions, burnings, drownings.

Through it all she kept fighting.

Until I finally broke her.

The look of utter defeat and acceptance in her eyes when she watched me fuck another woman in front of her. Revulsion and nausea rolled through me at the memory of that woman's skin touching mine. And all the others, so many others. Vomit rose sharply in my throat only for me to swallow it down. I swear I felt my dick try to crawl back up into my body so that I never used it like that ever again.

It was in that fucking moment that I literally saw Leah's love for me die. I killed it. I killed everything. That one moment stayed in the forefront of my brain and swirled with the next one, the one of me pressing the sharp tip of the knife into the delicate skin of her wrist while she screamed at me to kill her.

Knowing that I drove her to that made me want to find another knife to use on myself. Slowly.

"How much longer?" Chriton growled.

"Almost...done." Luke snorted and the seizing feeling stopped.

"Malachi?" Chriton's voice sounded above me. I cracked open my leaking eyes and stared up at him.

"I fucked up." I swallowed through a painfully tight throat, already knowing that I fucked up to the point that Leah refused to even live in the same Base as me.

"Yeah. You did. Big time." Chriton told me, his haunted eyes mixing with amusement.

My eyes narrowed on Luke when his face vision bombed Chriton's. "It's damned good to have you back. No offense, but I am pretty sure you housed most of your brains in your memories because that other guy was a complete putz."

"He has a point." Chriton pointed a thumb over to Luke who was now packing up a bunch of electrical equipment and rolling it out of the room. "By far the dumbest Drako zombie I have ever seen, or even heard of."

"Yeah. He was a dumb ass." I agreed, levering myself up and grabbing a nearby garbage can so that my continually roiling stomach could violently spew it's disgust out. By the time I was done, my whole chest hurt.

Chriton helpfully handed me a glass of water and a toothbrush that he pulled out from places unknown. I took the time to thoroughly scrub the leftover nasty from my mouth before rinsing with the water and spitting it all out into the garbage.

With shaking hands, I set the garbage can down. Not knowing what to say or do next, I stared down into my lap. I felt Chriton's hand squeeze down on my shoulder, his grip familiar and reassuring.

"How is she?" I asked softly, needing to know.

"Healing. Slowly." Chriton told me, sitting down beside me on the bed.

"Good. I am glad." I nodded slowly, my heart squeezing tight at the pain of loosing her. But then, I already lost her. Weeks ago. "You, uh...I know I don't have the right to demand this, but you need to love her deep enough for both of us."

"Believe me, I do. And she loves me back just as deeply." Chriton told me, sending another shard of pain through me.

"Why are you still here? Why didn't you take them home, to Andromada?" I finally lifted my gaze to his.

A different memory flashed through my brain, not mine, but Chriton's. Leah screaming angry words that ripped and lacerated my very soul as she threw clothing all around and violently pounded her fist into her chest. Chriton was sharing it with me.

"That was yesterday. She never wanted you to come back, to remember. Because she didn't want you hurt by what he did while you were brainless. But also, because, if you didn't come back then she could, not only let herself forget every torturous thing he did to her, but she could also forget you. She could console herself with the thought that Malachi was dead while his bastard of a twin, Apophis, was alive and living at the Base. If you came back that wasn't a possibility. Now she has to face the reality of the pain he gave her, the hatred he inadvertently brewed inside her mixing with the love she still holds for you." Chriton explained harshly. "She desperately tried to separate the two of you in her mind because she knew it wasn't you, it wasn't your fault. But in the end she couldn't completely do it, because deep inside Apophis was the soul she loved so desperately, your soul."

"And my soul recognized Mali and you but not her." I rasped out.

"Exactly." Chriton confirmed with a nod. "I didn't take them home because despite her mixed feelings and confusion about you, there is no home. Not for me. Not for Mali. Not even for Leah. Not without you. As long as Apophis was out there, there was a slim chance of Malachi returning to us. And I knew that while Leah needed him out of sight so that she could begin to heal, she didn't want him so far away that she couldn't get to you if she needed to."

"So now what?" I wearily asked the man beside me, completely lost but extremely grateful to have him still standing, or sitting, by my side.

"Fucked if I know." Chriton shrugged. "I am just flying by the seat of my pants here."

I couldn't stop my surprised laughter from bursting out at Chriton's statement. "Shit, we really are a pair, aren't we, 'Master'?"

"Hey man, you're the one who gave me the name in the first place." Chriton reminded me with a wink. "I just used it to my advantage."

"I did, didn't I?" I smiled warmly at the memory.

"Show her." Luke stated, stepping into the room.

"What?" Chriton asked Luke curiously.

"When Lysander and I first, well, started, he told me that he was extremely attracted to me and he wanted to be with me but I wasn't his soulmate. He didn't feel that connection with me. When we met Nova, that connection finally snapped into place for him. But by then it was too late, I didn't believe him. I told him that his words were meaningless. Truthfully, at that point, they were. If he wanted me to believe him and accept him after he hurt me so badly, he needed to show me." Luke explained, crossing his arms and leaning back into the wall. "Don't say anything beyond an apology because at this point words are meaningless to her. Instead, you need to do everything you can to show her how much she means to you. Every moment that you can. Whenever you think about her, share it with her." Luke tapped on his temple, showing us that he knew about the telepathic connections. "Send her little things that remind you of her or things that you know she will like. She still loves you. You just need to show her how much you still love her and how different you actually are from Apophis. She tried to separate the two of you but couldn't. Do it for her. Show her that he is not you and you are not him. Two completely different men."

"Fuck, I keep forgetting how smart you actually are." I whispered up at the man with an amazed voice.

"And you lot consistently complain about my bedside manner." Luke scoffed, turning to leave the room before stopping and turning back. "Oh, and one more thing. Show her exactly what she is missing."

"Malachi doesn't have a girlfriend and no way is he getting one." Chriton shook his head vehemently while I claimed, "Are you crazy? I already destroyed her by cheating on her."

"Noooo." Luke held up a finger, stopping the onslaught of our exclamations. "Apophis had a girlfriend. Not Malachi. Malachi does, however, have a boyfriend." Luke grinned slyly, dropping his finger and pointing at Chriton.

"Wait." Chriton shook his head at the same time I frowned and began to rise. "What?"

"Show her." Luke grinned and winked before spinning around and skipping out.

"I, uh." I swallowed and turned to look at Chriton. My mind flashed to the things I did as Apophis. That pale eyed woman wasn't the only one, she was just the one that Apophis centered on. She was the most beautiful, the cleanest, the most powerful. She was the one that always stood at Dante's side. There were others, other women, other men that Apophis was ordered to pleasure. And he did.

I pressed my hand to the empty stomach that was roiling with sickening disgust once again. I forced my mind to turn from the experience I was unknowingly forced to gain to the man beside me.

Chriton.

The thought of him helped. By replacing those repulsive images with him I was able to calm my stomach. Before Apophis, I never would have looked at another male like I was looking at Chriton.

"Yeah. Ok." Chriton breathed, running a set of frustrated hands through his hair, messing up the dark strands, leaving them to fall around the sharply attractive features of his face.

Not knowing what else to do, but knowing that he was still here, with me, I reached out to grip his jaw and turn his face to mine.

"What?" He frowned right before my lips covered his. His mouth froze underneath mine before it slowly opened for the tongue I was sliding along his smooth lips. He tasted good, really good.

Chriton's firm tongue investigated over the one I was exploring his with, rubbing and caressing together in a delightful way. I deepened the kiss, taking my time to learn him in deliciously new ways that were frankly arousing.

By the time I drew back, we were both breathing hard.

"Well, that was new." Chriton breathed, his tongue licking over his moist lips. A tongue I really wanted to taste again.

"Yeah, Apophis was experienced. Emotionless, but experienced." I cringed and straightened away from him, feeling that familiar burn churning in my stomach.

"Experienced, huh?" Chriton's eyebrows shot up with his amusement, thankfully drawing my attention back to center on him. "Are you still a virgin?" He asked, his eyes dropping to the curve of my ass with a mischievous gleam.

"Are you?" I shot back, giving him my own relieved grin. He wasn't mad at me for the things I did, the things I was forced to do while I was that brainless thunk.

"Yup." He nodded, giving me a wicked grin. "I have, however, experimented with that side of my sexuality."

"How far?" I asked curiously, feeling a familiar heat rising in my body.

"Oral." He stated bluntly before turning the question back to me, "You?"

"Yeah. I also know that, uh, male ass feels delightfully different." I shared with him, my mind filling with the image of him sucking my quickly rousing cock.

"Hmmm." He hummed, his eyes dropping back to my ass, his legs shifting on the bed. My eyes followed the tensed line of his thighs up to the bulge filling his jeans.

I felt my own stiffened dick twitch wildly in response to that sight, bouncing along the thin scrub pants I was dressed in.

"Fuck." I attempted to breath back my arousal, giving myself a shake and rubbing the palms of my hands harshly into my eyes.

Chriton chuckled and reached over to grip my shoulder in a way that I truly missed. I missed him. Our connection. Just as much as I missed Leah. At the thought of her, my amusement fell away.

"Hey." Chriton gave my shoulder a shake. "It's going to be fucking hard. But we will get there. With her."

"Fuck, I really hope so." I whispered, my hand rubbing at the pain in my chest.

"We will. In the meantime, we both have to work hard and be patient. Never give up." Chriton's fingers found my jaw and gently turned my face to his. He leaned forward and pressed a soft kiss to my lips.

"Never give up." I repeated against his lips, feeling that determination resounding in my soul.

———————

LUKE

WALKING DOWN THE BACK hall of Medical, I returned to my office and opened a voice link on my coms.

"Doctor." The female voice that answered was heartbreakingly soft.

"It's done." I told her, falling back into the office chair behind my desk.

"How is he?" Leah asked, her voice hesitant.

"He came out of it and immediately puked his guts out, which I will note is not because of the procedure. He is kicking his own ass harder than anyone I have ever seen. But he's not broken. He's ripped and bleeding, a visibly open wound. But he's stubborn and determined. He's definitely not giving up. Mind you, Chriton's a stubborn fucker as well and I think that is helping maintain that determination." I explained honestly.

"Good. And the things we talked about?" She continued in that voice, making my own heart hurt.

"Funny thing about a doctor's advise, as much as people hate it, they all still end up listening to it." I chuckled. "Quiet now, the show's about to start."

"And what I, uh, shared with you?" Leah whispered, her voice becoming emotionally thick.

"Yeah, you were right about that." I said in a low, careful tone.

"I, uh, figured as much." Her voice hitched dangerously before I heard her take deep shuddering breath in. "Are they...?"

"Yes, Leah. You were right about that too. They are examining it as we speak. I don't see them holding out long. Not with the connection between them." I shared with her.

"Good. This way they will at least have each other." Leah whispered.

"Leah, don't make me come down there." I straightened in my chair and glared at my coms as if the woman could actually see me.

"No. Nothing like that. It's just, if I can't, forgive." Leah rasped, her voice quivering. "Then at least he, uh, he won't be alone. He will have Chriton."

"And what will you have?" I demanded, my voice harsh.

"I don't know, doctor. Right now, all I know is that I can't stand the thought of either of them being alone. Beyond that...I just don't know." She whispered. "I, uh, I have to go now. Mali will be back soon."

"Ok, Leah. You know where I am, right?" I demanded, my voice injecting a silent order for her to call me if she needed.

"Yes, doctor. Thank you." The line cut dead.

Feeling concerned anxiety building in my chest I opened another call.

"Doc, after our last date I assumed that it would be a while before we connected again." Grayson's voice greeted.

"What can I say, men who are feverish and barely clinging to life are totally my game." I chuckled. "I just really want to get my hands on their hot bodies."

"Shit, doc." Grayson choked and coughed for a couple minutes before he chuckled. "You made me choke on my water."

"Come see me, big boy, and I will give you the Heimlich." I told him in a crooning voice.

"You always say the sweetest things." He said causing both of us to laugh. "Seriously though, what do you want?"

"Chriton's here. Malachi's back." I clipped out.

"Shit. Ok. I got her. Fuck, I hope she likes poker." He stumbled over his words, clearly dealing with this new information while worrying over the woman in question.

"And you?" I asked the Malachi's best friend.

"Nope." Grayson snarled angrily. "Not yet. Not with his shit so up in the fucking air. He can find me when he's ready. In the meantime, I will keep an eye on his woman. Keep her fucking breathing for him."

"Works for me. Thanks, Grayson." I told him gratefully.

"Yeah, yeah." Grayson emoted right before the line went dead.

Satisfied that I did everything I could, I sent a detailed message to Lysander before sending my own prayers to whoever deigned to listen.

CHAPTER 27

MALACHI

I returned to my empty suite, well not completely empty, Diad was thankfully there. It unfortunately still felt like an echo of how my heart felt. Painfully empty, and wrong. So fucking wrong.

Not only could I feel that noxious woman's residual presence staining the very walls themselves but the absolute physical destruction she left in her wake was also a keen reminder that she been here, in this sacred space. The bulk of the furniture and items in the main room and my old room were destroyed in some way due to her rage filled actions and the whole suite held this toxic, sludgy feeling.

"Well, you look like Malachi." Diad stepped out of the room he was staying in. He ran his narrowed eyes over my body in an intrusive way that made me want to smack him.

"Fuck off." I couldn't help chuckling at his obviousness. While it hurt more than I could say to have my family gone, I was glad to not be completely alone.

"Yeah, it's Malachi." Diad grinned happily. "How are you feeling with it all?"

"Like the biggest fuck up in the history of the universe." I sighed, falling back onto the couch and cringing when it gave a disconcerting crack. The thing was barely hanging on after that woman went hole hog on it during an episode.

"I can see that. I can also see that you have a plan." Diad noted, taking his own seat on one of the chairs that was missing an arm.

"I do, thanks to the good doctor." I was determined. I was alone for now but if I worked it right, I wouldn't stay alone. I was going to get my family back. "I am going to annoy the fuck out of her with everything I can think of. Then, when I have her complete attention, I am going to allow Chriton to fuck me, right in front of her. I am going to take everything I have and place it in the palm of her hand. Everything. My boundaries, my control, my fucking soul. Everything."

"I, uh, ok." Diad's eyes were wide with surprise. "That might actually work."

"First up, I am going to fucking grow my hair out. I hated short hair when I was in the forces and now short hair not only annoys the fuck out of me but it most likely reminds Leah of Apophis." I scowled and ran my hand over the top of my head and my clean shaven jaw. Maybe a beard was also in order. I wanted to make myself look as different from Apophis as possible.

"My second step is to make her a home." I turned my gaze to the grey walled suite around me. "Something that is all hers. No one else's." While most of the material items and furniture were a complete wash, I refused to have Leah come home to the same suite another woman lived in. A toxic suite that I now hated.

"Sounds like a plan." Diad grinned maniacally, obviously completely onboard.

That evening Lysander, Marko, and I sat down so that I could be debriefed on everything that went on in the Base while I was gone. The good and the bad.

One of the worst items was an incident with the First Team, my team. Some days after we were kidnapped the Base received some intel that there might by information on the location were Leah, Grayson, and I were being held hidden in a small Drako facility. My team went in, down by two.

It turned out to be a set up. The building blew up. Luckily, everyone was able to get out alive. A lot of them acquired severe injuries that they were fortunately recovering from.

Then there was Scope.

According to the report, he was closest to the bomb when it went off. While he thankfully wasn't blown to pieces, he did get a face full of shrapnel and a crushed hip due to the building trying to fall down on him. He also completely lost his eyesight due to the bright flash of the bomb.

Scope was healing, slowly. He currently walked with a cane due to a severe limp. He was also learning how to move around in his new perpetually dark world while doing extensive physiotherapy on the hip that Luke was thankfully able to rebuild.

Needless to say, Scope was dealing with the immensity of his physical changes. He was no longer the same man he once was. Strangely, he was cynically accepting of it all. According to Wings, he now portrayed a disturbingly silent character with a dangerous mix of self derision, sarcasm, and an amusing dry wit.

Royce reported that Scope refused to allow her to help him, but he seemed very determined to get himself back to fighting fit despite his vision loss. While it wasn't a deep concern, she did make mention that he might be attempting to overcompensate for the loss of something that defined him so much.

Either way, he was my next stop. Scope was happy to have me back but beyond that he was silently introspective. Not knowing what else to say, I simply sat with him and told him stories about my time with Declan, which he actually seemed to enjoy.

The next morning, I took the first of many videos I planned to send Leah and Chriton. With my coms recording, I walked down the lower floor hall. Only instead of stepping into our old suite that was down and across from the others, I opened the door to one that was right beside her best friend, Salem's. I kept recording as I toured the unfurnished, grey walled suite and its four bedrooms. I tagged it, *Beginning.*

Then I sent it to Leah and Chriton.

Show us. Was Chriton's return message.

So, I did.

Over the next few days, I officially resumed my position and spent time with Scope helping him adjust and learn. He was surprisingly quick and inordinately calm about it all. Instead of getting frustrated, he would continue working at something until he got it, even if it took him hours. Unfortunately, the only time I ever really saw Scope show any bit of his old self was when Wings showed up and egged him on or challenged him. That was when Scope showed the life he still harboured inside him.

I recorded myself choosing paint colors, opening them up in the new suite. I took video of Diad helping me paint the walls or of my own hand painting.

All of it was sent to Leah and Chriton with detailed descriptions of what I was doing.

While your hand work is top notch, it's still just a tease. I laughed when I received Chriton's demanding message.

That night, when I was done painting for the day, Diad took a picture of me from the neck down. I was dressed in a pair of ragged shorts and an old tank top, sweaty and covered in paint splotches.

Take it off! I laughed when I quickly received a return message. While it was Chriton making the demands, I also prayed that Leah was seeing these.

Going to the bathroom, I pulled my shirt off and used the mirror to take another picture.

LEAH

"FOR FUCK SAKES. STOP drooling over him." I rolled my eyes and reached out to grab Chriton's wrist to close down the picture that was open.

Malachi was standing in front of a mirror. No face, all upper body. His old, ratty assed shorts hung loosely from his hips. His skin gleaming with sweat and covered in paint. His abdomen tight, curved in a way that accented his ripped muscles. His darkened nipples tight and standing out on his large pecs.

I completely forgot how sexy he was. Something I forced myself to do in order to heal and move forward.

"No." Chriton laughed and jerked his wrist away. "I will stop drooling when you stop drooling."

"Jesus, are you really that horny?" I asked, my eyes dragging down his t-shirt covered chest to the throbbing length filling his pants.

"Yup. For you, for him, always. I will take everything I can get." He winked at me right before launching across the bed at me.

"No." I scrambled from the bed and pointed a firm finger at him. "Go out and get our daughter, it's time for supper. You can get laid after bedtime."

"Fine." Chriton straightened from the bed and walked to the tent flap only to pause and point at me. "Do not even think about masturbating to that picture. Because I know he sent it to you too."

"What? I would never." I gasped with fake innocence.

"Bullshit. You totally would." Chriton refuted my argument. "We will do that together."

"Fine." I raised my hands up in the air.

"Seriously, Leah, if I find out you touched yourself without me, I will make you regret it." Chriton ordered, his blue eyes filling with threat.

"How?" I bit my lip and asked out of pure curiosity.

"Hmm." He hummed softly. "I think it's been too long since I tied you down, filled your pussy with that toy you love so much, and fucked your ass."

I whimpered at the thought of that very memorable night. I came so hard that night that I passed out and scared the crap out of him. My pussy clenched, empty and yearning.

"Yeah, my girl needs some playtime." Chriton dragged his glowing eyes over my aroused, trembling body. Then the maddening man grinned and walked out, leaving me with that arousal.

"Ass." I called after him hearing his echoing chuckle in return.

That night we did play. And I didn't masturbate to Malachi's picture...without Chriton.

CHAPTER 28

MALACHI

After I finished painting, I continued with the videos. I also started adding gifts. Books, golf balls and clubs, toiletries, boardgames, a new video camera. I even joyfully sent one of my sweatshirts to the Ranch at Chriton's request.

I also started reaching out to the daughter I missed more than life. I sent her flowers that Callden grew in the garden and allowed me to replant into pots for her. I sent her books that I knew she liked to read and blankets to keep her warm. I wrote her letters everyday telling her about my days. I even broke down and sent her a hair dye kit, this one a pink that would go well with her skin tone.

According to Chriton the gifts were received with quiet introspection but were kept with love. A full week passed after I first regained my memory before Chriton visited for the weekend.

"Sexy." He grinned and gently pulled on the hairs of the short, well trimmed beard I grew.

He also brought with him the most precious gift. Mali finally wrote me back. That night, Chriton held me as I read and reread the letter with tears running down my face. Seeing her childlike writing telling me about her life at the Ranch, opening up and sharing with me was more beauty than I could bear right in that moment.

I woke up in the morning, my body completely wrapped around his for the first time in a long time. Instead of getting up, I stayed as I was, relishing every second.

"It's working, you know." He breathed softly, shifting around until he was facing me. "We watch the videos, we read the messages, we open the gifts, together. And every time, she smiles. At first it was heartbreaking, filled with heartbreak and hopeless dreams. But that smile has already become soft and appreciative."

"Thank God." I whispered, my eyes closing tightly.

"Her and Mali are hanging with Grayson this weekend." Chriton told me, dropping the next hammer.

"How is he?" I bit the bullet and asked the question I was avoiding.

"He's mad. Angry. Not just on his own behalf but on all of ours. Including yours. Right now, he's waiting for you to heal and get your shit together. He said it's up to you to come to him." Chriton explained with a slight wince.

"That's his right." I agreed with Grayson on that. I was the one that fucked up. It was up to me to find him and apologize, to acknowledge the wrong I did.

"True." Chriton grunted, subtly shifting around until his thick thigh was pressing into my sensitive ball sack.

I smiled and reached down to grip his thigh, holding him to me. "You know, as much as I want to take on this leg and everything else it leads to, I really need to wait for her."

"We both do. But that doesn't mean we can't play." Chriton waggled his eyebrows at me, rubbing his leg maddeningly against me.

"Play? Is that what you and Leah do?" I joked, tightening my fingers around him.

"Since the day you went in to undergo the procedure to remember, yes." Chriton surprisingly shared. "When the possibility of your return came about it no longer felt right. Not with you out there in the world and not with us, participating."

"So, no..." I led, rising my disbelieving eyebrows at him.

"Nope." Chriton shook his head.

"Playing." I nodded slowly, turning the word and its possibilities over in my head before rolling from the bed and pointing at the devious man that had been slowly crawling his fingers down my abdomen. "Not now, you fiend. Right now, we have shit to do. Gifts to find, letters to write, furniture to pick out, videos to record. It's a full day of fishing for the big one, Master of mine. So, get that ass up."

"Fine. But I expect you to show your full appreciation after we are done." Chriton growled, rolling from the bed and stomping to the bathroom.

"Only if we video it for her." I called after him.

"Oh, hey, before I forget again, I have a question." He called back from the bathroom where he was obviously peeing with the door open.

"What's that?" I asked, walking into the kitchen to start the coffee.

"Why are you sleeping in Leah's room?" He asked over the water running as he washed his hands.

"Apophis started it. When he first arrived, he kept waking up in that room. He was addicted to the smell in there. Diad was sleeping in your room so that one was off limits to him. When that woman moved in, he told her that she could use his old room. He didn't ever allow her or Chern into Mali's room or his new room, Leah's. Which turned out to be pretty smart considering how much that woman ended up destroying." I absently shared my memories of the man's thoughts and scratched at the short growth of facial hair that I was still trying to get used to.

"Seriously?" Chriton asked, coming out of the bathroom to stare at me. His coms was raised and pointed at me.

"Yeah, why?" I asked before scowling at him. "Did you just video tape our conversation...while you were peeing?"

"She doesn't care if I pee in front of her." Chriton turned his wrist so that it was facing him, "Right, love?"

That wrist was turned back to me just in time to catch my eye roll. "Back to my original question, why?"

"She believes you never remembered her, but maybe you did after you returned to the Base." Chriton clipped out, his voice sounding slightly excited. "Walk me through it, Malachi."

"Uh, ok." I thought about it while I turned to fix coffees for the two of us and handing Chriton his.

"Tell me about the smell." Chriton helpfully led.

"Oh, yeah. Shit, she's going to hate me for this, but here we go. He thought she stunk. Looking back now, I realize that while he was being put through the, uh, extensive brainwashing and training process with the lizards and Grays, she was kept mostly unconscious and locked in that cage." I pulled at the irritatingly short strands of my hair and shoved those extremely painful memories aside so that I could continue. "By the time Apophis first saw her, uh, after, she had already been locked in that cage for two, maybe three weeks. She was dirty and smelled very badly. She was also bruised and swollen, beaten by others. He was disgusted by her. Dante consistently called her an animal, so that's what Apophis saw. A dirty, repulsive animal."

I paused to take a deep, bracing drink of my coffee. "When we got back she was finally able to clean herself and receive medical treatment. She entered the room we were all in and she smelled good, really fucking good. When she disagreed with Apophis regaining my memories, he got the sense that she was doing it to protect him for some reason. Between that and the way you, his Master, treated her, he really started opening his eyes. When he first arrived at the suite, he could smell her. As I said, he become obsessed with that smell, protective. Then Diad showed him the video."

"What video?" Chriton frowned and asked.

"The one that Bane took our first day out at the Ranch. We were walking to the campsite and Bane gave Leah the bag of toys before videotaping our reactions." I described with a ghost of a smile, leaning back against the counter.

"Oh, that video." Chriton winced, his face blushing a deep red making me chuckle.

"Yeah." I grinned and winked at him before continuing. "Apophis, he didn't link himself to the man in the video, to me. He saw you and Mali, and he obviously knew who you two were. But Leah, he recognized Leah, inside." I pounded my fist to my chest to make my point. "She was clean and healthy, beautiful. He was immediately attracted and wanted to know who she was. When he learned who she actually was and how she was linked to the man that looked so much like him, he wanted to know about that man. He realized then that Leah wasn't protecting him, Apophis, that day in Medical, she was protecting the man in the video, me, Malachi. He saw her pain, your pain, and he didn't like that. It wasn't right. He felt the keen need to give you what you needed to be happy. Even though he didn't understand that word, that emotion, he knew he was seeing it in that video. So, he made the decision to destroy himself and bring me back to you."

Chriton twisted his wrist so that he was looking into the camera. "I love you, Leah, my precious. Be prepared for more video's because this mad man before me literally kicked me out of bed so that we could spend the day doing things for you and our daughter. Also, how hot is that beard?" He turned the camera back to me. "Say goodbye, Malachi."

Instead of saying anything, I stared into the camera and pressed my palm to my chest, telling her without words how much I loved her, how much I missed her.

Chriton lowered his wrist enough that he could type out a message to go with the video before he sent it off. Then he stepped forward and gipped the back of my neck. "I have to say this, that was dead ass sexy." He said hoarsely pulling me towards him and taking my lips with his. I moaned softly and twisted my head so that I could get even deeper into his mouth. I shivered and attempted to ignore the erection that popped up at a dizzying speed. The feel of his lips on mine, demanding yet giving, was phenomenal.

"You liked that, did you?" I said through my heavy breathing when I drew slightly back.

"Yeah, you almost made me come in my pants." Chriton grinned against my lips.

"Your taste almost made me do that." I returned his smile with a slight nip to those smooth lips of his.

"Hmm." He hummed, his lids falling over his glowing eyes, the hand gripping my neck sliding down over my chest.

"Nope." I brushed his arm away and side stepped his groping hand.

"Again?" He called after my fleeing body.

"Yup. I already told you, we have shit to do. Now stop distracting me." I lectured him as I shut the bathroom door behind me.

CHRITON

I LAUGHED AS THE DOOR to the bathroom slammed shut. I was really enjoying this playful side of him. I knew of it, I had seen it many times before, but I never had it directed right at me. It was a heady experience.

I couldn't lie to myself. It was only the thought of him and Apophis being two entirely different people who happened to share the same body that was stopping the pain of the knowledge that his body had been used to pleasure others.

I did, however, love the fact that Malachi, now that he was himself again, was doing everything he could to show us all how much he loved us. I also loved the fact that he was completely open to me, not just emotionally but physically. That was all because of Apophis' 'experience'. Apophis looked at me as his Master and saw me as an attractive male not just someone already placed firmly in the friend zone.

It also helped me realize exactly how sexually attracted I actually was to him. That first kiss was extremely surprising and frankly shocking. But it also blew my mind wide open to the possibility of him. The fact that the man was a damned good kisser helped quite a bit. Before I even knew what I was doing, I was kissing him back.

Now I just wanted more. And even though I knew I wouldn't get everything I wanted from him just yet, I was determined to enjoy the ride.

That day we did exactly what Malachi said we would. We videotaped us kidnapping Scope and bringing him with us to help test furniture. We attempted to make out choices based on what we thought the girls would like which, weirdly enough, ended up being most of the ones Scope picked. After we were done with the selection process it was all set to be delivered to the new suite. All new stuff.

Those videos were sent to Leah and Mali.

Malachi came across some hair clips and ties that he thought Mali would like. He was quick to pack those away for me to take when I returned to the Ranch. We both ended up in an argument over a set of lingerie for Leah. I wanted this lime green set that I thought would look phenomenal on her. Malachi argued that she wasn't the Kool aid man. When I tried to argue my case, he draped the hanger over his neck so the lingerie was hanging down his body. Then he jumped forward and yelled "Oh yeah!" While bowing his body out and shaking his fists in the air.

Needless to say, he won the argument, picking a black and pink set while I was dying of laughter on the floor at Scope's amused feet. It was honestly great to hear Scope laugh.

That video was also sent to Leah.

Wings eventually appeared and saved Scope from our madness, as Wings termed it. After that Malachi and I returned to the old suite to make dinner only for me to receive my own message from Bane. Pictures and one video that I shared with Malachi before sending it to him. We both bent over the counter and flipped through the visuals together.

The first was one of a mud covered Mali and Leah hugging each other and celebrating some sort of win while other muddy people cheered them on. The second was of Leah dyeing Mali's blond hair with the pink hair dye Malachi sent her.

The third was of the finished product. Leah was helping a pink haired Mali spin for the camera, both of them were laughing happily. The last was of the girls in Mali's bed, I could clearly tell that Mali was reading her bedtime book to Leah while Leah helped her with the words.

The last, the video, was of Leah. She was sitting in the security tent with three men and one woman. Bane, Grayson, Harper, and Dr. John James were all sitting around the table playing cards. Bane was clearly the one video taping it.

"Seriously, again? Fuck, Leah, give me chance here." Grayson groaned, throwing his cards down on a large pile of chips. The spot in front of him was intriguingly empty of chips.

"Oh, stop whining. You won last time." Harper laughed, nudging Grayson with her shoulder.

"And I liked it." Grayson pouted. "Do you realize that I haven't had to do my laundry in like three weeks."

"Now you will have to do it three times a week." Leah grinned, sticking her tongue out at him. "And you know how dirty and sweaty a couple of men can get. That's a lot of ball sweat for you to contend with."

"Come on." Grayson groaned, making the whole table laugh.

"Thank your lucky stars that it isn't Bailor. He's got one hell of a set on him." Bane pointed out.

"John, do you want to weigh in here?" Grayson turned to the doctor for help.

"Fuck no." John shook his head, giving Grayson his own grin. "You successfully proved to me that men are dirty and sweaty. There is no way I am risking another week of that."

"I am not that dirty." Grayson exclaimed in defense.

"Not to yourself. No one actually minds washing their own unmentionables or even their loved one's unmentionables because well, hello. But an acquaintance's or even a friend's? No matter how clean they are, it is still gross. No, thanks." Leah shuddered at that thought sending more laughter around the table.

"Anyone else want to test their luck?" John asked, shuffling the deck of cards. This question caused Bane, Harper, and Grayson to all immediately abandon their chairs and jump back from the table as if it was cursed.

Leah looked shocked for a moment before she burst into so much laughter that she ended up crying and choking.

Bane twisted the camera so that it was facing him. "She's totally annihilating us. And she's having one hell of a time doing it." He shared with a grin right before the video shut off.

Malachi was quiet beside me, his breathing heavy and slightly stuttered. "Hey." I wrapped my arm around his shoulders and drew him into my side.

"She's so fucking beautiful. They both are." Malachi breathed, his voice hitching slightly. "They look...happy."

"You didn't see it." I noted, tilting my head to lean against his.

"See what?" He asked hoarsely.

I rewound the video to the part he didn't seem to catch.

Leah was back on screen, sticking her tongue out at Grayson. "And you know how dirty and sweaty a couple of men can get. That's a lot of ball sweat for you to contend with."

When Malachi still didn't say anything I rewound it again. "...a couple of men..."

Malachi jerked at those words, his eyes widening in amazed realization. "I guarantee you, before we go to bed she will message me to being your dirty clothes with me when I return." I grinned over at him. "She will make the excuse of fucking with Grayson, but her words right there already told the story. She doesn't just claim one man, she claims 'a couple of men.'" I finger quoted.

"Fuck. I feel like I should pack everything now." Malachi let out a husky laugh, finally leaning his head back into mine. "I also feel like I should fart in the pair I am wearing now. Like a lot. Or better yet, smear some chocolate pudding on a couple pairs."

"That's absolutely brilliant and disgusting all at the same time." I laughed and nodded. "Let's wait for her message then tell her your plan. She's going to love it."

"I agree." Malachi grinned maniacally, straightening form the counter. "Now, feed me. I am starving." His order was punctuated by a sharp slap to my ass.

"Hey, who's the Master here?" I straightened and glared at him, my arms crossing my chest.

"Who's the Boss?" He shot back.

"Um, Master beats Boss." I pointed out.

He grinned and brought his hand up, waving his fingers at me. "That's not what my stinging hand tells me."

"Well, my hand is going to be stinging in a second." I threatened, raising my own hand.

"Fuck, stop trying to make me blow in my pants." Malachi growled, his hand dropping to grip the large column of flesh packing said pants.

"You started it." I whined, shifting my own erection into a more comfortable position.

We both grinned at each other and turned back to the counter to make supper.

After supper we sat on the couch and watched a movie. About fifteen minutes into the movie, Malachi twisted around and leaned back into me. I did my own shifting until I was relaxed back into the corner of the couch with one leg cocked up against the back of the couch and the other stretched along the floor. One of my arms rested over Malachi's shoulders and collarbone, my other rested on my leg and played with the fingers Malachi mixed in.

When my coms went off, Malachi brought my wrist around so we could both read the message. Malachi chuckled right along with me at the message Leah sent.

Grayson lost at poker. He now owes me a week of laundry. Is there any chance you can bring back some of Malachi's dirty clothes. (Not going to mention how hard that name was to type, but I will hint that it was just as hard as it was satisfying).

Malachi watched as I typed out our agreed upon message.

Malachi's all in. He even wants to get artistic with chocolate pudding.

Oh my God, yes! I am already picturing the look on Grayson's face.

Then it's a go. Love you, Leah, have a good sleep.

You too. Hold each other tight.

"Ok, I totally got that one." Malachi grinned down at the message. "When you didn't specify who loved her, she returned that sentiment, also without specifying."

"Yup." I agreed.

"I also got permission to cuddle with you." Malachi noted.

"Like any of us actually have a choice in the matter." I laughed, tightening my arm around him.

"You know, it's nice not to be the one doing the cuddling." He sighed and shifted deeper into my chest, his attention returning to the movie we were watching.

"You know what I find nice?" I gently ran my fingers up and down the roped muscles of the arm he was resting along my leg.

"Hmmm?" He hummed softly.

I bent down and whispered right in his ear. "Blow jobs." With that I nipped his ear.

"Yeah, those are nice." The fucker maddeningly agreed, arching slightly, his thighs spreading to give the heavy cock growing in his pants more room.

"Do I need to spell this out for you?" My hand found his neck and bent his face back to me. "Suck. My. Cock." I hissed out my order in his ear.

"Hmm." He hummed and licked his lips, his eyes darkening. His body abruptly twisted around and I found myself pinned to the arm of the couch by way of a thick forearm pressed to my windpipe.

I grunted when I felt his fingers yank at the waistband of my pants, pulling them open. His calloused fingers pressed into my abdomen and slid straight down my flesh to the root of my throbbing cock.

My head fell back in rapture when he fisted my dick tightly and milked straight up, freeing my tip from my underwear. My hips rose, following that wonderous pull of his hand and I felt precum spurt from my tip.

"How's this...Master?" Malachi asked hoarsely, his fist moving, twisting up and down my flesh.

"Fuck yes, Boss." I cried out, my hands gripping his forearm and the front of his shirt.

"Good." He praised, knocking my hands free long enough for him to pull his shirt off before returning to my cock.

My hands found him again, my fingers moving over his heated flesh. My eyes met his. Dark, pupils blown wide with his desire.

My teeth clenched tightly while my hips helped move my dick along the rapture of his calloused fist. With a quick move of my own, my spread legs circled his hips and flipped him.

"Fuck." Malachi groaned breathlessly when his back slammed into the floor.

While he was winded, I took the opportunity to pull off my own shirt and open his pants. An expert yank and he was laying naked on the floor under me.

Another flipping twist and my arm was locked around his neck holding his body back into mine.

"Smile for the camera." I ordered, my hand finding his fat dick and jacking him with slow, tight strokes.

"Fuck, Chriton. What are you doing?" Malachi gasped with pleasure, his hand clamping down around the arm I was pressing into his neck and trying to pull it away.

"Nah uh." I emoted, my arm tightening with warning. "Smile and wave. We are live." I jerked my chin to the coms I set on the coffee table in front of us. Our side was a blank tent wall, but Leah's side was centered straight on us. Malachi froze, his gaze focusing on my coms.

"Leah." He whispered in the softest voice I ever heard from him.

"Show her how you give me control." I whispered into his ear. "Show her how you give her control."

He swallowed and nodded shakily, his legs shifting and parting more, his eyes still searching the bare tent wall for her.

"Leah, precious, what do you want from him?" I turned to the camera.

It was quiet for a long time while I continued jacking Malachi's cock. His hips rose and fell, his breathing steady but becoming heavier and heavier. His hands tightened on my arms, his eyes completely focused the camera.

"Leah." He whispered, his body shaking with a mixture of pleasure and need. "Teach."

"Taste him." Leah whispered.

"Where?" Malachi asked roughly, his eyes flashing with joy at the sound of Leah's voice.

"His head." Leah answered Malachi causing his body to relax back into mine, his face covered in relief and elation.

"Anything." He whispered silently to the ceiling his head tipped up to it as if in prayer. My arms loosened and Malachi rolled up to his knees, shifting the coms around to a better position. I stood up so that I could kick myself free of my pants. My cock twitched with violent arousal as I stepped towards Malachi. I wanted him so bad that my legs were shaking.

Still on his knees, Malachi reached out to fist my dick right as he drew my head inside the heat of his mouth. That fist slid open to spread over my lower abdomen.

"Fuck." I snarled at the rapturous feeling of his mouth sucking on my dick. My hand gripped the back of his head as it twisted and bobbed, drawing me deeper and deeper each time. I couldn't stop myself from shuddering in pleasure when he gagged but still took my dick deep into the blissful constriction of his throat.

Stop. Leah's frantic voice ordered.

"Stop." I growled, forcing myself to step away from Malachi's talented mouth and throat.

Malachi breathed hard, his shaking hands falling away from me. His eyes fell from my penis to drop to the floor.

Leah, precious?

Does he even want this? I heard her ask, her quivering voice filled with terror.

Stepping forward, I gripped the back of Malachi's head and gently forced it back until his eyes met my gaze. His dark eyes held a mixture of fear and desire.

"Do you want this? Do you want me?" I asked him for her. "Do you want to suck my cock?"

His eyes flashed with understanding before they moved to the camera. "Yes, Leah. I want this. I want Chriton. Very badly." He told the camera, his voice shaking with emotion but filled with assurance. His head lowered and his palm hit his chest like it did earlier before his eyes returned to the camera. "You of all people know exactly how sexy he is." Malachi smiled and reached up to grip my sex.

"Trade places." Leah's voice came over the camera. This time louder and firmer, more sure of herself.

"As you say, Teach." Malachi smiled happily at the camera before turning that smile to me. I couldn't stop myself from caressing a thumb over the beautiful sight of his happiness.

Malachi rose to his feet while I lowered to my knees. I gripped the hard muscle pointing at me and drew the moist tip through my lips. Malachi's hips jerked under the hands I moved to them when I immediately swallowed him whole. I felt him stretching my throat delightfully and moaned around him before drawing back. My mouth became wetter at the feel of his substantial width drawing over my tongue.

After stroking my tongue around his sensitive head, I engulfed him again, my lips stretching around his thick root. Another withdrawal, this time completely off. I licked my lips and studied the saliva wet gleam of his reddened cock.

"Fuck, he tastes good, precious. He feels even better." I shared before bobbing back over his dick.

"Chriton. Master." Malachi breathed, his fingers sliding through my hair, his hips beginning to thrust in time with my movements.

"Do you like it when I suck your dick?" I asked, looking up into his dark eyes.

"Yes." He rasped, his eyes falling to my own sex that was stretching out from between my spread knees. "I want to suck your dick again. I want to taste your come on my tongue. Teach?"

"Do it." Leah's voice guided.

Malachi pushed me to my back, his lips finding my straining cock once again. "Malachi, Boss." I groaned as I was once again rapturously enclosed in the heat of his mouth. His head moved over my thrusting hips, his throat stretching around me, taking me deeper until I was fully fucking my cock in and out of his lips. Malachi growled around me adding an element of vibration that felt entirely too good. All the while his eyes watch me with a dark intensity.

Then his devious fingers delve between my legs. I shuddered with pleasure when his palm cupped my balls and his fingers found the spot on my taint that was right over my prostate. He rubbed that spot in a deep rotating massage while his palm worked my testicles. Pure ecstasy flared up my spine and burned through my brain. He felt so good. Everything he did only drove my rapture higher.

"Fuck, shit, Boss." I snarled, my control completely gone. My hands gripped the sides of his head and my hips took over. It took me six twisting pumps and I was coming.

My head banged back into the floor when he drew off the bulk of my dick. His free hand jacked my length into the harsh suction he was now employing around my oversensitive crown. More and more of my semen painted his tongue and was swirled around my head. Then it was all swallowed.

Malachi slowly removed himself from my still hard cock, his tongue carefully cleaning my flesh of any come that might remain.

I rubbed my shaking hands over my eyes before sitting up and yanking his mouth to mine. I could taste myself, but I didn't care because underneath was his taste. Malachi cupped the side of my face and kissed me back. Deep and wet, desperate yet filled with the love we felt for each other. When we finally released each other, I allowed my heavy head to fall to his shoulder.

"He's not done, Chriton." Leah's voice brought my mind back into focus, my eyes falling to Malachi's unsatisfied sex. I reached down and began to jack him. Malachi hummed with pleasure and his hips thrust in time with my milking. My other hand bypassed his balls to find his ass. The tight hole contracted under the pressure of my finger. A pressure that opened him up enough that my finger could delve through the burning tunnel of his ass and manipulate his prostate.

His eyes squeezed shut and his head fell back, his body shaking against mine. My lips took advantage of the display of his neck and feasted on the flesh there.

Malachi was so worked up that it took me less than a minute before his body was tensing even more and his thick white sperm was spraying out, splattering over both of our chests.

"Yes." I hissed, swiping up a line of that cream and popping it into my mouth. I extracted my finger from his clenching ass and soothed my hands over his shivering body.

"Fuck." Malachi breathed, his body slowly relaxing.

His gaze slid over to the camera, satisfied yet scared. "Leah?" He licked his lips as he questioned.

"Thank you." Leah whispered and the video call was shut down.

After we showered, Malachi and I curled up together in bed. We both fell asleep, satisfied and content. The happiness would come. I could feel it.

CHAPTER 29

LEAH

Another week passed with more and more gifts and videos for all of us. It was something I found myself looking forward to. The first video Chriton sent me that weekend, the one with Malachi explaining Apophis' reaction to me, sent my mind spinning.

I took a lot of time to think over this new information, to amalgamate it with the other information already knocking around in my head. I didn't want to rush any decisions. I couldn't bear the thought of making a mistake when it came to something this important.

When Chriton returned to the Ranch, he did it with a knowing grin. "Tell me, Leah, my precious, did you touch yourself that night while you were watching us make each other come?" He asked in my ear after he kissed me stupid.

"Nope." I told him honestly. And I didn't. It didn't feel right. They may have allowed me to somewhat control the situation, but that pleasure was purely for them, not me.

Malachi was now completely finished the new suite but refused to move in without us. He also started to tease me with visuals. Him, naked in a bubbled bath. The only thing visible was the flushed knob of his aroused cock. The tricky thing was nestled among the bubbles in a very fascinating way.

Then there was the video of him getting ready for the day. Wearing nothing but a towel while he brushed his teeth, washed his face, trimmed his short beard, and slicked on deodorant. I couldn't tell what I liked more, when he yanked at his slowly growing hair with a scowl or when he left the room. The latter included him turning around, whipping the towel from his waist to throw it over his shoulder and walked butt naked from the bathroom.

At the sight of Malachi's ass, Chriton burst into laughter while I gasped and covered my blushing face. Malachi got some new ink. It was placed across the top of his ass, right under the last planet in the solar system that ran down his spine. A white, shadowed mist that surrounded a set of realistic glowing blue eyes and sharp block lettering that spelled out one word. *Chriton.*

With every image he sent me, I could clearly see the how drastically different my beloved Malachi looked from Apophis. And not just due to the emotions Malachi easily displayed. His hair was still short but growing longer. The short beard he was now sporting failed to disguise his sharp cheekbones and jawline in a very attractive way. Chriton was right, Malachi was dead sexy with some facial hair.

Malachi was showing me. Step by step. He was showing how much he loved his daughter. He was showing me how much he loved me. He was showing me how much he missed both of us and wanted us to return to him. He was showing me him, the caring man I originally fell in love with. With everything he was doing and showing me, I could feel my head forgiving him while my heart was falling in love with him all over again.

I missed him. Desperately. And I wanted to return to him, but I just wasn't sure I trusted him, yet. I was also slightly scared that when I finally saw him in person all the hate would come raging back.

The last erotic visual I received was a complaint that Grayson shrank his underwear. My eyes automatically caught on another new tattoo of his that was right there, it curved over the top of the root of his cock. A very realistic split skin tattoo that was a detailed and literal showing of the muscles and veins that ran under his skin. If the wound would've been as real as the tattoo made it look it would've been very painful. A couple whisps curled from within the wound, someone else would mistake them for steam but I recognized them as soul whisps. Embedded among the muscles and whisps was one word. *Leah.*

Grayson looked at me with surprise when I finally tore my eyes from the tattoo to see the rest of the picture and I burst out laughing. Malachi was squeezed into an extra small, painfully tight pair of boxer briefs. They didn't even come up high enough to cover the root of him while his clearly pinched dick was trapped down his left thigh. Half of it was sticking out of the bottom of the brief's, red and swollen from his circulation being cut off by those shorts. It also included his face and a dramatically wide eyed wince.

I was sitting at my desk in the security tent that was set in front of Grayson's. Since the Ranch clearly didn't need a teacher because Mali was the only child living here, Grayson decided that security needed a secretary and a liaison between the Ranch and Operations.

"What?" He asked me curiously.

"Umm, you shrunk his shorts." I still hadn't been able to bring myself around to saying Malachi's name out loud. Fortunately, Grayson automatically knew who I was talking about.

"He told you." Grayson howled with laughter. "That's what he gets for pulling that pudding crap on me, fucker."

"Uh, yes and no." I covered my coms, protecting the picture Malachi sent me.

"He sent you a picture!" Grayson leaned forward and hissed with delighted glee. "Let me see."

"No." I vehemently denied, hiding my wrist from him. There was no way I was showing him the picture. It was all mine.

I yelped and raced out of the tent when Grayson leapt from his desk and lunged for me.

"Let me see." Grayson laughed from right behind me.

"No." I skidded around an incoming tall length of body and used it to hide behind. "It's mine. You don't get to see."

"He doesn't get to see what?" Chriton asked from beside Callden who I was hiding behind.

"My new picture." I snarled at Grayson and stuck my tongue out at him.

"Come on, it's just a picture." Grayson tried to lunge around Callden. His clawed hand just missed me as I darted to the other side of Chiton who was busy looking down at his coms.

Chriton laughed while his arm slashed out to block Grayson from reaching me. "Yeah." Chriton chuckled, shaking his head at Grayson. "You so do not get to see this."

"Damnit. You guys ruin all of my fun, ripping viable blackmail material right from my grasp." Grayson cried out, raising his clawed hands palm up and shaking them dramatically.

"That's right." I claimed with an arrogant grin.

"Fine." Grayson straightened and turned to Callden. "Are you here for her?" He asked, jamming a thumb in my direction.

"Yup." Callden smiled, dropping a heavy arm over my shoulders.

"Well, have a safe trip." Grayson clapped me on the shoulder before ambling back to the security tent.

Chriton bent over and pressed a soft kiss to my mouth before handing me over to his father. I didn't want to return to the Base, but I needed to. I was meeting with the school about the long distance program we were using for Mali. It was slow and glitchy and hard for her to work with. It was also frustratingly outdated.

When we got to the Base, Callden politely walked me down the hall to the school where he left me to my meeting. It took me and the principal a couple hours of working with Operations before we succeeded in getting the program updated and the glitches smoothed out.

I was walking back to the Guardian suite when a scuffle in a nearby hall brought me up short.

"Don't touch me!" Malachi's voice snarled. Hearing it so close and real, not through a camera, caused my heart to jump violently against my rib cage.

Needing to see, I peeked around the corner of the wall to see Malachi backed into the wall, his hands held straight up. The woman, Nephthys looked at him in confusion.

"What are you talking about, Apophis?" She asked, her ice blue eyes searching over him, her hands reaching out to grab him. "You need to help me."

"I said, do no touch me!" Malachi snarled again, his back sliding quickly down the wall and away from the woman's hands. "Do not call me that. I am not Apophis."

"You are Apophis. And you do what I say. Now!" The very confused woman angrily reached to grab at Malachi again only for her hands to freeze right in front of my chest. I didn't remember moving but here I was, standing between the woman and Malachi.

"I think you are confused." I told the woman firmly. "This man may look like the man you knew, but he isn't Apophis. Apophis is dead."

"I don't understand. He looks like Apophis and Apophis always does what I tell him to." The woman whispered numbly, her eyes flashing back and forth between anger, frustration, and confusion.

"I know you don't understand the difference and I get that it can be very confusing, but right now you have to understand that this man...M-M-Malachi...is not who you believe him to be. He never will be. And he has requested that you do not touch him, that you leave him alone. That is a request that you seriously need to listen to. No one here is going to put up with you accosting innocent people in the halls like this." I explained to the woman. When my eyes caught on Chern's incoming body, I gestured a hand behind her. "Chern is here for you. That other man, he is gone."

"I, uh, ok. I, uh, I don't understand." Nephthys looked like she was right on edge, her icy blue eyes darting over Malachi before frantically latching onto the incoming man.

"I am sorry." Chern apologized, talking her hand in his, his eyes darting worriedly between me and the man behind me. "I have her."

"Make sure, Chern. Take her straight to Dr. Daniels." I nodded at him in warning and watched as he firmly guided the confused and erratic woman away.

It was all over.

It almost broke me to see that woman let alone act nice and understanding. Fury swirled through me mixing violently with my relief and possessiveness. That woman tried to touch him, my man, my Malachi. Not Apophis, but Malachi. And Malachi did everything he could to stop it. Not because he knew I was there, but because he didn't want her fucking touching him. The fact that the woman thought it was her right to touch him despite his denial was infuriating. Right in that moment, to me, she was no different from the Dante.

All I could see was the pain that the two of them caused us. All of us. But especially Malachi.

So much pain.

Tears burned in my eyes and down my cheeks. Trembling took over my body and my legs collapsed under me. Hard arms circled my falling torso. Pain slashed through me clashing with my fury. The onslaught of emotions took me over until I couldn't even think. I was shaking, I was screaming. Shrieking with the violence of it all churning wildly inside me until my voice gave out. Then I just sobbed. Broken all over again.

Heated hands moved over the back of my bent head to settle on my neck. My pain and anger slowly leached out and I could feel my body tingling with warmth and healing energy. It slowly became easier to breath, easier to think. The jagged rips in my soul didn't feel so deep anymore. My body convulsing sobs slowed until I was simply breathing fast and erratic.

I relaxed back into the arms holding me until my exhausted head rested against the heated warmth of the body behind me.

Malachi.

I missed him so much. My tired, swollen eyes slid closed. I felt my body move as I was lifted against his hard chest. My fingers twisted tightly into the soft fabric they found there while my head nuzzled along until it found the steady, rhythmic beat of his heart. I never wanted to let him go, to be frank, I was fucking terrified to. I felt him walking, carrying me along the halls, down a set of stairs.

Then we were in a suite, the new suite, and I was being set on the softest bed I ever felt. When he went to draw away, my hand darted out to grip down around his thick wrist.

"Leah, baby." He smoothed my sweaty hair back from my forehead. "Talk to me."

My eyes blinked open and stared into his dark ones. No longer emotionless but filled with worry and love. "I missed you." I croaked out, my voice a silent rasp. "Everyday. I missed you. So fucking much." I forced myself to let go of him with one of my hands so that I could press my palm to my chest. "Every fucking day."

Malachi gave a sobbing cry as he buried his hands in my hair and pressed his forehead into mine. "I missed you too, Teach." He returned, his face tensed with his inner agony, his body vibrating with his emotions.

"I never stopped." I mouthed to him. "But I damned well tried. I hated him. I hated him for hurting me, for making me watch, for breaking me. I hated him for making you carry the memories of the things he did. I hated the very sight of him. And as a by product, I tried to shut it down, stop it, throw it the fuck away. But no matter what I did, how much I fucking tried I couldn't stop loving you. Never."

"Thank God." Malachi sobbed through clenched teeth, his shoulders convulsing. My hands climbed over his arms, to his chest and pulled on him until he climbed into bed with me. My arms and legs tentacled around him, holding his shuddering body tightly to mine as he cried. My fingers dug into the muscles of his back, my head tilting to cover the one he was burying into my neck.

His hands clutched at me, his legs curled up taking me with him into the fetal position. My eyes cracked open when the bed jerked and Chriton curled around Malachi from the other side.

None of us said anything. Words weren't needed. Not right then.

Malachi cried in our arms until he had nothing left. I felt his body relax and his stuttering breathing even out into sleep. I looked over him to meet Chriton's eyes.

"Mali?" I mouthed curiously.

"With dad." Chriton mouthed back, telling me that she was safe here at Base, staying with his family.

I smiled at him and stretched my arm out to bury my fingers into his thick, dark hair. "I love you." I mouthed.

"I love you too." He mouthed back, his eyes glowing fiercely.

Emotionally exhausted, I finally allowed my eyes to drift close. I fell asleep with a smile on my face.

CHAPTER 30

MALACHI

I woke up the next morning, body sore from my emotional breakdown. I was surrounded by the heartbreakingly familiar heat of two bodies. I felt complete in a way I didn't believe I would ever feel again.

My mind drifted to the image of Leah appearing in front of me, guarding me, protecting me from that woman. My heart jumped wildly in my chest at the sight of her there, so close that I could reach out and touch her. She was surprisingly gentle with the woman Apophis used my body to fuck right in front of her. At the same time, she was firm in her demand for that woman to leave me alone.

After Chern guided Nephthys away, Leah just sank into herself. She collapsed to the floor and my heart went with her. When I caught her, she started screaming. Her voice filled with soul deep pain and anger, her shaking body tensing and bowing with each scream that tore out of her. Feeling her lose it so completely like that, those emotions violently lashing out at the whole of the universe, I could do nothing but hold her tightly to me. I tried to show her that I was there all the while I was breaking right along with her.

Then her voice finally gave out and her screams turned to sobs. Deep, jagged, body seizing crying that ripped into my heart. I couldn't make it better for her, not then. I was just as damaged and broken as she was and barely holding back my own rage filled screams.

I was so thankful when Royce arrived on the scene. The gathered crowd automatically parted for the eerily pale woman. She was dressed in a long, flowing, black sundress that set off her loosely braided length of white hair.

With her usual bare feet, Royce stepped close and set her hands on us. First on Leah's neck then on the side of my face. I felt her healing heat inundate my body, searching and finding the jagged wounds on my soul. Deep wounds that still bled. I felt that pain ease. It didn't disappear completely but it lessened and the bleeding finally stopped.

My shaking arms tightened around Leah as she turned her weak head into my chest. I took a deep shuddering breath in, trying to get myself back together before carefully lifting her into my arms. Then my beautiful, amazing woman held me as I cried. I sobbed everything out into her. I gave her it all. My pain, anger, hatred. My helplessness, grief, confusion, gratitude, relief, love. All of it seeped out of me, tear by tear, until I fell deep into a healing sleep.

Now I felt lighter. As if a huge weight had been lifted off of my shoulders.

"Can I have sex now?" Chriton's voice sounded in the room causing me to roll my eyes and chuckle. I felt Leah's shoulders move as she laughed. It sounded horrible, scratchy and barely there.

"Nope." Leah shook her head in denial at him, softening the blow with a smile.

Leaning up on an elbow, I caressed my hand over her face, my thumb over her smiling lips. "I love you." I told her, looking deep into her grey eyes. I followed my words by pressing my palm to my chest.

"I love you too, Malachi." Leah mouthed, gripping my hand and bringing my palm up to her lips. I nodded sharply, my eyes squeezing shut with the absolute beauty of her words. Then I bent lower and nudged her lips with mine.

Leah smiled and pressed that last millimetre up to me. Then we were kissing. Finally. Slow and wet. Loving. Different yet the same. Somehow stronger, deep than ever before.

"Can I get some?" Chriton whispered, his face pushing into the sides of ours. I chuckled and drew away enough to meet his lips. "Pushy fucking asshole." I mumbled against his mouth before taking over the kiss and showing him who the true Boss was.

When our lips finally parted, he grinned and shifted to eat at Leah's mouth. She giggled and cupped his cheeks. "Crazy man." She rasped when he finally released her.

"Your crazy man." Chriton corrected.

"Our crazy man." Leah corrected his correction, her eyes moving to mine.

"On that note, I will leave you both with this. Group kisses are sooo much better than group hugs." Chriton rose from the bed and sauntered from the room. "That bed is fantastic. I do believe Scope nailed it when he made our choice." He called out from the bathroom where he was peeing with the door open.

"Holy shit." Leah gasped, sitting up and looking over the bed with wide eyes. It was admittedly huge. A California king. "How did you get this in here?"

"It's one of those fancy assed beds that come in a box." I told her with a grin. "We tested out one of the queen sized ones the furniture supply room had on display. Since there are three of us, and I figured if I ever got you back into my bed I was not going to let you out of it, ever, I should probably get a big one." I sat up and used a hand at her nape to pull her closer so I could speak against her lips. "Enjoy it, Teach, because this bed is now your home."

"Bossy man." Leah smiled and pulled at my chin hair.

"Always." I winked at her. "That's why I get to be the Boss."

Leah giggled and fell forward into my chest. My arms automatically enclosed around her.

"Come on. We have a daughter to retrieve and plans to make." Chriton yelled from the kitchen.

When Leah extracted herself from my arms I was right behind her. I was terrified of loosing sight of her. Needing to physically feel that she was here with me, my hand found her lower back. "Mali's here?" I asked quietly, feeling a mixture of excitement and unease.

Mali and I now communicated frequently throughout the day but I hadn't seen my daughter in months. Apophis didn't count.

"Yeah, man." Chriton turned from the coffee he was fixing. He walked over to me and gripped my arm when he saw the look in my eyes. "She's with dad right at the moment."

"Is she...?" I couldn't finish. My head turned to the side and I desperately swallowed back the emotions that tried to rise.

"She's excited." Chriton told me, his hand sliding down my arm to link his fingers with mine.

I nodded slowly, so many memories, mine and Apophis' flashed through my mind. "She knows." I croaked.

Soft fingers brushed over my clenched jaw, gently turning my head back and down. "She does." Leah said, her grey eyes filled with honestly and warmth. "She also knows the difference between Apophis and her dad. Apophis was the man that she met in Medical. He was the monster who...hurt her mom. Not her dad."

I stared down at Leah for long moments, searching deep into her eyes. She did the same, most likely seeing every emotion that was twisting inside me. Then she smiled, her fingers smoothed over the beard that roughened my jaw until she was cupping my cheek. She rose up on her tiptoes and pressed her lips to mine. At the brush of her lips and the feel of her breath exchanging with mine I felt my fear diminish and be replaced with resolve and strength.

"Ok." I whispered and nodded. "Let's go get our daughter."

"Good." Leah smiled and stepped away. My hand fisted tight in order to stop from reaching for her as I watched her walk away from me and into the bathroom.

My body jerked when Chriton's hand slid under my arm and around my chest to grip my shoulder. "I need you to help me." I told him, reaching up to cover his hand. "Make sure I don't drive her crazy, drive her away. I can't seem to let her out of my sight, out of my touch. It makes me anxious, panicky."

"I got you, Boss." Chriton agreed, resting his chin on my shoulder. "I was the exact same way when I got her back. Although, it didn't kick in until we got to the Ranch. It got so bad some days that I ended up following her around like a puppy. Those were the days that Grayson walked into security and laughed because I was holding her in my lap while she worked at her desk. I just...couldn't let her go. It slowly eased, but it hasn't gone away completely. I still have my moments. The same will happen for you."

"That's good to know." I said, turning my head to look at him.

"It helps that she just goes with it." Chriton grinned, his eyes flashing with amusement. "I have a feeling that she only does that because she feels just as anxious as I do. My recommendation is that you do you and she will do what she always does. She will go with it."

"Yeah, she does do that, doesn't she?" I smiled and kissed him. "Let me go, I need to pudding."

"Grayson was sooo mad at you for that." Chriton did let me go but only because he fell back with his laughter. "At first he was disgusted but then he realized what you did and he was furious. He's making all kinds of plans to get you back."

I chuckled as I headed into the other bathroom. "I wish him luck."

We reached the door to the Guardian suite.

Chriton rang the bell while I held Leah's hand tightly in my vibrating grip. My eyes were staring at the floor, frozen. Someone opened the door and stepped back. Chriton's feet stepped inside to a murmur of voices that my panicking mind couldn't seem to make sense of.

"Breathe, Boss." Leah whispered, her hand running up and down my arm, providing me the focus I desperately needed. I nodded sharply, trying to do as she said. Breathe. But it wasn't so easy.

At the sound of a small set of feet, my eyes squeezed shut before I forced them open and rolled them up to see her. My daughter. She was dressed in a pair of jean shorts and a pink top that matched her bright pink hair. And she was beautiful.

Her hand was clutching tightly at Chriton's, her beautiful brown eyes studying me before tipping to Chriton. Chriton gave her a grin and a wink. Her head snapped down to me and her voice sounded out loud. "Dad?"

My name. My daughter said my name.

"Shit, Malachi." Leah gasped and tried to catch me when my knees gave out. She might have slowed me a bit, but my knees still cracked harshly into the floor. My shaking fingers came up to press into my tear pained eyes. I felt Leah's body cover mine from behind, similar to what I did for her yesterday. At the same time a small, trembling body wormed its way between my arms and into my bowed torso.

My arms automatically surrounded the beloved body of my daughter. She was crying, sobbing into my chest, her little fingers and arms clutching at me.

"Mali-girl." I rasped, holding her tightly to my chest, my hand cupping the back of her head. "My Mali-girl."

"I missed you, dad." Mali sobbed.

"I missed you too, Mali-girl." I told her, soothing my hand up and down her back. "I love you, Mali. God, I love you so much."

"I love you too, dad." Mali sniffed, her sobbing slowing. She drew back enough that she could look into my eyes and cup my face. "That other guy was an asshole."

"Yeah." I choked on my laughter. "He was."

"Is he really gone? For good?" Mali asked, her eyes searching mine.

"For good." I nodded in assurance, my fingers smoothing through her bright pink hair, my lips stretching into a smile. "It looks good. Pink suits you."

"Thank you." Mali smiled, nuzzling back into my chest.

I carefully rose to my feet with my daughter tucked to my chest. Leah backed up, her hands slowly sliding away. Instead of loosing contact with her, which I was still unwilling to do, my hand darted back and caught hers. "Not yet." I warned her, pulling her around to my side.

Leah looked up at me and nodded. "Ok."

Bring our clasped hands up, I pressed a kiss to her knuckles. "Thank you."

We spent that day visiting with the Guardians. Mali and Walker played with Lucy, who was left with the Guardians when we took our vacation at the Ranch. After we were taken, Chriton asked Amber to keep Lucy until we were ready for her to return. That time had not come yet.

"I have a question." Callden eyed me from the table we were gathered around.

"Shoot." I told him, my eyes narrowing with the realization that he was right about to fuck up my life when I was still in the process of unfucking it.

"How did you lose your memories? Bane still retains his. At first Luke thought Chern's were somehow removed but now Luke is finding out that Chern never had any memories of his life before. Chern and, as it is turning out, Nephthys were actually born and raised in that life." Callden explained.

"The failsafe." Leah gasped with shocked realization and jumped up from the chair beside me. My teeth clenched and I was barely able to force myself to stay seated instead of chasing after her.

"What the hell is the failsafe?" Coren asked, straightening in the chair he was slumped in.

"It's a way to protect information. Uncle Declan came up with it. Well, not came up with it but, uh, studied it extensively. He called it 'the failsafe.'" Leah explained with a frown as she gestured and paced behind me. I adjusted my chair to the side so that I could see her and the table at the same time.

"He told you?" I asked her, confused at why Declan would do that.

"Yes." She exclaimed, pausing to point at me.

"What do you mean 'protect information'?" Callden asked with his own frown.

I opened my mouth to explain only for Leah to beat me to it. "Information." She resumed her pacing. "The higher someone climbs in any power structure the more knowledge they gain. And all of that juicy information is kept safely tucked away in one spot." She stopped and pressed her finger to her temple before resuming her pacing. "Uncle Declan knew that there were always ways for the enemy to extract that information, no matter how strong of a mind it was. Thusly, the failsafe."

"He studied amnesia." I bluntly informed the table.

"He posited that there was a specific spot in someone's head that when hit a certain way with a certain amount of force that amnesia might be achieved." Leah tapped her fingers to the back of her head.

"If the blow was done correctly, it could viably remove the connections between the area that retains memories and the rest of the brain. It would trap those memories, make them completely untouchable, inaccessible. The enemy would have no way to harvest that information and use it against us." I finished explaining, turning haunted eyes to Leah.

Now she knew everything. She knew that I did it to myself. I took myself away from her and left her completely at the mercy of an emotionless monster who wore my shell.

"I can't believe it actually worked." Leah exclaimed, cupping my face and climbing over me to straddle my lap. "You beautiful, brilliant man."

"You aren't mad?" I rasped in surprise, reaching up to grip her delicate wrists, my thumbs moving over her scars.

"No, Boss." Leah shook her head, pressing kisses all over my face. "You saved all of it. Everyone. Not just the Base or the Ranch, but all of the rest of the bases and the Alliance itself. With the information you carry, there is a good chance that the Drako would be able to destroy the whole of the Alliance. You locked yourself away to protect that information. Your life, Grayson, Mali, Chriton, me, all of us. You locked it all away in order to protect the rest of the world, even knowing that there was no possibility of ever finding the key to unlock it." The kisses continued while I smiled under her onslaught.

"Can you show me?" Callden asked, feeling around the back of his head.

"No." Amber snapped at her husband, slapping his hand away from the back of his head.

"That's not a very good idea, to be honest. I wasn't even sure it would work when I did it." I turned to look at Callden, my arms surrounding the woman who was curling into me, resting her head just under my jaw.

"Are you saying that you gave yourself a serious brain injury on a fucking theory?" Coren's voice was high with shock meanwhile Chriton almost fell out of his chair with his laughter.

"Uncle Declan showed me, well us, I guess, the spot and he told me how hard of a hit it would most likely take. But it was completely untested. So, yeah, I guess it would have been just a theory." Leah explained with a slight wince and my hand came up to cover the back of her head.

"Yeah, I did it purely on a theory and a prayer. I was kind of amazed myself when I got my memories back and realized that it actually worked." I shared with the stunned table.

"I can't, Amber. I just, I can't." Callden whined out, turning a set of dumbfounded eyes to his wife while Coren stared at me in shock. "I can't even call him a dumbass because his dumbasssery fucking worked. Pure fucking luck turned him from an absolute idiot into a hero."

By this point Chriton was laughing so hard tears were running down his face and he was bent over the table trying to catch his breath. "Fuck, that's awesome." He croaked out.

Later that afternoon, we left the Guardian suite and ambled down to our next stop, the Ancients suites.

"Yes. Yes. Yes." A clearly pregnant Salem exclaimed tearfully, pushing right past Wings, who opened the door, and launching herself into Leah's arms. The women hugged and rocked, all the while my hands gripped around Leah's hips.

"Group hug." Chriton yelled, running inside to tackle a surprised Scope. My hand automatically found Mali's when Chriton released her.

"Fuck." Scope yelped and the two stumbled back into Marko when Chriton lifted Scope into a giant hug. I heard one of the bathroom doors that connect the two suites slam open and Diad came sprinting through to crash into the side of the group of men.

Wings grinned and with a running jump, launched himself at the group, landing on Marko's back. Madron came out of the other bathroom and was quickly pulled into the group.

That was when I felt a hand fall to my shoulder and turned to see Catro standing beside me. "Come on." He grinned, pulling me away from my woman and daughter, guiding me to the group. My head twisted back to see Leah and Salem standing with their arms around one another, Mali tucked tightly between them. They were watching me with amused eyes.

"Malachi!" The group exclaimed and opened up, Chriton's hand darted out and yanked me straight into the middle where I was surrounded by them. Friends, family. They all held me tightly, officially bringing me back into the fold. And in that moment, I didn't want to be anywhere else. Not in the whole of the universe.

"Do you guys want to know what is better than group hugs?" Chriton voiced from somewhere in the group. "Group kisses."

The group as a whole let out a pained groaned. Other than Wings who grinned over at Madron. "That does sound interesting."

And with that the group broke up.

Turning to check on my girls, I saw that they had stepped fully into the suite where River and Royce joined them. Mali was sitting with Royce on the couch talking. River and Leah were leaning their heads together, looking down at the tiny baby in Leah's arms. Both of them bore soft looks of joy.

Salem was digging in the kitchen, pulling ingredients out for supper. Diad was quick to help her. Catro disappeared and reappeared with his children, Gabriel and Atlas. Atlas and Mali squealed happily and ran towards each other, best friends reunited.

Feeling twitchy and needing to touch her I stalked over to Leah and hugged up against her back, bending my head down to look at Paladin. Leah turned her head to gaze up at me, giving me the warmth of her smile. Her body followed her head and before I realized it, she was setting the boy in my arms. I held him carefully while Leah adjusted my hands and arms into a firmer position around the baby.

I stared down at the wriggling, gurgling child, the first baby I could ever remember holding. In that moment I realized that this was what I truly wanted. Our baby, our child. It's happily wriggling body moving in my hands.

"I want one." I whispered fiercely.

"Me too." Leah whispered back, her eyes coming up to meet mine.

"Only yours." I told her, voicing my thoughts and dreams on the matter.

One of the bigger reasons I found myself hating that woman, Nephthys, and wanting her no where near me was because Apophis almost gave her my child. A child I only ever wanted to plant in Leah.

The look in Leah's eyes mirrored my own churning feelings, shining with a mixture of pained relief and rekindling hope. "Yes. Please." She whispered in agreement.

"Now can I have sex?" Chriton joined us with a whisper, his head bending down to smile at Paladin.

"Sure." Leah smiled mischievously, pretending to reach out to take the baby from me. "You guys have fun."

"That's not funny." Chriton glared at her while my head flew back with my laughter. "Yes, it is." I choked out. "Patience, man." I nudged his shoulder and passed him the baby. "In the meantime, why don't you hold some living, breathing proof of what can come from your demand."

"My coming is the whole reason I am making the demand." Chriton grumped while smiling down at Paladin and shifting him so that he was laying against Chriton's chest.

"Well, if you listened to me none of it would be an issue." Leah pointed out with a mischievous shrug.

I pulled her back into my arms and delved my face into her neck. "Brat." I growled and nipped at her, making her giggle and attempt to curl away from me.

"Mom." Mali called across the room.

"Yes, Mali?" Leah straightened and looked over to our daughter.

"Can I stay over at Atlas' tonight?" Mali asked hopefully, her palms pressed together in prayer position, her eyes begging.

Mali barely finished her question when Chriton pointed at her and exclaimed vehemently. "Yes!"

The girls cheered while everyone else laughed. Royce rolled her eyes and Catro shot Chriton a knowing look.

"Does this mean I can move back now?" Diad asked from the kitchen counter. He was still staying with me, but I knew he was itching to get back to his own place.

In the end the man turned out to be a phenomenal friend.

"Yes." Leah told him, giving him a grateful smile. He was quick to return her smile with a wink.

"Give me." Marko, a slightly overprotective father, came over and liberated his son from Chriton's hold.

Chriton chuckled and clapped Marko on the back in an understanding gesture.

CHAPTER 31

LEAH

The suite door closed behind me with a soft click.

Chriton was already walking across the floor, stripping his clothes off and dropping them on the floor while ordering, "Get the led out." By the time he reached the bedroom door he was bare assed naked. And what a muscular ass it was.

Malachi, who had his hand resting on my lower back, thankfully maintaining that connection that we both needed, cocked his head and watched Chriton.

"You heard the man." I patted Malachi's chest and dropped my eyes down to his crotch. "Get the led out."

Malachi laughed, shaking his head down at me. He slowly slid his hand from my back before turning to face me. He pulled his own shirt off displaying the long stretch of his sexy torso. His palm came up and he curled his fingers at me in a come hither gesture while he slowly backed up.

I smiled and followed. My pussy clenched, empty and needing him. My eyes watched his hands open his belt and jeans and push the material from his legs. Those were kicked free before his tight, package hugging underwear were given the same treatment. By the time he backed into the doorway of the room, he was also completely naked and his deliciously thick penis was bobbing along his abdomen with his movements.

He slowed to a stop once we were inside the bedroom, his calloused hand coming up to cup my cheek, so gently. My hands fell to the heated bare skin covering his chest and my head tipped back for his mouth to take mine. At first it was deep and slow but quickly become demanding. Pure Malachi.

I shivered with desire when I felt Chriton's heat press into my back. His lips found my neck and his hands slowly caressed the clothes from my body until I was as naked as they were. Malachi drew away, his dark eyes opening, watching me with a deep intensity. Chriton's arms circled my waist, and I was being lifted and carried to the bed.

Chriton set me on the bed, propping me up against the headboard before stealing his own fierce kiss. "Stay." He ordered with a wicked grin before turning his head to the man who was still standing at the end of the bed watching us.

Chriton straightened and prowled to Malachi. He gripped Malachi's jaw and kissed him. I bit my lip and pulled my knees up, squeezing my thighs tightly together. All in order to ease the desire pounding through my sex.

The sharp lines of their jaws moved as if they were eating, which they kind of were. Their moist lips slid against each other, parting far enough every once in while to give me an erotic glimpse of their tongues licking at each other. It was one of the most arousing things I ever saw.

Masculine hands moved over muscled flesh. Malachi's fingers thumbed over Chriton's nipples before pinching down on those tight nubs. Chriton gave an pleasured gasp into Malachi's mouth.

Chriton's hands glided down Malachi's sides before groping the globes of his ass. Malachi grunted and his hips shifted enough that their dicks knocked into each other.

Sliding his hand around, Chriton took hold of both of their dicks, squeezing them together in his fist. That white knuckled fist milked upward causing Malachi to rip his mouth from Chriton's in breathless rapture, his head rotating back on his neck.

My hand slid between my thighs, my palm and fingers pressing into my sex. Trying to hold my need back, trying to calm the fire blazing through me.

Chriton's mouth fell to Malachi's neck, sucking and biting the flesh there. I could see Malachi's neck muscles work as he swallowed right before that growl I loved hearing rumbled out of his chest.

Chriton's hand continued jerking their cocks together. Precum spurt from one moist head or the other, adding more glistening lubrication to the mix. Both men were breathing hard as their heads tipped down to watch their dicks.

I couldn't help but whimper at the pure ecstasy written on their faces.

Malachi's down bent head tilted slightly towards me, his dark eyes running over me in a heated way that made me arch with need. Out of the corner of my eye, I caught the blue glow of Chriton's eyes following Malachi's gaze.

The slow dark grin that spread over Malachi's face was so sexy that it shot me right into orgasm. My fingers dug hard into my pulsing sex as it throbbed in delicious rapture. I cried out and my body arched and trembled. I was just coming down from it when my ankles were spread and I was pulled down flat. Malachi's dark eyes gleamed from between my shaking thighs and my hand was ripped away.

"Boss." I gasped and arched up to meet his incoming mouth. His hungry lips covered my pussy. The burning heat of his tongue licking over my sensitive flesh was compounded by the wiry brush of his beard. My hands gripped down on anything I could reach. The silky inch of growth at the top of his head, the thick arm crossing my abdomen, holding me down. My legs were laying over his bulging shoulders, my thighs spread around his head. His eyes stared up my body and into mine while his talented tongue flicked and curled over my sensitive clit.

"Does his tongue feel good, love?" Chriton's husky voice brought my head up to see him looming over me from the side.

"Yes." I whimpered, my hips twisting against the onslaught of pleasure that Malachi's mouth was driving into me. Chriton grinned and took my lips with his, eating my mouth as Malachi ate my pussy.

Then it got more intense. More rapturous. Chriton's hand cupped my breast, pinching and pulling at my sensitive nipple. Malachi's arms shifted down and his fingers introduced themselves to my pulsing entrance. Thick fingers that deliciously spread my muscles open as they delved inside me. Then they found my g-spot and everything sped up.

Malachi thrust his fingers in and out of me at a high speed, the curled tips dragging over my g-spot. It took thirty seconds for it all to culminate. The swirling pleasure coalesced into one big ball that popped open and sprayed everywhere. All over the bedding, all over Malachi. My pussy contracted and squirted my orgasm out while Malachi praised me and ate it up.

My eyes rolled back in my head and my body convulsed, my mind flew with mind breaking rapture.

Chriton eased his mouth from mine as my mind returned to focus, and my trembling body slowed. His glowing eyes stared down into mine.

I felt the hands moving over my abdomen, finding my hips. The cool air brushing over my wet, overheated pussy dispersed by the brush of smooth burning flesh.

I shrieked and came again when that burning flesh fucked inside my oversensitive pussy. My muscles spread painfully wide and my tingling nerves flared. The friction of Malachi's entrance was so mind blowing good that I was slightly afraid I wouldn't survive it.

Heat covered my torso and my unfocused eyes latched onto a set of dark ones. Malachi's hips were working in a slow, massaging rotation between the thighs I cocked around him. His chest was pressed down to mine, his hands surrounding my face.

"Boss." I whimpered breathlessly, my fingers clutching at his shoulders and neck.

"Right here, Leah, my love." Malachi rasped with a slight wince, his hands curling up and under my arms to grip my shoulders.

My eyes travelled over his shoulder to see Chriton kneeling behind him. Chriton grinned at me when he saw me looking at him. I couldn't see what Chriton was doing but I could certainly guess. Malachi's breath sucked in with a harsh whistle and his body tensed against me.

"Relax, Boss." Chriton soothed.

"Easy for you to say, Master." Malachi shot back at him.

"Yeah, it is." Chriton chuckled, doing something else that made Malachi's hips shift in a deeper rotation than usual.

I moaned at the stirring friction that Malachi's cock gave my insides. I immediately wanted it again.

"Your turn is coming." Malachi growled out his warning back to Chriton. Since I wasn't getting that toe curling stir, I did it myself.

"Fuck." Malachi groaned.

"What? I didn't do anything that time." Chriton grumbled.

"Teach did." Malachi rasped hoarsely, his head doing its pleasure filled rotation while my hips did their own rotation for the second time.

"That good, huh?" Chriton asked, bending over Malachi's back and pushing his arm between us to grip a hand over Malachi's staining pecs.

"Nuh." Malachi emoted on a gasp. His hands and arms tightened almost painfully around me. His eyes popped wide and his head fell back. His outstretched neck flushed red and pulsed with veins. His hips were pushed deeper into mine with the weight Chriton was giving him. Malachi's knees shifted and parted further.

"Fuck." Chriton groaned, his glowing blue eyes flashing brighter with pleasure.

"Does his ass feel good, Master?" I licked my lips and asked.

"Fuck yes." Chriton growled, the bed beginning to move with the slow movement of his body. "He's gripping me so fucking tight."

"Shit, fuck." Malachi breathed in a heavy gasping breath, his head falling down to rest against my collarbone. His hips started moving, restarting their delicious rotation once again.

"Shit." Chriton snarled with pleasure. "That does feel fucking good."

The bed started moving faster, the headboard began smacking against the wall. A slapping sound filled the room, flesh against flesh. Chriton's hips against Malachi's ass.

I could feel it building inside me. The deep rotation that Malachi was still struggling to maintain doing its job. Before I really knew it I was right on the edge. But then, by the sound of the way his breath was wheezing in and out of his chest, so was Malachi.

"Master." I gasped out in warning, knowing that neither Malachi nor I would last much longer.

"Yeah. Right there." Chriton returned through his clenched teeth. "Finish."

Knowing what Chriton wanted me to do, I began to rhythmically contract my muscles down around Malachi's massaging dick.

Malachi gasped out, his arms tightening around me. His hips shuddered and his tensed body curled even deeper around me.

"Yes." Chriton's cry came.

The feel of Malachi's cock jerking and throbbing within the tightened muscles I was gripping him with sent me spiralling up to join them in their orgasmic flight. That orgasm was driven deeper, soul deep, when I was filled with splash after splash of burning heat. I could feel my pussy sucking hard at that thick muscle, sucking

Malachi's sperm straight up into my womb and demanding more and more until he finally had nothing more to give.

That was when our souls pulled free and danced together. Our souls gleefully swirled and mixed together. Their joy of all being reunited was clearly evident. Once my soul returned it was beautifully heavier and lighter than normal. I could feel both of them inside me.

"My balls hurt." Malachi groaned, collapsing over me, his arms still holding me but now more in a loose satisfied way.

"Not your ass?" I asked him breathlessly, one of my hands soothing through his sweat damp hair, my other soothing through Chriton's. Chriton was collapsed against Malachi's back, his head resting along the back of Malachi's neck.

"My balls hurt more. Your pussy is very demanding." Malachi grunted.

"Isn't that the truth." Chriton slurred.

At that point my stupid leg muscle began to cramp painfully. *Owe, owe. Off. Off. Off.*

Both men were immediately gone from over top of me.

Leah? Chriton's concerned voice asked.

Leg cramp! I gasped, curling up to grip my thigh.

Damn. Malachi hissed and his strong fingers pushed mine aside to work over the cramping muscle.

Make sure you are working the Semimembranosus. Chriton advised from beside us.

What does it look like I am doing? Malachi grumped, his fingers finally helping ease the cramp and allowing me to relax.

It looks like you need to keep working that muscle.

Do you want to do this? Malachi growled, tilting his head up to glare at Chriton.

Yes. Chriton snarled back.

Then next time don't be so slow. Malachi mocked, sticking his tongue out at Chriton before returning his concentration to my thigh.

Fuck, I love you two. I sighed, leaning back on my hands and joyfully watching the two argue.

Malachi smiled and winked at me while Chriton grinned arrogantly. *Who wouldn't love all of this?* Chriton bragged, caressing his hand across his own chest.

Jesus. Malachi rolled his eyes and his hand shoved out into Chriton's arm. Chriton yelped when the push sent him rolling off the end of the bed.

I love you too, Leah. More than I can ever say. Malachi turned back to me, pressing his palm to his chest in his new gesture. A gesture of love that I loved seeing almost more than I loved hearing him voice that love.

You are such a suck up. Chriton groaned, pulling himself back up onto the bed.

You love it when I suck up. Malachi told him with a grin.

Yeah, I do. Chriton chuckled, leaning over to press a deep kiss to my lips. *I love you too, Leah.*

Once he released my lips, Chriton reached out to pull Malachi's forehead to his. I smiled when I was pulled in until our foreheads were all pressed together in a triangle. My hands came up to grip the back of their necks tightly, holding them to me as I breathed their breathes in. Life.

Their determination and resolve as they fought for me and each other irrevocably proved the strength and depth of their love. And I felt that love filling me until it overflowed.

CHAPTER 32

CHRITON

We moved back to the Base and into the new suite that Malachi built for us.

Everything was painted or tiled. The stone floors were covered with a dark toned floating hardwood floors and blue area rugs. The cupboards and shelving were a similar dark tone. The main room was painted an orangish tan color that reminded me of a sunrise. The countertops and tiles carried shades of the wall color mixed with blacks and blues.

The furniture was extremely comfortable and matched the blues found in the rugs.

Our room was painted a cream color with dark green accents. The bedding was along the same color scheme.

Mali's room was a pinkish cream with dark pink accents. Her bedding was rainbow colors with a heavy lean towards pink. She absolutely loved it.

The spare rooms were done up as well. One in blue and grey, the other in burgundy and beige.

When we took our last trip out to the Ranch to retrieve the rest of our stuff, Malachi came with us. He prowled down the pathways and walked straight into the security tent while we followed him. We reached the tent just in time for a mass of twisting and rolling bodies to come flying out.

Malachi and Grayson.

The two men wrestled over the ground with Malachi visibly allowing Grayson to land several blows to his face. Eventually though everything slowed and they both collapsed in a breathless heap on the ground. Malachi's arm rose to wipe the blood pouring from his nose and leaking from a large split in his mouth.

"Fuck, I needed that." Grayson groaned.

"Yeah, you fucking did." Malachi agreed. "I am sorry, man. I truly am."

"It wasn't you." Grayson sighed. "I know exactly what you fucking did, you bastard. Fucking fail safe."

"Then why did you hit me so hard?" Malachi turned a set of upset eyes to his friend.

"Fucking pudding!" Grayson snarled and rolled to land another fist to Malachi's stomach causing him to curl in on himself.

"Shit, you need to learn to take a joke." Malachi wheezed out a laugh.

"Fuck you." Grayson laughed, rolling to his feet and holding a hand down to Malachi. Malachi's grin was bloody but happy. He reached up and clasped Grayson's wrist. Grayson pulled him up and they were hugging. A hard, back pounding hug.

Grayson came with us to the tent to help us pack. We were all joined by Bane, Bailor, and Harper. When we were done, they said their goodbyes and saw us off.

After that our routine reverted to what it mostly was before the Ranch. Leah returned to her teaching, Mali returned to school. I resumed my Guardian work. Malachi, luckily, was already back in the swing of running the Base.

The weeks passed by slowly and our relationship finally found its calm as it deepened and strengthened even more. Life at the Base, however, was never calm for long.

Within a month Leah started getting tired and listless. But more concerning was the way she kept refusing to eat, claiming that her stomach was queasy. When I mentioned going to see a doctor, she refused, claiming that it was probably some stomach bug.

One morning, three days in, it all came to a head. I couldn't convince her to get out of bed. She whimpered and buried herself deeper into the covers whenever I tried. She even started crying in a very hoarse tone when I finally caught her.

"Please, Chriton, I am so tired. Just let me sleep." She begged, her chin quivering, tears rolling down her face. The woman was breaking my heart.

"You need to go to Medical." I told her firmly, lifting her up into my arms.

"No, please, Chriton. I will be ok in a few days. I just need to sleep." She cried, her fingers twisting in my shirt.

"Leah, you have barely eaten anything in three days. Malachi and I can barely keep you awake when you are home. You fell asleep in the fucking bath last night." I clenched my jaw and forced myself to walk to the suite door instead of giving into her like my heart screamed at me to do.

"I need pants." Leah cried. She kind of did since she was only dressed in one of Malachi's t-shirts and a pair of underwear.

"Not bad enough for me to risk releasing you and having you go straight back to bed. You are going to Medical." Angry at the situation, I shouldered the suite door open and prowled down the halls towards an incoming Malachi.

He was jogging back after dropping Mali off at school. "Good, you got her up."

"Yup. I just picked her up and refused to put her back down." I told him in a hassled voice as we moved down the halls and up the stairs.

"Malachi." Leah whimpered and reached for him. "Can I go back to bed? Please. I don't feel good."

"No, baby." Malachi caught her hand and brought it to his lips. "I am sorry, Teach."

Leah sobbed out a cry and buried her head into my chest, successfully killing us both. "She does feel warm." I told him while he soothed his hand over the back of her head.

"Then it's good we are taking her to Medical." He growled, his jaw clenching, angry at the sight of Leah so sick.

"What do we have here?" Luke asked when we entered the main area of Medical.

"She's sick." I bluntly told him.

Luke walked over and twisted his head so he could see Leah's face before guiding us into an exam room. "Symptoms?"

"She's warmer than usual." I stated, sitting down on the bed with Leah cradled in my lap.

"Tired, nauseous..." Malachi continued, sitting down beside us and rubbing her back

"Pregnant." Luke added on, gesturing to his nurse.

We both paused and frowned, looking at each other before looking down at the woman that was now fast asleep against my chest.

"Yeah, we are going to need a test." Malachi told Luke.

"And I am going to need some pee." Luke clanked the plastic cup his nurse handed him down on the side table.

"Leah, precious, we need you to wake up and pee in this cup." I gently woke the woman in my arms.

"No." Leah moaned softly. "You do it."

"Uh, I am pretty sure the good doctor really doesn't want my pee." I stated while Malachi chuckled. The maddening man completely ignored the glare I threw him.

"Sure he does. Everybody does." Leah slurred and patted my chest in assurance.

Malachi laughed even harder.

"Come on, Leah. Wake up and pee in the cup." I readjusted, trying to jar her back awake.

"Hmm." She simply hummed and burrowed deeper.

Malachi shook his head and finally helped by grabbing the cup and lifting her out of my arms. "Malachi, no." Leah cried as he carried her out of the room and into the bathroom. The door closed behind them and their voices echoed out to us.

"Yes, Leah." Malachi's voice argued back, his voice firm.

"I don't have to go." Leah whined.

"I don't care. Pee in the fucking cup." Malachi ordered.

"Please, let me go back to bed. I am so tired and everything hurts." Leah began crying again.

"She might also have a touch of the cold that's going around." Luke noted from beside me. "I will have to check her vitals."

"Teach, please, just pee in the cup then you can go right back to sleep." Malachi's voice pleaded.

"Promise." Leah asked shakily.

"I promise, Leah." Malachi whispered, his voice soft.

"Ok." Leah whimpered back.

Minutes later a haunted looking Malachi came back out of the bathroom with Leah safely tucked in his arms. She was already drifting back to sleep. "I left it in there." Malachi jerked his head to the closed bathroom door. Colleen, Luke's nurse smiled and went to retrieve the cup.

While we waited for the test results, Luke took Leah's vitals and drew some blood which made her whimper and try to curl deeper into Malachi.

Colleen eventually brought the results in and handed them to Luke. He looked them over before grinning. "Yeah, she's pregnant. Her temperature should be higher than normal but not as high as it currently is so she's also sick with that cold. Push the fluids. Lots of fluids. She need to take these vitamins, once a day. And try to get her to eat something."

"Thanks, doc." Malachi whispered, his eyes carrying a familiar sheen.

"Congratulations." Luke returned in a soft yet joyful voice. He rose from the stool he was sitting on and give us the room.

I threw my arm over Malachi's shoulders, covered Leah's head with my hand and leaned my head into his. There were no words. Just relief and joy. So much joy that my heart was bursting with it. Malachi drew in a heavy, shaking breath and tilted his head so that he could press his forehead to mine.

Leah spent the next days recovering from the severe cold that knocked her on her ass. It wasn't until she was starting to get better that Malachi and I shared with her about her pregnancy. Leah, our beautiful shining woman, stood in front of us, tears flowing from her eyes, her hands cupping her stomach. Her face was filled with such awe and joy that she practically shined.

Mali quickly became possessive of Leah and her growing belly, quiet often laying with her ear pressed to Leah's stomach in an attempt to hear the baby.

One day I realized that not only did Leah see me and provide me with the grounding my DNA needed but so did Malachi. Because of them there wasn't a day that passed by where I didn't feel loved and completely intact.

EPILOGUE

MALACHI

"Mom!" A surround sound of voices echoed throughout the large room. Each of them coming from a different direction.

"Shit." Grayson groaned and set his drink down on the small table beside him. "You get yours, I will get mine. Then we will meet in the middle."

"Are you sure? Because that only sounded like four." I grinned over at him. "And a tough soldier like you..."

"Nuh uh, I am not dealing with all of that myself." Grayson shook his head and stepped back from the long length of floor to ceiling windows we were looking out.

The valley far below was inundated with colorful plant life. I could hear the call of birds reaching through the window. The crystal clear lake that was at the one edge of the valley glinted with sunlight.

The beauty of the sight before me never ceased to amaze me. And the home that was built into the side of the small mountain that we now lived in displayed that beauty to perfection.

Chriton clearly lowballed his description of his home on Andromada, our home. Because that's what this place felt like. Home.

"What happened to the big strong man that used to take on any challenge?" I asked, setting my own drink down and following him through the walkway to the next large, open room.

"He had kids." Grayson growled.

"So?" I questioned curiously.

"Kids are mean. The other day my daughter told me that I needed to shave because my beard made me look fat." Grayson pouted, rubbing a hand over his newly shaved goatee.

"Ah, that's why you shaved." I nodded in understanding.

"Do, uh, I, um, do you think I have put on weight?" Grayson asked self consciously, pressing his hand to his flat stomach.

"Maybe in your ass, but you are totally owning it." I gave him a reassuring clap on his shoulder. With that we went our separate ways. He headed to the upper floor while I headed to the stairs leading down.

Grayson finished climbing the long curving set of stairs and paused outside one of the doors. I watched as he visibly braced before he opened the door to a horrified female scream. "I don't want yooouuu! Where is mom?" My brave second in command winced and stepped into the firing squad.

I chuckled and shook my head, finishing my descent into the dark. Well darker. The shades were pulled down over all of the windows save one, sending shadows throughout the room.

"He fell." My oldest son, Thorn, was pressing a blood stained cloth to his younger brother's thigh. "He thought he saw an Anichor and climbed onto the table to try to see it better. I told him not to and was coming over to get him down when he slipped off the table and fell on the toy there."

I crouched down beside my crying boys, my eyes automatically doing a quick assessment of the scene. One of the taller toy tables was pushed against the window. Underneath the table was an action figure toy made from blend, something similar to plastic but a lot more environmental healthy. The toy was covered in blood. There was also a trail of blood leading from the toy to the puddle the boys were now sitting in.

"Let me see." I stated calmly, reaching out to take the cloth from Thorn, my eight year old son. Thorn's eyes were red and worried. He was like just like Chriton, in everything but looks. In looks the boy was purely mine. My eyes, my hair, my features. Thorn was friendly, funny, open, but extremely protective of his younger brother. An accident like this happening under his watch was clearly having an adverse effect on him.

Lifting the cloth slightly, I examined the deep jagged wound running down my five year old son, Lach's, inner thigh. That calm that I was trying to portray almost went right out the window. The concerningly deep wound was definitely going to scar. Setting the cloth back, I took a deep bracing breathe and made sure to apply enough pressure to the laceration to stop the bleeding.

Lach gripped his thigh right above the wound tightly and let out a small whimper that darted straight through my heart. I absolutely hated seeing my kids physically hurt in anyway and I always had a very hard time dealing with it. I ended being shaky and on edge for hours and sometimes days after, until Chriton or Leah took me in hand and helped me work it out in a very physical way.

Chriton's edge trigger turned out to be outdoor overprotection, especially when we took the kids hiking in the Andromadan forests. This was not only because we were attacked and kidnapped while camping outdoors but also because of an incident that happened to him when he was a kid. Needless to say, he severely weaponized his person every time we went out.

Leah's trigger was the emotional pain the kids experienced. Both Chriton and I were forced to step in to stop Leah from acting whenever she heard of someone hurting one of the children's feelings. The day that Mali's first boyfriend broke up with her to date someone else was a bad one. That evening, however, turned out to be very interesting.

"You ok, Lach?" I asked him, looking up into his bright blue eyes. When he nodded his over long black hair fell over his forehead. Lach looked like his grandfather Callden but was so much like Leah that it amazed me. He was so kind and caring but carried this will of steel that came out when needed. I reached out to grip the back of his head, "I know this hurts." I told him knowingly.

"Yeah." He whimpered out.

"Thorn, I need the first aid kit. And maybe see if you can find your grandfather. I might need him on this." I advised my older son.

Thorn gave me a sharp nod and started to his feet only to stop when I caught his arm. "It could've happened to anyone, Thorn. Ask your Uncle Grayson about the scar on his thigh."

Thorn gave me another sharp nod and raced off.

"Brace, son." I advised before carefully picking Lach up and carrying him to the nearby bathroom. Lach gave a heartrending cry of pain at the adjustments making me want to destroy something.

I set him on a long length of countertop that was liberally covered in girl paraphernalia, most of which ended up on the floor when I swept it aside to make room for Lach. I was going to have to talk to Mali about her organization skills.

Running the water into the flat square sink set into the rubbery type countertop, I grabbed a clean cloth and the soap. Lach watched me with scared eyes as I wet and soaped up the cloth.

"This is going to hurt." I warned him before carefully cleaning the area. Lach whimpered and gripped his leg even tighter while tears of pain slid down his cheeks.

I was just finishing when Thorn came racing back in with the kit in hand. Swiping the crap off the other side of the countertop, I pointed at the spot I cleared. "Set it there."

Flipping open the lid, I began digging for what I needed while holding a new, clean cloth to Lach's leg with the other.

"Here." Callden came rushing in and found what we needed quickly, handing the items to me.

"You know I hate stitching." I growled at him, eyeing the supplies he was holding out.

"You need the practice." Callden stated firmly, pushing them into my hand and crossing his arms.

"Fuck." I snarled and stepped away from Lach so Callden could take my place holding the cloth.

Thorn watched everything with a keen eye while I carefully washed my hands and pulled on a set of sterile gloves. I opened packages and set everything out on a sterile pad before stepping back to Lach. Callden stood behind Thorn with his hand on his grandson's shoulder. He explained to the boy exactly what I was doing and why at the same time he guided me.

It took me forever, mostly due to my hands shaking so badly. I truly hated doing this on my own son. Eventually I finished and smoothed a large bandage down his leg. Ripping off the gloves, I immediately reached for Lach, needing to hold him. He sniffled and reached for me just as quickly.

Careful of his wound, I cradled him to my chest and reached out to find the back of Thorn's head to draw him into us. Both boys clutched at me. One in regret, the other in relief.

I felt Callden move out of the room and looked up to see Chriton pushing through the gathered group of kids and adults. His eyes took in the scene as he stepped into us. He cupped Thorn's face and lifted it up to his. He examined the boy's eyes for a moment before he hugged Thorn to him. "Ask Uncle Grayson about the scar on his thigh."

I chuckled and glanced over at Grayson to see him rolling his eyes and throwing his hands up in the air. "Come on."

"Uncle Grayson?" It was Lach who actually asked.

"We were raiding a city about four hours from the Base." I told the group. "It was an easy run. Mostly." Grayson crossed his arms and glared at me. "One of the carts we were using to fill the trucks began to roll away. Since the cart was filled with a bunch of items we really needed, I yelled at the team in general to grab it. By the time

Uncle Grayson started after it, the thing was already going pretty fast. Uncle Scope was following Uncle Grayson when he caught up to the cart. Uncle Grayson grabbed onto the handle just as it hit the grass. Unfortunately, because the cart was full and heavy it kept going, dragging him across the grass. Then they both just disappeared. One with a loud clanging crash and the other with this surprised yelp." I couldn't stop myself from grinning at the memory. "He was there one minute, gone the next."

"It was dark." Grayson tried to explain.

"Yeah, dark." Chriton rolled his eyes.

"Uncle Scope froze in his tracks and looked back at me with this horrified look." I continued with the story. "The whole team ran over to where Uncle Grayson disappeared to see him laying on a paved section about three feet below the grassed area. It was a pretty severe drop off between the two areas and Grayson obviously didn't see it. He was laying on the ground with a bleeding head and a wicked laceration up the outside of his leg. The mostly empty cart somehow ended up on top of him. Everything that was in the cart was strewn all around him."

Thorn was looking up at his Uncle with amazed eyes.

"Needless to say, the good Dr. Luke was highly impressed when we carried Uncle Grayson's ass into Medical and told him what happened." I finished explaining with a chuckle.

"Fucking Luke. He didn't stop laughing the whole time I was in there." Grayson growled.

"Language." Amber reminded Grayson. He turned to the side to see the women had finally returned. Leah, Amber, Grayson's wife, and my 15 year old daughter, Mali, were walking down the stairs.

"What happened?" Leah gasped when she saw all of the blood and medical supplies.

"Mommy." Lach whimpered when he saw his mother and held his arms out to her.

"Baby?" Leah immediately drew the boy into her arms and frowned in question over to Chriton and I.

"He fell off the table." I gestured to the table and the toy.

"Oh, my." Leah looked over Lach, finding his bandaged leg and brushing the edge with shaking hands. "Are you ok, Lach?" She asked with worried eyes.

"Yeah, mom." Lach nodded, curling into her chest, happy to have her comfort. "Dad made it all better."

I blinked at the tears that rose in my eyes and looked away from the group. Something about hearing those words, knowing that I actually did that when the whole time it felt like I was torturing him was amazing. Chriton's fingers caught the side of my face and brought my eyes back around to his.

He smiled and kissed me, wet and deep, before pressing our foreheads together. Thorn was quiet from where he was ended up being hugged between us. We stayed like that for a long moment before we both turned our heads slightly to see Leah watching us with that warm love in her eyes.

I slowly raised my palm and pressed it into my chest, right over my heart. Leah nodded sharply and leaned her head down to lay it on the top of our son's.

"Mali-girl." I lifted my head to look at the tall beauty my daughter was becoming. "We need to talk about your organization skills."

When she saw all of her stuff strewn over the floor of the bathroom Mali gasped in outrage, "Oh my God, dad!"

Chriton's laughter echoed throughout our home.

Don't miss out!

Visit the website below and you can sign up to receive emails whenever T. M. Kuefler publishes a new book. There's no charge and no obligation.

https://books2read.com/r/B-A-WJAP-QQHBC

BOOKS 2 READ

Connecting independent readers to independent writers.

Did you love *Endangered Essence*? Then you should read *Rational Existence*[1] by T. M. Kuefler!

[2]

Trapped deep in an underground testing facility, freedom was a dream for Royce. Life has been daily rounds of fighting to survive and hopeless agony for years. But all of that is sufferable, worthwhile, because those Royce loves are safe and free. That's all that matters.

That's not all that matters, not to the residents of the Rocky Mountain Base. Especially Catro, a giftless Andromedan Ancient suffering from a life long existential crisis. But then something happens to him and everything becomes clear to him. No longer lost and confused, he knows exactly what he has to do. The first step is to bring Royce back to him.

That's right!

Back!

After Eon's he is still trying to protect her, now with the chance of finally keeping her.

Warning: Some scenes may be triggering.

Also by T. M. Kuefler

Extra Elements Series
Connection Bound
Detected Conversance
Triumvirate Protagonism
Ambrosia Realized
Fairy Girl
Unchained Backdraft
Buck Off!
Flight Plan
Rational Existence
Endangered Essence

Knights Five
Cracked Tableau
Extracted Tableau

Standalone
Sunshine
Father

About the Author

An avid book lover and keen psychology student, Canadian T.M. decided it was time to pull up her big girl panties and put fingers to keyboard. During this time, the alarm on the phone gets a big work out, just so that T. M. remembers to pull her head out of the literary dreamland and back into reality.

CPSIA information can be obtained
at www.ICGtesting.com
Printed in the USA
LVHW030341261022
731543LV00004B/95

9 798215 807897